Walk Me Home

Walk Me Home

LIZA KENDALL

JOVE
New York

A JOVE BOOK
Published by Berkley
An imprint of Penguin Random House LLC
penguinrandomhouse.com

Copyright © 2020 by Elizabeth A. Edelstein and Karen A. Moser
Excerpt from *Home with You* copyright © 2020 by
Elizabeth A. Edelstein and Karen A. Moser
Penguin Random House supports copyright. Copyright fuels creativity, encourages
diverse voices, promotes free speech, and creates a vibrant culture. Thank you for buying
an authorized edition of this book and for complying with copyright laws by not
reproducing, scanning, or distributing any part of it in any form without permission.
You are supporting writers and allowing Penguin Random House to continue to
publish books for every reader.

A JOVE BOOK, BERKLEY, and the BERKLEY & B colophon
are registered trademarks of Penguin Random House LLC.

ISBN: 9780593098004

First Edition: January 2020

Printed in the United States of America
1   3   5   7   9   10   8   6   4   2

Cover art by MilosStankovic / Getty Images
Book design by George Towne

For Don, Chris, and Fleur.
This book is dedicated to the power of
friendship and family.
That friendship and family extends to the
wonderful and loyal readers who have
patiently awaited books and sent encouraging
letters, e-mails, and messages.
Love you guys!

Walk Me Home

Chapter 1

YOU CANNOT PUSH ANYONE UP A LADDER. THE WORDS echoed in Charlie Nash's head as she stared at the aluminum Everest in front of her. Someone famous had said that . . .

Charlie eyed the ladder cautiously, as if it might run toward her on its orange rubber feet and knock her down. "You want me to climb up on that?"

Eight slippery silver rungs: They winked coldly at her, daring her to brave them. Just one step at a time—up into the air—with nothing solid underneath her.

She was already feeling shaky enough just being here, in the Old Barn at the Silverlake Ranch. Days early for a wedding, of all things. She'd rather be buried alive than be here. But it was her cousin Will's big day, and Charlie was a bridesmaid, and her longtime friend Lila needed her help. Now Charlie had to balance on something? In these boots?

God had a sense of humor.

The ladder also made her think of a fire truck. Like the

one at the local station . . . where Jake Braddock lived. It was just down the street from Griggs' Grocers. She'd had to stop by yesterday to stock up on vanilla pudding for Granddad.

Charlie hadn't ducked her head into her T-shirt like a turtle, but she *had* deliberately worn oversized sunglasses and a baseball cap, idiot that she was—everyone in Silverlake, Texas, knew Granddad's classic green 1954 GMC pickup. Who else under the age of fifty would be driving it?

Lila Braddock raised her dark eyebrows, so similar to her older brother Jake's. "Yes," Lila said. "I want you to climb up on the ladder. Unless you can levitate and hang those floral swags for this disaster of a wedding without it."

Charlie grimaced. "Funny." Her cousin's wedding, so far, *was* a disaster, for more than one reason. Will's formerly normal fiancée had morphed into an epic Bridezilla.

She had invited, disinvited, and then reinvited fifty out-of-town guests, who had to be housed somewhere in this town of less than five thousand people. She had ordered a custom wedding gown from Amelie on Main Street, then tried to return it. When this proved impossible, because of that whole "custom" concept, she had bought another off the rack in L.A. and hadn't yet decided which one to wear. Amelie was furious, and she was the most even-tempered, tolerant woman Charlie had ever met.

Add to that the cake catastrophe . . . Bridezilla had also changed her mind three times in the last three months about her wedding cake. Kristina Robbins at Piece A Cake was ready to hand her a five-gallon tub of ice cream instead and tell her to have a nice life. It was a good thing Bridezilla wasn't planning to actually live in this town after her big day.

And Charlie hadn't even *told* Lila the latest piece of nuptial news. She simply couldn't find the words—even though she needed to.

Lila checked the time. "We've got to get these decorations up. I have the ladies' knitting circle coming in at noon for their regular meeting. We can't be working on top of them."

Charlie nodded and moved forward to grasp the ladder. It was harmless. *It's much more stable than you are. With nonslip feet.*

The metal frame was unyielding and chilly in the early October morning air, which had seeped inside. She dragged the ladder over to the rough wall of the old boardinghouse's dining hall, where the reception would be.

She loved this old place, though it was bittersweet being here. It had started life as a hay barn for the Braddock farm back in 1839, then been converted into a boarding-house for the ranch hands around the turn of the century, when the Braddocks had begun raising more horses than crops. The horse stalls had been closed in for separate bunk areas; the tack room was converted to a kitchen; and the "nave" of the barn became the central dining hall.

The rough wood on the outside had weathered over the years to a silvery dove gray, and it still retained the scent of cedar and straw.

The rich red golden interior walls soared to large windows that lined either side. At one end was a massive flagstone fireplace whose chimney shot straight up to the apex of the roof. Wide oak planks, beautifully finished, made up the floor.

Lila had brought in fine Oriental rugs and dotted them with hand-hewn rustic tables, comfortable oversized chairs, and glazed ceramic pots full of tall ferns and palms. She'd managed to make the place both elegant and cowboy-comfortable: a cross between palace and hunting lodge. While Charlie was a professional stager, she didn't have the interior design skills to have pulled this off. It was, in a word, stunning.

The fact that the Braddocks had hung on to the land over

the years was amazing, considering the blows successive generations had been dealt. But hang on to it they had, following the family credo: Thou Shalt Not Sell Land. Even if thou must doeth odd and dirty jobs on the side. Even if thou must liveth elsewhere and get basically adopted by another family.

Oh, Jake.

Charlie swallowed hard as she went to the long folding table where Lila had set out three dozen swags made of grapevines and adorned with white silk gardenias. Charlie tucked one under her arm, turned, and set one foot tentatively on the bottom rung of the ladder.

This is nothing, Charlie. Just do it. Jake had helped her climb up to the high hayloft over on the opposite side of the barn a couple of times before, in high school. Once she'd gotten past the climb, he'd made it plenty worth it.

Before. Before that awful day back in high school. Before she and her family had left town in the wake of a devastating fire that killed her grandmother and burned down all the good times along with the Nash family home.

"Why is there a funny look on your face?" Lila asked, appearing beside her and folding her arms across her chest.

Charlie took two steps up—not that skinny jeans were easy to climb in—then three and four. She looked down, wobbled, and clung fiercely to the sides of the ladder. The swag under her arm crackled in protest as she shoved it upward into her armpit, where it poked her painfully through the thin cotton of her black sweater. Small bits of leaves and twigs caught in the fabric. "What funny look?"

Lila tapped her foot on the flagstone floor. "That one," she said, pointing at Charlie's face. "Hey. Easy on the gardenias. They need to be unsquashed. Perfect. She said she was sure this time, and we can't give Bridezilla any excuse to switch them out for calla lilies or roses. I am so done with her."

"No kidding," Charlie said with feeling. "And *you* don't have to be her bridesmaid." Charlie and Felicity weren't exactly friends, but given that she'd introduced her and Will to each other at a college party, they'd insisted she be part of the wedding. Even if she sometimes regretted that introduction, she wouldn't dream of turning down her cousin's request. She took two more steps up the ladder, looked down at the stone floor again, and felt nauseated. She clamped the swag even more tightly into her armpit. The hook it needed to hang on was a foot away from her face. *Easy. No problem.* Except that she had to let go of the ladder with one hand in order to hang it. *Yikes.*

"Charlie? Are you okay?" Lila called.

"Yeah. No . . . I have to tell you something." Charlie eyed the hook. She clutched the ladder. She did *not* look at the floor again. She refused. *Hook. Swag. Simple. Let go of the ladder with your left hand, and hang the swag.*

Except she really needed to let go of the ladder with her right hand first, in order to pull the swag out from under her left arm and rescue the silk gardenias. They probably didn't bloom well if saturated with Secret antiperspirant.

"So tell me."

Charlie sighed.

"And are you going to hang that swag or yourself up there?"

"I'd break the hook right off the wall," Charlie said. "I've gained back the eleven pounds I lost, even though I swore off chocolate."

"You look great," Lila fibbed. "Now hang the swag already and spill."

Charlie uncurled her stiff, reluctant fingers and slid her sweaty right palm off the ladder. She tugged the swag out from under her arm and set it on top. *Yes. Good.* Except there was something white fluttering down. A gardenia. It hit Lila on the head and then fell to the ground.

"Really?" Lila said, narrowing her eyes. "Come down from there so I can fix that. And tell me what's going on already."

On the one hand, Charlie couldn't wait to get off the ladder. On the other, maybe it was good there was some distance between herself and Lila. "Geoff is being sent overseas on a military assignment. So he just dropped out of the wedding," she said. "They're going to need another groomsman." The words hung in the air between them.

"*What* did you say?"

Charlie looked down at Lila's stunned face. "I'm pretty sure you heard me. And Bridezilla is freaking out about the lack of human symmetry in her big show. Somehow, I'm supposed to pull a groomsman outta my—"

Lila was shaking her head. "No."

Charlie sighed. "Got any ideas?"

"No. This is not happening. I'm an *event planner.* Not a magician."

"Lila? I really hate to tell you this. But you'd better grab a top hat and a rabbit, as well as a groomsman. Because Bridezilla is having a meltdown of epic proportions, and she can't take it out on her groom . . . so she's taking it out on us. I spent two hours listening to her rant and cry last night. And she'll call you next, because you're her wedding planner by default; you come free with the site rental."

As if on cue, Lila's cell phone started ringing to a barking dog theme.

Forgetting her fear of the ladder, Charlie covered her involuntary smirk with one hand.

"I'm out of battery," said Lila, looking at her phone as if it were a snake. "I'm on another call. No, I'm on another planet."

Bark, bark, bark.

"I have supplied porta-potties, pink doves, and even a stand-in wedding ring," she continued. "But I cannot pull a groomsman out of my behind. It's not possible."

Bark, bark, bark.

Charlie put her hand back on the ladder and inched down it step by step until she safely reached the ground.

Lila bent and picked up the silk gardenia. She stared at it as though she expected it to speak, to give her a solution. And then a very peculiar expression bloomed on Lila's face. Charlie watched it grow as a bad feeling grew parallel to it, in the pit of her own stomach.

Lila pursed her lips as she took the swag back from Charlie. She efficiently reattached the wayward gardenia with a snippet of floral wire. Charlie's unease grew as she nodded with satisfaction. When Lila pursed her lips like that, it meant she was determined. And when Lila was determined, she got what she wanted. No matter what it was.

Lila had pursed her lips back in elementary school when she wanted a purple bike with a pink sparkly banana seat. Check.

She had pursed her lips in middle school when she'd wanted to go on the end-of-year trip to New York City and had been told there was no money for such a trip. Check.

And Lila had pursed her lips in high school when she'd wanted to date the quarterback, even though she was a somewhat dorky sophomore and he was a supremely cool senior. Check.

Charlie glanced toward the ladder, feeling a weird urge to climb back up it in order to escape from Lila and whatever she was about to say.

"Add magician to my résumé," declared Lila. "I can supply a groomsman after all."

"Give me that." Charlie snatched the repaired swag from Lila and scurried back over to the ladder. Up she climbed the first step, the second, the third. "You're kidding, right?"

"Nope."

Up the fourth rung Charlie went, and the fifth. "You have a spare man in your back pocket? I need to get a pair of those pants for myself."

"As a matter of fact, I do." Lila looked as if she were about to purr.

Charlie eyed the hook again. *Simple. Remove right hand. Take garland in it. Drop it on the hook.* Basically, the same as staging an apartment. A little design sense, a little elbow grease. Nothing to it.

"The Silverlake Fire Station does a lot more than just fight fires, right?" said Lila.

Charlie's heart hurled itself into her esophagus, and she choked on it.

"They always have. It's part of their mission statement. It's tradition, helping out the town. If you think about it, it's . . . it's . . . an *obligation.* They have to help the community wherever help is needed, so . . ."

No. Don't say it, Lila. Do. Not. Say. His. Name. Charlie extended the swag toward the hook, clutching the ladder for dear life with her other hand.

"Yeah, *Jake. He's perfect!*" exclaimed Lila. "He helps out everyone else in this town. Why not his own sister? It's about time we had a real conversation anyway. Jake will *totally* do it. He'll be perfect. What d'you think?"

Charlie made a strangled noise.

"Oh, come on. You can't avoid him forever," Lila said in a pragmatic tone. "It's too small a town, and being in the wedding means you can't just do your usual flyover. Imagine if you and Jake could finally get past the weirdness once and for all."

"Are *you* past the weirdness with Jake?" Charlie asked pointedly. "He's *your* brother."

Lila flushed. "No, but I'd like to be." That old Lila gleam appeared in her eyes, and she pursed her lips again.

Uh-oh. Lila had given Charlie her friendship in Charlie's darkest hour after that damned fire, when the Nashes blamed Jake, and the rest of the Braddocks were pressuring their little sister to close ranks.

"Maybe this is the thing that could finally do it. Charlie, I need this. Jake's the perfect solution. Please say you'll roll with this."

Lila didn't have to spell it out.

Charlie owed her friend . . . especially since she was the cause of the rift between Lila and Jake. But the thought of being in a wedding with him?

Charlie stared at the hook. It was a very sturdy one, its screws embedded in solid wood. Never mind the swag. Never mind the extra eleven pounds. She was going to hang herself on it after all.

Chapter 2

JAKE BRADDOCK LEANED BACK IN A DISTRESSED leather armchair next to the fieldstone fireplace in the great room of the main house. The scents of cedar and woodsmoke filled the air, as did the usual subtle tension between him and his brother Declan.

Jake remembered the day he got his badge under the mentorship of Old George at the fire station. He'd moved the rest of his stuff into the firehouse, and the look on Declan's face . . . it was as if his last hope for putting the Braddock family back together had died. Sometimes when Jake drove up from town, he felt like a visitor, coming through the iconic black iron gates with their silhouette of a bucking bronco and rider. When he saw Declan working alone in the shadow of the big barn, the wide swatch of land leading down to the lake rolling out behind him, it broke his heart. *Some of that's your fault, Jake.*

Now, watching his brother on the phone, Jake thought he still looked every inch like the man in charge Declan had always been, with that determined jaw and take-no-prisoners stare, but there were a few strands of silver threading through his dark Braddock hair and a few lines radiating out from those black Irish eyes.

We're all getting older, all five of us. Declan, me, Ace, Everett, Lila . . . and we're all still so alone. How did we get here?

Declan paced the plush, elegant book-lined great room, so at odds with the dirt under his fingernails and the bandanna rag sticking out of the back pocket of his worn jeans. Nicks and cuts from the barbed-wire fence he'd been fixing covered the muscular arm that held up his cell phone in a death grip. He spoke to their banker brother, Everett, in terse, controlled sentences; the tension with Rhett was *never* subtle, and Declan was the only one of the Braddock siblings who ever talked with him anymore.

"The lease of the north forty," Declan was saying, "will help us all pay off the mortgage, so that we no longer owe you."

There was a pause as Rhett said something on the other end of the line.

"It doesn't complicate things. The Sherman brothers will plant their crops for two years, and we'll see how it goes. If things are good, we'll renegotiate the lease at that point. If things get problematic, we can rely on the clauses I added to help us terminate the lease."

Another pause.

Declan kept his tone very even, but anger seeped in. "Everett, we are all in your debt. And you like it that way. But your money doesn't give you the right to call all the shots unilaterally. I'm asking you to sign off on this and trust me. I'm asking you to let me run things here effectively, or you will have to find yourself another rancher to manage this place. *No.* That is not a threat. But it *is* a line in the sand. You choose whether or not to cross it."

There was yet another pause.

"Thank you," said Declan. "I'll send the paperwork— fine. Electronic signature is fine. Goodbye."

Deck ended the call, tossed his cell phone onto the leather couch, and exhaled audibly.

"That sounded fun," Jake said.

"Always." Deck's mouth tightened. "He's very busy. Had to jump off to play a round of golf with some big clients."

"Oooh. Tough day, then."

"Everett," said Declan, and shook his head.

He walked forward, palmed the black iron poker, and nudged at a log in the fireplace, causing the flames to snap and crackle in protest. Declan cleared his throat. "You know, Jake, you've still got a room here, if you want it."

Jake paused, then nodded at his older brother. The nod was a shade too casual, as Deck's own words were. They both looked away at the same time, Jake out the plate glass window to the left of the massive oak front doors.

The pale gold and green vista of the Braddock family land stretched for miles until it greeted the sky in a senti- mental tinge of rose orange. The place was a patchwork of different pastures and crops.

There were picturesque fenced paddocks with cattle and horses grazing peacefully in them. There were neat rows of corn and wheat marching in orderly lines like obedient sol- diers. There was a gully that fed a stock pond, to water the animals and cool off kids on a hot summer's day. And then there were the rows of apple trees, bursting with fruit. The view, to put it bluntly, did not suck. Maybe he should come here more often, he thought.

"Thanks, man," Jake said, and let his gaze run to the weathered pier-and-beam architecture, the simple pleasing geometry of it. The ceiling soared to the original structure's

apex, a good twenty-five feet high. His brother had modern-
ized and updated the original bones, but also replaced what
seemed like acres of rooftop. He'd done a beautiful job.

Deck had left either side of the house open glass, framed
in by the same rough cedar. This created the illusion that
they lounged outside, the oaks shading and cradling the
house to both left and right. Jake felt as if he could shimmy
up one of the posts and right into the trees, as they had done
as boys. He felt a lump rising in his throat, an ache for the
innocence of his youth.

Jake's mouth twisted. Why didn't God hand out reset
buttons?

As they'd caught fireflies, lizards, and toads, as they'd
pitched tents of clothesline and old blankets, as they'd
rubbed bits of flint together to try to start campfires . . .
they'd had no idea what the future held. They'd had no idea
those simple times of togetherness were precious.

No, they'd just been goofy, rambunctious boys with the
peculiar blessing of a little sister to torment—the best gift
ever. They'd tickled little Lila, tackled her, and toughened
her. They'd taught her to be one of them.

He'd give just about anything to be ten again, clueless
and carefree. Anything. He'd set the table without whining,
even fold the napkins properly. He'd eat all the spinach in
the pot, not just the requisite three bites. He'd even wash the
dishes—just to have one last family dinner with all of
them—with Mama and Pop.

But that wasn't going to happen. Their parents were
dead, courtesy of a car accident on a country lane; the rest
of them were scattered. Deck lived here on the ranch all by
his lonesome with only Grouchy the mutt for company—so
named not because he had a nasty personality, but because
(except for not being green) none of them had ever seen a

dog that looked so much like *Sesame Street*'s Oscar the Grouch. Lila had even sewn him a "trash can" to sleep in, made out of furry gray material with a pillow lid. It lay on its side in front of the fireplace, the dog half in and half out of it, only his back legs and tail to be seen.

"Grouchy," said Jake. "Oscar glares at people from his trash can. You're in there wrong side out again."

Deck snorted and nudged one of Grouchy's hindquarters with the toe of his boot. The dog thumped his tail. "He's just backwards, like the rest of this family."

Jake raised an eyebrow. "Speak for yourself." He yawned. "I need to get going. Personally, I don't care if you lease the north forty to performance artists who plant purple Popsicles, man. Really."

"Well, I wanted to check with you. We'd never sell acreage, of course, but I can't plant all of it myself, and this will bring in a little more income. Which we need to pay off the loan to Everett."

Jake nodded. He strongly suspected that Deck had just used the idea of the lease as an excuse to get Jake over here. What he didn't totally understand was why. He could have called him and then e-mailed the documents to him.

Declan went behind his desk and sat down. He flipped a sheaf of papers to the signatory page and turned them to face Jake. There were names and spaces for all the siblings. "Sign and then initial the other four pages."

Jake leaned over and started signing.

"Lila's over at the Old Barn," Deck said, "prepping the space for a wedding. Another of her ridiculous, over-the-top events. But at least they bring in money, too."

Deck had little patience with overdressed, tipsy strangers skipping around the family property, and Jake didn't blame him one bit. But like the petting zoo and the apple picking, the party rentals at the barn helped to pay the bills on Silverlake Ranch. And Lila was brilliant at marketing and at managing the events.

Deck straightened some pens on his desk that didn't need straightening. "You could always stop by and say hello— and tell her that I need her to sign off on this, too."

Jake paused midsignature and looked up. "Can't you send her a text?"

Deck met his gaze evenly. "Is it really that big a deal for you to stop by?"

Yes. The word hung unspoken in the air. Lila had remained good friends with Charlie when she and Jake broke up. Water under the bridge? Maybe. But blood should have been a hell of a lot thicker than that water, given what had gone down.

Jake cracked his neck, finished initialing the pages, and stood up.

"She *is* your sister."

"Really," Jake deadpanned. "I hadn't noticed."

Deck let his loosely curled fist fall to the rough-hewn wooden desktop. "You know what? I keep this place up. I work to pay back the loan to Everett, while none of you will even speak to him. And I provide a side income stream for all of you. I surely don't ask a lot in return. You know that."

Jake looked down, then looked up at the wedding portrait of their parents hanging over the fireplace. Mama wore a secretive little smile. Pop's gaze was challenging somehow, as if he thought the painter of the portrait might be working up the nerve to ask his bride for a date—and he wasn't happy about it.

"So maybe you could do me a favor and at least try to remember we're all family?" Deck asked. "Try to remember that Lila was caught in a tough spot, and that Charlie was grieving and needed her?"

"She wasn't the only person who was grieving." The terse words escaped Jake before he could stop them, along with the resentment that punctuated them.

Deck stared him down. "Well, you're the one who made it either her or you, man. And you did it after the fact, which isn't really fair."

"When somebody accuses you of something you didn't do—something terrible—the people who care about you are supposed to stand by your side. I didn't start that fire, Declan. I told that to Lila's face right back when it all happened. I wouldn't have my badge today if I'd done what the Nashes accused me of. But Lila didn't stand up next to me when she should've; she straddled the fence. Stayed by Charlie's side instead."

Sure as hell, Jake had made his sister choose sides. He'd hardly had anybody left. He had needed to know there were still people in this world who cared about him. If it hadn't been for Old George taking him under his wing . . . he didn't like to think about it. The former fire chief had understood his pain, had patiently answered all of his naive questions about the fire, and had shared his time with a bruised and lonely kid.

Pain flashed in Declan's eyes, but it was gone as quickly as it had come. Jake flushed, suddenly recalling that the moment he'd realized that Lila was staying friends with Charlie Nash was also the moment he'd realized how Declan had felt trying to make enough of a home for his brothers and sisters to stay by *his* side.

Damn. The old wounds never stayed closed for good, no matter how many stitches they'd tried to put in over the years.

Jake sighed, bent down to give Grouchy a brief rub, and then got to his feet. "I didn't ask for your take on things."

"I know. You got it anyway."

Jake exhaled. "Yeah."

The truth was, he missed Lila. And the tight expressions passing for smiles when they crossed paths in public were getting really old. It wasn't the worst thing in the world to have an excuse to talk to her. Not that he'd admit that to his brother. "If it'll make you happy, then I'll stop by."

"Thank you." Deck seemed on the verge of saying something else, but evidently thought better of it. He got up, too, stretched out a hand toward Jake, then let it fall. "Good to see you, kid."

Wish you'd quit being a stranger. Jake heard it, even though Deck didn't say it. The pressure to come home. Even though he was now a fully grown adult. Well, if he'd felt that Deck could replace their parents, he'd never have left, would he? Searching, as all of them had, for the anchors that had moored them, the anchors that had sunk without a trace.

"Yeah. See you around, man." He clapped Deck on the shoulder and headed out.

Grouchy extricated himself from his trash can and followed him to the door. Declan was his favorite, but he greeted everyone, barked like crazy at strangers, and followed their vehicles until they were off the property. Jake was so busy trying not to step on Grouchy, spinning like a tornado at his boots, that he almost stepped on the cat.

Wait a minute. We don't have a cat.

Meow.

Jake stared down at a gray cat with golden eyes, swishing its fluffy tail at him.

"Where'd you come from?" he asked it.

It jerked its tail, as if to say, *None of your business.*

Grouchy lunged playfully at it, the cat swatted his nose, and then the two took off running.

"Deck?" Jake called, sticking his head back through the door.

"Yeah?"

"You got a cat?"

There was a pause. "Damn thing's adopted me."

"You do have a choice, you know. You've never been a cat person . . . Wait, is that a bowl I see? Two, actually. About cat size."

"I don't know what you're talking about," Deck called.

"Uh-huh." Jake grinned and shook his head.

"Okay, okay. Grouchy likes the critter. Gives him something to chase besides cars."

"Unbelievable. You don't let it in the house, do you?"

"Absolutely not. It does let *itself* in now and then, though."

"Declan, are you getting soft?"

Grunt.

"So what's your new buddy's name?"

"Just Cat. I draw the line at naming it."

"Good to know, tough guy. Good to know."

It was a short ride over to the Old Barn, which the Braddocks had been renting out for events for the past five years. It had actually been Lila's idea. Who would have suspected that the former tomboy could plan weddings and parties?

Jake aimed his Durango down the curving paved drive and then cut left onto a gravel road that led to the east bend of the property. He drove with one hand on the wheel, the other arm hanging out the open window, catching the crisp breeze. The sun was warm on his skin, the air fragrant with the scent of damp earth; Declan must be planting the oats and wheat around now. A western scrub jay and then a vermilion flycatcher danced by the windshield, wheeling and cawing in the ultrablue morning sky. Nothing to complain about—that was for sure. It was one of those days on which anyone was thankful to be alive.

The road wound to the left, then doglegged to the right, the Old Barn coming into view about a half mile ahead. Jake drove idly, wondering what, exactly, he'd say to Lila except for "Hello" and "Deck wants to see you."

He'd refused to even speak to her for a long time when she wouldn't sever the friendship with Charlie. She'd called over and over, trying to explain. Sure, he bumped into Lila now and again, but it wasn't the same. He'd just poured cement down in the hole where his heart had once been and let it harden. It was a lot more comfortable that way.

He never let his mind go to Charlie anymore. Never wondered where she was or how she was doing. He didn't want to know what she did for a living, if she'd gotten married, if she'd had kids. He just didn't want to know.

Jake's mouth flattened as he approached the Old Barn, slowed, and parked. *Get it over with. It's better than what you're signed up to do this afternoon, for chrissakes.*

Most towns this small had only volunteer fire departments. Silverlake, Texas, was different, and thanks to a tradition as old as the town itself—made official in the earliest city council documents, thank you very much—a squad of seven guys—himself, Old George, Grady, Mick, Hunter, Rafael, and Tommy—lived at the firehouse and received a civic salary. The trade-off was the understanding that when they weren't putting out the rare fire, the men were on call for anything the community needed.

This included such glamorous gigs as putting up the town Christmas lights; playing Santa; volunteering at the tri-county animal shelter; and once, regrettably, unclogging a toilet at city hall. (That one had been fiercely debated, since at the time of the Great Overflow, Vic, the local plumber, was seated only two blocks away at the bar in Schweitz's Tavern. And drinking a cold one. But Vic was clearly off duty and would bill for his services, whereas Jake was unfortunately free in both senses of the word.)

He climbed out of the truck, slammed the door, squared his shoulders, and headed toward the sound of his sister's voice. Lila was inside the barn by the wall, talking to a pair of booted feet on a ladder. The boots screamed city. They were black and high heeled, ridiculous for a barn. The body was blocked by a massive rafter.

"Hey, Lila," he called. "I heard a rumor—"

The feet jumped. Literally.

"—you were out here."

The feet came down all wrong.

"Holy—!" Jake sprinted forward as the ladder teetered.

A bloodcurdling shriek resounded through the cavernous space as the ladder fell.

"Oh God!" Lila exclaimed.

Without thinking, Jake dove as he might have to catch a football, twisting in midair to land on his shoulder, then his ass.

What he caught was no football. And it was worse than the flu.

After a decade of refusing to see her, speak to her, or think about her, Jake Braddock had caught a big curvy armful of none other than Charlie Nash.

Chapter 3

CHARLIE FELT ONLY BLIND PANIC AS SHE FELL. IT was the longest half second of her life.

And then she hit not the ground but Jake Braddock's chest. His muscular arms locked protectively around her, and she could feel his heartbeat pounding in time with her own. They lay there, unmoving and mutually horrified.

The wind had been knocked out of her. She couldn't breathe; she couldn't speak. Why, oh why, could her extra eleven pounds not have cracked open the floor so that she could've fallen right through it?

"Charlie Nash," he said at last. "What in the . . . Are you *okay*?"

The deliciously deep rumble of Jake Braddock's voice saying her name was something of a shock. A memory she'd either forgotten or forced out of her head. Of course, the last time they'd spoken, he was just sixteen. Charlie opened her mouth, but no sound emerged.

He was warm and reassuring underneath her. His chest

was solid muscle; so were his thighs under her backside. But how, out of all the people on the planet, could she be sprawled inelegantly on top of *Jake Braddock*?

Oh God. He smelled the same: like leather and sweet-grass and cedar and home.

She couldn't think.

"Charlie." That voice vibrated down every nerve in her body. Rough and sweet at the same time. Edged with a fear that a man like him could never admit to. His arms got tighter around her. "You okay?"

She managed to nod. He sat up, taking her with him so that she now sat between his legs on the floor. He was panting behind her; she finally gasped in some air.

"How—" She looked at the door, a good seventy-five feet from where they sat. Had the man been fired from a gun? How had he reacted so fast? How had he crossed that distance in a quarter second and managed to catch her?

Lila's expression asked the same question.

"Are *you* all right, Jake?" Charlie asked, her face suddenly burning. Thank God he was behind her. Thank God she didn't have to look into his—

He shoved her away. Got to his feet and stood over her, hands on his hips, dark eyes blazing into her. His unruly dark hair was slightly too long, and he needed a shave. The dimple at the left of his mouth still did weird things to her insides.

Oh.

Whom had she been thanking again? And for what?

And why did she have to be in a heap on the ground while Jake Braddock towered over her, looking not at all pleased to see her after all these years?

Jake's eyebrows drew together in a black Irish frown, and the kindness disappeared from his voice. "I'm fine.

What in the hell were you doing up on that ladder? In those idiotic boots?"

She still couldn't think, and it took a moment to fully drink in the sight of him: tall and rangy, in his practical and comfortable Ropers, snug battered denim, and a flannel shirt rolled to his elbows. His chest was broader than she remembered; he'd filled out over the years. There were other parts of him she refused to even acknowledge. He'd gone from boy to 100 percent man.

It took her another moment to register the word *idiotic*. And then another for it to trigger her anger, which was an easier emotion than total humiliation.

"My boots are Italian, not idiotic," was all she could think of to say. *Oh, Charlie, really?*

"Eye-talian? That so?" His mouth tugged up in a grin, displaying that one crooked tooth in front that she'd always loved and elongating his firm jaw. "Well, there are lots of fashionista cows, chickens, and horses out here who'll appreciate those."

A snort, quickly muffled, came from Lila's direction.

Charlie shot her a death glare before turning back to Jake. Her anger kicked up another notch at his sarcasm.

Jake and his smart mouth continued. "Me, I've just got on plain old American footwear here—it's not fancy, but at least I'm not unbalanced."

"I resent that."

"Do you?" His grin widened.

"I'm very stable," she snapped, and he lifted an eyebrow. "Mentally," she amended, then got even more furious with herself. Could she sound any stupider? "And I'm here to help with wedding decorations, not walk through cow pastures."

"Ah. Pardon me, your ladyship. Allow me to assist you

so that you can get on with things, then." He reached down a big, calloused hand.

Charlie ignored it and scrambled to her feet by herself, dusting off her jeans and sweater.

Jake gave her a slow, deliberate, very male head-to-toe assessment while the burn in her face spread to her neck and then over her chest. How dare he? She felt like a horse for sale. She stared right back at him. And then, unwisely, she asked, "Are you done, or would you like to see my teeth, too?"

"Your teeth?" He shook his head. "Nope. That's not at all what I had in mind."

"Really, Jake? Grow up," said Lila, stepping forward. "Why are you here?"

"That's a damned good question. I'm here because I had to sign some papers for Deck, and he needs you to sign them, too."

Lila frowned and folded her arms across her chest. "Why didn't he just text me?"

Jake folded his arms the exact same way. "I asked him that question, too."

They stood there awkwardly, looking like two book-ends, and Charlie was irrationally tempted to laugh, then equally tempted to cry. *She* had done this. She had caused the rift between brother and sister. She had screwed every-thing up. It was all her fault.

Charlie cleared her throat. "Well," she began, inching sideways toward the door. "This has been, um, great. But I've got to get—"

"You aren't going anywhere," Lila said. "As long as you're not injured and don't need to pay a visit to the ER."

"But I—"

"You just said you were fine." Lila smiled sweetly.

"True, but—"

"Swags," her pal reminded her. "Knitting circle. *Wedding.* Groomsman." Lila inclined her head toward Jake as he stared suspiciously at one of them and then the other.

Charlie pleaded silently with her eyes, shaking her head at an uncompromising Lila.

"Why is the hair on my neck rising as we speak?" Jake asked. "Why am I feeling very uncomfortable right now? Why do I feel like the pawn in some weird chess game?"

"Because you're not the stupidest man I've ever met," his sister replied.

"Thank you." Jake tucked his hands in his pockets. "But whatever it is, no."

"You can't say no before the question is even asked," Charlie told him. Irrationally. Because of course she didn't want him to say yes. *Remember that, dimwit?*

"Oh, but I can," he said.

"That's not fair." Charlie sounded ten years old, even to her own ears.

Jake's expression went from carefully blank to blazing with resentment and old hurt. "Life isn't fair, Charlie—or don't you remember that?"

She felt the words like a kick in the stomach.

Life isn't fair, Granddad had growled at a sixteen-year-old Jake right in front of her. *Figure it out! Now go home.*

"Play nice, children." Lila stepped between them. "Jake, we need a big favor."

"No."

"A little one, then."

"No."

"We need a hero," she wangled, clearly trying to appeal to any white-knight instincts Charlie hadn't just squashed out of him with her ample behind. Charlie shuddered just thinking about it.

"No."

"A groomsman for Will and Felicity's wedding this Saturday," Lila continued as if she hadn't heard him.

Charlie hadn't realized how loud a silence could be. Particularly in the vast space of a barn with unusually good acoustics. And it wasn't just the silence. The look on Jake's face . . . *oh, wow.* This was a bad, bad idea. She ran her index finger across her neck, desperately trying to catch Lila's eye: *Abort mission!*

Her "friend" grinned, shrugged off the murderous gaze aimed at her, and turned back to her brother. "C'mon, Jake," she wheedled. "It's only a few hours."

"In a suit. At a wedding." Jake pulled at the collar of his T-shirt. "I hate weddings. They make me itch."

This was news to Charlie. They'd planned in high school to get married in this very barn as soon as they turned eighteen.

"Don't make me go through Mayor Fisk and get you officially assigned." Lila smirked, clearly delighted with the Machiavellian idea.

"You wouldn't dare," Jake growled.

"Wouldn't I?"

Jake suddenly laughed, a sound Charlie hadn't heard in years. It sounded a little bitter, though, and that part she didn't remember from the past. Not until the very end, anyway.

"Jake?" prompted Lila.

"Sorry, I'm still recovering from the shock of being asked such an insane favor," he said. "Will seriously lost a groomsman days before his wedding?"

"Correct. He lost the best man, actually. He's being sent overseas."

"Damn." He nodded, but then . . . "Wait a minute. Isn't Charlie in the wedding?"

With a little less confidence, Lila answered, "Yep. She's the maid of honor. But we just need a body. A random groomsman, not a best man." She paused and then said, "This sounded better in my head."

"Clearly there's something *wrong* with your head. You're still asking me to stand up at Will's wedding. You're asking me to stand up with Nashes in a Nash wedding." Jake laughed, a hollow sound of disbelief.

Tears pricked at the back of Charlie's eyes as Lila's expression changed, as it finally dawned on her what they were really asking Jake to do: *forgive*. Could he?

Evidently not.

Charlie took a step back, a little disoriented, wondering how rude it would be to turn and walk out without another word. They should never have asked him. Jake might forgive Lila, but he'd never forgive *her*.

Jake shook his head. "Find someone else."

Charlie's face reignited.

"But the bride is freaking out," Lila said as her cell phone started barking again. Really, Bridezilla's timing was uncanny. "And we are in desperate straits here, dude."

"Do. *Not.* Call me 'dude.'"

Charlie dragged a hand down her face. Maybe she was reading too much into this. Nobody could blame the man for saying no—he was probably having trouble just standing upright after she'd leveled him like a sack of potatoes. She had probably flattened his "family jewels" in the fall.

"Would you respond better to 'butthead'?" asked Lila of her brother.

"Probably."

"Now I feel I'm getting somewhere!" Lila looked triumphant.

Jake snorted. "Only because you're deluded."

"Forget it, Jake," Charlie mumbled. "We shouldn't have asked. It should be anyone *but* you."

A long pause ensued.

Jake stared darkly down at her, now looking—of all things—offended.

"We can ask Vic," Charlie said desperately to Lila, willing to suggest anything just to end the conversation and give Jake an excuse to leave. Because one of them sure had to leave.

"*Vic?*" Lila was aghast. "I don't think so. There will be no plumber's crack on display at one of my events."

But Jake's expression morphed from offended to amused, and then to calculating. He opened his mouth as Charlie stared at him. She shook her head, suddenly knowing exactly which words were going to come out of his mouth. *He's enjoying my discomfort. He's going to say yes.*

"I'll do it," he said, his now-devilish gaze on Charlie. Then he turned back to Lila, and his tone softened. "For you."

Lila raised her eyebrows. For once, she had no snappy comeback. She looked at her brother, wide-eyed and speechless.

Charlie sucked in a breath. Masterful: Jake was exacting revenge on her and forgiving his sister at the same time. She was horrified—and she was touched.

And then he added, *"Dude."*

Lila and Jake burst out laughing.

Charlie swallowed the lump rising in her throat. It was the first time in more than a decade that she had seen them behave like family.

Chapter 4

CHARLIE'S HANDS SHOOK ON THE WHEEL AS SHE backed Granddad's old green beast of a truck, ironically named Progress, away from the Old Barn. The rip in the ancient vinyl seat next to her exposed its mildewy stuffing.

What a perfect metaphor; her own stuffing felt exposed. And she was surprised it hadn't exploded out of her when she'd hit Jake Braddock like an asteroid. Charlie squirmed again at the memory as she put Progress into gear and rumbled forward, kicking up gravel as she gained speed. Grouchy joined her as she passed the main house, where Declan lived. The dog escorted her off the property, barking and wagging his tail when she turned onto the main road.

She headed toward Our Lady of Mercy Hospital, where Granddad was recovering very slowly from hip replacement surgery. Complications because of arthritis, infections, and blood clots were keeping him there longer than normal, and he wasn't happy about it. Neither was the insurance company, but Kingston Nash was a VIP in Silverlake, and the hospital wasn't about to give him the bum's rush.

Charlie swerved to avoid an armadillo and took a sharper left onto the parkway than she'd intended. A small cooler full of Granddad's contraband vanilla pudding packs flew off the back seat and onto the floor, ice rattling.

She'd allowed the encounter with Jake to rattle *her*. There was something about the way his eyes had assessed her. And he'd shoved her away so quickly it made her ache inside. He still felt betrayed after all these years. He was still hurt.

That's what had her hands trembling. That was all. Charlie hated for people to be angry with her. She was a pleaser . . . and when she didn't please, it upset her, even though she knew that it was impossible to please everyone all the time. Eventually, she found herself in a no-win situation, stuck between two people who wanted or needed opposite things from her.

As she got up to speed on the parkway, the crisp autumn air billowed through the open windows and blew through her hair. The sun warmed her face and neck and she felt like a kid on a bicycle again, pedaling furiously into the countryside to escape her homework or chores. For a few moments she felt free, happy, and . . . home. A gust of wind somehow blew a smile onto her face, dissipating her anxiety.

And then as the parkway segued into Main Street and she slowed to make the turn onto Elm, she saw it: the site of the old Nash mansion. The blackened and burned-out foundation an eyesore, the peeling white posts of the one-time picket fence bitter, bony middle fingers extended like Granddad's gesture to fate.

He'd gotten countless offers on the land—from private

citizens, from two different churches, from the local bank. Even Mayor Fisk had sat him down to discuss creating a park or a new city hall there. But Kingston Nash refused to sell or donate or repurpose the land. And though he was still sitting on a pile of insurance money from the fire, he wouldn't even consider rebuilding.

Charlie pulled up parallel to the front "lawn," which consisted of a tangle of crabgrass, dandelions, and weeds. Babe Nash would be fit to be tied if she could see it. She'd always had giant pots of colorful geraniums or mums on either side of the wide steps that led up to the wraparound veranda. There had been other flowers, herbs, and vines flowing out of hanging baskets; *Good Housekeeping* and *Family Circle* magazines stacked on the wicker coffee table; Laura Ashley–print cushions on the comfortable wicker chairs and sofa.

Unlike some of its brick ranch neighbors, the house itself had been a pristine white three-storied Colonial, with dark green shutters and dormer attic windows. The hardwood floors inside shone with polish and set off Oriental area rugs to perfection. Grandma Babe's Queen Anne dining set was well used but still elegant.

What Charlie remembered most vividly were the aromas of bacon and eggs, pancakes, and cinnamon rolls in the morning, cookies or spice cake or apple pie in the afternoon. She remembered the simmering spaghetti sauce, beef stew, or chicken and dumplings in the evenings, along with the low background noise of Granddad's baseball or football games.

There, along that far blackened ridge, had been Babe Nash's kitchen. Charlie remembered watching it burn as she knelt in the grass, shaking in the arms of her brother, Brandon. And that adjoining area, now full of broken glass and debris, had been the dining room—backdrop to countless family dinners and holiday meals. Grandma Babe had cooked and served them in an actual apron, one with rustic roosters on it.

Charlie didn't realize that she was crying until tears silently streamed into the corners of her mouth and plopped from there into her lap. She couldn't bear to think about that apron; her grandmother had still been wearing it that night when Jake came through the flames and out of the house with her on his back. Grandma Babe had been wearing it when he laid her down on the lawn and collapsed, coughing, while Mom and Granddad gave her CPR. And when Mom, sobbing, had screamed at her to wake up: *Mama, please, God, just wake up . . .*

Charlie, openly sobbing now, slammed old Progress into gear and shuddered away from the curb. It was so painful to see the old place like this; she either needed to remember to stay away, or . . .

Or what, Charlie? Nothing would ever dull the pain or fade the memories or solve the mystery of how the fire had started, but maybe something new could be built. A new house. A garden. Anything but this festering wound in the ground.

The best tribute they could pay to Babe Nash's memory would be to rebuild the house exactly as it was. It deserved a fresh start.

A fresh start. Jake Braddock's face flashed into Charlie's mind. They'd once imagined living in that house together.

Charlie gripped the steering wheel. After her family had abruptly moved to Dallas, she'd never imagined coming home to Silverlake was possible. Now for some odd reason—even with Jake Braddock in town—the idea didn't feel as ridiculous as maybe it should have before she'd watched a grown-up Jake and Lila laughing their butts off like old times.

Because this wasn't about the past. This was about the

future. This was about Granddad and his happiness and turning something dark and troubling into something fresh and joyous. Lord knew, the old man could use some of that.

She was going to bring up the subject to Granddad during her visit. Surely enough time had gone by? And the old man needed a purpose in life, a bigger one than driving his nurses crazy and annoying the town council. This was it. Charlie would bring him both pudding and a purpose.

Charlie parked outside Mercy Hospital and killed Progress's engine. She climbed out, opened the cooler, and fished out two wet, cold vanilla puddings. She dried them with the dish towel she'd stuffed in the cooler pocket, then dropped the treats into her Tory Burch handbag, along with Granddad's monster set of keys.

Our Lady of Mercy Hospital was an uninspired block of a building that stretched six stories high and was in dire need of an update. The linoleum tiles were a shade of depressive beige; the walls, a sickly green; the artwork, sporadic and unoriginal. The elevator groaned more than the patients, and the few live plants reached desperately for the windows and doors as if trying to escape.

Charlie couldn't blame Granddad for not wanting to be here.

"Cook," she heard him say from all the way down the hall. "It's a verb! It means that someone does more than open a can or a box and slop the contents onto a tray."

Oh, yikes. He was not enjoying his lunch. Charlie thought guiltily about the vanilla pudding in her bag. She certainly hadn't made it from scratch. But she wasn't her grandmother, and this wasn't 1959.

"The hospital kitchen staff does the best it can, Mr. Nash," the nurse said. "But you know as well as I do that we don't have the budget for Kristina's triple-chocolate mousse at Piece A Cake."

Charlie stepped into the room in time to see Granddad poke at a rectangle of neon green Jell-O. He gave it a withering glare as it jiggled. "Not. Food."

She almost felt sorry for the Jell-O, but she felt sorrier for the nurse, a young blonde who was wearing a fixed, too-bright smile and a name tag that said BRIANNE. Charlie nodded at her.

Brianne nodded back.

"Nothing in nature is that color," Granddad growled. "*Nothing.* That was scraped out of an alien's bedpan."

"Hi, Granddad!" Charlie sang. "How are you doing today?" She kissed his wrinkled, red-veined cheek, getting a snootful of Listerine.

"Peachy," he growled. "Couldn't be better." He stabbed the Jell-O again. "'Cept they're still trying to poison me. Look at those weird yellow shreds in there!"

"I think that's pineapple," Charlie said in a soothing tone.

"That ain't pineapple, girlie. It's—" He searched among the ghoulish recesses of his brain. "It's probably chicken beaks."

Ugh. "I seriously doubt that, Granddad."

"Well, I wouldn't put anything past 'em. If it ain't beaks, it's old number two pencils!"

Brianne sidled to the door. "I'm just going to . . . check on another patient. You need anything else, Mr. Nash?"

He raised an eyebrow. "Yeah, but it'd get my face slapped."

The nurse fled as Charlie choked. "Granddad!"

He shrugged. "I'm a hundred and seventy, not dead."

"You're only eighty-one, you old liar. Now, if you won't eat the Jell-O, then how about that meatloaf?"

He pushed the tray away. "That ain't beef. It's probably ground sewer rat."

Charlie sighed. "Yep, I think you're right. You'll probably get the tails as spaghetti tomorrow, cleverly disguised under a thick blanket of red sauce."

"Ha!" Granddad winked at her. "Good one. What'd you bring me?"

If she didn't give him the pudding, he was going to starve. Charlie pulled the two containers out of her bag and peeled the top off one, handing it to him with a spoon.

"Thank you. It's not your grandmother's, but it'll do."

"You're welcome." Charlie let him take a couple of bites. "So, speaking of Grandma Babe, I went by the old—" She broke off, not knowing what to call it. House? There was none.

Granddad fixed a beady eye on her, continuing to spoon pudding into his mouth. "Yeah?"

"Place. Well, it's . . . sad. Awful."

He said nothing.

Charlie took a deep breath. "And I know it didn't seem right for a long time. But I think we should rebuild."

Total silence.

"You know, rebuild the house, exactly as it was."

Granddad set down the empty pudding cup with a *snap*. The spoon knocked it over immediately and clattered onto his tray. *"No."*

The single syllable contained enough hostility and anguish that she should have backed off. But she didn't. "She would hate having it look that way," Charlie said quietly. "The yard all scarred and ugly. She'd want her house back."

"Yeah? Well, I want *her* back. Ain't gonna happen." His face settled into bitter old lines.

Charlie opened the second container of pudding and set it on his tray. "Isn't it time to let the past go? Haven't we grieved long enough? Isn't it time to move on?" She hesitated and then said, "I was with Lila this morning, and Jake stopped by."

Granddad turned to face her full-on, his rheumy eyes overflowing with resentment. He opened his mouth, then closed it again. His whole body seized with tension. Then he picked up the second container of pudding and threw it at the wall. White goop splattered everywhere.

A couple of long moments went by as Charlie stared at it, stunned. She thought about yelling at him or stomping out of the room. But then they'd *both* be acting like five-year-olds. She took a deep breath; then she got up. "Really? Couldn't you have thrown the bird-beak Jell-O? Now you have nothing to eat."

Granddad hunched his shoulders and turned away from her. His ropy, veiny hands clenched the sheets. "Sorry," he muttered under his breath.

"Hey," she said, and moved to his side. "Hey." She put her arms around him. "It's okay."

He was unyielding; he couldn't or wouldn't respond to the physical touch. "Ain't never gonna be okay."

Charlie bit her lip and then took a chance: "Just listen for a second. Please. They're still broken, Granddad. Jake is still broken. Lila's still broken. From what I've heard over the years, all the Braddocks are broken. My brother is broken. *You're* definitely broken," she added with a wan smile, gesturing to his hip. "And I am, too."

"The Braddocks have been broken for as long as I can remember," Granddad said, his eyes narrowed. "Only one of them worth my spit is Declan there, and building on the land never did nothin' to make *his* demons go away. Not my problem, never was."

"What I'm trying to get at is that there's one broken thing I know we can fix. Grandma's house." Charlie gave Granddad a squeeze, then straightened. "You need a purpose anyway. Let's rebuild the house. What do you say?"

"I've got a purpose," he said. "If the Silverlake Town

Council will just listen to me. We have got to balance the budget in this burg. We've been running at a deficit for years now, and it's plain to see what needs to be done: get rid of that useless paid fire department!"

Charlie's heart sank. Not this again. Every time she swooped in for a visit, she got an earful of Granddad's plan to "get rid of that useless paid fire department." Thankfully, it never went anywhere. She got up and moved to the paper towel dispenser, intent on cleaning up the mess.

"If I could get out of bed," Granddad said, "I'd be going to the next town council meeting and have this handled in a jiffy."

"Uh-huh," Charlie murmured, her face to the wall as she scrubbed. It never did any good to argue with him.

"You listening to me, Charlie-Girl? I've done a lot of talking. Now it's time to do something. But I'm gonna need your help."

Something in Granddad's manner and in the tone of his voice made Charlie pause and give him her full attention this time. Something that made her more than a little uneasy. "Don't even think about what I think you're thinking about, Granddad," she pleaded. There was no way she'd out and ask, no way she'd take a chance on busting those old wounds wide open, not even in the middle of a hospital. But was that a hint of revenge in Granddad's voice?

Charlie let out a shaky breath, marveling at how fast her heart was beating. She loved her Granddad more than anything, but Jake loved the *firehouse* more than anything. She didn't want to be part of anything that took even more away from him than he'd already lost.

"I have been lobbying the council for a decade," Granddad ranted, "and they turn a deaf ear. But now I have statistics. Numbers that prove that every town around here of this size has a *volunteer-only* fire squad. This year, I will win. Imagine: seven guys in free lodgings, with benefits, *on salary* to lie around in their skivvies with their thumbs up their bums! It's not just offensive; it's criminal."

A cough came from behind her, and she whirled to see Jake Braddock standing there. In an instant, a familiar heat infused her cheeks. *Oh God. How much had he heard?*

He stood there, an ironic smile playing over his lips as he stared at Granddad. It didn't reach his dark eyes. His shoulders filled the doorway, and he seemed to suck all of the oxygen out of the room.

"Hi, Kingston," said Jake calmly. "How you doin'? I've, uh, temporarily gotten dressed and removed my thumb from my bum. I'm here for your physical therapy."

Jake's gaze moved to Charlie's face, and their eyes locked. For a split second, she imagined that the steel in his gaze had softened, and she thought her knees might buckle without them exchanging even a word.

The hot blush that had started in her cheeks began to spread over every inch of her skin. Her pulse kicked up, and her heart took a dive for her stomach.

Help, thought Charlie. *Granddad may need physical therapy, but if I keep running into Jake, I'm going to need the other kind before long.*

"You should probably close your mouth now, darlin'," Jake said, a corner of his mouth quirking up. "Unless you want me to take your temperature? You look a little flushed."

Chapter 5

JAKE HADN'T EXPECTED TO SEE CHARLIE AGAIN SO
soon, but there she was, blue eyes wide with alarm at
the sight of him. Her blond hair was windblown and half
hanging out of a clip at the nape of her neck, where a rapid
pulse beat. Looking mortified, she closed her mouth without a word.

What a day. He focused every cell in his body on looking
cool, detached, and professional. *I could care less about
her,* he told himself, *and I am not intimidated by Kingston
Nash.*

*I am not that confused teenager anymore. I don't need
his approval.*

He'd be damned if he'd let either Charlie or this wrinkled old coot see him sweat . . . or guess that each of his
feet had weighed a thousand pounds on the walk down the
hallway to room 217. Part of him still felt sixteen, still felt
guilty and helpless and lost. He guessed that around this
family, part of him always would.

He kept his expression nonchalant, as if he hadn't just caught her flying off a ladder. As if he didn't remember the way her hair smelled like sunshine, or how soft her skin was. The way she'd felt in his arms.

She ducked her head and mumbled something unintelligible.

He tried very hard not to notice how her jeans and sweater clung to her curves as she balanced on those silly high-heeled boots and scrubbed something that looked like mayonnaise or pudding off the walls. "What happened here?"

"I threw something too early," the old man snapped. "Could have aimed it at your head."

"Nice. I'm happy to see you, too." Of all the patients in the tri-county area, he had to get this one? Seriously? He could probably have weaseled out of it or traded shifts, but it stung his pride to do that.

I am not intimidated by Kingston Nash. He said it to himself yet again. Nash was just a crotchety old bag of bile and bones. He might've paid for the new roof on First Presbyterian Church, but he never had a kind word to say about anyone, and especially not Jake himself—even though he and his boys had physically put the roof *on* the church.

Seven guys in free lodgings, with benefits, on salary to lie around in their skivvies with their thumbs up their bums!

Old George would love that one. Jake tamped down his irritation.

"What in seven hells are you doing here?" the old man growled.

"You heard me," Jake said evenly. "I'm here to help with your physical therapy. You're on my rotation schedule."

Nash snorted. "Get outta my room."

"How 'bout you get outta that bed instead?"

The old man glared at him. "Which part of 'get out' did

you not understand, boy? They need to send me a professional."

"I am one. Had you forgotten? That's what my degree is in. That's why I volunteer here at the hospital, and not at the food pantry or the animal shelter or the rec center, like the other guys."

"Get this pyromaniac away from me, Charlie, before I . . ."

Pyromaniac? That hurt. Jake raised an eyebrow. "Before you what, Kingston? Beat me to death with your plastic drinking straw?"

Kingston gaped at him.

"Come on, old man. What are you afraid of? Let's get you out from under those covers so you can at least give me a good kick in the shins. What d'you say?" Jake moved toward the bed.

"I have somewhere better to kick you," Nash returned. "Charlie, get rid of him."

She stood up and tossed a wad of paper towels into the trash can near the door. "Granddad, you need to do the exercises in order to get better and walk again."

"I ain't gonna do 'em with that . . . that . . ."

"Very nice guy?" Jake suggested. "Model citizen?"

Charlie moved toward the bed and twitched the covers off her grandfather's bare, pale, bony legs.

"Stop that! Get away from me!"

"You've already thrown food today, Granddad. Can you please stop acting like a toddler and behave? Do your therapy?"

"Not with him." Kingston rang the bell for the nurses' station. Charlie shot an apologetic glance at Jake.

Jake dragged a hand down his face, then leaned against the wall near the door. He flattened his shoulders against it, sighed, and tried to ease a kink out of his neck. No dice. They all waited in tense silence for a nurse.

Mia Adams, whom they'd gone to high school with, came into the room within seconds. "Everything okay, Mr. Nash? Hi, Jake. Oh, Charlie—hello!" She smiled warmly. "It's been a long time."

"Mia!" she exclaimed. "Yes, it has. How are you? I didn't know you were a nurse."

"She *is* a nurse," Kingston growled. "That's why she's here in my room, wearing scrubs. And no, everything is *not* okay. I need a different physical therapist. Get this joker outta my room."

Mia looked from him to Jake and then back again. She was a very pretty redhead, with cinnamon brown eyes and a smattering of freckles across her nose. She took in a deep, measured breath while Kingston glared at Jake and then turned his gaze back to her.

Mia exhaled. "I do understand that there's some . . . history here . . ."

"History! Ha." Kingston snorted. "You could call it that."

"But if the hospital staff had someone else to send, they would have," Mia said. "We're short-staffed, so the options are very limited, Mr. Nash. We'd really appreciate it if you could work with us. With him. With, uh, Jake."

Kingston fidgeted and avoided her gaze. He looked around, perhaps hoping to find something else to throw. He screwed up his mouth, tucked his chin, and challenged them all from under his bushy gray eyebrows. "My hip hurts something fierce. I'm not wiggling or rotating *anything.*"

"Are you in severe pain?" Mia asked him. As she moved into different light, Jake noticed that she had huge dark circles under her eyes.

"Nah. I'm getting ready to run the Boston Marathon. Of

course I'm in pain!" He banged a fist on his tray. "That's why I'm extra specially delightful today."

Was he making a joke? Jake wasn't sure.

Mia put a hand on Kingston's shoulder. "Do you need some Percocet?"

"What I need is my youth back."

"It's on back order," Mia told him with a straight face.

"Ha! Good one."

"You won't stay sharp, but a little Percocet would ease your hip some. How bad is it?" she asked him.

Kingston glowered at Jake. "Well, that depends on what this fool's gonna do to me, don't it?"

Well, well. What a surprise. The old man's decided to co-operate. "Nice job, Mia," Jake murmured. Kingston Nash's reputation for being as sharp as a tack was a reputation he clearly didn't want to jeopardize.

Mia smiled back at Jake; next to her, Charlie bit her lip and looked away.

Jake forced himself not to wonder too much if she was jealous. He focused on Kingston and gave the man a nod. "We'll start with thirty minutes on a unicycle."

"Ha!" The noise of appreciation escaped Nash before he could strangle it. He looked annoyed. "So you're not only a drain on the taxpayers; you're a comedian."

"Yep, and since I lie around all day with my thumb up my bum, I have nothing better to do than torture old men."

Nash snorted.

"So you might as well let me earn my keep." Jake cast a professional eye at the withered muscles of Kingston's thighs and calves. They'd start with some basic stretches and rotations, then move on once he proved his stamina.

"Stop looking at my legs, you pervert," Nash groused.

"He can't help himself, Mr. Nash," Mia teased. "You're quite a looker."

Old Kingston rolled his eyes, but his cheeks went pink. *Unbelievable.* Jake began taking him through some simple exercises, trying not to look like he was eavesdropping shamelessly as Charlie and Mia caught up.

"So you're still living in Dallas, your grandfather tells me," Mia said.

"Yes. I work with a real estate development company. I stage properties, try to make them as appealing as possible before they go up for sale."

"You like it?"

Out of the corner of his eye, Jake saw Charlie shrug. "It's okay," she said. "I like the interior design aspect. But sometimes they have restrictions; I'm here to attest that there *is* such a thing as too much beige."

So she wasn't thrilled with her job.

"Do you like nursing?" she asked Mia. "Except when you have to deal with my granddad?"

"I heard that!" Kingston snapped.

Mia laughed. "Yes, I love it, actually. And it pays the bills—unlike Rob. We got divorced."

"Ha," said King. "Not sure why you work. That palace of yours is almost as big as my place . . . was."

Mia's laugh disappeared completely, and creases around her eyes joined the shadows underneath them. She said nothing.

"I'm sorry," Charlie murmured. "Wait, Rob from high school? Rob as in Robert Bayes, class president, right?"

Mia made a face, and then both women giggled like they were sharing a secret joke. "High school was kind of a high point for him," she said. "I keep telling myself it's not too late to meet someone really great."

Jake took a moment to assess Mia's attributes long enough to glean that she really had nothing to worry about. He caught Charlie's gaze as she noticed, and watched in fascination for a second as another deep blush suffused his ex-girlfriend's confused face.

Kingston cleared his throat. "We done?" he grumped.

Jake refocused on his task. "Not yet."

Man, how was it that there was anything even left between them? Enough to make Charlie flustered when he looked at another woman. Enough to knock Jake off kilter, thinking that she maybe gave a damn.

"How about you? Married? Kids?" Mia was asking.

"Uh, no," Charlie said. "I was engaged briefly."

Jake's hands tightened involuntarily on Kingston's ankle. Kingston yelped.

"Sorry," Jake muttered.

"But," Charlie continued, "it just didn't feel right in the end. He wasn't . . ."

Still working on Kingston's leg, Jake racked his brain for the possible endings to Charlie's sentence: *"He wasn't good enough." "He wasn't good to me." Or even, "He wasn't Jake."* What the hell was wrong with him? Why should he care if Charlie had been engaged? And clearly, she'd walked out on that guy, too.

Mia waited for her to finish.

"We were so different. He ran marathons, he was a health nut. He'd give me guilt trips if I put anything not organic or wholesome into my mouth . . . He wanted a size four Charlie, not a size ten one."

Clearly, the man was an idiot. Her curves were perfect. Jake fought the urge to throttle the unknown jerk.

"I just had this feeling that he'd try to edit me 'til the day I died . . . I don't know," Charlie muttered. "I guess I've had a little trouble figuring out what I want out of life. When I was young, I thought I had it figured out, but then, well. Sometimes things don't turn out the way you expect."

Mia gave Charlie a sympathetic smile and nodded. "So you came into town early for the wedding?"

"Well, I came in to check on Granddad after the operation and spend some time with him, too. But, yes, Lila and Felicity also asked me to help with the wedding."

"Isn't Felicity a trip?" Mia laughed.

"Someone may murder her before she gets to walk down the aisle," Charlie said with feeling.

"How long are you staying?"

"I-I'm not sure. I've banked a ton of vacation time, and things are kind of slow at work right now. So it just depends on how Granddad's doing." Charlie lowered her voice. "I'm kind of worried about him. He doesn't seem to be improving that much . . ."

"Think I can't hear you?" the old man hollered. "I'm right here in the room, you know."

But it was true. Jake frowned as he helped Kingston rotate his leg. He should have taken some steps on his own by now. It was a simple operation.

"Sorry, Granddad."

Engaged. Charlie had been engaged to marry another man. Jake couldn't seem to bend his mind around it. But of course she'd been with other men. Just as he'd been with other women. But he'd never gotten friggin' *engaged.*

"Well, I'd love to catch up more with you, Charlie," Mia said. "You should think about staying a little longer. We could get some of the girls together. We always had a good time."

Charlie looked at her grandfather and then back at her friend. "Actually, just today I was thinking maybe I'd stay a little longer after the wedding."

Jake sucked in a quick breath, and Kingston Nash said, "*I'm* the one using up all my energy. What's your excuse?"

"Fantastic!" Mia replied to Charlie. "We'll get together."

Charlie smiled that warm smile of hers. "Absolutely."

"Okay, Mr. Nash, it looks like you're in good hands," Mia said. She looked between Jake and Kingston, her eyes narrowing in suspicion. "We're good here? Nobody's planning to throw any punches?"

Jake looked at Kingston with his eyebrows up, and his patient took the cue to answer. "Fine," Kingston said curtly.

Well, that was at least a better answer than *He's trying to kill me.*

"Then I've got to get to my other patients." Mia and Charlie exchanged a hug.

"And I've got some errands to run," Charlie said, casting an uncomfortable look toward Jake.

Errands, right. The only thing she had to run was away from him. He could still read her like a book, and he could flat-out sense how unsettled he made her. The flush in her cheeks that had appeared when he walked in was still visible. She'd done nothing but fidget while talking to Mia. And she'd been steadily inching toward the door.

As always, the Goodbye Girl was itching to get gone, at least when it came to him.

"Great to see you, Mia," Charlie said.

"Yeah, it was. We'll take good care of your grandfather."

"I know you will. Granddad, I'll check on you later." Charlie walked over and kissed him on the cheek. She straightened and looked at Jake. "And thank you," she said to him, backing away. "See you . . . uh, soon. At the rehearsal dinner."

"Yep."

Jake steadfastly kept his focus on Kingston's scrawny legs, and—though he badly wanted to—refused to check out her rear view as she left.

Chapter 6

JAKE LOOKED UP FROM HIS NOTES ON KINGSTON'S progress to find that the old man's shrewd gaze was on him.

"You still got a thing for my Charlie," he said.

Jake's pen stilled, his fingers tightening on it. "No, sir. It's just, after all this time, a little weird seeing her, is all."

"That's horsefeathers."

"It's not, but you're entitled to your opinion, King."

"Damn straight I am. I didn't just fall off a turnip truck." Kingston glared at him. "And I'm only gonna tell you once. You stay away from my granddaughter. You've caused my family enough grief, you hear?"

The pen snapped in Jake's hand. "You know what, old man? I'm sick of the hostility and suspicion. I'm sick of the questions. I'm sick of you staring right through me or cussing and spitting anytime we run into each other in town. Even though you wouldn't talk to me twelve years ago and haven't since, until today, I know you heard me shouting outside your hotel window that night. The campfire was *out*. Now, you don't have to like the sight of me, or the fact that I remind you of a tragedy in your life, but I did live in your house, as a member of your family, for months. And you do have to ask yourself one question: Have you ever known me to be a liar?"

The old man dropped his glare, looked down at his gnarled, age-spotted hands. "I want some water."

"Have I ever lied to you?" Jake handed him the large covered cup with straw from his bedside table.

Kingston snatched it and took a large draft.

Jake snorted. "You'd love to say yes, wouldn't you? But you can't."

Slurp.

"By the way, I have no intention of going anywhere near Charlie, except for helping out at Will's wedding at my sister's request. But please understand that if I did, I wouldn't feel the need to ask your permission. Now, you have a nice evening, King. I'll be back tomorrow for another PT session."

The old coot locked eyes with Jake, still wielding his cup. For a moment, Jake thought he might throw it right at his head. But he just set it down hard; narrowed his eyes under those wacky, furry gray eyebrows; and gave him a barely there nod.

Well, I'll be damned. Looks like we understand each other.

Unburdened, Jake returned to the Silverlake Fire Station feeling a little lighter, despite the distant rumble of thunder and the threatening sky. As unpleasant as this afternoon had been in some ways, he'd finally had some kind of strange breakthrough with Kingston Nash. It proved that the man was actually human, not an escaped character from *The Walking Dead*. He was just a bitter, lonely old soul who needed a gentle, healing touch. Kindness and companionship. And someone to set him straight.

Before that last discussion, he'd done every rotation and exercise Jake had guided him through, and though it was with a constant grimace and more than a few insults, Jake felt as if he'd actually helped him. Who'd have thought it would be easier to find a way to move on from the past with Kingston than with Charlie?

Jake stepped inside the firehouse, which was technically the office. But it was also home, much more than a bachelor pad and bunkhouse. Its four brick walls and two levels of hardwood floors had been witness to friendship, rivalry, belly laughs, a lot of testosterone, and some occasional drama.

It even smelled like home. Jake sniffed appreciatively at the aroma wafting downstairs from the kitchen. Was that a tinge of possible redemption he scented, or his brother-in-arms Mick's famous meatballs? Mick made them with fresh parsley and oregano that they mocked him for growing in window boxes out back, and Romano cheese that came from Vittorio's, a tiny Italian market in town. Vittorio couldn't stand Mick and wouldn't let him through the door, but his second daughter had a crush on him and sold to him when her father wasn't there.

"Hi, honey," Jake called out to Mick, over the dull roar of ESPN upstairs. "I'm home!"

Not-Spot, their yellow Lab, gave a welcoming *woof* as Jake started up the old wooden stairs, his hand trailing the worn banister. Not-Spot had come home from the pet shelter one day with Tommy, the newest member of the squad. Tommy claimed that Not-Spot had lobbied to volunteer for them as a mascot until they found a dalmatian, which of course they'd never gotten around to doing. Who could break the big heart of a Lab?

The firehouse dated back to the 1950s and still retained much of the cozy, old-fashioned feel of the original layout. The lower level was essentially one big garage that housed Big Red, the fire truck; a couple of other city vehicles; and all their gear. The upper level consisted of a big eat-in kitchen with an L-shaped bar; a den that held a massive wide-screen TV, a navy sectional couch, and a computer desk; and a bunk room.

As Jake came into the kitchen and bent to scratch Not-Spot behind the ears, Mick wiped tomato sauce off his chin with a paper towel. "How was your day, dear?"

"I got to put my hand on Kingston Nash's thigh," Jake told him with a grin. "It doesn't get much better than that."

Old George choked audibly from the den and fell into a coughing fit. He'd officially retired as fire chief a few years back, but he still worked gratis—what else would he do? He'd never married, and the firehouse would always be his home.

"Yo, Georgio," Jake called.

Old George grunted. He hated being called that.

"Tell me you're kidding," said Mick. "Please."

"Nope." Jake ruffled Not-Spot's ears and walked over to the stove for a look.

"You should have ripped it out of the socket and fed it to the Lundgrens' hogs," Mick said.

There came a hoot from George at that.

"You know he's still lobbying hard to put us out of our jobs." Mick retrieved a fork, then banged closed a drawer with his hip. "Not to mention . . . how he's acted toward you over the years."

Mick knew all about how the Nash family had treated him. He'd couch surfed at Mick's house more than a few times after the Nashes kicked him out.

Despite Deck's best efforts to talk to him—even occasionally putting an actual hand on his shoulder—Jake had avoided him and the ranch. The Braddock homestead only depressed him, and Declan was no replacement for Mama or Pop. The more he tried to be, the worse it made Jake feel and the madder he got. Irrational, maybe. But it was what it was.

After the fire, he'd followed Old George around like a lost puppy, constantly asking questions about what could have caused the fire, how it could have been prevented, what they could have done differently. And George, being gruff but good at heart, had tolerated him.

Mick had tagged along, too. The two of them had trained for their badges together after George had kicked them into shape. And back when Jake's world was falling apart, the fact that Mick had never tried to be more than Jake's loyal wingman worked better than Declan's shell-shocked love.

"Yeah," Jake said. He tried to snake a meatball out of the pot, but Mick blocked him. "I'm pretty tired of the old man's BS. But even Kingston, underneath all that crap of his, is a human being—"

"Debatable."

"And someone's got to help him walk again."

Mick adjusted the flame. "Also debatable. If he can't walk, he can't heckle the town council. Ever think of that, genius?"

"True."

Mick took pity on him, finally. "Here, you can taste this. Does it need more oregano?"

Jake took the fork Mick extended to him. A chunk of meatball steamed enticingly. He inhaled it in a single bite, his eyes rolling up into their sockets with sheer pleasure. "Mmm. Man, I can't tell oregano from catnip, but I *can* tell you that these are incredible. As usual. I'll take five right now, on a hoagie roll, with extra cheese and sauce."

"Four," countered Mick. "But they're oversized. And you'll wait until dinnertime with the rest of us."

"Yes, Mom," Jake said with a grimace. "Do I gotta do my homework first?"

The sound of a video call coming in on the television interrupted Mick's response. "Ace is early," he said, and looked at Jake in alarm. "Injury?"

"We'll find out," Jake said, accepting the call from his brother. Ace appeared on the screen, his baseball uniform dirty and accessorized by a black eye and disheveled hair.

"Hey, bro," Ace said. His other eye, bright blue, winked. But it wasn't a merry wink, or a reassuring one.

Jake cursed. "This doesn't look like a simple superstition call. You okay?"

One of Ace's pregame rituals was to call Jake. They'd shoot the breeze a little, Jake would tell him that all the family members were alive and well, and then Ace would go off to hit home runs, catch fly balls, and man second base with the Lone Stars, the major league team out of Austin.

Jake and Ace had maintained the same pregame ritual since they were kids in Little League, ever since their parents had died.

Alive and well. Ace said he had to hear Jake say it or he couldn't play.

Jake sometimes suggested that Ace come home and see for himself. Declan never missed a game and had Ace's stats pinned to the wall in his office, and Lila baked brownies to take to Schweitz's on game day. But Ace never came home. Neither did Everett.

It was never a good sign if Ace called too early, and a

couple of times when he hadn't called at all, Jake had been
legitimately worried. Those were the times when his brother
never even made it onto the field.

Ace took a long swig from a bottle of water, the wreck of
a house party showing behind him on the video screen. And
was that—*oh, man*. A baseball bunny was still sprawled,
barely covered, in his bed.

"I'm alive, but I can't say I'm well. Don't think I'm playing today, bro," he said.

Mick made a worried sound behind him, and Jake looked
around.

"Hey, Mick," Ace said.

Mick might have a loud mouth in general, but he never
shared Ace's business with the press. "What the hell, Ace?"
he asked, still hovering over his meatballs like a nervous
mama hen.

Ace ran his fingers through his hair. "Got into a fight last
night."

"Not with her, I hope," Jake teased, trying to keep his
concern under wraps.

"What?" Ace blinked and then looked over his shoulder.
"Oh. Right. No, not with her. We got along just . . . great.
She's been a nice distraction from this." He held up his
hand. One of his fingers looked distinctly bent, and the others looked black-and-blue.—

Jake winced. "Son of a— What the hell did you do? And
why isn't that splinted yet? You need a doctor."

The cell phone lying on Ace's bed rang. "That'll be the
team doctor now." He grimaced, and said to Mick, "Sorry
about the game." To Jake, he just said, "Sorry." And then he
hung up.

The blare of ESPN came back on automatically once
Ace logged off.

Jake slowly shook his head.

"Maybe some guy spilled a beer on him," Mick said. "Or got too pushy about getting an autograph. Or got pissed that Ace was flirting with his girlfriend. Who knows . . ." He went back to his meatballs. "I do know that they're gonna retire him a lot faster if he can't behave. Too bad we couldn't send Coach Adams on the road with him. Keep him in line."

Coach Adams—Mia's dad—had been a mentor for Ace growing up, as Charlie's dad had unofficially adopted Jake. The high school baseball coach still lived vicariously through his protégé.

"Yeah, no kidding." Damn, that television was loud. Jake picked up the remote and absently killed the sound so that he could think.

"Hey!" Mick said. "I need that to drown out all the voices in my head."

"There's nothing on the planet that will override those."

"Amen to that," Old George called from the other room.

"I should just accept the voices?"

"Exactly. Just as the rest of us do." There was a silence as Jake stared off into space before he said, "I'm having one hell of a day."

Mick put down his cooking spoon and wiped his hands on a towel. "Um, just so you're not caught by surprise, I'm gonna make it worse. Charlie Nash is in town for Will and what's her name's—Felicity's—wedding next Saturday."

Jake stiffened.

This statement had the effect of producing Old George from the other room. He was rumpled, his shirt untucked from his khakis and his shock of gray hair flattened in the back. He tugged at his mustache. "Serious?"

"Hey, man. Yeah," Jake said. "I ran into her at the hospital."

Mick's eyebrows flew up. "And?"

"And nothing," Jake answered.

George snorted. "Last time she was in town, you volunteered for extra shifts."

"It was the holiday season. I was trying to help the rest of you out."

George's eyebrows climbed toward his hairline.

"You were trying to avoid her," Mick said.

"Well, hello, Mr. Serious All of a Sudden. No, look. It's fine now. I've seen Charlie, and it's fine." Jake shrugged, forcing himself to look like he didn't give a damn. He only wished it were true.

George said nothing, just went and stuck his head into the fridge. He knew better than to try to fish out a meatball.

"Fine? Okay. Yeah." Mick snorted. "I've been around the block with you, Jake. I know how it all went down."

Not this again. What is with *everyone?* "It was high school, man. It's been over a decade."

"You said you'd never get over it. You looked like you'd never get over it. Are you getting over it?"

"There's nothing to get over, I'm telling you."

"'Cause if you are, I think we should throw a big party and invite every single girl in the county."

Jake forced a smile.

"Charlie included. If you're over her, then I'm gonna take my chances."

"Ha!" Old George pulled his face out of the fridge.

Jake quit trying to smile. "Don't even think about it."

Mick grinned. "Called your bluff. That was way too easy."

Jake stepped over to him and palmed the back of his head, shoving it down toward the steamy pot. "Time for a facial, Mick!"

The two of them struggled, laughing and cursing, until Not-Spot bounded over and barked them apart.

"It's okay, buddy," Jake told him, as they all panted at

each other. "I'd never kill the guy who bakes you home-made dog biscuits."

"And I'd never kill a poor lovesick fool," Mick added.

George snuck toward the meatball pot, taking advantage of the distraction. And scored.

Charlie's image flashed into Jake's mind's eye. Again.

I was engaged . . .

He wanted to kill the unknown guy.

I've got some errands to run . . .

Any excuse to get away from him. It was borderline insulting.

And that look of almost comic dismay on Charlie's face when he'd agreed to stand in as a groomsman.

We shouldn't have asked. It should be anyone but you.

Nice. The only thing worse than being asked was specifically not being asked. "I am not lovesick!" Jake growled.

Not-Spot cocked his head and looked at him askance. Then he barked once more.

"See," Mick said. "Even the dog knows you're lying."

Chapter 7

PIECE A CAKE WAS BOB'S DONUTS BEFORE KRISTINA Robbins's family came to Silverlake during Charlie's sophomore year in high school. Kristina herself was about as different from the potbellied donut slinger who'd come before her as you could get. She had narrow brown eyes, a sensitive poet's mouth, and waist-length blond hair, which she wore in a braid down her back to keep it out of the way. She rode her racing bike to work every day, but even without the exercise, she was six feet tall and rail-thin with a completely unfair metabolism. Since she had a hyperactive thyroid, Kristina could eat a cake a day and still manage to lose weight. Charlie would have killed for that particular medical problem.

"More coffee?"

Charlie grinned and pushed her mug toward Kristina, who was holding a classic coffeepot that looked deceptively unexceptional. "Absolutely."

It might look like any old coffee, but Kristina was nothing if not particular about her beans. Which was why Charlie hadn't bothered making breakfast for herself in Granddad's apartment since she'd arrived. It was weird enough sleeping there; she refused to cook there. So she visited Kristina every day.

Okay, maybe it wasn't just the coffee. Charlie licked the last bit of chocolate croissant off her fingers and checked the time. Granddad was probably still sleeping. The hospital could wait for one last cup. For now, Charlie could relax and enjoy the uplifting atmosphere.

Kristina had worked with a local artist to design all the furniture out of painted plywood: There was a bench made to look like a chocolate éclair; all the individual chairs had painted "cupcake" backs; and the walls were covered with bright graphics of cakes cut out of plywood. Some of them tilted crazily and jutted out three-dimensionally from the walls.

The real art was in the refrigerated display cases, though: cakes so beautiful that visitors took pictures of them. To say Kristina was gifted was an understatement. Kristina was a Michelangelo, freeing sculpture from marzipan and icing.

Beyond the rows of booths lining one side of the bakery, the sun was shining through the windows. The storefronts lining the opposite side of Main Street looked quaint and welcoming, with their carved historical signs and brightly painted exteriors.

It was surprising to feel this much at peace in a place where she'd had the worst experience of her life.

And the best, Charlie.

She wondered what Jake was doing now. If he was up, on duty at the firehouse, drinking his own mug of coffee. Or if he was still in bed.

An unwelcome thrill passed through her as she thought a little more about that image. The last time she saw even so much as a bare-chested Jake, he was still on the cusp of becoming the adult he was now. Jake. In bed. Jake, now a *man*. Jake, bare-chested . . . man . . .

Sigh.

A sharp whistle pierced the air. Kristina had her hand on her hip and a giant platter of cookies balanced on her up-ended palm. "Wherever you just were, Charlie? I think I want a ticket. This what you had in mind?" She gestured to the cookies.

Charlie laughed. "That's perfect. Thanks." She swallowed the last of her coffee and took her tab to the counter. "So, is everything settled with Felicity's cake?"

Kristina managed a lopsided grin. "Settled? I don't think it's going to be *settled* until the moment she says 'I do.' As she passes me walking down the aisle, she's probably going to ask me to switch the frosting. I was telling Lila we should throw a cake rejects party for the latest round of samples I made . . ."

She paused, her hands tangling in the plastic wrap she was using to package up the cookie platter. "You know what? Yeah! That's *on*. I'm gonna invite all the single ladies in town for a cake rejects party." She looked up at Charlie with renewed enthusiasm. "Maybe serve a little champagne."

"I'm definitely in," Charlie said.

"Spread the word," Kristina said, frowning at the dispenser as the plastic wrap ran out. "The more, the merrier. Date and time to come, but it has to be soon. Buttercream is fussy." She looked around, and went off in search of a new box.

Charlie's gaze fell on a rack of loaf cakes behind the counter, one tier full of banana bread fresh out of the oven.

It looked like the ones her own mom once made. The ones Charlie wouldn't touch but Jake used to eat in two bites with a huge glass of milk after school.

Kristina was back, adding one more layer of plastic wrap, and now ringing up Charlie's bill. "Anything else?" she asked, following Charlie's stare to the banana bread loaves. "Hmm. Is that a yes?"

"Just one," Charlie blurted, wondering what had come over her. "Thanks. But, um, could you bag it separately?"

Jake does not want banana bread from me. Jake does not want anything from me. Why am I buying this?

She paid for the goods, apologized for being such a space case, and headed out to tackle whatever this new day was going to bring.

Outside the bakery, Charlie gave a slight shiver. The sun was shining, yes, but it was warring with some ominous-looking clouds, and a chill laced the air. For everybody's sake, she could only hope the weather would get over itself long enough to get Felicity married already and the rest of them off the hook.

Her phone buzzed. Charlie stood on the sidewalk on Main Street, balancing the goodies while reading Lila's text:

Stop at Maggie's? Please?! New color. Sigh.

The text was punctuated by several unhappy emoji, including one of a disgruntled bride with Felicity's exact coloring.

No problem, Charlie replied, adding the grin-and-bear-it emoji.

She walked to where Progress was parked a few yards away and stowed the baked goods on the passenger-side seat. Charlie stared at the banana loaf for a moment and then slammed the door shut. She drew her sweater together and headed for the florist, still trying to shake Jake from her mind. She wondered just how he had found the grace to overcome her grandfather's hostility and get the old man to work with him. Because that was the word for it: *grace*. He'd ignored the insults to him and his squad, and he'd half bullied, half jollied Kingston into finding some of his own grace—which was in short supply.

She wondered, a little cynically, if Granddad had caved only because he thought Mia was cute, and she'd asked him to be flexible. But whatever the reason, Charlie was relieved that he was going to get his physical therapy. If they didn't get him up and walking, he'd never get out of that bed . . . which wouldn't improve his temper. And if he had a good session with Jake, then maybe he'd back off from his mission to eradicate the paid fire department—a goal that would make her encounters with Jake even more awkward than they had to be.

Just outside Maggie's shop, Petal Pushers, a young mother was putting a gorgeous floral centerpiece in the back of her car, a toddler in her other arm. The little boy wriggled and squirmed, positioning himself over her shoulder so that he could see Charlie. He aimed an impish smile at her and pointed. "Gah!"

"Gah," Charlie said back with enthusiasm, her heart melting.

With his dark cloud of hair and dark eyes, the faintly stubborn set to his chin, he looked . . . *oh*. Coloring so similar to Jake's. It occurred to her that she didn't actually know if Jake was married, though he didn't wear a ring. A lot of men didn't. For all she knew, that woman could be Jake Braddock's wife! *Okay, whoa now, Charlie. Lila would never keep that from you.* Her imagination was going crazy after seeing him again for the first time in a decade.

"You forgot your credit card, Mrs. Kincaid!" Maggie Cooper called, running out from Petal Pushers with her tattooed arm outstretched. The mother stuck her toddler in the car seat, then gratefully took the card and exchanged some words with Maggie.

Charlie was ridiculously relieved, then wanted to smack herself in the forehead. What was wrong with her? Jake lived with a bunch of other men in the firehouse, first of all. Second, why would it be any of her business whether he was married or not? He couldn't stand her, and she lived in Dallas.

As Mrs. Kincaid pulled away, Maggie waved at Charlie. "You're here to pick up Lila's latest sample?"

Charlie held up her phone. "Just got the text."

Maggie rewarded her with a huge grin. "You have no idea how glad I am to see you instead of Felicity." She held the door for Charlie, and the two of them walked to the counter inside.

"These really are gorgeous, Maggie!" called out the only other customer in the shop, a slim woman with a choppy blue-black bob looking at a display of handmade ceramic vases.

"Thanks, Aimi!"

It always cracked Charlie up that Maggie was short not for Margaret but for Magnolia. Because it would be hard to find a woman less suited to the name, which sounded Deep Southern, old-fashioned, and somehow very blond. Maggie was Texas-born and -raised, was covered in artistic (though mostly floral) ink, and had spiky dark hair and a silver nose ring. She'd had both of her arms tattooed with climbing roses, and an inked honeybee "buzzed" right under the hollow of her throat.

The floral shop was a tiny piece of real estate, but Maggie made the most of her space. Petal Pushers was covered, floor to ceiling, with potted plants and bucket after bucket of cut flowers. There were decorative bonsai, and vines hanging from pots hooked to the ceiling. One wall was just roses, in every imaginable color. The perfumed scents of lilac and peony, rose and lavender were tempered by the earthier smells of damp dirt and cedar. "It's like a mini paradise," Charlie said, taking a deep breath.

Maggie beamed at the compliment, her expression falling only as she pushed forward a rose that was colored a horrific shade of bright kelly green. Not unlike Granddad's Jell-O. "The latest sample," she said. "When I think of that poor rose drinking that dye . . . ugh."

Charlie looked at the monstrosity. "For a wedding?"

"A Martian wedding, maybe," said Aimi, sidling up to the counter with her selection in her hand. She peered at the rose in open disgust.

"I'm not going to make any jokes about a wicked witch," Maggie said. She paused for a moment, and then . . . "Okay, maybe I am."

All three of them laughed. Aimi carefully set down her ceramic vase and leaned against the counter, giving Charlie an easy view of her perfectly drawn cat-eye liner and a pair of pouty lips that should have been either fake or illegal but were clearly neither. The two women recognized each other at the same time. Little Aimi Nakamura, not so little anymore. And nobody should look that good in ripped jeans and a white T-shirt.

"Oh, jeez. I heard you were in town," Aimi said. She sighed. "I should hate your guts, Charlie Nash."

For her part, Charlie tried to process the metamorphosis that had taken Aimi, who was two years behind her in school, from scrawny teenager to absolute knockout swan. "Wait, what? Why?"

From the corner of her eye, Charlie saw Maggie bite down on her lower lip.

Aimi shook her head. "Everybody knows you're the reason why Jake's a total commitmentphobe." She crossed her arms over her chest. "Lord knows, I did my best."

"I—"

"Six months. Well, it's more than anybody else got."

"You and Jake—" And *who* else? Obviously, Jake dated other women. And obviously, he'd done so in Silverlake, given that this was where he lived. Obviously. *You have no right to feel anything at all about that, Charlie.*

"At least Jake and I are still friends," Aimi finished. It wasn't meant to be an insult. Just a fact. Aimi's confident gaze swept up and down Charlie's body and then alighted on her stunned face. "And here you are looking like you look, perfectly nice and normal, and making fun jokes about the craziest wedding this town's ever seen." She heaved an enormous dramatic sigh and looked over her shoulder at Maggie. "I'd told myself she probably ended up with terrible skin and an even worse personality. Alas."

"Nope," Maggie said, resting her chin on her hand propped up on the counter. "Charlie's a good egg."

"Is she? Was this your idea?" Aimi asked, pointing to the heinous green rose.

"I'm happy to say that I don't generally have ideas like that," Charlie said.

Aimi grinned and faux shuddered. "In that case, you and I can probably be friends, too."

"This time, I actually hope Felicity changes her mind again," Maggie said grimly. "But the client is now contemplating what she termed a 'bold' color scheme and wanted to see extreme green. Here's extreme green. Please get it out of my shop as soon as possible. It hurts my brain."

Charlie laughed. And with the rose wrapped in cellophane plus a pot of parrot tulips for Grandma Babe's grave, she headed to Lila's office.

* * *

Lila's office was located several blocks down from Maggie's, atop a vacancy set up for a small restaurant. The owner of the building didn't live in Silverlake anymore, and Lila was renting out the office space until a new tenant could be found.

Charlie once asked her why she bothered renting when she had all the space she needed at Silverlake Ranch for free. Lila said it was more professional to have an office in town, and changed the subject.

Walking into the Silverlake Events office gave a person the impression of having accidentally walked into a party storage closet bursting at the seams. Sequins and satin, dried flowers and fake birds, photos of past events and printouts of sample schedules covered every inch of the walls, and the chairs, too. Only a burnt-orange sofa crammed against one wall—probably earmarked for visiting clients—remained pristine. Well, pristine except for the cowboy hat and the boot-shaped pillows, the latter complete with spurs that had been embroidered with silver thread.

That said, in spite of the sheer volume of materials, the place gave Lila what she wanted most, a quiet place to plan events and do business away from Silverlake Ranch.

Charlie pushed open the door with a token knock to find Lila sitting at her glass desk—literally a thick piece of glass placed over two large urns full of yet more party paraphernalia—looking as harried and disheveled as she'd ever seen her. "Are you sure you're ready for this?" Charlie asked, easing the door shut before it slammed.

Lila cocked her head, a pained expression on her face. "How bad?"

"Bad." Charlie dropped the rose on Lila's paperwork.

Lila studied the atrocity and then looked up at the ceiling. "Is Will sure he wants to commit himself to her for the rest of his life?"

Charlie sat on the sofa's armrest and shrugged. "It has not escaped my notice that Will is not yet in town, though he's getting married in a matter of days. I hope he didn't bite off more than he can chew."

"I feel that there's a really gross joke in there somewhere," Lila said, wrinkling her nose.

"Well, it'll all be over soon." As soon as the words were out of her mouth, Charlie felt a pang in her heart.

"Yeah," Lila said. And then she went silent.

"What's on your mind?" Charlie asked.

"I've been thinking about family . . . in general. And about *my* family in particular." She hesitated.

So Charlie prompted with a soft, "Go on."

"If it weren't for this wedding, I don't think Jake and I would be talking much still. Maybe there's actually a chance my family can pull itself together after all this time. Literally and figuratively." Lila smiled wryly. "Wouldn't that be something?"

"I would so love that for you," Charlie said softly. "I bet Jake would love that. And Declan. Well, I haven't seen him yet, but it's all he ever wanted."

Lila fiddled with the pen in her hands. It was purple with an enormous tuft of feathers on the end, clearly some sort of event leftover. "It's been hard enough trying to reconnect with Jake," she said. "I can't imagine being close to Declan again. I dunno. Declan will always leave the door open for us, but I think we broke his heart for good. We just didn't appreciate what he was trying to do." She cleared her throat, still fixated on the pen. "He was barely an adult, trying to take care of us all. He worked his fingers to the bone to keep the ranch afloat, to keep food on the table, to keep our family together . . ." Lila's voice cracked.

"You were so young," Charlie said. "We were all so young."

"Everything we did and said told Declan he wasn't good enough. We all left him. One after another, looking for greener grass, a *real* family."

"Lila, Lila," Charlie said, taking her friend's hand across the desk. "You'd lost your mom and dad. You were hurting. Everything seemed wrong. Nobody knew what to do. And Declan tried his hardest, but it wasn't what you wanted at the time. I remember how it was."

Lila pulled herself together, clearing her throat. "Maybe it wasn't what any of us wanted. But maybe it was what we needed. Maybe if we'd all just stayed and tried a little harder. He was the only one who even really *tried*. Maybe if Everett hadn't left for boarding school and Ace hadn't spent so much time at baseball camps and on the road with travel teams. If I hadn't chased mother figures in every woman I saw, inviting myself to dinner with strangers while Declan's sloppy joes and Hamburger Helper got colder and colder when no one showed up. Maybe if Jake hadn't moved in with you . . ."

A lot of things might have been different if Jake hadn't moved in with the Nash family. It was almost an accident how it all happened. Jake coming home to hang out with Brandon after school every day because things at the ranch were so dark. He'd told her all about it. About Declan trying to do too much. Running the ranch, putting food on the table, wiping Lila's tears and frankly spoiling her, to compensate for the absence of their parents. Everett fighting with everybody because he couldn't cry over the loss. Ace mentally checking out and shadowing his coaches and finally leaving to train for the pros.

Then it was just Declan and Lila waiting at home in a mess of uncertainty and sorrow. But Jake didn't go home. He stayed for dinner at the Nash mansion—once, twice, and then all the time, like a member of the family—until her parents even gave him his own bed and treated him like Brandon's twin brother. And suddenly, he lived there, part of the stable, normal family he craved. The one Declan couldn't give him.

Charlie rested her hand on Lila's back until her friend heaved a great sigh and pulled away.

Lila quickly plastered that old let's-look-on-the-bright-side smile on her face. "Well, it is what it is, right? Just like everything else."

There was something a little off about Lila's forced cheer. Charlie cocked her head to one side, studying her friend's face. "Like *what* 'everything else'? Is there something else bothering you?"

Lila's cheeks turned pink, but she didn't say a word. Just tapped her pen against the paper like a manic squirrel. Charlie looked down at the purple feathers attacking the paper. Lila followed her gaze and froze when she saw the bits of feather littering her desk.

They both looked at each other again, and Lila's body crumpled a little, almost in surrender. "I was all set to tell you that I'd met someone. Finally, right?"

"Uh-oh," Charlie said.

Lila looked up, a desperate, reckless spark in her eyes as she forced the words out: "The guy I've been seeing. I mean, it started out as a fling, and then I thought it was getting serious . . . I was going to tell you that I've finally got a boyfriend who works in Dallas a lot, so you and I might be able to hang out more . . ."

Charlie took Lila's hand, waiting for the kicker.

"Well, he texted me and confessed he's *married*. He was

supposed to pick me up for a date two nights ago, and I waited and waited, and then he finally sends this text saying he's not coming. That he was afraid his wife would discover our affair, and he begged me not to tell. So. Gross. And then when I tried to reach him after that, he ghosted me."

Charlie moistened her lips. "Oh, Lila," she said, shocked.

"I messed with someone's family, Charlie. I didn't know. I swear." She shook her head, her eyes sparkling with unshed tears. "He was a pathological liar and cheater. Obviously, I'm out now, but . . ." Lila took a huge breath of air, steeling herself. "Like I said, always looking to build a family in the wrong place. That's a Braddock for you." Charlie's heart ached for Lila as she pulled herself together. "Anyway, I want to just, you know, put it all behind me."

This wasn't just about the latest lying not-boyfriend. This was about *all* the stuff Lila liked to put behind her.

"Let's get a drink sometime soon," Lila said. "Sit down for a sec and take a breather from this wedding."

"Maybe we could also talk about what happened with this guy for more than a few minutes," Charlie suggested gently.

"Yeah." Lila shrugged. She sniffed and blinked her lashes a couple of times, and still no tears fell. "But not now. I've got to keep myself together long enough to get Felicity married. Speaking of the wedding, are you doing okay crossing paths with my brother?"

Classic diversion technique. But Charlie studied Lila's face, saw how much it had taken her to even admit to the shame she felt about her cheater ex, and went with the change of subject. *Am I okay crossing paths with Jake? If you count wanting to kiss him and break down crying all at the same time as doing okay, then I'm okay.*

"Yeah," she said. And then more gently: "But at some

point, we *are* going to talk about what you just told me. And you're going to be all right, too. Got that?"

Lila nodded. Then, to cut the tension, she picked up the nuclear rose and tossed it in the trash.

Charlie burst into laughter, and Lila joined right in.

Chapter 8

THE CRISP OCTOBER SKY WAS STREAKED WITH STRIPES of pink-orange clouds when Charlie bounded down the steps from Lila's office and hopped back into Progress to point the green machine toward the hospital. She was running later than she'd meant to, and didn't take time to fix it when she parked a little wonky.

Slinging her purse over her shoulder, Charlie anchored the pot of tulips against the passenger-side door, grabbed the cookie platter, and shut the truck door with her foot.

She headed to the nurses' station and found an exhausted-looking Mia filling in a chart at the desk. The poor girl looked as if she rarely slept, though she was unfailingly cheerful and almost frighteningly competent.

"Good morning to *you*. Those are Kristina's, aren't they?" Mia exclaimed when Charlie came forward with the cookies.

"They're for you," Charlie told her. "You deserve combat pay for dealing with my grandfather."

Mia laughed. "Oh, no. He's not that bad. Definitely not

a whole platter of Piece A Cake cookies bad." But, smiling, she made room among the clipboards and brochure racks. "Thank you. The other nurses will be thrilled."

"Well." Charlie hitched her purse up onto her shoulder. "I just wanted to tell you and the rest of your team that I really appreciate your taking such good care of Granddad, Mia. I know it's not always easy. By the way, Kristina's going to throw a cake rejects party. You should come."

"A what?" Mia looked mystified.

"She has a baker's dozen of sample cakes that Bridezilla has rejected. So she wants us to come and help eat them so they don't go to waste. It's a good excuse to have a girls' thing, right?"

Mia laughed. "Sure. Count me in! I need to follow up with Lila about the gifts in the bridesmaid bags anyway. I'm making all the beeswax and honey favors. Felicity wants the lip balm and the candles."

"You mean, *today* she does. Tomorrow she'll want face spray or lotion."

Mia half laughed, half sighed. Then she just nodded.

Charlie left the nurses' station and walked back to room 217, where Kingston lay in bed watching a cable news show at thunderous decibels.

"Hey, Granddad!" Charlie called over the meaningless gabble of some lacquered talking head. "What did I miss?"

Granddad cast a suspicious look in the direction of her cheerfulness and harrumphed.

"How are you feeling now?" Charlie asked in a pointedly loud voice.

"Just as lousy as before," Kingston informed her, finally turning down the volume with the remote that lay on his bed. "Why do you ask?"

"Because you got out of bed, right? With Jake? And at least took a few steps?"

"Yep. Aggravated things all over again."

"That's partly your arthritis. But he helped you, right? And he's . . . nice. You seemed to be getting along."

Kingston snorted with gusto. "Nice? You think I was born yesterday, girlie? He's sucking up to me to soften me up, trying to make himself indispensable, so that I won't go after his job. You think I don't know what he's up to, that one?"

Charlie sighed. "I disagree. I think he actually wants to help you. Is that so crazy?"

"Don't be gullible."

"Fine. Then why did you agree to work with him? Why didn't you just send him away?"

"Because I need to get my withered old butt outta this hospital bed so that I can kick his tax-sucking one."

"So you're using him? That's . . . that's just wrong, Granddad."

"Damn straight. He's not half-bad as a physical therapist. So he can do *that* for a living, and I'll even write him a letter of reference! As long as he gets the hell off this town's payroll, I don't have a problem with him."

Charlie looked him straight in the eye. "Yes, Granddad, you do. And, as I said before, isn't it time we let the past go? Move on?"

The old man's mouth worked, and his hands clenched around the remote.

"Don't you dare throw that," Charlie said.

"Let the past go," he repeated. "Move on."

"Yes."

"Those are real nice notions, Charlotte. Real nice. But you see, not a day goes by that I don't miss Babe. Your grandmother. My *wife*. The woman I *loved*. The woman I married and shared my life with and expected to grow old with! You hear? And she's *gone*. Just gone. Because of stupidity and *carelessness* and that *no good piece of*—"

"Stop it!" Charlie said. "If you blame Jake for the fire, then you also have to blame Brandon. They both made the campfire in the backyard that night. Do you understand that?"

Kingston said nothing. Nothing at all. But his breathing was fast and shallow, his color almost purple. His nostrils were flared and his jaw was so tightly clenched she was afraid he'd break his dentures.

"Granddad? You okay?"

"No, Charlotte, I'm not. I will never be okay. I can, and I do, and *I will continue to* assign blame *for as long as I draw breath*, to the useless, lousy fire department that couldn't get a few blocks over to save my wife before she died of smoke inhalation! So don't give me any grief about *using* some jackass who's paid to do nothing twenty-four seven, three hundred sixty-five days a year. Do we understand each other?"

Charlie exhaled. They sat for a long moment in silence before she nodded. "Yes, Granddad. I guess we do."

"Fan-flippin'-tastic. Then you also understand that since I can't get my useless bony old butt outta this bed on this coming Friday, you will be going to the town council meeting as my proxy. You will present my facts and numbers there, and you will vote in my place."

Charlie gaped at him. "Wh-what?"

"You heard me."

She felt the blood draining from her face. He wanted her to do battle in his stead, go up against Jake and the firehouse guys, lobby for the elimination of their jobs? "I can't do that," she said.

"Why the hell not?"

"Because, I—" Why couldn't she? Because she still remembered the way Jake's arms had felt around her when he'd caught her? How his body had felt underneath hers? The heat of him, seeping through her clothing and into her heart?

Maybe all of those things were true, but also because she didn't believe what Granddad believed. She didn't believe the things that Jake and the other firefighters did were a waste.

"I just can't," Charlie said.

"You can, and you will." Granddad's tone didn't allow for argument. It was the same tone he'd used when telling her as a child to brush her teeth, to go to bed, to change the TV channel from something inappropriate for her age.

But Charlie was no longer a child. She was an adult woman who didn't like being ordered around. "You'll have to find someone else."

"*What* did you say?"

Charlie shook her head. "You know that I love you, but I'm not going to go and lobby for the elimination of the fire department, especially after Jake Braddock was just here helping you try to walk again."

Granddad's color, which had been subsiding from beet red, darkened to purple. "You're gonna give me a heart attack, girl," he said through gritted teeth.

"You're not going to have a heart attack, Granddad," Charlie said, patting him gently on the chest.

"I ask you to do one little thing for me, and you say *no*? If you say *no*, I'll just find somebody who will!" the old man blustered.

This sounded a little worse than usual. "I'll think about it," Charlie said in a rush, desperate to change the topic.

Granddad wasn't having it. "This ain't the end of this conversation."

"Granddad—"

He folded his arms across his chest, his eyes narrowed, and glared at her.

"Are you giving me the silent treatment?"

He didn't answer. And his color was still making Charlie nervous.

"I know this is so hard for you," she said. "All of this. And I hate that you're stuck here almost as much as you do. Ask me anything else."

Stony silence.

Charlie sighed. "I was thinking of visiting Grandma Babe," she said softly. "I know you missed visiting her because of this injury. I picked up some of those striped tulips she loved. Anything you want me to tell her?"

Granddad's arms stayed firmly over his chest; his jaw stayed clenched.

"I'll tell her you love her," Charlie said.

And though he still wouldn't say a word, something deep in his eyes softened.

Charlie left Mercy Hospital and walked back through the parking lot, casting a wary eye up at the gray sky. Thunder rolled again in the distance, and a few raindrops spattered her on the way to old, dilapidated Progress, which sat lonely in the parking lot, a throwback to another era.

Progress. What irony. Who had named the old truck? It might have been her grandmother . . . Granddad had always laughed at the name, as if it referred to a private joke between the two of them.

A wave of pure longing washed over Charlie, and as tired as she was, she headed away from town toward the cemetery for what would hopefully be her final errand for the day.

But she never could just pass the ruins of the old mansion without stopping. Especially not today, with Grandma Babe's tulips on the seat beside her. Planting them in October was probably silly, but they should survive for a while. As the burned-out foundation of the old mansion came into view, she found herself pulling right onto the lawn, such as it was. She climbed out of Progress and slammed the door on it, which seemed fitting, given her lack of success in getting Granddad to move on and leave the past behind. The high heels of her "idiotic" boots sank into the mud that underlay the weeds, but she could hardly bring herself to care.

She made her way through the yard to the tallest wall still standing, which was the back one. It was only three feet high now, and filthy, but Charlie plopped down on it anyway. Her jeans were black and couldn't get any darker, besides which they needed a good washing.

This had been the family room, when the house was intact. A large picture window had been to the left of where Charlie sat. It had faced out to the back lawn, where there'd been a white gazebo for entertaining. A flagstone path had led to it.

To Charlie's right had been an old brick fireplace, most of which had survived until Granddad got blind drunk one night and attacked it with a sledgehammer. Concerned citizens driving by had alerted Bode Wells, the sheriff, who'd come out to try to reason with him. When reason didn't work, Bode had been decent enough to let Granddad finish the job—and his pint of Jack Daniel's—before driving him to his apartment and not to jail.

That was how people in this town were: decent. They looked out for one another. They cared. And they had looked out for and cared about Granddad for years now. Which made it all the more important that he not take that for granted, that he not spit in their faces and cling to his bitterness.

Charlie wondered how to reach him. In her mind's eye, she saw Grandma Babe enter the room in her rooster apron, peering over her horn-rims at him as he fussed and crabbed

over an article in the newspaper. *All right, King,* Charlie heard
her say as she handed him a whiskey on the rocks. *That's
enough, you old curmudgeon. Now it's time to say thank you
to the good Lord that you have eyeballs to read that rag,
and the leisure to do so, and a comfy leather chair to sit in
while you complain about the politicians.*

Tears sprang to Charlie's eyes, and Babe told her that
was enough of those, too, thank you very much.

But what do I do? Charlie implored her as the sky continued to rumble overhead. *How do I get him to move on?
To free himself from the past?* She found herself praying for
a solution, praying for him, praying for a way out of what
he was asking her to do at the council meeting.

That's when the rain blew in, seeming to mock her efforts. The black sky shattered into a million liquid silver
bullets, pelting her as she ran back to Progress and fumbled
with the ancient handle to get the door open. She was
soaked by the time she scrambled in.

Charlie grabbed a mangy, musty old jacket of Granddad's
from the space behind the seats, wrapped it around herself,
and let the storm have its thunderous temper tantrum outside.
It flailed and thrashed and blustered and poured while she sat
safely in the old metal cocoon and peered out at it. Despite
the raging weather and her state of exhaustion, despite
Granddad's antics, she felt comfortable here in Silverlake. As
if she belonged. And as if some invisible force were calling
her home.

She liked Dallas, and her job was okay, but all she did
was work, and she'd never put down roots there. It was too
easy to skate on the surface of things: make small talk and
run meaningless errands, and turn to the TV or her iPad for
company in the evenings. Charlie again found herself with
the fierce urge to rebuild the house that should be standing
in front of her, porch beckoning, lights welcoming. And

maybe if they rebuilt the house, then her parents or even Brandon would come home.

Pragmatism reared its ugly head as she mused. What would she do here to make a living? And how could she escape seeing Jake in a town this small? They'd run into each other anywhere and everywhere: Schweitz's, the bank, Shear Glamour, Sunny's Side Up Diner, The Tooth Fairies . . .

So? said a belligerent part of her. Jake Braddock didn't own the town. Besides, they'd managed to stand in the same tiny hospital room at the same time, and the world hadn't come tumbling down. Maybe they'd even get to the point where they could be friends. If Granddad could accept Jake's presence, she should be able to as well. As long as her family didn't insist on repeating the past and destroying everything Jake cared about.

But Granddad's demand that she be his proxy still weighed heavy. She didn't want to defund the fire department! That would cause Jake to lose his job. Who could she ask to stand in for her?

Charlie closed her eyes, listening to the now-steady beat of the heavy raindrops on the hood, roof, and windows of the truck. The din soothed her somehow. She heard Grandma's voice saying, when Charlie was small, that into every life some rain must fall. That it helped wash away grime and grow new flowers. Charlie remembered asking her, as a little girl, what thunder was for then. And Babe paused a moment before telling her that thunder was just the sky being a bully.

So what about lightning? she'd asked.

Lightning, her grandmother had said, was dangerous. Made you open your eyes and see things that might have been previously hidden. It could strike viciously and reduce your illusions to ash.

What's an illusion, Grandma?

Shh. Go to sleep, sweet pea. Go to sleep.

So Charlie did.

She awoke with a jolt maybe an hour later. She'd been sleeping upright in the truck, her head bent forward. There was a trickle of what must have been very attractive drool in the corner of her mouth, and she had a terrible crick in her neck. It took her a moment to realize where she was: snoring in Progress, like a drunk, on the former front lawn of the Nash mansion. *Nice.*

The rain had stopped, though the trees were still dripping. Charlie stole a look at herself in the rearview mirror and wished she hadn't. Her hair looked like a bird's nest, her eye makeup was smeared, and her nose was so shiny it reflected the emerging sunshine. "Hello, gorgeous," she muttered. "Let's *not* take a selfie."

She fumbled for her cell phone to make sure the hospital hadn't called. No messages. Good. Her stomach gurgled, then rumbled like an outboard motor. She was in dire need of some food and a shower. Charlie dug her index fingers into the corners of her closed eyes, trying to relieve the tension she felt, and then turned the key in Progress's ignition. The dependable old engine roared to life, and she put the gearshift into reverse, then stepped on the gas. But there was no familiar lurch backward, only an acceleration of the engine.

Charlie looked down, thinking maybe she'd popped the truck into neutral, but no. She tried again, with the same result. Progress made no progress. What was going on? She tried a third time, stepping harder on the gas, but the back wheels of the truck just spun in place. Oh no . . . Surely not? Surely . . .

Charlie killed the engine and climbed out of the truck, only to sink her high-heeled Italian boots now ankle-deep in mud. She eyed them with an emotion too weary for despair and peered at her back tires, also sunken deep into the mud. Her efforts to reverse had only made the tire trenches worse. Wonderful.

Okay. What to do now? She supposed she could call the local garage—was it still owned by the Larsens? Or she could try to help herself first. She looked around for any big flat rocks or planks of wood. Hmm. No planks, but there was a rock a few feet away that looked promising. Charlie tried to take a step forward but found that it was challenging. She looked down at the boots she'd been so excited to score on sale and cursed them. They *were* idiotic under these circumstances. What she wouldn't give right now for a pair of flat-soled rubber rain boots—the uglier the better!

Charlie sighed, pulled her left foot out of the sucking mud, and bent over to unzip the boot. She stepped out of it, grimaced, and planted her socked foot into the muck. Then she bent to unzip the right one. She left the boots where they stood, next to Progress, and squelched over to her chosen rock, where her feet sank yet again. She looked ruefully down at her manicure, which she'd paid good money for last week in the city. *Screw it.*

Charlie bent over the rock and started scrabbling in the dirt. Problem: The rock wasn't so flat. In fact, it was possible that it was more of a boulder . . . She heard the noise of a vehicle approaching, and looked under her arm at it. A Dodge Durango, red. Oh no. That wasn't—surely not—it couldn't be—

Jake Braddock.

Noooooooooo!

Not again. Not here. Not now.

Charlie realized the picture she must be making at the moment: butt in the air, bootless, with muddy socks, scraggly hair, filthy blackened hands, and a beet red face, because her head was hanging upside down. She had some choice words for her choices in this situation.

Plan A: She could run before he recognized her. Too late. Progress was a dead giveaway. Besides which, if she ran in her socks, she'd slip in the mud, wipe out, and look even worse, like a giant skid mark.

Plan B: She could dig like a manic mole to hide. If she started right this second, she figured she could sink her face and head at least to the ears, which would mean she couldn't see or hear Jake laughing at her. But the downside of that plan was not being able to breathe, and she utterly refused to die looking this bad.

Plan C: Charlie could embrace her white knight a second time, pretend to adore being a damsel in distress and a cliché. No. No, she absolutely refused.

She had a cell phone! She could call AAA for a tow— well, no, because she wasn't a member. Wait, yes, she could! She'd join now, right this minute. Where was her wallet? Her phone?

The Durango had pulled forward and stopped. A figure that looked an awful lot like Jake Braddock got out of it and shut the door. Tall, dark tousled hair, broad shoulders. T-shirt under a flannel shirt rolled to the elbows. Arms so cut with muscle that they were defined even under the plaid.

Charlie straightened, turned at the waist, and with effort, unstuck one foot and set it down in front of her. Then with determination, with what she thought of as sheer brio, she unstuck the other one, but she slid on the first, lost her balance, and pitched forward onto her face. Mortification had never smelled so much like weeds, wet earth, and— ugh—deer dung.

This-is-not-happening-this-is-not-happening-this-is-not-happening! she sang to herself. *Nope-not-never-not-not-not-nope! I am dignity itself, shimmering in the wind, the very spirit of grace. This is so not happening. I am vi-sualizing this not happening. I can create my own reality with my thoughts . . .*

There was a suppressed rumble of amusement above her. "Charlie?" Jake's voice quivered with the effort not to laugh. *Smart man.* "Is that you?"

She raised her face and spat out a blade of grass. "No."

"I didn't think so."

"I am a complete and total stranger, Jake Braddock. Get that straight. You have never seen me before in your life."

"Okaaay," he said cautiously.

"That's the only way I can deal with the humiliation of *this* situation on top of the humiliation of the *other* situation. Got it?"

"Yep." He paused. "Would you like a hand?"

Charlie pushed herself to her knees, squatted on her haunches, and just looked at him.

He gestured at her. "Oh . . . oh, boy. You—"

"Don't say it. I don't want to know."

His lips twitched and his dark eyes danced, and yet he managed to adopt a kindly expression, which was the biggest insult of all—aside from his being so hot here when she was . . . *not* hot.

"Hi, beautiful," he said.

"I hate you," she said.

"You can't hate me. I'm a total stranger, remember?"

"Right. But you look highly suspicious and generally loathsome. So I'm pretty sure I hate you anyway."

"Fine. I'm good with that."

She decided it was time to stand up, and did so, ignoring his proffered hand. "I'm too dirty." She was absurdly proud of herself for making it to her feet without his help.

"I don't have a problem with dirty girls," he said with a totally straight face.

She glared at him.

He cleared his throat. "That went over well. So can I ask what happened to your shoes?"

He followed her gaze to the Italian boots, sprawled where she'd left them next to the truck. "Ah." His mouth worked. "And you decided to leave the truck . . . why?"

She pointed to the rock. "I thought maybe it was flat and I could put it under one of the wheels."

"Well, that explains everything," he said dryly. "And nothing. Why are you out here?"

"Because . . . because . . ." She gestured at the blackened foundations of the mansion. "I have this crazy idea that I should rebuild it," she blurted.

Jake's mouth tightened, and the good humor drained from his expression.

She suddenly felt terrible. Of all the places for him to find her, out here was the worst. "There are a lot of good memories here, too, Jake."

"Yeah," he said baldly. Abruptly. "So, you need a tow?"

Chapter 9

OF ALL THE PLACES IN THE TEXAS HILL COUNTRY that Jake did not wish to stop, Charlie had to stall him at this one.

It was bad enough driving past the burned-out husk of the Nash mansion almost every day on some odd job or other. He usually turned the radio up loud long before he approached and made a point of looking for deer in the trees across the road, or checking the lake for signs of a top-water bite. He kept his head turned away.

Jake still woke up some nights to those licking, devouring walls of fire, that skin-melting heat. It was indescribable, impossible to convey the horror of it. He'd felt like a human marshmallow, crisping and blackening on the outside, his blood boiling and his organs bubbling inside. For precious, hideous seconds, he'd stood gaping and steaming in his own sick fear. Then, impelled by some stronger emotion, he'd hurtled back into the house to find Grandma Babe.

The back wall of the house was in flames. The fire had knocked out the electricity, so the only light seemed to come from hell, and it was precious little because of the thick, suffocating, nightmarish smoke. It wasn't just smoke, either . . . it was a hot blanket that had dropped him to his knees. But on his knees he'd gone forward, crawling like a blind, crazed baby, searching for Charlie's grandmother, feeling his way along.

He got to the bottom of the stairs, where he heard a high-pitched whining, a bark, then a disembodied canine scream and the skittering of paws. A rattling of chain, then a *thump, thump-thump* and a howl as Mr. Coffee came hurtling down the stairs and hit Jake head-on. Grandma Babe had clearly pushed him, trying to save him. So she was still okay . . .

The dog was tangled in a sopping-wet towel, and Jake dragged the animal, towel and all, backward, in the direction of the front door. Jake tugged and scrambled, heaved and gasped, until he got the squirming, whining bundle through the door. He pitched them both forward, rolling them down the porch steps.

The dog was hysterical, and the once-cold wet towel was steaming. Charlie rushed, white-faced and panting, to take Mr. Coffee. Jake himself was banged-up, bruised, gasping. But Grandma Babe was still in there, upstairs. Without thinking, Jake ignored the screams from the front lawn, pushed past a wild-eyed Kingston Nash, hurled himself up the porch steps, and crawled back into the inferno.

The walls pulsed with horrific heat. It was a toxic, burning malevolence that tore the oxygen from his lungs. He was hopping with adrenaline and a weird fury at the fire. He couldn't beat it—no way—but he wasn't going to let it take anyone he loved. Jake crawled once more to the stairs.

He didn't remember making it up them. All he could

recall was feeling the texture of the carpet at the top of them, and then something soft—Babe Nash's thigh. She lay there quiet amid all the terrible cracks and pops and thunderous whooshing. He shouted her name. No response. *Oh God.*

Jake knew he couldn't stand up—the smoke was too thick and too scalding. The only breathable air was close to the floor. The only way to get Babe out was—he didn't think about it. He simply positioned himself at the head of the stairs, facing down and facing the floor. Then he pulled her up onto his back, holding on to her arms as best he could with one hand, and slid down the stairs on his belly, balancing somehow with the other hand. It hurt. It wasn't dignified. But it worked.

He had little memory of getting from the stairs back out the front door. All he remembered was clumsy weight and awkwardness, and a sheer terror that drove him like some primal motor. Then they were on the front lawn, with people screaming. Charlie's mom rushed to do CPR on Babe, while tears streamed down Charlie's dad's face as he embraced Brandon.

Jake collapsed onto his back in the grass, desperate to drink in all the night air available, with the moon and the stars as chasers. Instead, he coughed and hacked out smoke. Rolling onto his stomach, he gasped in dirt and bits of grass along with the clean air he craved. Then he coughed those out, too.

He became aware of a hand slapping him on the back. *Jake? Jake! Are you all right?*

It was Charlie. She was crying.

You got her out! she said, over and over. *You got Grandma out.*

Except he hadn't gotten her out in time.

Jake shook off the memory of the Charlie of the past and

focused on the one standing comically before him in the present.

Yep. The best of times, the worst of times. That was Charlie in a nutshell. The idea of her rebuilding the mansion . . . the idea that maybe she was rebuilding to stay, well, that was the kind of nightmare scenario that used to keep him awake at all hours once he'd stopped being haunted by the opposite: that she was never coming back. And yet another part of him (well, a couple of different parts of him, truth be told) had the notion that after all this time, Charlie Nash keeping him up all night wasn't the worst thing he could think of anymore.

God, Charlie, the truth is, it feels good to see you. I never thought I'd be able to say that. But it feels good to see you, looking so alive.

And I still hurt so badly inside.

He surveyed the bright-eyed natural disaster standing in front of him and alternately wanted to yell at her and take her in his arms. Jake had never wanted to kiss a swamp creature before. But here he was, wanting to back Charlie Nash up against the nearest tree, lick the mud from her mouth, and have his wicked way with her. There was something very wrong with him.

But even covered from head to toe with sludge, with a piece of grass stuck to her cheek and her zombie eye makeup, he wanted her. Even growling like a small bear from mortification, Charlie was gorgeous, which entertained him and aggravated him at the same time.

"Yeah," she said after a pause. "I could use a tow."

He nodded and headed for his Durango before he said or did something stupid, and repositioned the trunk so that his bumper faced the front of Progress. Then he got out, and unlocked and opened one of the big toolboxes that rode directly behind the cab. Out of it, he pulled a long length of chain with a hook on either end. This wasn't the first time he'd had to give someone in Silverlake a tow, and it wouldn't be the last. He and the guys sometimes towed cars for the Larsens' garage.

He walked back to poor old Progress, which was sorely in need of a paint job. A memory surfaced: he and Charlie's brother as teenagers, washing and waxing this very truck for extra money.

Charlie had squelched back over to it in her disgusting socks. He caught her taking an aghast look into the side mirror and couldn't contain his laughter any longer as she put a hand up to her mud-encrusted hair.

"Sweetheart, don't bother. You look like you've been dragged through a hogpen backwards and then trampled by a mule."

Startled, she jumped and almost fell on her face again, but she braced herself on the running board. "I, uh . . . I wasn't checking my appearance. There's, um . . . something under my contact lens," she said, clearly attempting to recover half a shred of dignity.

He shot her a knowing glance, which she did not seem to appreciate. He crouched down and hooked one end of the chain under Progress. Then, accompanied by its metallic rattle, he walked the other end to his trailer hitch and secured it. When he turned around, she was staring wistfully at the burned-out foundation of the house.

Bile rose in his throat as he gazed at it, too. His stomach clenched. He tried to ignore both sensations. They'd go away if he simply didn't acknowledge them. So would the emotions roiling inside.

He'd sat at the Nash kitchen table, right there in the middle of the foundation, eating meatloaf and baked potatoes and peas. He'd sat at their Thanksgiving table, in the dining room sixteen feet to the right, eating turkey and stuffing. He'd played backgammon and chess in the family room at the far left, with Brandon and Dave, their dad. He'd watched sports and played poker with them and Kingston back there, too—a game which they'd always pretended was Go Fish or Uno if Babe walked in. She hadn't approved of gambling.

Jake swallowed, then inhaled raggedly and looked up, finding the now-invisible bedroom that the Nashes had once told him to call his own. They'd taken him in, a stray, and practically adopted him. He'd been so happy in that bedroom next to Brandon's. The denim comforter on the twin bed and the blue plaid flannel sheets had always smelled clean and fresh, thanks to Babe, like spring in the country. The bottom of the lamp had been red ceramic; the bureau, simple blond wood. An oval woven rag rug had warmed the hardwood floor, and on the wall had hung a turn-of-the-century oil painting of boys playing in a schoolyard. That room had been Jake's idea of heaven.

Charlie squelched over to him. She put a hand on his arm, which sent an unwelcome and inappropriate jolt of electricity through him and brought him back to the present. "Remember the time when Mr. Coffee snatched the Butterball turkey right out of the sink and ran under the house with it?" she asked.

"Yeah." One corner of his mouth lifted.

"And you and Brandon had to slide under there and pry it away from him?"

He nodded. "Mr. Coffee. The chocolate Lab from hell. I still miss that dog."

"Me too. He lived a good long life, though."

Jake nodded. "How is Brandon?" he asked carefully. Brandon, his best friend—until he wasn't. Until the tragedy, after which the whole Nash family had moved away and cut him cleanly out of their lives. Ostensibly for Brandon's sake, because he was distraught, emotionally unstable.

She shrugged, an expression of grief and frustration settling over her features. "Depends on the season. He's, uh, struggled, but he seems to be doing better now."

Jake examined a smudge on his work boot. It was rust-colored and shaped like a fist. He'd never noticed it before, but now it was fascinating. He took a deep breath as his stomach roiled along with a rush of dark feelings. "If it's ever appropriate, if it ever feels right, or if he ever asks about me—tell him I said hey."

Charlie swallowed. "I will." Her blue eyes held grief, wistfulness, guilt . . . and something else that he couldn't name but wanted to.

Without being conscious of it, Jake reached out a hand and cupped her cheek, rubbed gently at the mud there with his thumb, at the smudged mascara.

Charlie's breath hitched, and she closed her eyes.

And then somehow his other hand was cupping her other cheek, and he was stepping into her space, all the dark feelings, all the dark memories of their broken lives fading away. Jake felt like he was in a beautiful dream, with this girl he'd loved like no other in his hands where she belonged. *If I could go back in time . . .*

Guiding her mouth to his, he bent to kiss her very gently.

He smiled against her lips; she tasted like earth from her face-plant. She smiled, too. He raised his head, lifted his T-shirt, and wiped her mouth with it. She let him, her gaze fixed on his bare abdomen. She flattened her palms on it, and he sucked in a breath. Then she slipped her hands around his waist and sighed as he kissed her again, more urgently this time. The touch of her hands on his skin was almost too much to bear. He wanted to devour her.

He backed her against the side of Progress and pressed every inch of himself against every available inch of her, not caring that it was wet or cold or that she was mud-encrusted. If he thought anything at all, he thought, *Mmm* and *Mine.*

Then a tremor, a shudder, racked her entire body, and he belatedly realized what he was doing: kissing the Goodbye Girl, Charlie Nash. The girl who'd cared so little for him that she'd left without a word, and wouldn't take his calls or letters once he had managed to track down her new address. The girl who'd shut the door in his face when he'd hitchhiked into the city to find her.

What the hell was he thinking? He *wasn't.* Jake backed away, wiping his mouth on his flannel sleeve. Feeling that he needed to spit out the taste of her, because it made him want more. A lot more. "That," he said evenly, "was a mistake."

Charlie sagged against her grandfather's truck, her expression shell-shocked, staring down at the useless Italian boots still stuck in the mud.

Jake strode over to the Durango and flung open the driver's-side door. "I'd move those, if I were you. And you'll need to get into Progress so you can steer once we've gotten your back wheels free." He got in and slammed the door—on the brief flare of attraction between them, and on any possibility of it escalating further.

Charlie bent forward, pulled the boots from the muck, and tossed them into the bed of the pickup with about as much ceremony as she'd given their breakup all those years ago. A boy's feelings? His love for her? *Thunk, chunk.* The old metal reverberated as the boots hit it.

Jake started his truck and drummed his fingers on the wheel impatiently as Charlie clambered awkwardly into her grandfather's truck. Was she really going to try to drive in those muddy, slippery socks? He rolled down the window and tooted the horn.

She manually rolled down her own window, raising her eyebrows.

"You might want to take off your socks," he drawled. "It's awful dangerous for a city girl to—"

Something came whizzing at him through the window. Jake dodged just in time and caught the projectile in his hand. *Banana bread? What the . . . ?*

"I'm not a moron, Jake. But thanks," Charlie said, looking pleased with herself. She bent down, peeled off her socks, and tossed them onto the passenger-side floor mat.

Jake stared down at the banana bread in his hands. It looked really similar to the kind Charlie used to ask her mom to make for him. "You hate bananas."

"Yeah. So throwing it at your head was a win for both of us."

The ridiculous feeling of well-being that shot through Jake as he stared down at his "present" was almost enough to make him forget what a mistake that sweet, sweet kiss was.

Almost. A wave of anger swept through him as he remembered how easily Charlie had once switched from hot to cold.

"Jake," she said haltingly. "What *was* that, just now?"

A mistake. Mistake. Mistake. "Banana bread," he said, knowing quite well that wasn't what she was asking about.

He slipped on the aviator sunglasses that sat in his console. Then he put the Durango into drive. "Ready?"

She shrugged.

"Start her up and put her into first gear," he told her, though this time it was without the attitude.

And Jake got on with rescuing her, though what he really wanted to do was drive away at a very high speed, leaving her and his memories mired in the past, where they belonged.

* * *

Charlie's mouth burned from the kiss, and she could still taste Jake on her lips. Her stomach quivered, and she gripped the wheel tightly, as if it might slip from her grasp, as he had. The man who'd been kissing her moments ago had gone up in smoke, his essence untouchable and faceless behind the twin mirrors of his shades.

She wasn't allowed to keep him back then. What made her think she could have him now?

The Durango did its job with a roar. Charlie sensed a similar aggression below Jake's too-cool surface as he manned the operation. With a mighty lurch, Progress pulled free and then shuddered forward, the chain clanking and rattling to the ground.

Jake got out and unhooked the two vehicles.

"Thank you," she called.

"No problem." He slung the chain and hooks back into his toolbox and slammed the lid.

She tried not to enjoy her view of his backside in the snug, faded denim, tried not to notice the small hole in the shoulder of his flannel shirt that was somehow endearing instead of sloppy. She definitely didn't pay any attention to the way the slightly curling dark hair at his nape met the muscular back of his neck, or the cocky way he held his head as if he knew she was checking him out.

"Jake . . ."

He turned, his face so neutral and professionally pleasant that it made her ache deep inside. "That was a mistake. Let's not do that again," he said matter-of-factly. He checked his watch, a plastic digital number. Nothing flashy or designer for Jake. Just pure pragmatism, right down to the Timberland work boots he always wore. "I'm late for a . . . thing."

She nodded, even though she knew there was no "thing," and he *knew* she knew there was no "thing." The layers of awkwardness were surreal. Charlie stepped on the gas with her bare foot and lurched forward, then made the most inelegant shift into second gear and finally third. Then she fled, heading in no particular direction, just away from Jake. Away from her own guilt about the past and the role she'd played in making it even worse for him. For Brandon's sake.

"Stop beating yourself up, Charlie," she said aloud. "The past is the past." A clean break, everyone had said, was best for her brother.

But *had* it been best for him? Really? And what about poor Jake? What about *her*? Everyone had made such a fuss about Brandon and his struggle in the fire's aftermath. Her parents had been all-consumed by their worry and their grief. Charlie herself had just stayed out of everyone's way. She'd seen a therapist for a while, but had filled only one scrip for an antianxiety medication, only to have Brandon swipe the pills. She never refilled it.

Grandma Babe used to say there was no better cure than a homemade apple pie. Maybe Charlie ought to do some baking tomorrow. Maybe she'd make, oh, say, twenty-five pies. Maybe that would do the trick.

The potted tulips on the passenger seat nearly tipped over as Charlie hit a pothole. Charlie smiled. *You don't approve of my attitude, Grandma?* She sighed. *You're probably right.*

Without further incident, Progress led her to the gates of the Silverlake Community Cemetery and then down the curving tree-lined drive to where the huge stone Montmorency Mausoleum kicked things off, so to speak. One of the founding families of Silverlake back in 1839, the Montmorencys had seen to it that they anchored the cemetery and were remembered in style, with a Gothic arched entrance to their eternal resting place. A very large stone angel guarded it, wings outspread. Brandon, the soul of irreverence, used to say that it looked tired, that maybe it needed a break.

After the Montmorency clan, who'd erected the town library and the first city hall, came the slightly smaller tribute to the bootlegging Brockhursts, who'd opened the first tavern (and, it was rumored, the first brothel). No angel outside their mausoleum, just a very large urn. Then there were massive looming blocks of dark granite for the three brothers Stockdale, who'd owned the first bank, livery stables, and dry-goods store. After that, Charlie lost count. They'd been forced to learn about Silverlake's founding families in school, but the local history lesson had needed to stop somewhere.

Charlie stared out at the sea of gravestones, looking for the corner plot shaded by a large oak that was Babe's. There it was, over there. Progress took her right over, and she made sure to park in a paved area—no more mud today.

She grimaced as she gazed down at herself. Really? She'd come to visit her grandmother looking like this? Charlie opened the door, grabbed the tulips and a spade from the foot well, and hopped out. Yes, her toes were grime-encrusted. Her pants would need to be burned. Her sweater, once a fashion statement, now looked as if it had been dug out of some long-deceased person's casket. And then there was Granddad's nasty old barn jacket to top it off.

"I feel pretty," Charlie sang, under her breath. *"Oh so pretty . . ."*

Grandma would laugh.

Charlie walked slowly toward the oak, appreciating the softness of the green grass under her feet, even though it was wet. She was still shivering, still humiliated and confused by her feelings for Jake and the utter wrongness of them. But she tried to ignore all of that.

Babe's headstone was a light gray granite, and oddly enough, there were fresh white lilies in a container in front of it. BARBARA NASH, the marker read. 1934–2004. BELOVED WIFE, MOTHER, GRANDMOTHER. Charlie jammed her hands into Granddad's coat pockets, wiggled her bare toes in the grass, and stood there in all her vagabond glory, just staring at the stone block. Four words, to sum up a woman's whole life and all of the love she'd given to everyone she'd ever encountered.

So inadequate. There was so much that the headstone did not say:

Had wanted to be a nightclub singer in her youth. Got married and sang in the church choir instead. Secretly retained her affinity for slutty shoes and too-bright lipstick, to counteract that rooster apron. Held her entire family together. Made everyone mind their manners. Chased after anyone who didn't behave with a wooden cooking spoon.

Couldn't bear to kill any living creature, even if it had six legs and jumped out at her from behind the flour jar. Always looked at her glass as half-full (even when it was upside down, transporting a cricket back outside on a piece of paper).

Babe Nash, tiny lady with the heart of a lion. The kind of woman who'd have a tug-of-war with a terrified chocolate Lab during a house fire, crawling on her arthritic knees under a monstrous antique four-poster bed to pull Mr. Coffee out, throw a wet towel over his head, and push him toward the staircase and freedom.

Charlie used the spade to make a hole in the ground and quickly transplanted the tulips from the pot to the natural soil guarding Babe's name.

She wiped her hands on her dirty clothes and then sat down next to the headstone. "Sorry I look so terrible, Grandma. But I promise you that my underpants don't have holes in them, and you would have really liked my Italian boots if you'd seen them yesterday.

"I won't stop anywhere else on my way to the shower, I swear. I won't embarrass you. And I'm going to rebuild your house if it's the last thing I do in my lifetime. Okay?"

Babe Nash herself didn't respond, but a squirrel in the branches overhead beaned her headstone with a seedpod of some kind. Charlie didn't find that respectful, but she decided to take it as an "amen."

She got to her feet and grabbed the empty pot, not bothering to brush off her backside, and stared again at the white lilies. They had to have been placed there recently—no later than yesterday. But by whom? Certainly not by Granddad, who couldn't walk on his own down the hospital hallway, much less outside in the cemetery. She couldn't see him paying someone to do it—that was just out of character. Charlie puzzled over it for a moment longer, then turned to walk away. That's when she noticed it: a very large fresh bootprint in the damp earth.

As she fired up Progress and headed back to town, she thought about it some more. The print was definitely a man's. No woman had a foot so large. That print had been made by a man's work boot. But whose?

Back at Granddad's complex, she deliberately ducked down in Progress and hid until old Mrs. Dwyer had finished walking her schnauzer. Grandma Babe would haunt her forever if she let Mrs. D, a former archrival in the garden club, see her granddaughter like this.

Then she hopped out and scurried into Granddad's sparse little apartment. She was so dirty that she left tracks on the walkway and inside on the hallway floor. She grabbed a clean garbage bag and stripped in the bathroom, tossing each discarded item of clothing into the bag. She'd just pray that they didn't destroy the apartment's laundry facilities.

It wasn't until icky brown water was streaming off her in a blessedly hot shower that she realized something. Jake's red Dodge Durango hadn't been coming from town when he'd stopped to help her. It had been coming from the direction of the Social Security office and the cemetery. Jake wasn't over sixty-five, so that ruled out a visit to Social Security. And he'd been wearing work boots on his very large feet.

It broke Charlie's heart. Twelve years after the tragedy, Jake was still putting flowers on Babe Nash's grave.

Chapter 10

SLEEP. I NEED MORE SLEEP, THOUGHT JAKE, ROBOTI-
cally hefting the final sack of groceries out of the
Durango and heaving it across the garage to Tommy to pass
up to Mick in the kitchen.

"Last one," he heard Tommy shout upstairs. Jake
checked for any missed apples or bottles that might have
rolled under the seats, then slammed the truck door.

Last night had been a total bust. He could not get yesterday out of his brain. That moment on the dirt road, with
Charlie in his arms and his mouth covering hers, the soft
sound she made when he kissed her . . .

He'd told her it was a mistake, because what the hell else
was he going to say, confused as all get-out, thinking he
should still be angry but liking way too much the way it felt
to hold a grown-up Charlie in his arms. You'd think he'd
kissed her enough back in the day to not react like a
lovestruck high school virgin now.

All night long, his brain had reminded him it was a

mistake. But his heart—and, oh hell, his body—seemed to have a different opinion.

Charlie'd thrown that brick of banana bread through his window, and for a split second he was sitting at Grandma Babe's kitchen table with a glass of milk and a half a loaf on his plate, Charlie giggling into his ear, her arm draped around him. For a split second, he'd remembered the simple joy that a completely ordinary day could bring.

Jake pushed open the door leading from the garage to the living space, tempted to flop onto the worn navy couch and pull one of the plaid pillows over his face, so he wouldn't have to look at Grady's latest terrible abstract painting. The thing was a "study" in blues, purples, and blacks, with a dribble of bright green stinking up the middle. In short, it was weird. But they'd all have to look at it until he got inspired to do another one. Tommy kept suggesting nudes, to no avail.

Jake bypassed the couch and was headed for the kitchen when he heard Ace and Mick on the horn. They were talking about how many more games the Lone Stars would need to clinch the pennant race.

Ace saw him enter the frame and gave him a chin nod.

Jake smiled. "You look better than last time," came out of his mouth at the same time that Ace ran his fingers through his newly cropped hair. Those fingers were attached to a hand attached to an arm that was in a massive splint. "Oh, crap," Jake added.

Ace grunted and continued to fidget, running the top of his good hand across the newly landscaped scruff on his chin. "I was telling Mick earlier that I'm thinking of coming home for a visit."

Jake had heard that one before. Although Ace hadn't been injured the other times he'd said it. "Seems to be all the rage."

"What's all the rage?"

"Coming home."

Ace's eyes widened. "Rhett came home? No way."

Jake barked a laugh. "Everett? He's *never* coming home. Unless you know something I don't know. Are you in touch with Rhett these days?"

Before Ace could answer, Mick leaned over the couch and said loudly into the video-chat microphone, "He means Charlie. Charlie's back. They bumped into each other yesterday."

"Charlie who?"

Behind his head, Jake could tell Mick was making some kind of big motion with his arms.

"Charlie *Nash*?" Ace asked. "I hope you kicked her to the curb!"

"Not exactly," Jake said.

"Why is Mick smiling like that?" Ace asked.

"He didn't kick her," Mick said. "It was a different word he used. But it also started with a 'k.'"

Jake punched Mick in the shoulder, which was sort of like punching a very dense piece of wood, in more ways than one. Shaking out his fist, he said, "They've still got you on the injured list. You doing your PT like they're asking, or am I going to have to take a leave of absence and come make you?"

"Hey, that's not a bad idea. You should come out *here*," Ace said. "Everybody should definitely come to me." He was not nearly as skilled as Jake was at deflecting serious questions.

"He can't come out there," Mick said. "He's too busy canoodling with Charlie."

"Oh, Mick, you're the *worst*, man," Jake said, shaking his head. "I kissed her *once*, and it was a mis—"

"Mick wasn't lying? You really kissed Charlie? Charlie

Nash Charlie?" Ace leaned back and let out a *hoo-boy!*
"The same Charlie Nash who broke your damn heart into
so many pieces I think some of the shards are still stuck
between the floorboards of Declan's living room? That
Charlie Nash? You *kissed* her?"

Jake crossed his arms over his chest, leaned back against
the sofa, and gave Ace a stony glare. "You done?"

Ace was wearing that lopsided grin of his. The one that
could slay any female—and even some of the males—for
miles around. "What else did you do with her?"

"Charlie and I had our shot. Our time ended years ago,"
Jake said. "So I told her the kiss was a mistake, and that
was it." Well, that wasn't exactly it. Because he couldn't
stop thinking about it. Thinking about it to the point of being unable to sleep. He kept that part to himself.

"I *totally* hear what you're saying, my man," Mick said,
making it clear from his expression that he totally didn't.

Jake snorted. "Sorry to disappoint you both, but I'm not
going to let her affect me."

"Hmm . . . that's not quite the same as saying you're
unaffected," Ace drawled. He drummed his fingers on his
chin and narrowed his eyes, looking like Sherlock Holmes
trying to solve the mysteries of the human heart.

"Can we talk about something else?" Jake said. "Like
your muscle tone or your RBIs or something? Want me to
say hey to Coach Adams for you?"

"Yeah. But I don't want to talk about baseball," Ace said
flatly, his smile vanishing. "I gotta suit up for the bench
now anyway."

Mick and Jake shared a concerned glance.

"Speaking of which . . ." Ace's face suddenly looked
boyish again. "I know I'm not playing, but . . ." He shrugged.

"Declan, me, Lila, and as of two days ago, Rhett—
we're all alive and well," Jake said quietly.

"Amen," murmured Mick, rapping his knuckles against the wood knife block.

Ace nodded, looking embarrassed and relieved. Then a devilish gleam appeared in his eyes, and he leaned forward. "Jake, a word of advice?"

"Oh, no," Jake said.

But Ace was undeterred. "You see Charlie Nash again, get Mick to help you establish a fire line, and stay *well* back. 'Cause, brother, you are gonna get *burned*." He winked and killed the connection before Jake could get in the last word.

"He hangs up on me every single time," Jake muttered.

Mick was still laughing as the two of them finished jamming the groceries into the firehouse refrigerator and then jumped into an SUV to head out for Felicity Barnum's fire-safety check. He wasn't looking forward to meeting the woman who was giving the whole town fits with her crazy demands, but Old George had asked him to step in today, and Jake didn't have a good reason to say no.

Turned out, he just didn't know he had a good reason; Mick was intolerable. The twenty-minute ride was a litany of inappropriate fire-related puns pertaining to what Jake had or hadn't claimed to have done with Charlie Nash. Jake just sighed and kept his mouth shut and his eyes on the road.

Well, he never should have kissed her.

After what seemed like an eternity, Jake pulled the SUV up to the barn. Mick grabbed the paperwork and a clipboard, and they hopped out, heading straight for the side entrance that connected an outer equipment shed to the main barn.

It wasn't a shed anymore, just like a lot of the property wasn't just a working ranch anymore. It was now what Lila called her "staging area," which Declan had reluctantly transformed into a sitting room for a bride before her big moment walking down the aisle.

He had paneled the walls and painted them a soothing pale blue color. Lila had brought in a 1930s-era walnut vanity with an oval mirror and placed a chair with a needlepoint seat in front of it. She'd placed an antique silver-plated brush, comb, and hand mirror set on the vanity. And in a corner, she'd set up an old-fashioned art deco changing screen with a painted motif on each panel.

Jake pushed open the shed door and said to Mick over his shoulder, "I'm counting on this to go fast. I have to go see Mrs. Baxter for her PT. And it'll take a while, since I know she's gonna want to read my tea leaves or something."

Mick suddenly gasped, and Jake nearly reached for his radio to call for Big Red based on his partner's expression alone. When he turned back around, he saw the cause of Mick's horrified face.

It wasn't on fire, though it would have been better if it were.

It wasn't alive—in fact, it seemed more suitable for the undead.

Charlie stood in the middle of the room next to the changing screen, wearing what had to be the worst dress Jake had ever seen. Behind her were several identical awful dresses hanging from a couple of bridle hooks on the wall.

Jake choked on involuntary laughter, forced it into a cough, then dragged a hand down his face. "You. Are. A. Vision."

"Holy guacamole," was all Mick could contribute.

Jake's male mind went straight to the expanses of pale nude skin exposed by the dress: neck, arms, legs . . . cleavage. He then tried his best to process the short strapless dress she wore, made of a shiny silver fabric that exploded with apocalyptic red tulips. A ten-inch ruffle festooned the hemline like a length of folded fire hose—and looked just about as elegant.

Standing next to Charlie was an extremely made-up woman in city clothes. She had the body of a *Sports Illustrated* swimsuit model, glossy black hair, and stop sign red lips. This could only be the high-strung, beautiful, and spoiled Felicity Barnum, a.k.a. Bridezilla. All of Silverlake had been buzzing since she'd breezed into town earlier in the day.

"Good to see you again, Charlie," Mick said, his mouth twitching with amusement. "Long time no anything."

Along with the god-awful dress, Charlie wore an expression of complete horror. "Hi, Mick. What are you doing *here*?" She breathed the words more than said them, looking between the two men.

Jake couldn't tell if it was how she felt about the dress or him, but he figured both he and the dress deserved it, at least a little. There were no words.

"Fire-safety check," Mick said, knocking Jake's shoulder. "Right, Jake?"

"Right," Jake mumbled. "We should probably go . . ." And yet his eyes stayed glued on Charlie in that dress, and his feet stayed glued to the floor.

"And you must be Felicity," Mick added, when neither Jake nor Charlie did anything to help move this strange eyesore of a situation along.

"Yes, I'm the bride," said Felicity, pressing a manicured hand to her chest and fluttering her eyelashes. "Felicity Barnum. Soon to be Mrs. Will Spence." She held out her hand, nearly blinding the men with her massive sparkler, and giggled. "Hello, *Mick*, is it? And *Jake*, obviously Will's told me all about *you*."

Charlie winced. Jake shrugged it off.

"You are just in time to give me a second opinion," Bridezilla said. "These are the bridesmaid dresses. Don't you just love them?"

Charlie squirmed, tugging the hem of the dress down. Jake followed the motion to the curve of her thigh.

"*Don't* you just love them?" Bridezilla repeated, more nervously this time.

Jake looked at Mick. Mick looked at Jake. After a couple of stuttering attempts at speech, it was Charlie who pulled herself together. "They're . . . amazing. Really unique," she said.

"The red tulips will echo the red in my new lace dress!"

"They're perfect," Jake finally said.

First, Charlie could wear a garbage bag and still look fantastic. Second, he knew how stressed Lila was about all of Felicity's changes; a change to the bridesmaid dresses at this stage would put her over the edge. So, in his mind, they *were* perfect. And, yeah, if he went back to focusing on the parts of Charlie the dress didn't cover, there was a lot—*a lot*—to appreciate.

The only downside, if you could call it that, was that the dress was clearly making her chilly; she seemed to be trying to cover herself up where the skirt hit high and the top hit low.

A quick elbow from Mick got Jake's attention back on track. "What happened to not letting her affect you?" Mick asked in a low voice.

Jake tried to shift his focus back to fire safety. He looked away from Charlie's body to her face. Well, her face was certainly on fire. See? He could be professional.

"And the best news?" Felicity was saying to Charlie. "I ordered red satin elbow-length gloves for all of the girls! I found them online. I have them in the car."

"Fabulous!" Charlie managed.

"Actually . . . I'm dying to see if the gloves are the same red as the tulips on the dress. They'd better be. If you just stay right here, I'll look for them now!" Felicity was gone in a flash.

As the door shut behind her, the guys hooted with laughter.

"Stop it," said Charlie. "This is so not funny."

"Yes, it is!" Jake said.

"Talk about a pain in the butt." Mick shook his head. "Are you second-guessing being in the wedding yet, bro?"

"No. It was a peace offering to Lila," Jake said.

"I think I'd have chosen war . . ."

"I thought Old George did the safety checks," Charlie said.

Jake let his laughter fade. Charlie was starting to look really distressed. "You're really not laughing, are you?"

"I'm trying, but . . ." She shook her head, her arms wrapped tightly around herself.

Suddenly, Jake would have given anything to wrap his own arms around her. "Hey. Listen. You don't have to worry. The dress is bad, but nothing ever looked bad on you."

Charlie managed an uncertain smile, and all of a sudden there was a lump in Jake's throat the size of Felicity's ego.

At the same time, he and Charlie said, "Listen, I—"

They looked at each other in silence until Mick cleared his throat and muttered, "Uh, right. So . . . I think I hear Lila yapping in the main barn. I'll get the show on the road. Leave you two to . . . whatever . . . Okay, uh, bye."

Before Jake could find the words he wanted to say, Charlie stepped behind the changing screen.

"Thanks for the banana bread," he said, and then rolled his eyes at how stupid he sounded. *Thanks for the banana bread?* "Okay, so—"

Charlie let out a soft oath. "Um, do you mind getting the

zipper?" She backed out a little ways from the screen so he could reach.

Jake stared at the way her hair swept forward, exposing the pale skin at her nape. "Sure," he said roughly. He awkwardly grabbed for the zipper tab, his fingertips sliding down her skin as he loosened the dress.

Charlie shivered and disappeared back behind the screen. Her voice was a touch breathy when she said, "Thanks for taking care of Grandma Babe's grave, Jake. It was you, wasn't it?"

"I . . . uh . . ." Jake shook his head the way Not-Spot did after a dousing. Didn't seem to do a damn thing to clear it when he could see tiny glimpses of skin where the three sides of the screen were hinged together. Her blond hair cascaded past the hinges. Charlie must've flipped her hair the way she used to after blowing it dry. "It was on my way," he muttered.

Charlie poked her head around the screen, giving Jake a quick view of one bare shoulder. "Jake Braddock, we both know that was not on your way. You did a kindness, and I thank you for it."

Jake turned his back on the screen, sending a silent request up to the heavens for some of Declan's stoicism. What was he even still doing here? Once a zipper's down, a zipper's down. *Wait, don't think about it that way.* "If you're good," he said, "I'll go ahead and just meet you in the barn."

"I'm not good," Charlie said.

I'm not good, either. "We can't change the past," he said roughly.

"Is there anything you think we *can* do?" Charlie asked.

Jake dragged a hand down his face. *Maybe if you talked to me. Really talked to me about everything. Explained why. My whole life, I feel like I've been waiting for you to tell me why. Why did you let me go?*

"Jaaaaake!" Lila's voice called from the barn.

"Coming!" Jake yelled back. He sighed and turned back toward the screen. "You're not even going to be in town that long. In the meantime, as Grandma Babe always said, it don't cost anything to be friendly." *Well said, Jake. That sounds mature. You're like a grown man or something.*

Charlie came out from behind the screen, fully dressed, her hair tucked behind her ears, looking fresh and adorable and utterly, utterly kissable. *Damn it.*

"I'll take friendly," Charlie said. "I can do that. I'd love to do that. There will be no more of those pesky . . . confusing . . . complicating . . . inappropriate . . . mistakes. Scout's honor." She sliced her hand through the air like she was using a cleaver on a piece of meat. "Just friends. Or, well, at least, friendly."

"Jake! Where *are* you?" Lila yelled. "We gotta get this safety check off my list!"

Charlie smiled at Jake and headed for the door. "Duty calls, eh?"

Jake followed behind, trying to find his own smile. She'd just suggested exactly what he thought he wanted, everything he knew was for the best.

So why didn't it feel right?

Chapter 11

WHEN CHARLIE ENTERED THE MAIN BARN, FELIC-
ity was already there with a pair of red satin
elbow-length gloves slung over her shoulder.

Oh, good. Charlie stared forlornly at the gloves. *We'll
all look like Vegas showgirls. I don't suppose there's anything I could say to convince her to leave them out of the
wedding . . .* She looked up at Bridezilla, who was fluttering
around Mick as he attempted to check a wall socket, apparently second-guessing everything he said or did. *Nah.*

Felicity had swept her black curls into a side ponytail
and tumbled them artfully over her left shoulder. Her ruby
red lips had definitely been augmented somehow since college, and with just a little more work would successfully
approximate talking sofa cushions. Charlie told herself to
be nicer, but the way Bridezilla had been treating Lila,
Kristina, and the rest of the proprietors in town, she was
rapidly depleting her stores of goodwill.

Lila waved Jake over, and the two began to walk the

periphery of the reception hall. The fire department was scheduled to do a fire-safety check because of all the extra electricity required for Felicity's elaborate and dramatic event lighting. But Charlie had expected the crew to stay in the barn, not to barge into a glorified closet during a try-on of Felicity's (*please-oh-please-oh-please-let-it-be-over*) final choice of bridesmaid dresses.

Although come to think of it, Old George barging in on her in that dress would have been only slightly better.

Mick glanced over while Felicity was talking and widened his eyes at Charlie. She guessed he was having a hard time with the contradiction of Felicity's obvious physical charms juxtaposed with what was coming out of her mouth. Charlie'd known Mick well in high school, and there was something both wonderful and sad about how easy it was to just plug back into the old friendships.

Good old Mick the Menace, high school's most beloved practical joker. He'd been the driving force behind filling the football coach's old Corvette with rank, sweaty gym clothes that had been collected for days beforehand.

Mick had put on muscle and seemed to have matured since then. He'd been an eyeful and a half in his youth, and he'd only improved. Charlie couldn't help but chuckle as she recalled that he'd set an unofficial school record for kissing girls. Well, not her. She'd always been too busy kissing Jake.

Charlie shook her head, wishing her every thought would stop leading to Jake. Sure, they could say they were going to be friendly and not make any more "*mistakes*." But she still couldn't get their last kiss out of her mind. She just wished it hadn't felt so right.

Felicity snorted at something Mick said, tipped her head back to laugh, and went stone-still instead. "Oh no!" she screamed.

Both Mick and Jake reached for their radios in the instant before they processed that this what not what they would call an emergency.

"It doesn't look right," Felicity said, pointing to the swags. "Not with my new color concept. And it's so perfumy. The guests will get a headache. We can't give the guests a headache. And, frankly, some of the petals are starting to turn brown. So the gardenias are going to have to come down anyway. There's still time to do roses, right? You know, real red roses."

Mick's expression went south. Apparently his willingness to always give a sexy woman the benefit of the doubt just couldn't hold up in the face of Felicity's entitlement.

Charlie almost laughed out loud.

Bridezilla gazed at them expectantly, her question still hanging in the air.

Lila appeared temporarily speechless and then finally found her voice, clipped as it was. "Yes, of course we can switch all of the gardenias in the swags out for real red roses. As long as you cover the cost of the gardenias. You did ask to have them put up earlier than advised, and that's why they've started to turn. As I warned."

Boy, did Lila have a lot of big white teeth when she gritted them in that particular way, drawing her lips back until they almost nudged her ears. Charlie'd never noticed how sharp Lila's incisors were. Then again, she'd never seen that . . . almost carnivorous . . . look on her face.

The bride-to-be made a face at the idea of paying twice but then shrugged.

From behind Felicity, Jake winked at his sister and gave her a thumbs-up.

Charlie liked seeing that. At least Jake and Lila were starting to behave like brother and sister again.

"Then do it," Felicity said.

"Of course," Lila said after a tiny pause. She did not look up at all the gardenia-festooned swags that they'd hung already.

Charlie carefully didn't look up at them, either. But Jake did, his eyes twinkling with brotherly malice. It was oddly endearing.

Lila scratched subtly at her nose with her middle finger.

"But are you sure you want to use real roses, Felicity?" she said. "Because if so, the swags"—Lila gestured at them—"will have to be redone on Friday and then stored overnight somewhere. Maybe in Ray the butcher's meat locker—ha ha!—since I don't think Maggie has the refrigeration space for such big items at Petal Pushers."

"Ray Delgado would love to store a bunch of wreaths on his meat hooks," Mick assured them all in a dry tone. "I'm sure he'd be very accommodating."

Felicity missed the sarcasm, but Jake punched Mick lightly in the shoulder, as if to tell him to shut up. Charlie's lips twitched.

"Or," Lila continued, aiming a death stare at Mick, "the flowers would have to be wired onto the swags really, *really* early on Saturday, before Maggie opens, and then we'd need to rehang them all. So maybe we can use silk ones? It's more practical, and though it's still extra work, it doesn't throw us into emergency mode."

Any more than we already are, Charlie thought. But those words remained unspoken.

Felicity's phone rang. She put up a ruby-manicured finger to indicate that silence was required. She held her bedazzled cell phone to her diamond-studded ear. "Hello, Amelie." Her pillowy lips flattened. "I think we have a misunderstanding about the alterations on the gown. Since you *refused* to give me a *refund* on it, I honestly thought you'd modify it for free. I mean, how hard is it, really, to shorten the thing into a summer cocktail dress?"

Charlie, her smile still painted on, exchanged a look with Lila, who seemed to be strangling a growl. And Felicity's tone was not going to do her any favors with the long-suffering Amelie.

Jake's eyebrows shot up, and Mick frowned.

"Yes, I know it was custom work," Bridezilla said. "Yes, I know I approved the sketches and signed your order form. Yes, I do know you have other customers—not for long, when I put the details of my experience on Yelp, but—*excuse* me? You don't know how to make me happy? I just explained it to you very clearly, Amelie. Shorten the dress for me! Right away, so I can take it on our honeymoon cruise. Honestly, I can't keep laying out more cash on gowns. My father is going to draw the line."

Daddy should probably have drawn a line back, say, when Bridezilla was a toddler. But clearly, he hadn't.

In the background, Jake began to whistle softly, a sure sign that he was irritated. He'd done it back in high school. Funny how Charlie remembered that.

"Split the difference for the alterations? That's the best you can do?" Felicity snapped. "Really? You know what, *fine*. I don't know what is wrong with the people in this town, but they are just not bride-friendly. I don't have any more time to haggle with you." She ended the call and gave a dramatic sigh. "I am so tempted to elope."

Hope dawned in Lila's eyes, but Charlie knew better.

"But poor Will," Bridezilla said, "would just die. It's always been his dream to get married in this Podunk town—"

"Podunk?" repeated Mick. "Don't you mean, say, picturesque?"

"Uh, no offense." Felicity waved a hand, as if it would erase her words or the insult behind them.

Charlie looked down at the floor. *Careful, Bridezilla, or you might "just die," too.*

Mick moved away to test another wall socket.

"So what were you saying about silk roses and butchers, Lila?" Bridezilla asked, her perfect silky black eyebrows drawing together in a frown, which she quickly smoothed away. "No. Look, I've decided that I don't care for the iridescence of silk. I want the velvety, natural look of real flowers."

"Well, these particular flowers are going to be ten feet above the heads of the guests," Lila pointed out. "So I'm not sure anyone will see their texture."

"The overhead lighting will shine on it," Felicity insisted.

"But we'll have those overheads turned off. We're doing the sconces only, right? And the can lights in the potted trees around the dance floor. Then the spotlights and the twinkle lights everywhere outside. That's what we talked about."

Bridezilla chewed on her artificially plump bottom lip. "Yes, but . . . I want real roses. There's nothing like the scent of fresh flowers."

Unless they are too scented. Like gardenias.

Charlie watched Lila close her eyes and then make a note in the wedding file. Then Lila tried one more time. "Well, again . . . remember that these particular flowers will be ten feet overhead. We can use fresh ones for your bouquet and the church pews and the centerpieces on the tables."

Felicity shook her head. "They all have to match exactly. And some of those silk ones look so cheap."

Jake laughed silently behind her, which was, unfortunately, infectious. Charlie did her best to shove a giggle back down her own throat. She absolutely could not laugh—or growl—at the bride. She told herself to be understanding. Ugh. *Felicity is just a nervous girl at heart, trying to choreograph her big day.*

"All right," Lila said, "let's check with Maggie right away and see what she can do."

The barn door creaked and then slammed, and none other than Declan Braddock walked into the barn, clearly surprised to see Jake. "Jake," he said, shaking hands with his brother. "Twice in one week. But then . . . I heard you were part of the wedding." He looked at Charlie, his face impassive.

Shame burned her cheeks. He'd been aloof since the fallout after the fire. Since the Nashes had cut off his brother. Go figure.

He hesitated, then surprised her. "Welcome back to town, Charlie," he said, holding out his hand.

You're a good man, Declan. "Thanks," she said. She shook hands and forced herself to look into his impenetrable dark eyes.

But he'd already turned back to Jake. "Usually we do this with George. We square on the safety check? If there's anything we need to do, I'm on it."

"Oh, Lila . . . *Lila!*" Felicity was frantically waving from the other side of the barn.

Lila didn't seem to hear her. A glazed expression on her face, Lila didn't seem to hear anything.

Charlie tapped Mick on the shoulder and, when he bent down, whispered in his ear, "Can you keep Bridezilla busy for second?"

Mick sighed and whispered, "This would be a lot more fun if she hadn't started talking."

But he took Felicity aside, and when he had her occupied, making a discussion about wattage overload sound as sexy as anyone could make it, Charlie pulled Lila away from her brothers.

"I know she's starting to get to you, and I don't blame you, but you look like you're one tube of frosting away from slamming a wedding cake in her face."

Lila took a deep breath and looked down for a minute. When she lifted her gaze again, Charlie saw a storm under the surface. She wondered if Lila was going to tell one of her brothers that the reason for the dark dusting under her slightly puffy eyes wasn't just about Felicity's endless requests. But then she figured Lila didn't want anybody getting arrested. She had to know that in spite of everything, Jake and Declan would—at a minimum—punch the lights out of any man who hurt their sister after they finished hanging the moon for her.

And Lila was apparently steering well clear of her personal issues, because she was all business when she answered. "I got a call yesterday that the *Knot* is interested in photographing a ranch wedding for a feature. And this one— if we *ever* get the details nailed down—is perfect, if they can send a photographer on such short notice. This is such an opportunity, but if Felicity doesn't stop messing around, I won't get to take care of the little things. And it's the little things, the things you can't even see, the things only I would know about, that will make this shine for the magazine. Imagine how many bookings I could get out of it!"

Charlie imagined the bookings—and then she also imagined how much Declan would hate them. "Poor Declan," she said with a small laugh.

"Poor Declan? Are you kidding? He's done amazing things with this land, but my events keep the money rolling in. He keeps building. Reinvesting, he calls it . . ." Lila turned to look at her brothers. "Well, look at that," she said softly. "Jake and Declan together. Jake never comes out to the ranch for the safety stuff on my events. This is really cool."

Charlie hesitated for a moment and then finally asked a question she'd been thinking about for years. "Do you ever blame me?" Charlie asked. "You've never said you did. But you could have blocked me out, just like I did Jake."

"You were in an impossible position, and you know I get it. I don't understand everything that happened. I don't understand why your family blamed Jake like that, because, Charlie, he loved you and he'd never have hurt you or your family. Never. But I know how your parents were and I know how it was for you, and I just get it. And . . . I didn't want to lose your friendship, either. I didn't grow up with a mother, much less a sister."

Charlie, he loved you. Charlie had to take a deep breath to save herself from getting swamped by emotions. *We were kids. He loved me then. Now we're adults. He doesn't love me now.* "Jake doesn't get it," she muttered.

"In all fairness, Jake was jerked around a lot," Lila said. "He thought you Nashes were his forever family, and then you all abandoned him. And that just left us even more broken . . ." She swallowed hard. "Declan wanted nothing more than to keep our family together, and to be honest, your family stopped that from happening. Your parents took in Jake and broke the Braddocks even further apart than we were, only to spit him out at the first big test of loyalty."

"*You* won that test, Lila," Charlie said softly.

Lila looked at Jake. "At a cost, pal. A cost we're still paying." She gave Charlie a hug. "But I love you, girl. And I'm glad we stayed friends."

A big smile was back on Lila's face, but Charlie could tell she was still off her game. The way her friend's sad eyes tracked her brothers at the far end of the barn proved it. *I've*

*got to remember that. Lila always looks like she's ready to
take on the world; I can't forget she's as human as the rest
of us.*

"Hey, ladies!" Mick called. "I think that's everything."
He had a familiar look on his face. One Charlie remembered from high school. The one that said, *Been there, done
that, save me.* "You ready, Jake?"

Jake was staring across the barn.

"Something we missed?" Mick asked.

Charlie couldn't be sure, but she thought Jake said "I
wish" under his breath.

Everyone followed his gaze, becoming equally riveted
on the scarlet lace flamenco dress and matching mantilla
Felicity had told Charlie about earlier this morning. It currently hung on a hook, partially obscured by a beam until
you turned just the right way. Underneath it was a box containing a pair of Jimmy Choos, no less. It was Bridezilla's
third wedding ensemble. Amelie must be furious.

"I almost forgot!" Felicity cried. "The gloves!"

Lila took a deep breath and exhaled slowly and noisily.

Felicity pulled the satin bridesmaid gloves from her
shoulder and held them up in her outstretched hands. And
she was worried about silk roses being shiny? Those things
were going to glow in the dark. "Charlie, my dress is beautiful, isn't it?"

"Very." No lie: It truly was.

"Unusual," Felicity said. "Original, right, guys?"

"That it is," Mick offered.

"Absolutely," said Jake.

"And the bridesmaid gloves . . . they match. Do you
think they match? I can't tell if they're a shade off. They're
very close . . . but *do* they match?"

"The dress is red, and the gloves are red," Mick said
encouragingly. "Everything's . . . red."

"You're saying they match, then? That's what you're saying," Felicity said.

Mick nodded up and down and sideways. "Um . . . yeah. Red . . . and red."

Yes. Charlie nodded. *Satanic red.*

Declan cleared his throat. "I need to get back to work. Congratulations again, Felicity. Excuse me."

If Felicity noticed the speed with which Declan got himself out of there, she didn't let on. She was busy running her palm over the ruby red creation. "I adore it."

"Well, that's the most important thing," Lila said.

Bridezilla smiled and looked at Charlie. "So," said the Nuptial Nightmare, "I think you should put the bridesmaid dress back on with the gloves this time, and see how it all looks next to my new gown."

"No!" cried Jake, Charlie, and Mick in unison.

Into the awkward silence, Jake cleared his throat and said, "We forgot to, uh, look at the hose . . . nozzle . . . attachment . . . thing . . ." He steered Felicity to the wall where the fire extinguishers hung, with Mick trailing behind, his shoulders heaving with suppressed laughter.

Lila looked at Charlie, her eyes wide. "What the . . . ?"

"You should have seen it. No, I mean, *nobody* should have seen it. She asked me to try the bridesmaid dress on, and what could I do? Oh God. I can't believe Jake saw me in it . . ." Charlie put her hands over her face and took a deep breath. "I realize that as a bridesmaid, it's my sworn duty to look bad so that the bride looks even lovelier. But this? Lila, there are no words."

Lila giggled. "Try."

"I looked like a badly upholstered sofa. There's this massive ruffle. My thighs, they looked . . ." She spread her hands a yard apart. "I looked like a space alien with open sores. Like I stole a curtain from a brothel and wrapped it around myself. Like I—"

"I think I get it. But . . . how did Jake and Mick see?"

Charlie's face burned red, not just from humiliation. Some part of it was the realization that Jake had seen more than a bridesmaid typically revealed. And that he liked what he saw in spite of the hideous dress.

And yet he'd said their kiss was a mistake.

"They came through the sitting room entrance while I was changing," she mumbled.

"Oh, man, I miss everything," Lila said.

From the opposite side of the barn, Felicity clapped her hands and yelled, "Lila, I forgot to tell you. I've changed the bridesmaid-groomsman pairings. Just from a height standpoint, it makes sense to pair Charlie with Jake. He needs to be the best man."

Charlie's last breath left in a whoosh.

"It makes sense, right?" Bridezilla said. And then she looked down at her phone and started texting someone as if it were nothing, as if she'd asked for a different appetizer or some spare Band-Aids.

But she'd asked for everything. And no amount of wishing or pretending could make the words go away.

Under his tan, Jake had gone a shade lighter.

Pleaser or not, Charlie shook her head. "Let's not do that. Jake and I don't—"

"It'll be fine," Jake seemed to force out. "We're friendly now, right, Charlie?"

There was a horrible awkward silence. Charlie wanted to cry. They'd talked about getting married in this barn. They'd once held hands just a few paces across the floor from where they were standing, pretending to walk down the aisle at their own wedding.

"But—" Charlie began.

Jake looked blank.

"Oh boy," Mick said suddenly. "I can sense a big emergency waiting for us. Big, big emergency. Later." He put one hand on Jake's back and shoved him in the direction of the door. "Sorry to run, but as they say in the business, duty calls." Mick looked over his shoulder with a grin and said in Felicity's general direction, "You're gonna have a real memorable wedding, Miss Barnum."

And just like that, Jake was gone. Charlie stared at the door, which was still vibrating from being slammed.

"Wonderful," Felicity said. "Because Chrissy and Steven are engaged, so we can't split them up. And then there's my stepsister, Martha, and her husband, Todd—same issue. And finally, there's Richard, who's all of five-six, so I have to put him with Alicia, since you'd tower over him. So I'm promoting Jake to best man, and you and Jake will walk down the aisle together. Okay?"

Charlie gritted her teeth. *Not okay. Not remotely a good idea.*

Bridezilla's bedazzled cell phone rang again. *Sweet, sweet relief.* Charlie nudged Lila. "I don't know about you, but this seems like a perfect time for that drink."

Lila looked at Charlie. "Drink? I need a whole bottle."

Chapter 12

JAKE WAS NURSING HIS SECOND CORONA WITH THE firehouse guys in the back corner of Schweitz's Tavern. Schweitz's was a Silverlake landmark, one of the oldest German businesses in the Texas Hill Country outside Fredericksburg, and the Oktoberfest season was in full swing.

The interior was lined with reconstituted barn wood. The tables were either old whiskey barrels topped with hammered copper or picnic tables flanked by benches. The walls were hung with the requisite neon beer signs, but also wagon wheels, mirrors lined with horseshoes, and black-and-white historical photos of the town. Every Monday night at Schweitz's was polka night, and on those special evenings, the sound system played nothing but German folk music. Tonight's was a mix of rockabilly, country, and rock. The legendary Stevie Ray Vaughan figured prominently.

Otto Schmidt, old Steffen Schweitz's nephew, manned the bar and spoke German to his uncle with a Texas accent, to often hilarious effect. Schweitz winced at every syllable that came out of Otto's mouth.

"Hey, Otto!" called out Old George, his mustache quivering with mischief, his blue eyes dancing. "Tell Schweitz that Texas beer is better than German beer."

"Das Bier in Texas ist besser als in Deutschland, Onkel Steffen!"

Schweitz rammed his head through the swinging doors at this insult, and bellowed, *"Ufff! Zum Teufel damit sagst du! Ein Sakrileg!"* The hell you say! A sacrilege!

They all fell about laughing.

Old George smirked. "Hooo, doggie . . . he's pissed now."

"Be careful he doesn't spit in your beer," Grady warned.

"I'll just jam a big ole pretzel into his snout so he cain't."

Schweitz growled at their merriment and retreated to his cooktop.

Jake wasn't expecting it when his sister walked in with Charlie Nash and made a beeline for the bar. To his knowledge, neither of them had ever been big drinkers, so he was surprised when Otto poured out shots of what looked like tequila. Lila tossed hers back, choking a little, and asked for another, which she stared at for a long moment before she downed it, too.

Charlie sat next to her with an untouched shot glass, her hand patting Lila's arm. God, he remembered how good she was at turning dark times into sunshine. That was something special about Charlie. She understood people. She noticed what they cared about and shone it right back when they needed it most.

The big brother in him wanted to go find out what had Lila staring into a shot glass; the distance that still stood between them after the Nash bust-up forced him to sit back and let Charlie work whatever magic she could. At least for now. But he'd keep his eye on things over there, and in all truth it wasn't just to watch over his sister. The back booth at Schweitz's was the perfect vantage point for people-watching. Most of it was screened from general view by several tall plants.

Mick nudged him. "You see that?" He gestured toward Lila and Charlie with his own beer, a Rogue Dead Guy. "I never would have pegged either of them for the type to do random shots on a Tuesday night."

Jake shrugged.

"I've said it before, but I'll say it again. Charlie's got a real nice ra—"

"Shut it, Mick," said Jake.

"He's just trying to get a rise out of you," said Grady from across the table.

"He's probably already got a rise, staring at that girl," Tommy said.

Jake glared at the other off-duty firefighters from the team. Grady was back to focusing those deep thoughts of his on his whiskey, and Tommy was laughing as he played some kids' video game called *Goat Simulator*. Tommy didn't have a drink, which meant he was on call for the community hotline.

They were all good buddies because of living and working together at the firehouse, but they couldn't be more different. Grady was a rangy six feet four, brainy as hell, with fists like iron, and Tommy, only five feet ten but built like a fireplug, couldn't sit still without a distraction of some kind.

He and Mick had swapped places with Rafael and Hunter, who were now on duty, probably eating more than their fair share of Mick's latest masterpiece as fast as they could while waiting for any call or alarm.

"*Goat Simulator*? Why would anyone want to simulate a goat?" asked Jake, perplexed.

"'Cause you can head-butt people who annoy you," Tommy said. "It's awesome."

"If you're six years old," said Grady, swirling his ice cubes.

"Lighten up, old man." Tommy flashed his grin. "It's more interesting than the stock market. You're obsessed. Hey, this is too funny: You can take the goat up the stairs at the school and head-butt the principal right off the top of the building."

"Seriously? It takes that little to entertain you?" Mick scoffed.

"Uh-huh. Cheaper to play with goats than currency, dude," Tommy said. "So what's for dinner, Mick?"

"I look like the Barefoot Contessa to you?"

"No, but we like your grub. Problem is, the meatballs are already gone."

"Tonight is out of a box unless someone wants to grill. I'll make lasagna tomorrow."

"You're Irish, Mick, not Italian. Try a shepherd's pie sometime?"

"I got your shepherd's pie right here . . ."

Grady shook his head at Jake as the banter went on like this until Tommy changed the subject midstream. "Hey, should we be worried about the town council meeting later this week?"

"Nah," Mick said. "Not with Kingston Nash still over at Mercy Hospital. We should get a break this year."

"I don't know," Jake mused. "He may install an outboard motor on his cot and drive it right down Main Street to city hall."

"Yeah, well. The good news there is that Tommy can always just head-butt him with an imaginary goat," Mick jibed.

"Simulated!" Tommy said. "A *simulated* goat, gentlemen."

Jake's eyes narrowed as Lila, over at the bar, did a *third* shot. "One sec," he said, getting up.

He shoved his hands into his pockets and walked over to the bar, where Lila was now inhaling the spicy pecans that Schweitz's put out. "Hi," he said.

He was greeted by a slightly glassy stare, and then the Heisman: Lila extended her hand like a stop sign, pushing it almost into his face. "No guys in our clubhouse right now."

Jake raised his eyebrows, absurdly offended by this statement.

Charlie bit her lip, and color swept into her cheeks.

"Clubhouse?" he said. "If I'm not mistaken, this is a bar, very much open to the public. Which is roughly half made up of . . . let's see . . . guys."

"Okay, no stinky brothers in our clubhouse right now," Lila said. "We are having a chat."

"Well, pardon me. But I can't help noticing that there's a lot of tequila involved in this chat."

Lila grimaced. "That would be—and I mean this with all due affection but absolutely no respect—none of your business."

"Well, then. I guess I've been told." Jake's gaze went to the door of Schweitz's as it opened, only to reveal his ex-girlfriend Bridget. Her eyes brightened alarmingly when she caught sight of him.

"No offense, stinky bro."

"None taken," Jake responded on autopilot, even though he found himself way too interested in whatever mysterious topic Lila had to discuss so privately with Charlie. He calculated the distance back to the Fire and Rescue crew's hidden booth, wondering if he could sprint back there before having to interact with his ex.

No such luck. Bridget raised a hand in greeting, and his

own hand jerked up as if pulled by a string. Worse, he'd been ejected from the girl chat, so he had to move away from them. He was alone and exposed.

So were Bridget's legs. They were long and a little too tanned, and she wore a denim skirt that was a little too short. With pink cowboy boots that were also quite short.

Pink.

Bridget saw him looking at her legs—which was unavoidable, in his defense—and smiled knowingly as she walked over. "Jake," she said, laying a hand on his arm.

Pink fingernails, too. They matched the boots exactly. He didn't know why, but he found this calculated and disturbing. "Bridge." He nodded. "Been a long time. How are you?"

His back was to Charlie, but he was hyperaware that she might see Bridget touching him, and he was weirded out by that. He barely resisted the urge to peel his ex's pink-tipped fingers off his skin.

"Great!" Bridget exclaimed. "So nice to run into you! Let's catch up. Buy me a beer?"

"Uh . . . sure. You still drink Pearl?" It was a historic San Antonio beer, even if it was now hard to find—and an endangered species.

The wattage in her smile grew. "Good memory," she said huskily.

Honestly, the only reason he remembered that was because it was such a girlie name. How to get out of this?

"You get the beers. I'll snag us a booth," Bridget said. With a practiced flip of her perfect long auburn hair, she sashayed toward one near the front door.

Great. It'll be all over Silverlake by tomorrow that we're seeing each other again.

Jake sighed inwardly and went to the far side of the bar, away from Charlie and Lila and whatever private, keep-out conversation they were having. Charlie's flush had deepened, and he couldn't help but notice that she was torturing her lime with a swizzle stick. Stabbing it, digging little pieces of pulp out.

"Still got Pearl here, buddy?" he asked Otto.

Otto rolled his eyes. "Yep, we still got some, though its future is up in the air."

"Then I'll take one of those and a Shiner Bock. Thanks."

Jake's eyes met Charlie's as he picked up the beers, and she froze, then looked away and dropped the swizzle stick onto her napkin. She leaned in deliberately toward Lila, furrowing her eyebrows at whatever his little sister was saying.

For a moment, he fought irritation that Lila wasn't entrusting *him* with her confidences. He was her brother, after all. And the old anger rose in him that she'd refused to shut Charlie out, the way all the Nashes had him.

Oh, get over it. All she's guilty of is being a good friend.

There was a part of him that enjoyed seeing them with their heads together, like old times. He didn't get to claim Lila just because he was her brother. And it wasn't like he'd worked hard to stay close to any of his siblings.

Bridget flipped her hair again as he sat down, and he just managed to miss touching her hand as he slid the Pearl across the table toward her.

"Thanks, Jake."

Her lipstick was the exact same shade as her nail polish and the boots. Did women sit around matching up stuff like that?

"You forgot a glass," she said.

What was he, a waiter? "Oh, yeah. Sorry." Jake got up and headed back over to Otto. "Got a glass?"

"Apologies, my man. I shoulda remembered that Bridge doesn't do cans or bottles."

"Evidently, I should have remembered, too," Jake said dryly.

Otto produced a glass and polished it with his bar towel. "You, uh, goin' there again?"

"No."

"But she's perfect." Otto winked.

"Yeah, that's the problem. Whenever I see her, my collar feels a little tighter. Even when I'm wearing a tee." Was it his imagination, or had Charlie's ear perked up like Not-Spot's? Was she trying to overhear their conversation?

The idea was intriguing.

Glass in hand, Jake headed back to Bridget, wondering how he was going to extricate himself after one beer. He was absolutely not buying her dinner, or she and the whole town would have them engaged to be married by morning.

Engaged. Like Charlie had been, to some health nut who wanted her to be a size four.

"Thanks, Jake—you're a doll." Bridget poured her can of Pearl into the tall, clear glass.

He barely refrained from wrinkling his nose. *Never, ever call a man a doll.* "No problem."

She smiled. "You know the old rule: Nice girls don't drink out of cans or bottles."

Who says I want a nice girl? "How'd you get to be so nice, Bridge?" He kept the edge out of his voice.

"My grandmother and her Southern etiquette, I guess."

"But this is Texas. The Wild West."

She laughed. It wasn't that funny. But he chuckled, too, to be polite.

"Cheers, Jake."

He clinked his bottle with her glass. "So what's new with you?"

"Well, as a matter of fact, I just passed the bar exam." She shot him a dazzling white smile.

"Congratulations. That's impressive—I didn't even realize you were in law school."

Her smile dimmed. "You didn't wonder where I was for the last three years? You hadn't heard I was up at Texas Tech?"

He shook his head in apology. "Well, you know . . . I've been really busy."

"Me too," she said with a brittle laugh. "Law school is no picnic."

"No, I'm sure it's not. So will you hang out your own shingle?"

"I'll be joining Daddy's firm." She said it quietly, with eyes modestly downcast.

"Oh, right." Of course. In addition to having perfect legs, hair, nails, lips, and etiquette, Bridget had a perfect job lined up and a perfect family. It was all a little nauseating, especially because she knew it. She was a real catch.

Too bad he didn't want to catch her.

There was a weird undercurrent between them as they exchanged another set of fixed smiles and small talk. It took him a while to pinpoint it: resentment.

Bridget, knowing she was perfect and utterly available, was angry at him for not pursuing her. Hell, he was almost angry at himself for not pursuing her: the smart, beautiful, accomplished daughter of a personal injury attorney who owned a hefty chunk of downtown Silverlake. He was probably stupid. She could aim a lot higher than him.

But he'd broken it off with her four years ago because there was something missing. Something big. An emotional connection.

Someone like Bridget, whose life had unrolled so flawlessly, like a red carpet, couldn't connect on some level with a rough-and-tumble, damaged guy like him. But there was no way to explain to her why that was . . . because she had no idea that she was missing the life experience he had. The grief and the hurt and the cynicism—or the relief of working through it all and coming out the other side. For lack of a better word, it was *depth* she was lacking—and it wasn't in any way her fault.

So he felt guilty, sitting across the rough wooden table from her and not being attracted to her on more than a surface level. He felt bad that he didn't enjoy her company. He could feel her frustration and puzzlement and the wound to her ego, just as much as he could feel the perspiration and the chill of his beer bottle.

He felt the crazy urge to apologize to Bridget. Some version of the "It's not you; it's me" speech he'd given her four years ago. But that would be even more offensive, since he'd be giving voice to the currently unspoken and unacknowledged rejection that hung in the air. *Shut it and keep it shut, you jackass.*

He found his gaze straying back to Charlie, who was still deep in conversation with his sister at the bar. Lila's shoulders were hunched and her head was cocked at a dejected angle, and Charlie put her hand on Lila's and squeezed it.

This was more than a bitch session about Bridezilla.

Charlie's hand remained on Lila's, and Jake remembered the way it had felt on his own. In his own. Her skin soft, her fingers tapered, her nails free of any polish.

He became aware of a deadly silence across the table from him. Bridget took a perfect sip of her beer and waited. For what?

"Uh," he said, at his most articulate. "So . . . how is your dad?"

Judging by the flash of hostility in her blue eyes, this was exactly the wrong question to ask. "I was just telling you that, Jake. But I guess you weren't paying attention."

"Bridge, I'm sorry. Got a lot on my mind."

"Clearly."

He could almost see the gears turning in her head, telling her to warm up her smile and play it casual.

"Want to talk about it?" she said.

His gaze returned to Charlie, to the way the barstool hugged her curves. "It's complicated."

Bridget followed his eyes; her own narrowed at the sight of competition. And as if Charlie felt them looking at her, she turned her head. Lifted an eyebrow.

Jake raised his Shiner Bock in a wry toast.

"Are you serious, Jake?" Bridget said. "You're thinking about going *there* again?"

"What?" He so didn't need this right now. "No. Of course not. I'm just a little worried about Lila, is all."

"Is that right? Yeah, your little sister's got herself into a situation, or hadn't you heard?" Bridget washed down the faint tinge of malice in her tone with another sip of her beer.

Jake stiffened. He didn't like hearing Lila spoken about in such a tone. He sure as hell didn't like Lila having a *situation* that people like Bridget knew enough to gossip about but that *he* knew nothing about. Jake was racking his brain for a polite out from a conversation that was about to go south, fast, when a shadow fell across the rough wooden table—a curvy, Charlie-shaped shadow, which brought with it the scent of jasmine and fresh lime. And to his surprise, his heart skipped a happy beat.

"Jake, I'm sorry to interrupt, but I think Lila needs you."

Jake tried to process this. His little sister . . . needed him? Since when? And when the hell had seeing Charlie started to feel good? First, he'd gotten used to the dark memories of her. And then he'd gotten used to feeling blank. But good? Good was . . . bad. Terrible, in fact.

"Lila needs me?"

"Yeah. Believe it or not, she does."

Chapter 13

CHARLIE COULD STILL READ JAKE LIKE A BOOK.
When Bridget had walked into Schweitz's in her
pink cowboy boots and made a beeline for him, Charlie had
known a moment of doubt. What man wouldn't want to buy
those long, tanned, taut legs a beer? But the trip back to the
bar for the glass, the awkward body language, the forced
laughter, and the entitled tilt of the woman's perfect chin . . .
they'd all told her a different story.

And when Jake had toasted her with his Shiner, he may
as well have had HELP ME branded on his forehead.

Sure, Charlie had hesitated. It really wasn't her place, not
anymore. But he definitely looked like he needed an out.
Besides, her excuse wasn't exactly a lie, and if she'd guessed
wrong and he wanted to stay with Bridget, that would be a
useful piece of information for her unruly heart to know.

It took Jake mere seconds to extricate himself after that,
and before the poor girl could manage the second syllable
of "goodbye," he was by Charlie's side on the way back to

Lila. Oh, why did he have to look so delicious? All snug denim again, rolled-up flannel sleeves and biceps and strong forearms . . . T-shirt over his wide chest and dark hair curling at his collar. Why did he have that firm jawline with the five o'clock shadow that she wanted to trace with her fingers? Why those instantly assessing dark eyes that could go from warm to distant in half a second?

Right now they were brimming with gratitude. "Thank you," Jake said.

Charlie smiled. "Ain't nothin' but a thing."

"A big thing. I'm in your debt."

"Not by a long shot," she said as they wove their way back through the crowd.

"What's wrong with Lila?"

"It's not for me to say. She'll tell you herself when she's ready."

Behind them, the door of Schweitz's banged shut as Bridget made her exit, her Louis Vuitton shoulder bag slapping against her hip as she strode away.

Jake sighed.

"But she's perfect," Charlie teased.

"Not for me," he said as they reached the bar.

Lila shoved a little sequined makeup kit back in her purse and looked up.

She had powdered her nose and buried her blues from sight. The tequila was already hitting her. It was visible in her loopy grin as she eyed Charlie and Jake standing side by side. "Hi, Jake. Huh. You guys look like you're rehearsing your new roles for the wedding." She seemed to scent the air for a moment. "Wow. I must have said that out loud. You could cut the tension between you two with a spork."

Behind the bar, Otto laughed, turning it into a cough when Jake and Charlie glared at him. He quickly busied himself slicing limes.

"Hi, yourself. You've always been so subtle," Jake said to Lila. "But everything's fine. Right, Charlie?" He raised his eyebrows at her.

"Everything's fine," Charlie repeated.

"Fine, huh?" said Lila, swaying a bit on her barstool. "Deny it all you want, but I know better, and you're going to have to deal with it eventually."

"Is Felicity driving you to drink?" Jake asked, neatly changing the subject. "Did she get worse after Mick and I left? What's up?"

"Yes, she is driving me to drink, and my blood pressure is what's up." Lila left it at that, and Charlie didn't volunteer that as bad as Felicity was, the wedding wasn't the only thing that had brought Lila low.

Tell your brother, Lila, Charlie thought. Talk *to him.*

"Seriously, Charlie, is there anything you can do?" Jake asked. "To warn your cousin Will about the level of crazy he's about to bring into your family?"

"Uh . . . how exactly am I supposed to do that?" Charlie asked. "Besides, she's different with him. Almost normal."

"There is nothing normal about her," Lila said. "What is she *thinking*? A hellfire red wedding dress? I think it's bad luck, but what do I know? Otto, can I have another shot, please?"

Otto poured it. "And you, Jake? Can I get you anything?"

"Guess I'll do another Shiner."

Lila tossed back her shot and nodded for another.

Jake shook his head. "Jeez, Lila . . . That's number four. So who's driving you home?"

"Possibly you," said Lila, "since you look like you have nothing better to do."

Jake looked heavenward. "Not this again. I've already heard it from Kingston Nash."

Charlie's stomach roiled at the sound of Granddad's name,

which of course reminded her all over again of his agenda and the role he wanted her to play. *Ugh—absolutely not.*

"Ah," Lila said, grinning and plopping her elbows sloppily onto the bar. "More of the same? That you're paid to be a lazy layabout? Paid to be here in this bar drinking beer?"

Jake frowned. "Hey! I happen to be off shift right now. You know as well as I do: forty-eight hours on, forty-eight hours off. And I don't know how many times I have to tell you this, but we stay pretty damn busy. Who did your safety inspection earlier today out at the barn? Who talks to the schoolkids about Smokey Bear? Who checks all the gear and equipment daily? Who rides out with the ambulance half the time as a backup paramedic? Who did the water rescue last month when the flooding swept away Mrs. McGowan's old Honda?"

Lila smirked. "Calm down, bro. I think you're totally worth it. It's just fun to wind you up."

"Yeah, well. I get enough of that. I'm going to punch the next person who asks me what my going rate is for sleeping on the job."

"What is it?" Lila asked, laughing, dodging behind Charlie and using her as a human shield.

"I'll get you, little sister," Jake said, narrowing his eyes in fake menace. "When you're least expecting it."

"Oooh, I'm scared. Now, d'you want to buy our drinks 'on the taxpayers' dime'?" Lila almost pulled Charlie over backward as she maneuvered them both behind a potted palm. Normally, Charlie would have laughed. But given the topic and her granddad's obsession with it, she didn't find it funny. Especially since she knew the old man would never let it go.

"Lila, let go of me," she said, slapping at her friend's hands.

Jake eyed her curiously.

"What's the matter?" Lila asked.

"Nothing," Charlie said.

Jake's gaze made everything she wore feel too tight and hot and scratchy. The sips of tequila had burned a hole down her throat and into her gut. She felt edgy. Perhaps she shouldn't have rescued Jake from Bridget. He'd said thank you, but maybe he was just being polite. What if he thought she was throwing herself at him? *"What?"* she said.

Jake shrugged.

Lila tilted her head toward him and then toward Charlie, assuming that weird bloodhound-scenting-the-air stance again. "Hmm . . ." Then she craned her neck toward the back. "Is that Old George I see in the back booth? I'm going to go say hello."

"No!" Charlie hissed under her breath. "Don't leave me alone with your brother."

"What's that?" asked Jake, even though Charlie was pretty sure he'd heard her.

"Be right back!" Lila said with a wink.

Charlie was going to murder her. Lila had been fiercely loyal to their friendship, but she was also bullheaded and merciless when she got an idea into her head. And she seemed to have the idea that—

"So it's just me and you, kid," Jake said.

Charlie took her seat at the bar and threw back the rest of the shot of tequila that was still sitting there.

"Want to tell me why you and my sister are doing shots on a Tuesday night? Felicity's bad, but I don't know if she's this bad."

"Nope."

"And why you're pulling at your clothes and shifting in your seat."

"Am I?" Charlie asked.

"Yes. Why?"

"Because you make me uncomfortable, Jake. Isn't that obvious?"

A normal guy would have backed off. Jake didn't. "Guilty conscience?"

She exhaled. "Yeah, maybe. It's not like my family treated you well."

"Let's leave your family out of this. *You* didn't treat me well."

His words landed like a bowling ball in her stomach.

Oh God. Were they going to get into this now, after all these years? Couldn't they just ignore it for a little while longer? Not rip open the old wounds?

Bad enough that she had to walk arm in arm with him down the aisle and eat with him at the rehearsal dinner on Thursday night. And then there was the wedding itself to get through on Saturday evening . . .

"If I buy you another shot, will you talk to me? Really talk?" Jake asked in a softer tone.

"About what?"

"The past."

"What is there to say?" Charlie asked.

"Plenty. I think you owe me an explanation, don't you? Otto, one more for the lady."

An explanation. Yeah, he probably did want one.

This day just got better and better. "I don't want another shot," she said. "Make it water. Thanks."

Jake's eyebrows shot up, and he folded his arms across his chest. Widening his stance, he rocked back on his heels. "So?"

Otto eyed her quizzically, and she wished he'd just go polish the other end of the bar or something. He stayed put, of course.

Both of them waited. Charlie almost wished something would catch fire so Jake, off shift or not, would go running out of the bar as fast as she'd like to. But that was terrible.

She didn't wish a fire on anyone. "Uh. Um . . ." She shook her head and waved her hand dismissively.

"That's not a great start," Jake said as an almost predatory expression crossed his face.

Otto got bored and went to check on tables. Inexplicably, when he returned, he set a second shot in front of her. Charlie stared down at the tiny glass of poison. "Really, just water."

"Lila ordered it for you," Otto said. "From the back booth."

Charlie pushed it away. "Of course she did. No, thanks. She's on a roll. Take it to Mick."

Otto grinned, removed it, and replaced it with a big glass of H_2O.

Of course, as soon as the tequila was gone, she wanted it back. Jake was larger-than-life next to her, and she could smell the familiar scent of sweetgrass and a hint of leather, the laundry detergent of his shirt, the underlying scent of his skin. He leaned close to her, and she also caught a hint of mint and beer. "Talk to me," he said.

I want to, she caught herself thinking. *Maybe if we just say all of it out loud, it will make the pain go away. And if the pain goes away, maybe we can start over.*

No! Stop it, Charlie, you fool. Don't get any closer to Jake Braddock. It wasn't just a question of the past; it was a question of the future. Of loyalties and betrayals. Granddad was still actively trying to abolish Jake's job. He wanted her help to do that. And even though she had no intention of granting that request, he wouldn't take kindly to her rekindling a . . . friendship.

She gulped some cold water as Jake awaited an answer. Loyalties and betrayals. The concepts seemed very abstract. Sort of pompous. All the man wanted to do was *talk.* Why was that so bad? *Someone* should tell him why they'd all cut him off and shut him out. She'd always felt terrible about it.

Charlie opened her mouth to say . . . what? . . . when she was rudely interrupted. A classic Def Leppard song, "Pour Some Sugar on Me," kicked on, inciting Lila. She yowled the refrain from behind the potted palms in the corner.

Jake winced, and raucous male laughter broke out over the music.

Oh boy. As one unit, Charlie and Jake turned to stare.

Lila's head and shoulders twisted unsteadily over the green fronds, black hair cascading over her shoulders, one bare because her sweater had slipped off.

Charlie shot off her barstool and headed over.

Jake followed quickly.

Lila was up on the table, swaying, while Tommy hooted and clapped—Old George looked shell-shocked, as if the Gerber baby had just donned pasties and a thong.

Lila had grabbed a saltshaker and was employing it as a microphone as she sang the lyrics tunelessly and gyrated.

"Hey, get down!" Charlie told her. "You're going to hurt yourself."

Lila's chin jutted out. "I'm juss havin' shum fun."

Jake caught the napkin holder as Lila kicked it. "*Off* the table. Now."

His sister swung her booty at him and shook it, tossing her hair. "Go away. You're no' the boss o' me."

Wincing, Grady salvaged his bourbon just before it went airborne, courtesy of Lila's left Windex blue wedge heel. "This would be so much better if we hadn't all known her since she was five," he said.

George removed what was left of a platter of wings and hot sauce before she could plant her right heel in it. He shot another traumatized look at Jake. Shaking his head, he excused himself.

Tommy just laughed. "*I* haven't known her since she was five. C'mon, Jake," he protested. "Don't spoil the party."

His eyes roved helplessly up Lila's curves as she kept gyrating.

In answer, Jake thunked him between the eyes with the napkin holder before setting it down on a chair.

"Ow!" Tommy said, but he took the hint.

"Lila, you're embarrassing yourself," Jake said. "Not to mention me."

"Thiss isn't 'bout you, dude! Thiss me, eshpreshing my inner Leppard!"

"And that's a beautiful thing," Charlie told her, deadpan. "But—"

"Nein!" they heard Schweitz yell from the kitchen. He came barreling out, wiping his hands on a liberally stained chef's apron. "Restaurant insurance vill not cover! *Get down, bitte!"*

"Don't be a schtick in the mud, Schweitzie!" sang Lila. "Come up here with me!"

She leaned forward, exposing a terrifying amount of cleavage, and grabbed Schweitz's ball cap in one hand. She shoved the saltshaker between her breasts and grabbed his gray beard, yanking him forward for a big smooch on the lips as salt sprinkled his head. *"Pour some sugar, babieeee!"* she yowled.

"Schweitzie" blushed fire and looked dazed.

"Okay, you're done." Jake moved in to forcibly remove her, but the bar owner was in the way, petrified but now very much under the spell of Lila's dubious charms.

Charlie knew that Jake and his brothers had trained their little sister well in evasion, almost from birth. Lila instinctively dodged him, spinning on her toe and jumping off the table. Before he knew it, she was running for the massive, long main bar.

"Incoming!" Charlie called to Otto.

"Huh?" He looked up just in time to behold Lila vault toward him, seat her denimed cheeks to the left of his perfectly sliced limes, and spin triumphantly to her feet. "Holy cow!"

Lila's eyes narrowed on him. "Who're you calling a cow, little man?"

"Uh—"

"I am a *goddess*. Now give me that." She pointed to a bottle of Don Julio Añejo.

"Don't even think about giving her that, Otto!" Jake growled, in hot pursuit.

"Goddess."

Otto nodded. He extended his hand toward the Don Julio, but Charlie rounded the bar and swiped it before he could.

"No," she said to Lila. "You've had quite enough."

"There ish no enough! I have been dealing wiss Felithicy *Beeyotch* Barnum, and there ish not enough tequila on the planet to make up for it." Her expression mulish, Lila cartwheeled to the other end of the bar, more salt spilling from the shaker wedged into her cleavage, and commandeered a bottle of El Tiempo that sat near Pullman Duff, the town's accountant. Rumor had it that he was so cheap he bought Thunderbird in a paper bag for dinner guests and poured it into a decanter to disguise what it was.

Pullman goggled at her and protected his own shot of El Tiempo as she unscrewed the cap of the bottle.

"Lila, so help me God," Jake said, "if you drink that, I'll—"

"Sinch when do you care?" Lila asked.

Jake blanched. "I *care*."

Lila blinked, going a little soft. "Oh." But after a beat of silence between the two siblings, Lila suddenly grinned at Jake, shoved the cap into her pocket, and winked as she took a long swig. Then she whipped the saltshaker out of her blouse and held it up to her lips as she yodeled along with the music.

"*Pour some sugar on . . .*" Lila leaned back dangerously and dramatically for the last notes of the song, seeming to forget the last word of the lyric.

"Dang," Otto muttered. "Look out: She's headed straight for *America's Got No Talent.*"

"I heard that," Lila snapped. As she began to struggle upright, the cap of the shaker fell off, spraying her face and filling her mouth with salt. "*Thit!* Thath not thugar!"

"Yeah, no," Jake said. "It's not, Lila."

"Will you marry me?" Tommy called, as she spewed salt and curses all over the bar. He came running up and tossed some dollar bills at her.

Otto gingerly offered her a bar towel and then retreated to a safe distance.

There were no words for Jake's expression.

Charlie exchanged a glance with him. He inclined his head toward the debacle that was his sister. Charlie nodded in understanding.

He moved in on the left, Charlie on the right, and they muscled Lila the Lush off the bar, not that she made it easy.

"Leggo o' me!" she howled, shoving her elbow into Jake's gut and still spitting out salt.

He grunted in pain. "I'd like nothing better, trust me. But if Charlie and I don't get you out of here, then Bode will, and you'll spend the night in jail."

"Maybe I wanna!" Lila returned. "Maybe it's the only thing that'll shtop me from killing Bridezilla!"

A pig snort escaped Charlie, who went to get Lila's purse while Jake steered his sister toward the exit.

"Hey! I'm serious! Will you marry me?" Tommy asked, stepping in front of them.

Lila blew him a salty kiss. "Yesh!"

"Get out of the way, Tommy," Jake growled. "I'll deal with you later."

"But I'm in love!"

Jake palmed Tommy's face and walked him backward. Then he threw Lila over his shoulder, and Charlie opened the door.

"Mind if we take your wheels?" Jake asked Charlie. "I rode with George, and frankly I'd just as soon Lila didn't have access to her car tonight if she wakes up later and wants a chocolate milkshake."

That earned him a thump on the back from his sibling. "You. Are. A. Caveman."

He nodded and slid his gaze toward Charlie. "I've been called worse."

"Pumme down, Cavey," slurred Lila.

"Trust me, I can't wait. But I'm not gonna drop you to the pavement. Charlie, where are you parked?"

"Over here." She led them to where Progress hunched, between an old Firebird and, of all things, a Tesla. She opened the passenger-side door and stood aside.

Jake placed his surly, ungrateful burden onto the seat and pushed her over into the middle, with rough brotherly love, as she grumbled at him. His mouth twisted as he looked around the interior of the ancient, musty truck, and he pulled his head out abruptly.

"Want to drive?" Charlie asked softly, extending the keys to him.

He blinked and pursed his lips. Then he accepted the keys, his hand brushing hers.

Her skin tingled, and he drew back quickly. So she knew he'd felt it, too.

He rounded the hood of the truck to get to the driver's seat, but Lila had other ideas.

"I yam ffiiine to drive," she announced, gripping the steering wheel and honking the horn.

Jake sighed. "Spoken like every other moron who's just downed seven or eight tequila shots. Now move over."

"Not a moron," Lila protested as Charlie got in the passenger side.

"Okay," said Jake. "Whatever you say, little sister. You're a very wise person who just happened to crash into a bottle of tequila for no apparent reason on a Tuesday night."

"Oh, there are reasons," Lila muttered darkly. "Bridezillas, and . . . and . . . boyfriendzillas."

Charlie bit her lip.

Jake raised an eyebrow. "Boyfriendzillas, huh? They sound terrifying."

"A horror show. You have no conshept at all."

This seemed to catch his interest. "So who's your boyfriendzilla, Lila? I didn't know you'd been dating anyone."

Lila emitted a mysterious gasp and then a tiny burp. "Dating nobody. Slip of the bum."

"Ah. A slip of the bum. Sure. Now move over." Jake shoved her back into the middle of the seat, over her protests.

"You are so bossy! Fine. If you're gonna drive, I'm 'onna sing."

"Nooo!" Jake and Charlie said in unison.

Lila giggled and then began to caterwaul her favorite Def Leppard lyrics again.

"Oh, dear God." Charlie dropped her face into her hands as Jake got in. "Drive fast. Please."

Chapter 14

J AKE DID DRIVE FAST, STARTING UP OLD PROGRESS and heading for the small three-bedroom house that Lila shared with Amelie, creator of Bridezilla's first wedding gown. Thank God that Lila's cat-strangling segued into gentle snoring within a couple of minutes. Her head kept lolling onto Charlie's shoulder, but Charlie was just glad for the peace as they drove.

Lila's shared house was made of limestone, and featured a turquoise front door with a fan-shaped glass window at the top. A lonely cedar tree stood guard in a yard that had a garden bed filled with river rock and was adorned with a single Mexican ceramic pot. A painted metal peacock sprouted from this, seeming to grow out of the soil. Evidently neither resident had the time—or inclination—for gardening.

Amelie greeted them with a mouth full of pins, her tight dark curls twisted into a knot on top of her head. Some had escaped and danced near her ears, her skin

gleaming mahogany under the porch light. She rolled her
eyes at the sight of her roommate passed out in Jake's arms.

"Evenin', Amelie," he said.

"Mmm mmm *mm*?" she answered.

"Not sure how to translate that, but I believe it was
something close to WTF."

"Mmm hmm!" Amelie moved out of the way and gestured to them to come in, pointing the way to Lila's bedroom.

"Hi," said Charlie, following Jake inside past a dress-
maker's dummy clad in iridescent aqua mermaid scales.
They had to step over her tail.

Amelie pulled the pins out of her mouth and dropped
them into a porcelain dish on the console table next to it.
She spread her hands wide and raised her eyebrows.

Charlie sighed. "Lila had a bad day with Bridezilla and
a bad night with tequila. Her inner Leppard came out, and
now we're all Def."

"Say no more. I'll get water and aspirin." Amelie headed
for the kitchen.

"Thank you!" called Charlie, and braved Lila's bedroom
with Jake.

He'd deposited her on her queen-sized Victorian bed and
was clumsily trying to unbuckle one of her Windex blue
wedges.

"Here, let me do that." Charlie took over.

"I'll never understand women's shoes as long as I live."

She laughed and glanced over at him as she easily undid
the straps and slid the shoes off. Jake's expression said everything he'd probably never put into words to his little sister.

It was tender, exasperated, amused, concerned, and pro-
tective all at once. He adored her.

Charlie's breath caught in her throat, and the familiar
guilt that she'd come between these two haunted her. And
that she'd allowed Lila to straddle the fence to her friend's

own detriment, while she, Charlie, had firmly sided with her own brother, Brandon. Loyalty came in many shades and forms, didn't it?

Jake, suddenly seeming aware of her scrutiny, evaded it by grabbing Lila's trash can and bringing it to her bedside as Charlie put the shoes in her friend's closet. "Hey, Charlie," he growled. "This *boyfriendzilla* thing Lila mentioned? If she needs someone to give somebody a talking-to about something . . . I'm available."

She nodded at Jake, closed the closet doors, turned, and came face-to-face with a spindly shelf full of party planning books, among them *Awesome Occasions!* and *Elegant Evenings.* Then, notably: *Weddiculous: An Unfiltered Guide to Being a Bride.* Charlie smiled.

Lila's room was similar to her office. Odd wedding and party accessories sprouted everywhere, a testament to Lila's job. A yellowed antique wedding veil trailed from one of the bedposts. A painted cowboy boot filled with silk violets adorned her dresser, along with a pair of white elbow gloves. In the far corner of the room, a book lay sprawled as if it had been thrown against the wall. Charlie chuckled as she identified it as *Miss Manners' Guide to Excruciatingly Correct Behavior.* Evidently, Lila had fallen short? What a shocker.

Jake found a blanket on a pale green French country–style chair in the room and draped it over his sister. "Let's hope for her sake that she vomits."

Ugh. But Charlie nodded.

"She'll feel better in the morning if she does," Jake said.

Amelie came in with a glass of water and three aspirin and set them on the nightstand. "So she sang?"

Jake scrubbed a hand down his face. "That's a questionable verb."

Amelie laughed. "I'll keep an eye on her. Don't worry."

"Thanks. What's with the mermaid costume?"

"Silverlake Middle School is doing a performance of *The Little Mermaid*. I'm helping out with the costumes."

Charlie put a hand to her heart. "That's so sweet."

Amelie's lips flattened, and she looked up at the ceiling. "It's a pain in the butt," she said. But the quirk of her mouth gave away that she loved doing it. "Not as big a pain as Bridezilla, though!"

"Amen to that."

❧

With Lila safely in bed under Amelie's watch, Jake helped Charlie up into Progress's passenger seat and got into the driver's seat once more. Without his sister in the car, sitting here with Charlie suddenly seemed so intimate.

He inhaled the familiar smells of old vinyl, rusty metal, musty seat foam, and eau de gasoline. How many years had it been since he'd sat in this truck, tooling around with Kingston? He remembered the old man teaching him how to check the oil and the tire pressure, back when Jake had been "one of the family." Before the fire.

Ha. Likely he had been their pet project, their charity case. He'd worn Brandon's hand-me-downs and gladly taken his castoffs: the older-model Dell computer, for example. His old Nokia flip phone. Things that Deck couldn't afford to buy for any of the Braddock kids. At the time, Jake had been over the moon to have them . . . but had those "free" items come at a price? The price of equality?

Jake fired up the engine abruptly. Progress roared, visibly startling Charlie. He'd almost flooded the engine as a wave of unnamed emotions flooded him. But he preferred them unidentified. They were easier to brush aside that way.

"Why so jumpy?" he asked Charlie. "You okay?"

"No," she said baldly.

"Why not?"

"I can't even begin to explain it." She fiddled with the straps of her big tote bag and stared out the window.

Frustration mounted in him. "You could try."

Silence.

They'd reached the firehouse now, but instead of hopping out, Jake parked across from the driveway and cut the engine. "You said you'd talk to me. About the past. So . . . ?"

She tucked some hair behind her ears and examined her fingernails. "I don't know where to start."

"Yeah? Well, *I* didn't know where—or why—to *end*, Charlie." The words escaped him, raw and harsh, without permission. Embarrassing after all this time. But since they were out, the hell with it. "One minute I was a part of the family," he said, "an honorary Nash. And the next, I was an outcast. Shunned. Persona non grata."

Charlie's shoulders hunched. She let her bag drop to the floor of the cab and tucked her hands underneath her thighs. "I know," she said. "I'm so sorry."

"You've said that. You've said it more than once. But what I want to know is *why*! We put out that campfire, Brandon and I. I know it was out. Not a single ember. I even kicked sand over it. And I'm the one who got your dad out of the house, wheelchair and all—"

"I know," she whispered. "It wasn't fair," she said, her voice breaking. "None of it, Jake. I know that. I'm so sorry. But . . . I couldn't . . . All of it combined was like a force of nature that I couldn't stop."

She leaned her head against his shoulder, and Jake put his arm around her. At last, disjointedly, the story was coming out. The story nobody would tell him, the one he'd waited so long to hear.

"I was fifteen years old, Jake, and Granddad was raging

and looking for someone to blame. There was an insurance investigator, a psychologist, all the police and the firefighters, everyone asking questions. So many questions, and so many fingers pointing . . ." Charlie shook her head, choking on fresh tears. "Pointing at you. It was awful. So awful. From the get-go, they forbade me to even talk to you, for legal reasons."

Jake's heart stuttered. The injustice of it was like a kick in the stomach. He let his arm drop away from Charlie, and he sat there reeling, fighting a sudden urge to smash the windshield. "Why? Why would they think it was me? The campfire was out! I swear it. Brandon saw it. He was there."

Charlie refused to meet his gaze.

What? No . . . it just wasn't possible. Had Brandon lied and said Jake was responsible? Aw, hell. Did it really matter at this point if he had? The whole town had whispered that it was probably Jake's fault. Fair or not.

Charlie kept talking, even though now he wasn't sure he wanted her to.

"The authorities had a theory. I don't even know where it came from. And even when there wasn't enough evidence to prosecute, the idea just wouldn't go away. Once it got in Granddad's head, in Mom and Dad's head . . ." Charlie was absolutely sobbing now.

"What theory?" Jake asked, his voice sounding cold and foreign in his own ears.

"Envy," Charlie blurted.

Jake's heart, having stopped, now resumed like a sledgehammer trying to crack his breastbone. *Envy?* What was she saying? That they'd thought—*no.* Not possible. Bile rose in his throat. "You thought I—? How could you think that?"

"I didn't! The insurance investigator was trying to get me to say stuff about you. Stuff that would incriminate you.

I told him that he was full of it. He suggested that I was romantically biased and naive. He suggested that we'd all taken in a lonely, unstable kid who had something to prove, who wanted to impress the family, cement his place in it. That you set the fire so you could be a hero."

Jake heard her words as if from a great distance, trying to cut himself off from the vicious pain they caused. *Lonely. Unstable. Something to prove.* The truth of the insights hurt almost worse than the crazy supposition that the investigator had arrived at.

Impress the family. Cement his place . . .

"Because, you know, Mom and Dad had given us both a talk a few days earlier. Do you remember? Do you remember The Talk?"

Oh, yeah, Jake remembered The Talk.

"Jake, you're like a second son to us," Dave Nash had said, a regretful, tender expression on his craggy face. His hands, resting on the arms of the wheelchair, shook a little, but who knew whether it was from emotion or MS?

"Yes, darlin', you are," Maria Nash chimed in, enveloping him in one of her ample hugs. Jake loved her wide smile, the tiny smudge of coral lipstick that always ended up on one of her front teeth. He loved her messy, curly blond hair, the crinkles at her eyes, the way she looked at him as though she saw into his heart and approved of what was there.

This hug felt different, though. It felt . . . official. He couldn't put his finger on it, but he didn't want to let her go, even though normally he felt a little awkward at the physical contact.

"Sit down, Jake," Dave said, a little too gently.

So he did, a nameless dread rising in him.

"It hasn't escaped our notice that you have, uh . . . feelings . . . for Charlie."

Heat suffused Jake's face, and his palms instantly became damp. Prickles of sweat started in his armpits, too.

"Or that she has them for you."

Okay, this was humiliating, but not a crime. Maybe Dave or Maria had seen him and Charlie making out behind the rosebushes yesterday. They'd just—

"That's fine, son, just fine. But you're both at an age where, given the circumstances, it's just, uh, inappropriate *for you both to be living under the same roof."*

Oh God. This was beyond awful. His armpits were now full of glue. Sweat trickled from Jake's nape down to his lower back, pooling there, soaking into his T-shirt. "I haven't—uh, we haven't—"

Okay, so he'd thought about it. More than once. Even often. But, no, he'd never pressured Charlie . . .

Dave Nash closed his eyes and flapped a hand.

"I mean, it's not a problem!" Jake blurted.

Maria gazed at him in her kindly but firm way, her expression soft and at the same time steely. "It is *a problem, honey. And that's normal. But what's not normal is . . ." She paused and looked to Dave, who took up her slack.*

"For you two to live in the same house."

He stared at them, these two stand-in parents whom he'd grown to love. "So—what is this?" Jake said. "You're firing me from your family?"

Maria made a sound of pure distress and got up as if to hug him.

Jake jumped out of his chair and backed away. A lump had grown in his throat, one that made it impossible to swallow. "Please . . ." His voice cracked, and he hated himself for it. "Please don't do this. When my parents died, you said your house was mine now, that I would always be welcome. You said I was family."

But Dave and Maria just looked at each other and then down at the floor.

They *were family. Not Jake. Jake was once and always a Braddock, not a Nash. And there wasn't any Braddock family anymore. The familiar swell of loneliness that always seemed just a heartbeat away nearly swamped him now. There must be something he could say . . .*

"I promise—" Jake began.

"Don't make promises that you can't keep, son," said Dave.

The hurt got the better of him then. "Don't call me 'son' *if you don't mean it!" Jake spun around on his heel and ran for the door.*

"I do mean it!" *Dave called after him.* "Please try to understand the awkwardness of our position here . . ."

But nothing was more awkward than being a teenager in love for the first time.

Or being a teenager marked "Return to Sender."

⁓

Jake had a sudden urge to find the creep investigator and choke the life out of him for seeing his sixteen-year-old weaknesses and for using them to build a completely fictional case against him. Employing sense to build nonsense.

Charlie's voice brought him back to the present. "There may have been no conclusive evidence in the investigation, but the idea was enough. A psychologist told Mom and Dad to keep Brandon and me away from you, to not see you again, so that we could recover from the trauma."

She stopped talking, thank God. They sat there in Progress without speaking.

"My God," Jake murmured, still reeling. He felt empty, crumpled, turned inside out. "I'm sorry I ever asked."

"Jake," Charlie said softly. She put a hand on his knee. "I didn't believe those jerks—the insurance guy *or* the shrink who agreed it was possible."

He drew in a couple of shaky breaths. "Yeah, I think you did."

"No!" She slid sideways across the old bench seat and gripped his arm. "I didn't."

"Why didn't you talk to me, then? Why, when I came to Dallas, did you *shut the door in my face*?" The last part came out as a bellow; he couldn't help himself.

Charlie's tears had dried up, but her skin was pale in the moonlight, and her blue eyes were haunted. "Because I had to make a choice: my own family or you. And Brandon had just threatened to kill himself."

Kill himself? Brandon?

Her words sucked the oxygen out of him, out of the argument, out of the truck. "Oh, man. I'm so sorry. I didn't know." Jake leaned his forehead against the steering wheel.

"Of course not. How could you have known?"

"Why? Why would he do that?" But Jake knew. He knew.

"Everyone was asking him questions, same as you, about that campfire. I guess he felt responsible, somehow, for Grandma's death. And he'd lost you, too."

Jake's heart clenched with pity. "That's awful, and it's untrue. George wrote up the report," he said, carefully editing his words. The Nashes had been through enough. They didn't need to know the whole truth. Including Charlie. "He's told me to my face that it was just an accident. An accident that stole away a really wonderful lady. I wish I could turn back time and run a little faster. I'd do anything to have saved your grandma, Charlie."

Jake dashed sudden tears away from his eyes.

"You didn't fail Grandma Babe . . . You did the best you could for her." She put her arms around him and laid her head on his chest, listening to his heartbeat.

He slid his arms around her, too, and for a moment he rested his chin on top of her head. It was the best feeling in the entire world, holding Charlie in his arms like old times. "I swear to you by all that's holy, Charlie, that I had nothing to do with the fire," Jake whispered.

"I know that," Charlie told him. "I know it deep in my bones. I always have."

As he absorbed her words, a part of him that had been coiled tight for twelve years suddenly relaxed, leaving him weak inside.

He savored the warm, fragrant feel of her in his arms and found her lips with his own. *Hello, Goodbye Girl. God, you taste good.* His whole body hummed, and he wanted more of her. He deepened the kiss, pulling her tighter, savoring the curves of her body.

"Jake," she whispered, her breathing quick and shallow.

"Shh." He slid his hands into places he knew he shouldn't, but he couldn't help himself. Warm handfuls of Charlie . . .

"Jake!"

He groaned and pulled her bodily into his lap. He wanted her naked in the worst way.

And of course that was when the firehouse alarm went off, at lust-destroying decibels.

That was when the floodlights came on and the garage door went up, exposing Big Red in all its glory. That was when Old George came running out first, a priceless expression crossing his face when he saw them.

"Well, that's progress," he called, in a tone as dry as

dust. "But we got a night drill for a disaster-preparedness scenario, remember? Out near the Lundgren property. You coming or what?"

Jake looked down at the beautiful woman in his arms and sighed.

Chapter 15

ELEVEN HOURS LATER, JAKE AND THE BOYS STUM-bled into Sunny's Side Up Diner. They were dog-tired, dirty, and sweat-encrusted. And they all wanted pie for breakfast. There was nothing better after an all-nighter than coffee and a huge slice of Sunny's caramel-apple-cinnamon pie.

Coach Adams was reading the paper at the counter; he raised his coffee mug to them. "Boys."

"Coach. How ya doin'?" said Jake.

"Be doing better if Ace would get serious," Coach mumbled, his mouth downturned, his eyes like raisins in his beefy face.

"Yeah, well . . ." Jake didn't know what to say.

He lifted a hand in greeting to his former PT client Jorge Ramos, who had almost fully recovered from a stroke, with Jake's help. Jorge, on his cell phone with his mouth full, winked and waved a triangle of toast at him.

Jake turned, then pulled up short at the sight of his brother Deck sitting alone at a table in back, his big hands wrapped around a steaming mug as if it were his only friend in the world. That hit Jake in the gut.

Old George saw Declan, too, and gave Jake a nudge toward his brother that he didn't need. But he nodded anyway and peeled off to go sit with him. The others got a table in the front window.

"Hey, man," Jake said, bumping fists with Deck. "What brings you to town so early?"

"I ran out of toast to burn. And I can never get my eggs right. My sunny side up turns into runny side up."

"You can run a ranch, but you still can't conquer a couple of eggs?"

Deck gave him a look. "Don't you smell nice. Long night?"

"Yeah. It started with Lila dancing on a table at Schweitz's and then got better with a nighttime drill out near the Lundgrens' property. Couldn't let the mythological nuke get their hogs. That'd be way too much bacon for one town."

Declan smiled and took a sip of his coffee. "So you had to put Lila to bed?"

"You don't sound surprised."

"Sunny heard at least one version of the story from her neighbor, Otto. He said you and Charlie took her home."

A moment of silence ensued. Deck waited him out.

"Yeah . . . so. I've been patching things up with Charlie," Jake said, almost testing out the words for himself.

Declan's hands seemed to tighten on the coffee mug in front of him. After another long moment he said, "Give you some peace?"

"Yeah." Well, there was peace, and then there was the feel of Charlie's mouth. There was the fact that it was complicated . . . Even if they managed to forget the past, she didn't even live in Silverlake anymore.

"Works for me, then," Deck said.

"I wasn't sure what you'd think about it." Jake greeted Sunny as she delivered a huge plate of breakfast to Deck with a slightly lovesick smile. She was easily two decades older than Declan, but she was undeniably attractive, the crow's-feet at the corners of her eyes enhancing her smile. Sunny had gotten her nickname because of her buoyant personality. Nothing, it seemed, could get her down.

Jake looked at what she'd brought his brother. Three eggs, perfectly sunny-side up. A mountain of golden hash browns. Three slices of crispy-browned bacon. Forget about pie. "I'll have the same, please," he said.

"You got it, sugar." With a flash of her dimples, Sunny headed back to her kitchen.

Declan dug in. "Does it matter what I think?"

Jake fiddled with the silverware in front of him.

His brother inhaled the mountain of hash browns soaked in egg yolk. He chewed and swallowed. "I've never had . . . the kind of . . . love"—Declan said the word as if it tasted funny—"for anyone that you had for her, and I don't even know that I'd know to grab for it if I saw there was a chance. But you're not me." He smiled that rare smile of his. "You asking for some sort of blessing?"

Jake laughed, almost choking up a little at Declan's open expression. "What? Why would I be doing that?"

"No reason," Declan said, returning to his breakfast with a smile still playing on his lips. "No reason at all."

The two men ate in silence for a while. For the first time since Ace and Everett had put Silverlake in their rearview mirrors and Declan's heart had shut down, it seemed like there was a chance the word *brother* could become more than just a word again.

* * *

Charlie, Mia, Amelie, and a sheepish Lila all stood in Kristina's gleaming stainless-steel baker's kitchen at Piece A Cake. The kitchen was a professional space, undecorated, in sharp contrast to the explosion of color that was the bakery/café.

"Welcome to the cake rejects party!" Kristina announced. "By the way, this is against all health-code regulations. We should do this out in the café, but I don't want my other customers overhearing any choice words about Bridezilla."

"What?" Amelie pretended to be shocked. "None of us have *anything* bad to say about that darling girl. She's my favorite customer." She coughed. "Luckily, we're almost through with her, so I brought champagne to share while we sample her ten rejected cakes."

"Eleven," Kristina said evenly. Charlie had never heard that edge in her voice before now.

"Right. Eleven. Which one do we start with?"

"Anything with chocolate?" Mia asked, hope on her face.

"Anything with raspberry?" Charlie chimed in.

"Yes and yes." Kristina opened her cavernous industrial-sized refrigerator and slid out two trays of small cakes, beautifully frosted—most in white or pale cream ganache. Each was missing a thin slice. A tiny bride stood on one, a groom on another. Yet another cake sported a life-sized engagement ring. Next to it was one with a wedding ring. An adorable pink purse adorned the next, and so on.

"Kristina, they're stunning."

"Gorgeous!"

"Way too pretty to eat."

"How can you stand to cut them?"

"Like this!" Kristina said, and hacked through the middle of the tiny bride's cake with a wicked-looking knife.

Tiny Bride lost part of her veil and her shoulder. "Oooh. That makes me feel *so* much better."

Everyone laughed as Kristina slaughtered more cakes and put pieces on paper plates.

"So if she rejected eleven cakes, which one did she finally decide on?" Charlie asked.

Kristina took a deep breath. "Apricot Champagne. The first one I suggested, incidentally." She took another deep breath, then exhaled it slowly, as if cleansing herself of evil. "So. We'll start with Vanilla Hazelnut, Luscious Lemon, and—"

But the girls had already dug in.

"Ohhhh!"

"Oh my God!"

"Thith ith unbelievable, Kristina!"

"Better than sex."

"If I die right now, I'll die happy . . ."

Kristina tried to resist preening but failed.

Charlie firmly told herself to stop thinking about calories and tried another cake. It was a velvety, flavorful surprise on her tongue, but she couldn't identify the ingredients. "Wow, what is *this* one?"

"Bridezilla's third idea: Anise Pear. Glad you like it. Not a fan of anise, myself. But as it turns out, neither is she!"

"She's crazy," Charlie declared, and took another large bite.

"I think it's good. I have no complaints." Amelie popped open the champagne.

"No alcohol for me," Mia said. "I go back on duty in an hour. But I'll have some of the Chocolate Raspberry."

"Patience," Kristina told her. "I'm getting to it. But we have six more in line before it."

"I'll be visiting Granddad while you're on shift," Charlie told Mia, trying not to think about the council meeting on

Friday morning. Her dread of it only grew. "How was he last night? I meant to call, but got . . ." She cast a sidelong glance at Lila, who still looked a bit green. "Distracted."

"He's doing pretty well. He keeps saying he's going to make the wedding on Saturday, and he's stubborn. We won't let him out before then, but . . . he just might."

"You guys do a fantastic—and patient—job of looking after him. I'll keep my fingers crossed," Charlie said.

"Hair of the dog, Lila?" Mia asked, offering Lila a glass of champagne.

Lila shook her head. "That expression alone makes me want to hurl."

"Does that mean you don't want any cake?" Kristina asked.

"How does everybody know about this already?" Lila exclaimed.

"Seriously?" Amelie grinned. "You *did* dance on a table—and the main bar—at Schweitz's. There were people in there. And people walking by outside. And this is a small town."

"Heard Tommy proposed to you," Mia said with a laugh. "And that Otto really does think you're a goddess—as long as you don't sing."

"Hey!" Lila protested. "I was actively recruited for choir."

"To play the triangle," Charlie reminded her dryly.

"Cake?" Kristina asked. "If we keep your mouth full, you can't rediscover your inner Leppard."

There was more laughter as Lila accepted a loaded plate. "That *was* quite a night," Lila said, turning to Charlie with a look on her face suggesting she was probing her memory for all the details. "I dreamed you hooked up with my brother."

Four additional pairs of eyes swiveled to Charlie's face.

"I dreamed you almost got X-rated with a saltshaker at Schweitz's," Charlie said. "Only it wasn't a dream."

"I did not! I only used it as a microphone."

"Yeah, until it spilled into your mouth."

Giggles echoed throughout the kitchen, reverberating off all the stainless steel.

"Isn't it kind of weird to dream about your brother hooking up?" Mia asked.

"Yes," Lila said. "Yes, it is. So maybe that wasn't a dream, either."

Four pairs of eyes ping-ponged back to Charlie's face. "Ugh. I wouldn't want to dream about *my* brother hooking up," Charlie mumbled.

"*I'd* like to dream about your brother hooking up," Amelie said. "Brandon is hot." She cleared her throat in the awkward pause. "What? I saw a picture."

"If you saw a picture of him, he was a lot younger then," Charlie said, shifting uncomfortably in her chair. "He hasn't been back in a while."

Another pause ensued.

"Next up is a groom's cake: Chocolate with Malt-Ball Frosting," Kristina said, slamming a new cake with one slice removed down on the table. "Not *my* idea."

Charlie looked at Kristina with grateful eyes. Brandon was still very, very good-looking by anybody's measure, but he was also still very, very broken.

Somehow, they worked through all eleven cakes, groaning with pleasure and guilt over all the sugar.

Lila was going for seconds on a Red Velvet groom's cake when her cell phone rang. "'Lo?" she managed around a large mouthful.

Even though it wasn't on speaker, Charlie heard Jake's voice clearly. "How's your head, dumb-ass?" His affection was clear, despite the crude words, and it warmed Charlie's heart.

Lila chewed and swallowed. "Aw, Jakey. You haven't called me that in years! It makes me feel so special."

"Don't feel so special that you sing."

"I'm really starting to feel ganged up on now. Others have commented, too." She looked around darkly.

"You don't say," Jake said. "Are you still bringing that tuxedo over, or are you going to send someone who can still walk in a straight line without hurling?"

"Oh, please. It wasn't that bad."

"Uh-huh."

"But now that you mention it"—Lila looked up at Charlie with a gleam in her eye—"I'm gonna send Charlie."

Charlie sucked in a breath, but Jake didn't miss a beat. "Great. Send her soon. I'm on call this afternoon. So really, how are you feeling?"

"I feel *awesome*."

"You lie. And you snore."

"I'm hanging up now, bro."

"I'm pretty sure I just heard you say, 'Thank you, Jake, for taking my drunk butt home and putting me to bed.'"

"Nope. I don't think you heard me say it. But I do appreciate it."

"You're welcome."

"Even if it was just an excuse to hang with Charlie!"

Charlie blushed.

"I'm hanging up now, sis."

Lila smirked. "You do that." Then she ate another piece of cake.

༄

The firehouse door was up, and Big Red was gone. Charlie hopped down from Progress and grabbed the tuxedo, in its garment bag, from the passenger side. She walked into the garage, took a look around at the orderly piles of equipment, the boots and jackets and hats hung carefully on brass hooks. Jake's name on the back of his fireman's jacket was faded but still legible, and it made her smile.

This is Jake's world. This is where Jake is happiest.

He'd sounded good on the phone to Lila, joking and laughing. But a pang of doubt hit Charlie hard as she stood in the empty garage, gripping the unwieldy bag. What if, in the light of day, he regretted kissing her again?

"Hi."

Charlie wheeled around. Jake stood there in his uniform, framed in the doorway leading up the stairs to the living quarters. Oh, did he look good. *And all that used to be mine.*

"Hi." Charlie moistened her lips, suddenly nervous. She held up the garment bag containing Jake's tuxedo for the wedding. "Special delivery!" She released a calming breath. "If you're going to tell me last night's kiss was a mistake, too, then this would be your moment."

Jake stuck his hands in his pockets and cocked his head. "Well, now, let's see."

He has to think about it?

Suddenly, Jake burst out laughing. He came down the last few steps and took the bag off Charlie's hands, hanging it on a utility hook by the light switch. "You should see your face!"

"What's wrong with my face?" Charlie asked, relaxing now. He did not seem like a man with regrets.

"Oh. You want me to get specific?" Jake walked—no, prowled—toward her with a mischievous grin on his face.

"What are you doing?" Charlie said, laughing even as she backed up, dodging a grease stain and an orange safety cone.

"You know my job is to right wrongs, so let's see." He caught her in his arms and gently pressed a kiss on her nose. "No, that wasn't it. That didn't feel wrong. Maybe here . . ." He kissed her right under her ear. "I'd better keep checking . . ."

Oh, thought Charlie, on a sigh. *This is what it would have been like. Oh my. This is what it could be like.*

Could there really be a second chance here?

Jake whispered softly against her ear, "Missed you so much."

Her breath caught, half on a sob, half on cloud nine. She couldn't find the words, but as his lips slid down her jawline and he took her mouth with his, for the first time since she'd given him up and sent him away, she imagined the possibility of taking that chance.

They couldn't change the past, but maybe, just maybe, there was a future here.

Chapter 16

WHEN CHARLIE STOPPED BY TO CHECK ON GRAND-dad, her heart rose at the sight of him: He was sitting bolt upright in bed, TV remote in hand. He was more animated than she'd seen him since he'd gotten so cranky about Jake turning out to be his physical therapist.

Then she discovered why: He was eviscerating the talking head on the news. The talking head wearing a fire chief's helmet and a grim, weary expression. Five people had been killed in a high-rise condo fire in downtown Austin.

The chief began. "We are very sorry to say—"

"Damn straight you're sorry!" Granddad growled. "A sorry bunch. What d'you do, ladies—change into evening gowns before heading out to *not* save the day?"

Oh, good Lord. Not more of this.

Charlie almost turned on her heel and ran away. Then she realized that she might be the nurses' only savior from his obnoxious behavior. Stifling a sigh, she went in.

"Too busy posing for a beefcake calendar?" he accused the unknown chief on the screen.

"Hi, Granddad!" Charlie aimed a bright smile at him and bent to kiss his withered cheek. "How are you feeling?"

"Aargh."

"Really? That's wonderful."

He pointed at the television. "More nincompoops—"

"Who's got vanilla pudding? Huh? D'you think it's me?" Charlie extracted two of the packaged desserts from her handbag, along with a plastic spoon and a Halloween-themed napkin. "You hungry?"

"Aargh!"

"Use your words, Granddad."

"Don't patronize me." He scowled. "I got plenty of real choice words I can use. *French* ones, if you take my meaning."

"Grandma Babe would not approve of them." Charlie took the remote control off his bedside table. "Mind if I turn this off so we can visit?"

"Yes."

She raised an eyebrow at him and clicked it off anyway.

"Hey!"

"Granddad, I won't be in town forever. Let's just hang out and talk. You can get riled up at the news any old time."

He grunted.

"Pudding?"

He nodded. "Thank ya."

She peeled off the plastic film on the top, then handed him one. "Maybe I'll try making Grandma's one of these days."

"That so? All's I remember is that it had lots of milk and egg yolks in it." His expression went dreamy. "She'd warm up the milk, and I sure hated that smell, but then she'd somehow turn it into heaven."

"She sure did. So how's your hip doing?"

"Better. I plan on getting out of here for young Will's wedding."

"That's only a few days away. You sure?"

"Yep. I don't want to disappoint Sadie. Though that young lady of Will's—I got my doubts about her. She'll lead him around by the nose, if he ain't careful."

Charlie bit back a smile. "She's a little headstrong."

"Spoiled rotten, by the look of her."

Charlie didn't say a word.

"So I'm glad you're here, girlie. We need to go over my talking points for the town council meeting."

Oh no. No way. "Granddad—"

"I got research now from neighboring towns and counties: facts, figures, statistics, reports. Armed and dangerous, I am! Or, uh, you'll be."

"Granddad," Charlie said, "I told you that I would think about it, and I have. I do not feel comfortable presenting a case to do away with the Silverlake Fire and Rescue crew's salaries."

"Oh, you don't feel comfortable, do you? Well, I don't feel *comfortable* with a plastic hip socket. I don't feel *comfortable* without your grandmother."

"Look, Granddad—"

"I'm asking you to do one small thing for me. One."

"It's not small!"

"You still hung up on that mooching layabout?"

"He is no such thing, Granddad. And, no, I'm not hung up on Jake Braddock. But—"

"Then you'll do what I ask."

"It's not a reasonable request!"

"Oh, now I'm unreasonable, am I? The cheek and the disrespect of your generation is astonishing."

"What? I—"

"Who's family here? Who's your flesh and blood?"

"How does that have anything to do with—"

"It's got to do with loyalty, damn it."

"*No*, it—"

"Whose granddaughter are you?" he shouted, his nostrils flaring.

"Granddad, please calm down!"

He raised himself up on his elbows. "Who raised your mother? Whose house did you grow up in?" He was almost hyperventilating. "Who had a role in feeding you, clothing you, teaching you manners? Huh?"

"Please—"

"Who taught you how to ride a bicycle?"

"Lower your voice—"

"Was it Jake blasted *Braddock*?" Spittle and hatred flew from his dry gash of a mouth.

"And don't elevate your blood pressure—"

"*Any* of those layabout firefighters?"

"Granddad—"

"Answer me! Was it?" He was almost unrecognizable, with his bushy old eyebrows drawn down, his eyes narrowed to slits, his face contorted.

"No." She was afraid he was going to have a stroke, or a seizure of some kind.

"So your loyalty is to whom here?"

"I told you, this isn't a question of loyalty."

"Yes, it damn well *is*!" He suddenly clutched at his chest and swore.

"Granddad!" Charlie bolted toward him. "What's happening?"

He opened and closed his mouth but said nothing, which threw her into a panic.

"Mia!" screamed Charlie, running now toward the door. "Help! Get his doctor! Get *any* doctor—I think my grandfather's having a heart attack!"

A different nurse came running from the room next door.

Granddad's color was still purplish, and he fell back against his pillows.

Tears streamed down Charlie's face. "You're okay, you're okay," she repeated over and over. "Please be okay. I'm sorry. I'm sorry . . ."

He nodded at her. Weakly raised an index finger to point at her.

"Fine, I'll do it. Whatever you want," she promised. "Just stop getting upset."

"Desk drawer," he rasped as two more nurses and an ER doctor rushed in. "File. Take it. Friday."

Charlie nodded, weeping as the medical personnel circled around him, trading instructions in tightly controlled voices, the crash cart obscuring her view. "All right, Granddad," she managed to choke out. "I'll be there. As your proxy. I promise."

I'm sorry, Jake. I'm so sorry.

Oh God. Some things never changed.

Once Granddad was stabilized, sedated, and sleeping, Mia ordered Charlie to get out of the hospital and get some sleep. Initially, she refused. But in the face of more pressure from Mia, she reluctantly headed back to her grandfather's apartment.

Thank God he was all right.

Granddad's place was small, spare, and tidy, though it smelled of sour old man. It was a bachelor's space, populated by three fishing rods, a gray tackle box, and some books: history, politics, and biographies. It had standard-issue beige carpeting and was furnished with a dreadful brown velour recliner, a matching love seat with a hand-knit afghan over the back of it, and a large television. On the shelf holding the books was an eight-by-ten silver-framed photo of the whole Nash family in happier times.

It depressed Charlie to see it, but she'd gone numb after the scene in the hospital; after seeing Granddad on the brink of death, she had no more tears left.

There wasn't much in the tiny galley kitchen besides a jar of change and some small white apartment appliances: stove, microwave, dishwasher. Plus a case of Ensure facing off against a case of vanilla pudding. Vanilla pudding—the family comfort food.

What a crazy few days. She'd fallen off a ladder and into Jake's arms. He'd dug her out of the mud. They'd babysat a drunken Lila. They'd played True Confessions. He'd kissed her twice, and she hadn't exactly minded . . . but now she was going to have to attack his livelihood or alienate her granddad! And then stand up with him in Felicity and Will's wedding. How, exactly, was this all going to work? God help her.

So your loyalty is to whom here? Granddad had ranted.

To both of you, Charlie thought. *How do I choose?*

That pudding was going to come in handy. Even if she had already eaten her weight in cake.

Charlie's skinny jeans were cutting off the blood flow to her legs. She felt as if an overambitious boa constrictor had swallowed her lower half and now regretted it. Plus, two of her toes had gone numb from being crammed into her high-heeled pumps.

She kicked those off in the bedroom, peeled off the accursed jeans, and padded into the kitchen. She lunged at Granddad's vanilla puddings and ate two in quick succession, barely registering that she was doing it. And that's when the idea came to her: She would ask someone else to be his proxy. Mia? Kristina? Amelie? She wasn't picky. Even Vic the plumber—he had his quirks, but he was a sweetie.

That was her out. She'd find a *different* proxy, and then everything would be okay.

Her thoughts turned to her late-night conversation with Jake.

I swear to you by all that's holy, Charlie, that I had nothing to do with the fire.

She believed him. She couldn't help but believe him.

But if Jake wasn't responsible, then that left only Brandon. Didn't it?

Ugh. She didn't want to acknowledge that suspicion.

She ate a third pudding while she thought about how to broach the past with her brother. Would it send him into yet another tailspin? She didn't know.

But she now had more questions . . . ones to which she wasn't sure she wanted the answers.

They came to her anyway. Lack of evidence—that was the reason her parents had given her for not pursuing charges against Jake. That was even Jake's belief. But somehow she knew there was more to the story.

The investigators and the psychologists went away. But her parents had still moved them almost overnight to Dallas.

Charlie got to her feet and went into the living room to look at the picture of the family all together. Granddad had his arm slung around Grandma, and they stood smiling next to Dad's wheelchair. Mom sat on the right arm of it, leaning in toward him. Brandon lay propped on his elbow in the grass at Dad's feet. And she, Charlie, sat cross-legged next to him.

Aunt Sadie, Dad's sister and her cousin Will's mom, had taken the picture one Thanksgiving. She must have given Granddad a copy, since everything had been destroyed in the fire.

Charlie looked closely at Brandon's face. It was youthful, carefree, faintly bored. His mouth tugged upward. He was waiting for the world to hand him a happy, prosperous future. He looked like a completely different person than he did now.

Today's Brandon rarely smiled or laughed, and when he did, he seemed to want to punish himself for it.

Charlie began to add it all up: Brandon's inability to move past the incident, his refusal to even talk about Jake, the way he hurt himself, the general wreckage of his life . . . it all spoke volumes. So did their parents' silence on the topic.

With shaking hands, she dialed Brandon's number.

Brandon answered on the third ring. "What's up, Charlie?" His voice was deep and a little sluggish. "How's Granddad?"

She pictured him lounging on the gray couch in his apartment, probably in a Cowboys sweatshirt and jeans that hadn't been washed in a week. His hair would be too long. He'd have a beer in front of him, sitting among crumbs on the coffee table.

"Granddad is super weak. He had a heart attack earlier today."

Her brother seemed stunned. "Is he all right?"

"Yeah . . . he's doing better. There's a chance he'll still be able to go to Will's wedding. So that's hope right there."

"Okay," her brother mumbled. "Good. Glad to hear it." A TV program gabbled in the background; Brandon's TV was almost as large as his couch.

"Are *you* coming in for the wedding on Saturday?"

Silence.

She sighed. "Did you even RSVP, Brandon? He *is* your cousin."

"I forgot."

"Well, I'm sure you'd still be welcome. I don't really think Granddad will be out of the hospital by then, so I doubt he'll make it. But you could visit him while you're here—I know he'd love to see you."

More silence.

"Brandon? You there?"

"Uh, yeah. I'll think about it."

"They sent out the invitations six weeks ago. You haven't had enough time to think about coming?"

"Get off my ass, Charlie." And then after a pause he asked, "You okay being back there so long?"

"I'm fine," she said. Which was more or less true. She took a deep breath. "So I've run into Jake Braddock a couple of times." Her tone was a little too casual, especially in light of the fact that their family hadn't brought up his name in twelve years.

From her brother came a swift intake of breath. Then silence again.

"Jake, uh, says hello."

Brandon's silence grew to ominous proportions. Then Charlie heard the *click-click* of a lighter, and the sound of suction as he drew on a cigarette.

"Bran?"

Her brother abruptly hung up on her.

Seriously?

Charlie removed the phone from her ear and stared at it, her inner knowledge and anger growing. Had her brother had something to do with the fire? Had he lied, all of these years?

She grabbed a fourth vanilla pudding and ate it as she paced from the kitchen to the family photo and back again. If she confronted Brandon, would he try to hurt himself again?

She paced back and forth, back and forth. Threw the plastic pudding cup in the sink and paced some more. It was on lap thirty-seven that she decided: She wasn't going to participate in this family whitewash any longer. If Brandon had just come clean from the beginning, he might have healed.

Charlie lay down on Granddad's bed and gazed at the portrait of Grandma Babe, who smiled at her serenely, unsurprised at human weaknesses or failures. *Time will tell,* she seemed to say.

Charlie closed her eyes and thought about the terrible night of the fire. Jake had been evicted two days earlier, after The Talk, and both of them had been upset, to put it mildly.

But her parents, Dave and Maria, had made it very clear that Jake was still welcome to visit. That they had great affection for him, and that he could come over to visit anytime. He just couldn't sleep there.

So Jake—chin up and legs spread wide—had shown up on the doorstep to test that invitation. He'd rung the doorbell close to dinnertime and rocked back on his heels, hands stuffed in his pockets, probably to hide the fact that they were shaking.

His bravado didn't fool Charlie for a second, and her heart broke for him. She'd let him in, her parents and grandparents had converged on them, and she'd gone to find Brandon. He was in the backyard, facing the setting sun, and when she called him, he'd turned quickly and concealed something. Said he'd be right in.

Charlie hadn't thought much about it at the time. But now she knew exactly what he'd hidden. It came to her in a rush of clarity, brought on by that *click-click* of his lighter and his audible drag on the cigarette.

Her fingers fumbled the phone when she dialed Brandon's number again, surprised when he picked up and said in that gravelly voice, "I shouldn't have hung up on you."

"Will you let me say what I have to say?" Charlie asked. "Let me finish?"

He was silent, but he didn't hang up.

"Maybe you were smoking the night of the fire, Brandon. Maybe something happened."

There was a curse from his end of the line, and then a crash, as if he'd thrown something against the wall.

"What was that?" she asked.

"Nothing."

She waited a beat. Then two. "If something happened that night . . . oh, Bran, I know it had to have been an accident," she said, her voice somehow full of compassion.

The tension on the line between them grew almost tangible, a blue-black ominous thing. A thing neither of them really wanted to risk touching. But she had to, no matter how painful it might be. She approached it with extreme caution.

How could she feel sorry for her brother and yet be so angry with him at the same time? How could she love and hate him simultaneously? "You didn't . . . kill . . . if something out there happened like that—maybe with a cigarette or a lighter or something—you didn't *kill* anyone. It was an *accident*. And you were a *kid*, a scared kid. But you're an adult now. It's time to grow up."

Her brother was silent.

"Brandon, it doesn't make you *bad*. Just human. Okay?"

He exhaled audibly.

"I love you, Bran. Nothing will ever change that. Mom and Dad and Granddad and Aunt Sadie and Will—we all will still love you. But you have to tell the truth. For everyone's sake. And for your own."

After yet another long silence, her brother finally said, "I hear you."

Charlie felt weak with relief. "Come in for Will's wedding, Brandon. Talk to Jake. It's a long story, but he's a substitute best man."

"A *what*? For *Will*? You've gotta be kidding me."

"It's a weird story. He's helping out."

"Right."

She sighed. "Come in for the wedding. Then I'll help you talk to Granddad. Mom and Dad, too. Just come."

"I'll think about it." Was that a trace of hope in her brother's voice? She prayed that it was.

"One last thing," Charlie said. "Promise me that right now you're okay. That you won't do anything stupid."

He promised.

"I love you, Bran," she told him again.

"You still love Jake, too," he said. "I could hear it in your voice."

His bold statement was like a bucket of cold water in her face. Things could be so different if she hadn't had to make that promise to Granddad. *Love* wasn't even on the table, much less in her hands. "That's ridiculous," Charlie said emphatically. "Now, let's both get some sleep."

She hung up the phone, knowing that she'd done the right thing but feeling as spent and limp as linguine. At least the call hadn't been for nothing.

She'd taken a huge risk. She'd stopped avoiding the past. She'd addressed the bruised, painful tension between her and her brother. It might have exploded in a mess. She could have destroyed the ghost of their relationship.

But she hadn't.

It had turned out okay . . . maybe even better than okay. They'd have to wait and see.

Brandon's reaction still vaguely puzzled her. She'd expected an extreme: either total denial and a permanent rift— or a flood of true confessions. But he was still . . . what was the word? Hedging?

The question was why, but she wasn't going to solve the riddle tonight.

Exhausted, she turned out the lights and shoved her head under Granddad's pillow.

Sleep did not come easy. She did not love Jake Braddock. She might be attracted to him. She might want to resolve the issues of the past. But just because she wanted the truth to come to light did *not* mean she loved the guy.

Chapter 17

JAKE FINISHED UP A FIRE-SAFETY INSPECTION IN A local warehouse the next day and drove back to the firehouse, bracing himself for the wedding rehearsal and dinner. Ridiculous what a case of nerves he had. He was paid to keep calm in every sort of life-threatening emergency, yet here he was, sweating bullets over a nonevent.

Why in the hell had he agreed to be a stand-in groomsman? Oh yeah. For a little petty revenge on Charlie, who so clearly hadn't wanted him as a substitute at the time.

Except after that last kiss, Jake didn't want revenge. He had no idea what she wanted, though. The worst part was no longer standing up next to Charlie; it was seeing whatever members of Charlie's family were going to show up.

Jake owned only one jacket, a standard navy blue blazer. He put it on with a light blue dress shirt and gray slacks, debating whether or not he'd have to strangle himself with a tie for Bridezilla. He owned only two of those, and one was dotted with reindeer and Santas.

Muttering darkly to himself, he snagged the other tie—boring blue and gray stripes—and shoved it in a pocket of the jacket. He looked in the bathroom mirror and recoiled. That was not him staring back. No way. It was his brother Everett, about to go into some business meeting.

Jake scowled and ran a hand through his hair, messing it up so that he looked more like himself. Then he trudged down the stairs, wishing he were going anywhere but to rehearse for somebody's wedding.

Mick and Tommy were downstairs with Not-Spot, watching the ball game while Mick made chili, which smelled phenomenal. Even more reluctant to leave, Jake inhaled the aroma of garlic, chilies, onion, tomato, and beef.

"Save some for me," he said, without much real hope. The guys ate like raptors, and Not-Spot was a criminal counter surfer who devoured anything within reach.

Mick turned around and whistled. "Look at you, Princess Buttercup! Aren't you lovely."

Tommy grinned. "Off to prom, then? Did you get her a corsage?"

Jake shot them double fingers, but it didn't do any good.

"Do we need to have the birds-and-bees talk, son?" Mick asked.

Jake looked around for his keys. "I'm only doing this for my sister, guys."

"Doing it for his sister," Mick mused. "That just sounds wrong."

"It does," said Tommy. "But speaking of doing and sisters—" He waggled his eyebrows.

Jake palmed his keys off the kitchen counter and narrowed his eyes at Tommy. "You stay away from Lila, or there will suddenly be one less hose in this firehouse. Understand?"

"What if she likes me?"

"I can fix that." Jake headed for the door.

"Don't do anything we wouldn't do," Mick said. "By the way, we do it all, so go crazy. And give Charlie my love!"

"Charlie from the bar the other night?" Tommy asked. "Gotta agree with you. She does have a nice ra—"

"That is *enough*, gentlemen!" Jake said, glaring at Tommy.

Tommy laughed. "Well, if you like her so much, then why do you look like you're about to go in front of a firing squad?"

"Because I probably am." Jake shut the door on them and headed for the Durango.

Minutes later, he pulled up at the Old Barn, where Charlie was waiting for him in the parking lot that Lila had marked off using more of those damned swags on hammered posts. Waiting there in a stunning classic black knee-length dress that hugged her every gorgeous curve.

Jake felt a lump growing in his throat. *Swallow it, idiot.*

He did, but another one welled in its place. He told himself he'd seen too many sappy movies, but he knew that his feelings had nothing to do with Hollywood and everything to do with Charlie.

She looked regal in her simple black dress. Her uncomplicated beauty absolutely undid him, as her words had last night.

You didn't fail Grandma Babe . . . You did the best you could for her.

He loved her for saying it. He just wished the rest of her family felt the same way.

She offered him a warm smile, and when he parked, she walked over.

Jake leaned over and opened the passenger-side door. Charlie hiked up her skirt a little so she could climb inside. "Hi," she said.

Jake's gaze was riveted to the expanse of smooth, bare thigh she'd revealed. "Hi."

"Ready to rhumba?"

He reached out to touch her left leg, tracing his fingers from the hem of her dress down to her knee, gratified when she shivered and made no move to push his hand away. "Ready as I'll ever be." He'd leaned forward to kiss her, when the barn door flew open and Lila peered out.

"Charlie? Charlie, we need you in here right away!"

Charlie sighed, scooted for the door, and slipped out of the truck.

"What is it about weddings that make women crazy?" Jake asked.

She shrugged. "I don't know. But excuse me."

"Give me a minute. I'll be right in."

"You okay?"

He nodded.

"It'll be okay," she said softly.

"I'm not afraid of them, Charlie."

She gave him a level look that said she didn't believe him, but she shut the door and went into the barn.

She knew him too well. As Jake braced himself to face the entire Nash family, a sandy-haired guy pulled up in a silver BMW. Instead of getting out, he just sat there, gripping the wheel and staring straight ahead.

Jake did the same thing. *I am not afraid of any member of the Nash family,* he told himself. *I have done nothing wrong. If they behave strangely, it's on them . . . It has nothing to do with me.* He got out of his truck, and the sound of his door closing seemed to jolt Mr. Beemer out of his trance. He got out, too.

"Hi," said Jake. "Here for the rehearsal?"

"Uh, yeah. I'm the groom. Will Spence." He smiled and stuck out his hand, and Jake froze, because he looked so much like a younger version of his grandfather Kingston. And because they'd met once before.

But Jake took his hand. "Jake Braddock, rented grooms-man, your grandfather's physical therapist, and your wedding planner's brother. We've met, but it's . . . been a while."

"Right, right. We have met. At my grandmother's fu-neral." Will didn't withdraw his hand, but his expression congealed. "Listen, I guess this is all a bit weird, but when Felicity gets an idea . . . Anyway. But, uh, thank you, man. For subbing in at the last minute. We appreciate it."

Jake nodded slowly. "No problem. Glad I can help."

Together they entered the Old Barn, where almost ev-eryone else was already gathered. "You know my parents? Sadie and Theo Spence?" Will asked politely.

Jake didn't, though of course he'd seen them at the fu-neral, too. He'd stood in the very back of the service, trying not to throw up from nerves, doing his best to ignore the whispers and sidelong glances. *Brandon's friend . . . They set a campfire in the backyard . . . May have had something to do with the house fire.* Jake looked around; Brandon wasn't here.

"Mom, Dad," Will said a little too jovially, "this is Jake Braddock. He's subbing as groomsman for Geoff, since he was transferred overseas."

"Oh dear. Oh, yes. Jake Braddock. Hello." Sadie looked like a plus-sized version of Babe Nash, taller and with a little more stuffing. She seemed frazzled, and to avoid making eye contact with Jake, she kept beaming artificially at an older couple who looked as if they'd just stepped out of *Town & Country* magazine. Must be the bride's parents.

"Nice to meet you," Jake said, because he couldn't say, *I'm sorry to this day that I failed to get your mother out of her burning house alive.* It didn't seem appropriate for the occasion.

Sadie's husband, Theo, was a tall, gaunt fellow with cup-handle ears and a faintly condescending expression. "Ah. Good to meet you," he managed, examining some lint on his sleeve.

"Likewise." *Why didn't I bring along a flask?* Why wasn't there a bar right here in the barn?

Jake got to meet Town & Country Twosome next. They were indeed Bridezilla's parents, fashionably dressed and sporting magnificent blindingly white dental work.

"You know my fiancée, Felicity?" Will asked, as he and Jake approached her.

Jake nodded. "Yes, we've met. Good to see you again." Felicity was resplendent in hot-tamale red lipstick and a silky silvery cocktail dress. It left very little to anyone's imagination. It clung to . . . everything. So much so that Jake had to look away.

Felicity seemed oblivious, but her husband-to-be's color rose as the pastor and his wife took the same tack as Jake did; they avoided looking directly at the bride for fear of ogling anything ripe or low-hanging.

Jake thought about talking to the pastor about this bizarre situation and what a very strange sense of humor God had, but he reminded himself that this occasion was not about him. He also reminded himself that he'd thoughtlessly and foolishly said yes to the devil, a.k.a. Lila.

He excused himself and searched among the gaggle of bridesmaids for Charlie, but he didn't see her. He was relieved when she and Lila came in, and went over to them immediately.

"Jake," Lila said, smooching him on the cheek. "How are you?"

He grimaced. "Is it too late to find a different groomsman?"

"Yes," Lila said.

"Because this is extremely awkward."

"I know. But at least this way, the Nash family has to recognize your existence." She punched him in the shoulder and then flashed him a surprisingly sympathetic smile.

"I'd actually rather they didn't. It was cleaner that way."

"We're not talking about your wishes here. We're talking about what's right."

Jake was shocked at the vehemence in his little sister's tone. *Huh.*

"They should not only thank you," she said, "but kiss your butt, every last one of them, and I intend to see that they do just that." She exchanged a meaningful glance with Charlie, one that he found highly suspicious. Then Lila rushed away, because Bridezilla was demanding that someone bring her the antique fan she'd be holding.

"Charlie," Jake said. "What in the hell is going on here?"

But Charlie galloped away, too. So Jake wandered over to his sister and the bride.

"Felicity," Lila said, trying to reason with the bride, "you'll be holding your bouquet while you walk down the aisle, so you don't want to have the fan until later."

Bridezilla pouted. "But the fan is a vital accessory for my dress, just like the mantilla!"

"Well, but the mantilla will be sitting on your head. The fan is something that you have to keep track of."

"Lila, I've already choreographed my steps with the fan . . . There's no rule that I have to hold my bouquet in both hands, is there?"

Lila pinched the bridge of her nose between her forefinger and thumb. "No rule. But you'll want to hold your groom's *hands* once you're up at the altar. Remember?"

"Of course I remember. But my maid of honor can take both the fan and the bouquet, can't she?"

"She'd need a third arm to be able to arrange your train, then . . ."

And so it went. Jake was truly amazed at his sister's reserves of tact and patience.

Finally, Felicity was organized to her satisfaction, though she didn't seem to notice there was no groom. Lila had to run around shouting Will's name until she found him shotgunning a flask in one of the old stalls with a loose chicken pecking at his polished oxfords.

At last, the wedding party was assembled. Lila waved over Rufus Jenkins; he'd swapped his electric guitar for a violin, but the amused grin he usually wore was the same as always. Then, Lila physically moved every bridesmaid and groomsman onto the painter's tape Xs she'd stuck on the barn floor. When she was done, the wedding party was perfectly aligned under an archway made up of silver and red glitter-dipped balloons. Jake could still smell the glue, which meant that this, too, had been a last-minute demand; in any case, it explained why the pastor's wife, Olivia, had an excessive amount of glitter on her face to go along with that weary expression.

After passing out bunches of wildflowers to use as stand-ins for the bridesmaid bouquets, Lila began to explain the details of the processional. Jake could appreciate what an organized professional his wild little sister had become, but it sure was an awful lot of detail for a walk across the barn floor.

He looked over at Charlie and smiled. She was staring at the wildflowers in her hand with a tight expression. He cleared his throat gently, and she looked up at him. Her body relaxed, and she smiled back. It got to him, feeling so in sync with Charlie. Like it used it be, where a look or a touch meant as much as—or more than—a word.

Okay, then. This is going to be fine. Even better, it'll all be over soon.

Lila finished her dissertation on the finer points of moving gracefully down an aisle and sent the wedding party to the back of the barn for a test run. Will sure wasn't saying much at the end of the line back there. Poor guy.

After a lot of giggling and jostling among bridesmaids and groomsmen, Rufus played the intro to the wedding march and everybody shut up and took an arm. One by one, the pairs stepped out until it was just Charlie looking up at Jake with wildflowers in her hands and a sheen of tears misting her eyes . . .

Oh God. Jake inhaled a shaky breath. The Old Barn. The wildflowers. And this beautiful, beloved girl. This should have been their wedding.

What was he doing, kissing her in his truck, acting like a second chance was really on the table? This wedding would start; this wedding would end. Charlie would say goodbye and go home to Dallas. And life in Silverlake would go on without her.

Charlie took a step forward and then looked back at him as Jake didn't move alongside her. He had a second to make up his mind: See this night through and make the best of the time he had before she went home. Or walk away like a coward.

You don't walk away from anything, Jake Braddock.

Jake gave Charlie a smile, escorted her down the aisle, and tried not to think too hard when her hand slipped away from his arm and he had to leave her to walk alone to the other side.

Chapter 18

CHARLIE DROVE WITH JAKE IN HIS DURANGO TO the restaurant after the rehearsal, which made it feel like an official date. Part of her wanted it to be one; the other part shouted loudly at her to *stop it already* with the romantic BS.

But it was difficult. Because the only thing better-looking than Jake Braddock in a flannel shirt and snug denim was Jake Braddock in a navy blazer and dress slacks, his blue button-down open at the collar to reveal his bronzed neck.

Jake, dressed like this, was simply . . . unfair. Charlie found herself fixating on his collarbones and wanting to lick them, which was completely and totally unacceptable. He was not an appetizer, and the only thing she should be using her tongue for was to speak out on his behalf, which she intended to do before everyone left town again. Her family did indeed owe Jake a big apology.

Bridezilla had chosen to have the rehearsal dinner at Jean-Paul's, the white-tablecloth restaurant in town that was in the Hotel Saint-Denis on the square, opposite Schweitz's Tavern. The hotel was a charming old brick building covered in ivy, and Jean-Paul's had a capacious ground floor that seated easily a hundred and fifty people. On the second floor, accessible by either a wide wooden staircase or a gorgeous mahogany-paneled turn-of-the-century elevator, was a more intimate room that Aunt Sadie had booked this evening for Will and Felicity.

They walked into the restaurant, and Charlie stopped dead in her tracks. Jake bumped into her from behind.

Felicity was draped full-length along the bar, like a nightclub singer on a piano, while the wedding photographer snapped pictures. She was a sight to behold, in that shimmery silver silk cocktail dress. She looked stunning, with her red lips and black hair, but it was a little—okay, a lot—too much for a gossipy town like Silverlake and a rehearsal dinner. Even if it was her own. Will and her luxuriously dressed parents were stepping in and out of the photos at Felicity's command. Poor Will looked dazed; he was a deer in his fiancée's headlights.

The few customers already here for happy hour had obligingly moved to one end of the bar to watch the show. It was hard not to.

Charlie raised an eyebrow at Jake, who blinked, then hid a smile behind his hand.

Jean-Paul had retreated to a corner with a couple of the waitstaff. Charlie saw him check his watch. It was the upstairs room that had been rented, not the entire restaurant, and he'd have lots of regular customers coming in on a Thursday night.

She waved; he waved back somewhat grimly. Charlie headed up the stairs with Jake, looking forward to a drink, but alas, that was not to be, at least not yet. They found Lila frantically pulling white gardenias out of the fifty or so antique glass bottles that marched down the center of the vast banquet table.

A waitress ran after her with a bucket, into which Lila was tossing the gardenias. And Aunt Sadie ran after both of them with a different bucket, full of red roses and greenery. She was replacing the gardenias with the red roses.

"Hi again, everyone," Charlie said. "You look . . . busy."

"Help!" called Lila. "Ouch. These suckers have thorns on them."

Aunt Sadie looked almost tearful. "Hi, darling girl. We're in a bit of a crisis."

"I can see that. But it's okay," Charlie told her. "The bride is occupied in front of a camera downstairs and putting on quite the show."

"Oh, good." Aunt Sadie set down her bucket and hugged Charlie. She still smelled like baby powder and looked exactly like a larger, plusher version of Grandma Babe. "Didn't have a chance to do that before. So . . . can you help?" She said not a word to Jake.

"Of course." Charlie set to work, with an apologetic glance at Jake. He strode over to the bar, not that there was anyone behind it. He looked as if he might serve himself.

Uncle Theo, who was also lurking there, had already taken advantage of it—possibly more than once. His ears had flushed bright pink from Scotch whiskey, as had his nose and bald scalp. With a flourish of his glass and a rattle of ice cubes, he bolted away as if Jake were infected with something.

Great.

Charlie could feel Jake's dark gaze on her as she worked with the others. "What happened?" she asked Lila.

"Maggie at Petal Pushers was overwhelmed at having to redo all the wedding flowers on such short notice, and there was a . . . what's the polite way to put this? A *dispute* over billing. So she tried to refund the money for the rehearsal dinner flowers, but Bridezil—um, Felicity—couldn't find anyone else to work with her on such short notice. Maggie compromised, agreeing to fulfill the original order, because the gardenias had already been delivered." Lila sighed. "But . . ."

Aunt Sadie was quivering with suppressed emotion. "But my future daughter-in-law threw an old-fashioned hissy fit the likes of which I've never seen!" she snapped.

"Oh my." Charlie set a soothing hand on Aunt Sadie's plump shoulder.

Lila nodded. "And so your mother," she told Charlie, "personally drove these roses here from a florist in Dallas."

"My *mother*? I didn't think Mom and Dad were coming until tomorrow!"

"They weren't," Aunt Sadie said acerbically. "But Maria took pity on me."

Speaking of Charlie's parents, at just that moment, the elevator rumbled and squealed before disgorging them, Maria pushing Dave in his wheelchair. "Hello, sweetheart!" said Mom.

Still tall and trim, she wore a brown velvet dress that set off her curly blond hair. A burnout-velvet scarf with an autumn leaf motif completed the outfit.

"Surprise!" Dad said. His short hair had gone more salt than pepper, and he wore a dark suit with a silk tie Charlie'd brought him back from Italy. His dress shoes were polished to a mirror shine, and she laughed when she saw that his socks were printed with tiny wine bottles.

"Hi!" Charlie moved forward to hug and kiss them. Then she glanced over at Jake, who had turned to stone in the corner. "I, um, have a date for the wedding. Don't know if you heard that one of Will's groomsmen got shipped overseas. You remember Jake Braddock, don't you?"

The smiles dropped from their faces, and they went silent. The entire room did.

Please, Charlie prayed, *do the right thing. Be polite.*

"Jake," Dad finally said, rolling forward in his wheelchair to greet him. "It's been a very long time."

Thank you, God.

Mom's mouth trembled; she seemed to be struggling for something to say. Mom had always had a soft spot for Jake. But of course she wouldn't have chosen him over her own son. And she, like the rest of them, had gone along with the recommendation of Brandon's psychologist.

Jake stood rooted to the ground like a six-three pillar of salt. "Yes, sir," he said at last. "It certainly has been a long time. Twelve years." His expression was terrifyingly impassive, his smile utterly professional. He took the hand that Dad extended and pumped it as briefly as possible before releasing it.

Charlie's heart broke for him all over again. She knew that inside that tough, rugged, manly exterior still lurked a devastated sixteen-year-old. Not that anyone would guess.

He raised his chin and let his hands hang loosely by his side; he cocked a hip. Mr. Casual. "Great to see you again," he said, just the faintest trace of irony in his tone.

Oh, Jake. Charlie fought the urge to run to his side. She walked instead. But she made things clear: She stood with him.

❦

Jake refused to even glance in Charlie's direction. If he'd felt awkward before, he now felt blindsided. Though to be fair, the arrival of her parents didn't seem to be Charlie's fault.

But here he was, stuck unexpectedly in a room at close

quarters with the family who had adopted him, then ostra-
cized him. Ripped his heart wide open, when all he'd ever
done was his best for them.

He found it hard to breathe. He fought the urge to run.
But he was no coward; he never had been. He would have
had to see them at the wedding anyway. Still would. But
he'd planned on doing his part in the ceremony and then
disappearing into the main house with Deck—or better yet,
just leaving.

He'd taken Dave Nash's hand with as much enthusiasm
as he'd take the hand of a salesman or a repairman. Dropped
it just as quickly. Gave him credit for manning up and rolling forward. As Dave should have, frankly. After all, Jake
had saved his life.

He appreciated that Charlie had crossed the battle lines
to stand with him.

But it was Maria's trembling lips that undid him. Jake
closed his eyes so he wouldn't have to see her emotion,
because it might elicit some in him. And he simply couldn't
afford that.

He kept his eyes closed as he heard her heels click forward; her hands settled on his shoulders, and she reached
up to kiss his cheek. She still smelled of vanilla and
grapefruit—some lotion she'd used for years.

Maria hesitated, probably because Jake didn't move a
fraction of any muscle in his body. But then she put her arms
around him and hugged him as if she'd never let him go.

No. No, no, no . . . This was the very last thing he'd
imagined. He'd much rather that she'd spit in his face or
punched him. Screamed curses at him. That, he'd inwardly
steeled himself for. But not this.

This was the worst thing imaginable.

He couldn't have hugged her back if he'd wanted to. His
body felt hewn from marble, and her hug was a chisel that

cracked him in half. Agony gripped him in some nameless place he didn't know existed. Pain that he hadn't felt since his own mother died. And his father.

"Stop," Jake said, and his voice betrayed him; it broke.

But she didn't. "Oh, honey," Maria murmured. "Oh, Jake." As if she understood. But how could she?

Damn her for being loving. And damn Dave, too, for being decent.

Where were your love and decency back then, when I needed them? Tell me that! The fury came out of nowhere, shocking him. Choking him.

Jake peeled Maria off, refusing to speak to her or even look at her. He sidestepped her and headed blindly for the stairs, but oblivious Felicity and her parents and the blasted photographer were blocking them, the bride posing like Scarlett O'Hara against the ornate railing.

"Jake!" Charlie ran after him but stopped in her tracks when he raised his hand, palm out, and shook his head. Something in his expression must have scared her.

He turned for the elevator, but it was on the fourth floor. He was trapped like an animal.

Jake veered for the men's room and careened inside. He punched the nearest wall, then punched it again, ignoring the explosions of pain in his knuckles. He had reared back to punch it a third time when the door opened awkwardly, banging against something, and he saw Dave Nash in his wheelchair. Dave opened his mouth.

"Get out," Jake said. "For the love of God, Dave. Leave me alone."

There was a long, awful silence.

Then Charlie's father nodded as if he, too, friggin' *understood*. He couldn't possibly.

Nobody understood—nobody. How alone and rootless and lost Jake had been. Nobody got how vulnerable Jake had been after the loss of his parents, after the center had dropped out of his world. How mad he'd been at his brother Deck for even trying to parent them—Deck, lame substitute father, the blind leading the blind.

Jake had been vulnerable to any crumb of affection from Brandon's parents or grandparents. So blindly stupid he'd been, to put any stock in their assurances that he was like another son to them . . .

Dave finally granted Jake's wish that he leave. He rolled himself backward, colliding with the door again, wrestling with it. In a different moment, in a different life, Jake would have held it for him. But he just couldn't in this one.

Oh hell. He could, and he would. Jake stepped forward and opened the men's room door.

He was still holding it open when he heard Uncle Theo, of the two double Scotches and the hot pink ears, say loudly, "I ask you: What kind of person saves a *dog* over a human being?"

Chapter 19

CHARLIE WASN'T EVEN AWARE THAT SHE'D RUSHED Uncle Theo like an offensive lineman. She ripped the drink out of his clutches and threw it in his idiotic face, dimly registering his outrage as ice cubes avalanched down his dress shirt and bounced onto the floor.

"How dare you!" he spluttered.

The room was a symphony in shock, people's mouths hanging almost comically open.

"How dare *you*?" Charlie fired back. "Have you ever saved even a burning slice of *toast*? Jake Braddock pulled my *father* out of the house first. Your brother-in-law." She turned to Aunt Sadie. "Maybe, just maybe, you could express some gratitude to him instead of holding a grudge against him. Grandma's death was awful, but it wasn't Jake's fault. She was a grown woman who made a conscious decision to go up the stairs to try to save our dog. She knew that it was a risk! And Jake was a sixteen-year-old, doing his best—better than any of us, by the way—who had a dog dropped down the stairs onto his head. So he dragged Mr. Coffee to the door before going back in for Grandma, figuring that he'd get her next. It wasn't a crime; it was a judgment call! And he had every expectation that she was coming down the stairs right after the dog."

The room was frozen.

"Jake was half-dead of smoke inhalation himself when he brought Grandma out. But nobody seems to get that. Or care. We owe Jake Braddock a huge thank-you, an even bigger apology for the way we've treated him, and drinks on us"—she paused and looked straight at still-spluttering, wet Uncle Theo—"for the rest of his life."

"Nice speech, but he's the one who started the fire!" Uncle Theo countered.

"No, he didn't," Charlie said. "There's no proof of that. It's a nasty little piece of fiction someone dreamed up that stuck. Maybe it was you!"

Aunt Sadie gasped and tottered backward to a chair, while Theo's face drained of color.

"Why, you little *bit*—"

"Careful, Theo." Dad's voice was low and hostile. "That's my daughter. And wheelchair or not, I can still kick your butt."

"We need," Charlie said, "to start asking some very tough questions here in this family. Especially of members who aren't here." She looked straight at Mom, who looked away, and then at Dad, who met her gaze steadily but sadly.

"Charlie's right." Dad rolled forward, into the center of the room. "Jake saved my life that night, and he tried like hell to save my mother's. We were selfish in our shock: All we thought about was our own healing, our own grief, our own closure. We allowed rumor, suspicion, and pure speculation to misguide us into some very bad decisions. And I, for one, am sorry about those bad decisions."

"I am, too," Mom said quietly.

Bridezilla chose this very moment to emerge from her staircase photo shoot, sweeping into the room with Will in her wake. "Why is there, like, ice all over the floor?" she shrilled. "Oh my God, the flowers still aren't done! What's going on? Why is everyone acting like somebody died? This is a party, people!"

Behind Felicity, Jake came out of the men's room, looking grim. He didn't make eye contact; he just took the stairs down, two at a time.

Charlie went after him.

❧

He was in the Durango and backing out of his parking spot when she ran outside after him, people in the lower level of the restaurant rubbernecking.

"Jake!" she called.

But he was out of the slot. He slammed the truck into drive, intending to speed forward.

Charlie stepped in front of it and put her hands flat on the hood. *"Stop."*

She felt the shudder of the vehicle as he slammed it back into park, then emerged, furious.

"What in the hell do you think you're doing? I could have killed you!" Jake gripped her by the shoulders.

"Defending your honor," she said calmly.

How could a man look so outraged and yet so tender at the same time?

That's when he kissed her, his mouth hard and possessive on her own. Then he pulled back and shoved her away, leaving her bereft and breathless and wanting much more.

"I don't need you to be my white knight, Charlie."

"Yeah, I think you do."

"I'm not some damsel in distress—"

"True. You'd make a really ugly damsel," she told him. "And with those pecs, you'd bust right out of a corset."

That surprised him into a bark of laughter.

"But I do think you're in distress, Jake."

His dark eyes held a world of pain. An ocean of anger and regret. "That's a melodramatic word. Seriously, I'm fine."

"Are you? I have my doubts. And I think it's about time that someone stood up for you."

"*Aargh.*" He scrubbed a hand down his face. "What you did in there—that was just . . . embarrassing."

"Why?" She was genuinely confused. "All I did was set the record straight with the idiots in my family."

"Yeah? Well, damn it, I love you for it, but you basically ripped off my balls and dropped them into your handbag. Now it's going to be even harder for me to face them."

"I don't understand: You'd rather that I let them trash-talk you?"

He shrugged. "Sticks and stones," he muttered.

"But words *do* hurt people. You, in this case. And I have a problem with that. So I countered with a Scotch in Theo's face," she said.

A corner of his mouth tugged up. "What a waste of good Scotch. Single malt, no less."

"You're *welcome*, Damsel Jake—"

"Don't you even *think* about calling me that," he growled, backing her against the hood of the still-running truck until she squeaked. Pinning her there between his muscular thighs. Which was both delicious and distracting, to say the least. Distraction was probably what Jake wanted, but Charlie wasn't about to let him change the subject. Not now.

"Hey!" She pushed at his chest, but it was like trying to move a tank. Breathless, she looked up at him. "I'm defending your honor—"

"I'm not feeling very honorable right now."

"And trying to comfort you in your distress—"

"There is *no* distress here."

"Right." She grabbed his right hand, and he winced. She turned it over, appalled at the sight of his bloody, split, swollen knuckles. *Oh, Jake . . .* But he wouldn't appreciate her clucking over them. "Roger that. No distress at all." She kissed his injuries and heard Jake's swift intake of breath.

"I'm extremely pissed off at you," he said. He looked down at her, those black Irish Braddock eyes making her knees weak. He pressed every available inch of himself against every available inch of her.

Oh my. "Yes," she said a bit weakly. "I can feel your, um, anger. Up against my—"

"Don't ever do anything like that again, Charlie. Understand?"

"Not really," she managed.

"I fight my own battles. I don't need anyone, especially a girl, to do it for me."

"That is *so* politically incorrect."

"I don't care. It's the way it is." His face was inches from hers, and he was taking up all of her oxygen.

"Not to mention ungrateful," she added.

"Ingratitude is one of my specialties," he whispered against her lips.

"Is it?"

"Yeah. Would you like to hear some others?"

She smiled. "I think I just might. By the way, the hood of this truck is hot."

"So are you, Charlie. So are you."

"Then why are you driving away?" she asked. "Why are you ditching me? Got another date?"

He shook his head slowly. "No other date."

"Then can you please take me—"

"Yes," Jake said, again covering her mouth with his and then kissing her senseless. "I can definitely take you."

Chapter 20

A CHEER WENT UP FROM THE DOWNSTAIRS BAR AS they walked back into the Hotel Saint-Denis. "Get a room!" someone shouted.

Charlie's face ignited. Well, what did she expect? After all, they'd been making quite a spectacle of themselves right outside the plate glass window.

"Working on it," said Jake.

And within minutes, they were alone in a beautiful French country–style room with a king-sized bed, and she was seeing Jake without a shirt on for the first time since they were teenagers. What had been cute once—fine—had filled out to magnificent.

He smiled as her mouth dropped open at the sight of his muscular chest, perfect six-pack abs, taut belly. And his arms. Dear Lord, those biceps. "C'mere," he said.

Her mouth had gone dry; her legs trembled. Really, a torso like his should be illegal. She was definitely going to lick his collarbones.

"Gonna make me come get you?"

"Huh?" She'd been staring at him like the village idiot. "Oh. Yes."

So he did. "I like your dress, Charlie," he said softly, "but I'll like it better on the floor." He stepped behind her, moved aside her hair, and kissed her neck. Then, with the rasp of her zipper, the dress puddled around her feet and she stood there in her high heels and not much else.

Feeling bare, feeling exposed. That's right—she should concentrate on what was wrong with her body, so that she didn't lose all control and climb him like some sex-starved orangutan. Gnaw on his triceps.

"So beautiful," he said.

"Who, me? Ha. I've gained eleven pounds—"

"Shh. I love every last one of them." He ran his big hands down her arms, then over her stomach, hips, thighs, and . . . *oh*.

Was this really happening? She vaguely recalled that there was a reason it probably shouldn't . . . but for the life of her, she couldn't think of it right at the moment.

Jake pulled her against him, snug to his chest, and she thought she might pass out from the pleasure of touching him, really touching him, after all these years. His chest felt so warm and decadent against her back. His fingers threaded through her hair, sending frissons of pleasure radiating from her scalp to her whole body. Jake's lips brushed her neck. Every nerve ending she possessed awoke with joy.

Then he pushed her onto the bed, and undressed her completely.

They were no longer teenagers. Charlie was no longer worried that her dad would come rolling down the hallway to discover them, or that her mom would pop nosily out into the garden, armed with her knitting needles. Granddad wasn't there to clean his gun.

They were no longer teenagers, but she felt as if they were, because it was new, even after all these years. Because the waiting and the heartache and the separation amplified the experience. And because he was Jake Braddock, her first love.

Afterward, she fell asleep in his arms, wishing she could stay there forever. It wasn't until she woke at 5 A.M. that cold, hard reality hit. The town council meeting was at ten. The meeting during which she had promised her grandfather she would stand in his stead and threaten Jake's livelihood—because she'd never asked someone else to do it. The meeting that she'd somehow never said one word about to Jake.

Oh, dear God. Charlie sat bolt upright, clutching the sheet to her overabundant chest. *And what are you going to do about it now, huh? Write him a sweet little note? Sure. That'll do the trick. No hard feelings.*

She looked down at Jake, his face unguarded and relaxed in sleep. Dark stubble had made an appearance overnight, making him look wonderfully dangerous and disreputable. Even his thick dark eyelashes were sexy. Something very much like a smile curved his lips.

She bit down on her own foolish smile, which had come unbidden. *What were you thinking, Charlie? How could you have let this happen?*

She cast about for ways to get out of this situation. She could just not go. Pretend to be ill. But she pictured Granddad's reaction—if he got furious, would he have another heart attack? A stroke? God forbid. And she'd promised him that she'd attend the meeting. Make his case. A promise was a promise.

She could wake Jake up right now and try to explain to him. Apologize in advance. But she knew that wouldn't come close to solving anything. And he was sleeping so peacefully.

Charlie slipped out of bed and slowly got dressed. What to do? She was undecided until the very moment she opened the door.

Coward.

She couldn't just sneak out and then blindside him at the meeting. That was simply unforgivable.

She shut the door again. She leaned her forehead against it. Then she turned and walked to the bed, feeling as if she were headed for the guillotine. She sat down next to him.

"Hey," he said, opening his eyes. He yawned, pushed a hand through his unruly dark mop of hair, and smiled at her. It broke her heart. "Want to order blueberry pancakes? Lots of butter and syrup? A split of champagne with fresh orange juice for mimosas?"

"Jake, I have to tell you something," she said.

"Well, don't look so damn serious about it. And why do you have clothes on?" He grinned and reached for her. "Let me fix that."

She shot off the bed and backed away. "Jake."

The smile disappeared from his face. "What?"

"I, uh, wanted to tell you this before now."

"Okaaay. Out with it, then. You're secretly married? You're having an alien's baby? You're—"

"I'm going to be at the town council meeting this morning," she blurted. "Instead of my grandfather."

He stared at her.

"Presenting for him. His case against funding the fire department. I intended to find someone to go in my place, but with everything going on . . ."

Jake's face went completely blank.

"Because obviously, he can't, being still in the hospital. I . . . just wanted you to know."

"You wanted me to know," he repeated, swinging his legs out of bed.

"Yes."

"You sure as hell didn't seem to want me to know *last night*," he bit out.

"Jake, last night wasn't planned—by either of us."

"No, it wasn't. But *this*, this has been planned now for how long?" His voice was quiet, his tone deadly.

When had Granddad first asked her again? Charlie tried to remember. "He asked me a few days ago. I said—"

"A few days ago."

"I said no. I was very clear. But then he brought it up again, and when I said no again, he got so upset that he literally had a medical episode."

"And you never thought to mention it to me?"

"It just happened—and there hasn't been the right opportunity!"

"You mean you didn't have the nerve to tell me."

Charlie looked away. "No."

"But now, just hours before I have to defend my right to make a living, now is the perfect time for this information. Beautiful, Charlie. Really. And after last night."

"Jake, I don't want to do this."

"Then why are you doing it?"

"I tried to say no, and Granddad freaked out—"

"So what? You're an adult. Not a child. Why do you keep letting your parents and your grandfather make your decisions for you?"

"That's not fair!"

"It's absolutely fair." Jake got up and hunted down his pants. "You made a choice twelve years ago—you chose them over me. And now you're doing it again." He stuffed one leg into the trousers.

"Excuse me? Who did I choose to stand with yesterday evening when I threw the drink in Uncle Theo's face? I stuck up for you! I told them we all owe you an apology . . ."

"Yeah, and where is that girl today? Who the hell are you? How can you defend me one day and attack me the next?"

"I'm not going to attack you. I'm going to stand there as his proxy and deliver his report."

"You could have said no!"

"I tried. You don't understand—Granddad literally started having a heart attack when I refused him!"

"How convenient." Jake stuffed his other leg into the pants and yanked them up.

"It was terrifying, not convenient!" Charlie shouted. "I had to get the nurses, the doctor. It was *real*."

"And what *we* have isn't real. That's crystal clear to me as of right now." Jake grabbed his shirt.

"Jake. Please. That's not true."

"Why are you even telling me this?"

"Because I needed to be honest about it."

"Honest." Jake let out a short, unamused bark of laughter. "Are you really using that word? You, Charlie, have to be the most two-faced person I've ever met!"

"Again, that's not fair. I could have taken the easy way out and left this morning—"

"Congratulations on your nobility. I have nothing else to say to you." Jake had buttoned his shirt and was now stuffing it into his waistband.

"Jake. Listen to me. Granddad has been lobbying against the fire department for the last decade, and nothing has ever come of it. Nothing will come of it this morning, either."

Jake shoved his feet into his dress loafers, grabbed his jacket, and shoved his socks into one of the pockets. He palmed his keys, strode to the door, and flung it open. "Tell yourself whatever you need to, Charlie. We're one hundred percent done—so knock yourself out, babe."

And then he was gone.

Chapter 21

WHAT CHARLIE HAD TO DO THIS MORNING WOULD have been hard enough if she weren't already emotionally devastated.

Silverlake's city hall was a gray building with two fluted, flat columns on either side of the door that were echoed in the window trim. The architecture managed to look both pleasant and faceless. Charlie wished that she were faceless, too, as she forced herself up the stone steps, hanging on for dear life to the metal railing in the center of them. She did not want to be here. She did not want to do this. And yet here she was. *Thanks, Granddad.*

She prayed that once Jake cooled down, he would understand. She was just going to spew some figures and research. Nobody had listened to Kingston Nash in more than a decade; nobody would take Charlie seriously today. Her stomach roiled, sliding greasily from side to side, and her head pounded. Her legs trembled with each step she took, and her feet felt as if they belonged to someone else. She clutched her tote bag to her shoulder, her hand sweaty on the strap. In it were the reports Granddad had compiled about other small-town fire departments staffed by volunteers.

She opened her bag for inspection and passed through a wide hallway flanked by offices with people busily working in them. She lifted a hand to wave at Teresa d'Alba, who was the mayor's assistant. Teresa waved back cheerfully. "Go on in, hon. They're about to start the meeting."

Charlie's knees knocked together. "Okay, thanks." She walked to the double doors of the large room where town meetings were held. A long table stretched across the front of the room. Seated at it were the six council members, the seventh being Mayor Marisol Fisk in the center.

Charlie aimed a tight smile at everyone and hunted for a seat in the back of the half-filled room. She found one and sat down. *Don't want to be here, don't want to be here, don't want to be here . . . Stop it. You* are *here.*

She felt like a traitor. A jerk.

You're not a traitor. You're a proxy. A stand-in. Here to deliver a speech that you did not write.

Tell yourself whatever you need to, traitor.

The mayor called the meeting to order, and the council took care of some minor business having to do with parking permits and raising the fee at the city dump.

Charlie allowed herself to relax; she told herself that she'd be able to present Granddad's reports to an audience of almost nobody. Then the door opened, and Jake walked in with Mick, Tommy, Hunter, and Grady, who wore red fire department polo shirts identical to his. They were clean-shaven and brawny, and radiated good humor and competence. Not to mention that they were all hot enough to be in a pinup calendar: *Men of Silverlake Fire and Rescue.* She swallowed the bile that rose in her throat at the hostile expression on Jake's face when he registered her presence.

* * *

Jake tried to get his head around it: Charlie Nash was about
to screw him over yet again. Which was not only unbelievable but unforgivable, considering how she'd spent last
night, in his arms. And never once had she mentioned until
this morning that she'd be here. Gunning for his job and the
jobs of his friends.

How could she?

Jake sat there still half-stupefied as Mayor Fisk called
the next item on the agenda: the review of Silverlake Fire
and Rescue's budget.

Charlie remained frozen in place for a moment, and then
she got up slowly with a notebook and headed for the podium. Her blond hair was up in a twist, her face was pale,
and she wore a navy skirt with a plain white blouse. She
looked like a lawyer, not a lover.

Mick nudged him. "Didn't you just, uh . . . ?"

Hunter raised an eyebrow.

Jake said nothing.

Tommy leaned forward, too. "Wasn't she your *date* last
night, dude?"

"Jayzus," muttered Grady.

The expression on Jake's face must have alarmed all of
them, because they fell silent.

Blood began to pound a steady rhythm in his head as
Charlie adjusted the microphone to her height and opened
her notebook. She glanced out vaguely at the audience—
anywhere but at him—and cleared her throat.

"I'm Charlotte, uh, Charlie, uh, Nash. Most of you know
my grandfather, Kingston Nash, a longtime resident of Silverlake. He can't be here today, since he's had surgery and
is busy terrorizing the Mercy Hospital staff . . ."

This elicited a few chuckles.

"So he asked me to come in his place." She paused and looked down, compressing her lips. Then she looked up again, searching the crowd for Jake's face. Her next words were clearly addressed to him.

"I'd like everyone here to know that these statistics and opinions are my grandfather's, and not my own. I don't agree with him. Again, I am only here at his request, as his, uh, his proxy."

Jake eviscerated her with a glance. *Make any joke, any excuse you want, sweetheart. There isn't one that will get you off the hook with me. It doesn't exist.*

She averted her gaze. Then she began to speak again, her voice shaking. "It's no secret that a full twenty-four percent of the Silverlake municipal budget is spent on our firefighters. Yes, *twenty-four percent.* While we are, of course, very grateful to the brave men and women who protect our town, this percentage is simply not—" She looked hesitantly at Jake again.

He gave her his best dead-eyed stare.

"Not sustainable from an economic standpoint, and leaves less—if not *no*—money for equally important things like teachers, nurses, police, hospitals and health clinics, administration, parks, libraries, community events, and historic preservation."

Murmurs arose in the audience.

Charlie continued. "I think you will all agree that teaching the next generation, healing the sick among us, protecting those who can't protect themselves—none of these things can be neglected or ignored." She paused, unscrewing the cap from a bottle of water and holding it up with a shaking hand to her lips.

There were more murmurs, some fidgeting, some shaking of heads.

"This doesn't have to be an either-or situation!" Mick said.

"Please refrain from comment, Mr. Halladay," said Mayor Fisk. "Miss Nash has the floor. You will have a chance to respond."

"The huge costs of our fire department," Charlie continued, "are in large part due to the firefighters' union, which makes negotiating lower numbers difficult, if not impossible. The cost and maintenance of firefighting equipment alone is astronomical. When you add to that the cost of the salaries we pay to our firefighters; the maintenance, mortgage, and taxes on the firehouse; the taxes on the land . . ."

Jake watched Charlie's lips move, his sense of betrayal rising, almost choking him. He tuned out the actual words—after all, he'd heard many of them before, out of the mouth of Kingston Nash.

"Most towns the size of Silverlake have all-volunteer firefighting departments, and there is good reason for that. The reasoning gets even better when we look at some statistics. Because of the use of higher-quality flame-resistant building materials and much stiffer safety regulations and inspections, the number of fires in the last decade has actually fallen by over forty-one percent. But the number of firefighters in the region has increased by thirty-seven percent . . ."

She was good. Jake had to hand her that. She presented the facts baldly, professionally, in a detached, almost apologetic way.

"And their salaries have increased by over nine percent. The cost of their benefits has also risen, and the town has to pay for all of this somehow. The firefighters' union routinely ignores the ability of small towns like ours to come up with the money . . ."

Charlie had settled into a dry monotone, which was a far cry from her grandfather's usual theatrics. Unfortunately, it was far more effective, since the old man's drama revealed his bias. And everyone who saw him at the podium both pitied him and wrote him off because of the past.

Charlie was hard to write off. She continued to list damning sets of numbers that made the fire department seem overfunded and even superfluous.

"I will leave you," she said finally, "with the disturbing example of what happened in a neighboring county: the municipality that resisted the demands of the firefighters' union and took the matter to arbitration, as required by law. Not only did they not win, but the firefighters were awarded a retroactive ten percent raise, and the city had to pay their legal fees—which ended up bankrupting it. Do we want that to happen here in Silverlake?"

Jake's sense of betrayal mounted again. Last night he'd been *kissing* the lips that were spewing this poison.

"Can we afford to have that happen here?" Charlie read aloud from her grandfather's report. "My grandfather doesn't think we can. We must act swiftly and decisively, once and for all, to create an all-volunteer firefighting force that is staffed by people who put our community first, and not their own—"

She stopped, her color rising.

"Miss Nash?" prompted Mayor Fisk.

"Not their own personal agendas, salaries, and pensions," she whispered, head bowed.

Jake erupted out of his seat and stalked to the doors. Mick followed him, setting a hand on his shoulder as he threw open the right door and stormed into the hallway. "Bro, you gotta—"

"You have to give the rebuttal, Mick. I'm too angry. And I never want to see that woman again."

"Wha—but—I'm not much for public speaking. You know that!"

True.

Jake stood in the hallway clenching and unclenching his fists like a bad cartoon character, almost levitating by fury alone. He fought for control over his temper. Storming out of the council meeting wouldn't do the firehouse any good—in fact, quite possibly the opposite. He had to go back in. He had to make their case and rebut Charlie's. The survival of the firehouse was at stake: their home and their livelihoods.

Jake didn't run from a fire, and he didn't run from a fight. No matter how angry he was, he wasn't going to run from this one—even if Charlie had betrayed him.

The Nash family, once his haven, had become his curse.

Jake took several deep breaths and told himself to focus as Mick stood there anxiously. He was a great guy, but meatballs were his strength, not public speaking. This was on Jake. So he pulled open the door and went back in.

Charlie had gathered her notes and made her way back to her chair. Her face was pale and drawn. She tried to catch his eye; she mouthed the words *I'm sorry*, but he refused to acknowledge her in any way. Charlie Nash was officially dead to him. He would cut her out of his life as cleanly as her family had once cut him out of theirs.

Mayor Fisk nodded at him. "Mr. Braddock, would you like to respond on behalf of Silverlake's fire department?"

"Yes, I would," Jake said as he walked to the podium and looked out at the audience. "And it's Silverlake Fire and Rescue, by the way."

"Duly noted. Please proceed, Mr. Braddock."

"Miss Nash has just spouted a lot of numbers at you all," Jake began. "And she is free to do that. But I'm not going to talk to you about numbers. I'm going to talk to you about our community and what we do, which is much more than rescue cats from trees or knock hornets' nests off garages. There's a common misperception that we're paid only to sleep and watch TV when we're on shift. Nothing could be further from the truth. We maintain our equipment, first of all—and there's a lot of it. We teach fire safety in the schools, we study the schematics of public buildings so that we're familiar with how to save lives should a fire or other disaster occur in them. We check hydrants, hoses, and sprinkler systems all over the town. We do auto-extrication training, swift-water rescue training, and high-rope rescue training. We maintain our EMS certifications and help in all kinds of emergencies . . ."

Jake looked out at the faces in the audience. Most were attentive and sympathetic. He had their attention. His words were effective. He relaxed a little. Made sure the edge was gone from his voice. Anger would only alienate folks and make him look unapproachable and arrogant. He needed to be one with the people, or better yet, their hero.

"When Mr. Sanchez got T-boned at the intersection of Ninth and Main, it was me and Mick here"—he pointed to his buddy—"who pried him out of his '98 Oldsmobile with the Jaws of Life. When the floodwaters swept away Mrs. McGowan's Honda with her and her grandchildren inside, it was us who went after them and got them out. And when, in his infinite sixteen-year-old wisdom, Teddy Flint climbed the old water tower on a dare and punctured his thigh on a rusty bolt, it was Grady and Tommy who went up after him, got him down, and took him to the hospital."

Jake paused. "These are the kinds of things we do for the community without question, no matter what time of day or night. We also do a lot of other things, taking time away from our families, just so that people around here won't wonder if we're really earning our pay. Christmas lights? Check. Volunteer work at the hospital? Check. Volunteering at the animal shelter? Check."

His audience was quiet but approving. "Now, you've just

listened to a bunch of statistics researched by Kingston Nash, a man who's clearly biased against Silverlake Fire and Rescue because of a tragedy in his past. A terrible tragedy, it's true—but one that happened over a decade ago, one we've all got to get beyond.

"I'm very, very sorry for his loss. But funding or defunding Silverlake Fire and Rescue should be about more than a personal grudge. It's about your security, about life and death to you, your friends, and your neighbors. Let me ask you a question, folks. Would you ever dream of asking people in this town to be happy with a volunteer-only *police* force? I'll leave you to think about that. Thank you for your time and consideration today." Jake stepped back from the podium, confident that he'd defended himself and the boys quite adequately.

"Hold up there, Jake," called old Billy Hodgkins from the back row. He'd played pool with Kingston Nash on Thursday nights for as long as anyone could remember. "When exactly *was* the last fire in Silverlake? I mean, one of any significance?"

"Well," Jake said, rubbing the back of his neck. "I'm not sure what you mean by 'significance' . . . "

"'Scuse my five-dollar word," Willy said dryly. "I guess I mean *big-ass*. As in, requires seven guys and a large red truck to put it out. When was the last one? Answer me that, will you?"

Jake searched his brain. "Just because there hasn't been one doesn't mean—"

"'Cause it seems to me that the last big-ass fire requiring you guys was the one at the Nash mansion, twelve years ago. And there are a lot of questions about that fire still."

Jake felt the blood drain from his face. Then a hard pulse kicked up in the left side of his neck, powered by anger.

Would the suspicion and speculation ever end? Could no one cut him a break, give him the benefit of the doubt, after all of his years of service here in Silverlake? He opened his mouth to respond, but Willy pressed his advantage before he could.

"Twelve years. For *twelve years*, we've been paying hundreds of thousands of dollars in salaries and bennies to keep you and your boys in style at that downtown firehouse. So you've done a rescue or two, removed a hornets' nest from an old lady's garage, and you keep your red truck all clean and shiny. Like *she* says"—Willy jerked a thumb at Charlie—"the numbers don't add up. Sorry. Nothing against you guys personally. But where do we draw the line?"

"Our jobs are just as much about fire *prevention*, Willy," Jake ground out. "So if you look at our track record that way, it's phenomenal."

Willy guffawed. "You takin' credit for stuff that *hasn't* burned down now?" The old man stood up, his bushy-bearded chin jutting forward, his hands on his hips. "Folks, am I the only one in here who smells the BS?"

Too late, Jake saw the trap he'd laid for himself, all in the name of defending the firehouse. How in the hell could he recover now? He searched for a way, but the blood pounding in his ears and the fresh wave of anger at Willy's dig, on top of Charlie's betrayal, made it impossible to think.

He saw red for a hazy moment, then white—Charlie's miserable white face looking right back at him. He hadn't even realized he was staring at her, trying to burn a hole through her with his gaze. He averted it now.

The council meeting disintegrated around him, and still he couldn't think. Couldn't find a way to sway the audience. Mayor Fisk finally pounded her gavel to call the meeting back to order, but the damage was done.

Jake walked on leaden legs back to his seat, where Mick,

Hunter, Grady, and Tommy said not a word. They all sat in tense silence as Mayor Fisk called for a vote.

Their silence turned to disbelief as the vote went against them by three. Once the new year arrived, they'd all be officially unemployed.

Chapter 22

FROM THE BACK OF THE ROOM CAME A FEMININE noise of distress, somewhere between a cough and a wail. Jake knew instinctively that it was Charlie but didn't turn to investigate.

He got up on legs that didn't feel like his own, that seemed to walk of their own accord to the double doors. He just followed Mick and the other firemen, feeling numb. The blood rushing through his head, the pulsating anger, the viciousness of Charlie's unexpected betrayal—all of it had vanished and been replaced by this yawning pit of nothing. He wasn't sure he'd ever feel anything again. He was conscious of breathing, conscious of having a heartbeat, but he didn't feel human.

He didn't register or remember anything about the drive back to the firehouse. All he could think about, as he turned into the familiar circular driveway, was that this would no longer be his home—the house he had lived in for more than a decade. The guys—Old George, Mick, Grady, Tommy,

Hunter, and Rafael—would no longer be his brothers. They'd no longer share a purpose in the community, or even have a role here. What in the hell were they all going to do?

Despite the presence of Mick and the other guys next to him as they entered the firehouse, Jake hadn't felt this lost and alone since he'd been kicked out by Dave and Maria Nash twelve years ago.

Not-Spot came bounding over to greet them, his entire body wagging in enthusiasm, his tongue spilling out the side of his mouth like extra glee. *You're home! You're home!* Except this was no longer home. The dog's excitement seemed almost obscene, given the circumstances. Jake had let them all down. Why would anyone or anything be glad to see him?

Jake sank to his knees, ostensibly to hug Not-Spot, to pat him and scratch him behind the ears, but in reality it was because he didn't feel that his legs would hold him up any longer. The dog licked his face and wriggled with joy, tail whipping anything within reach.

Jake leaned his forehead briefly against the dog's neck and breathed in the comforting scent of his fur: canine love mixed with earth and leaves. But Not-Spot squirmed free to get to Mick, Tommy, Hunter, and Grady, just as excited to see them. Jake wasn't special, and now that he wouldn't have a job or a title or a paycheck, he'd better get used to that.

He stayed down on his knees as the other guys gave the dog his due affection. It seemed a monumental, if not impossible, effort to get up. Stand tall. Like a man. But without a job, without a home, without a purpose in life, he didn't feel that he qualified as a man.

"Hey." Mick's tone was gruff.

Jake looked up to find him holding out a hand. He wanted to take it but found that he couldn't. "I . . . let you down. I let all of us down today."

"No. You didn't," Mick said. "Now get the hell up off the floor. I've got something to say, but I'm only gonna say it once, which means we've all gotta be in the same room. So let's go upstairs."

Jake nodded, but he still couldn't take Mick's hand. So Mick grabbed his instead. He damn near dragged Jake up the stairs.

Rafael and Old George sat at the kitchen table, looking sweaty and beat-up. "Man, you wouldn't believe—"

"We probably would," Mick said. "Listen, there's no easy way to say this: We lost the vote today. The town council decided that as of the new year, Silverlake has an all-volunteer fire department. No salary. No benefits. Kingston Nash—courtesy of his granddaughter—has finally won. We're . . . done."

Old George gaped. *"What?"*

"You're kidding me," Rafael said.

Jake stared wordlessly at them.

"No joke, gentlemen," Grady said. "Sorry to say. Jake here put up the good fight. But the numbers are a problem, and we know that and we've known it for years. Charlie Nash, reading from her granddad's script, made it sound like we're money hogs. We're the death of police and school-teachers and Santa Claus and the Easter Bunny, too."

Old George finally closed his mouth. "But . . . what the hell are we going to do?"

"That's a damn good question. If we want to stay in this burg, we'll need to find other jobs. We've all got EMS training. We're practically professional PR guys, with all the work we do for the community . . ."

"But what'll happen with the firehouse?"

"Beats the hell outta me."

"Maybe the town will put it up for sale. Maybe we can go in together and buy it."

"Yeah, sure," Hunter said bitterly. "That's gonna happen. Since we're all rolling in cash."

Jake sat down heavily on one of the kitchen barstools. "Guys . . . I'm so sorry. I let you down today. I don't know what else to say."

"You didn't do any such thing, man." Mick turned to Grady. "Did you see him let us down? No. Kingston Nash just finally got his way. Maybe he bribed half the council. Hell if I know."

"It's not fair to insinuate that the council is crooked," Jake said wearily. "Though Billy Hodgkins isn't exactly unbiased, since Kingston regularly pays his bar tab. Wish I'd thought to point that out, but it's too late now."

They all stared at one another.

Jake dragged a hand down his face. "Mick, you got something to say?" Maybe he could get them all united and on the same page.

"Yeah, I do. This sucks, and I say we demand a revote, based on . . . on, I dunno. Something."

As rousing speeches went, it left something to be desired. "I don't think it works that way," Jake told him.

"Yeah, well, it should."

Silence ensued.

Once again, it was up to Jake to lead them onward. To think of something. To bring them all together. If only he weren't so tired. So demoralized. So heartsick.

Get up. Give them a speech. He didn't know where the voice came from, or whose it was, but it was insistent. *Go on. They're looking to you for answers.*

Leave me alone, he told the voice. *I don't have any answers.*

Yes, you do. Now get up and open your mouth and they will come.

Jake got up. He was probably crazy. But these guys were

looking to him for leadership. He sucked in some air. "George. Mick. Grady. Hunter. Tommy. Rafael. We may have just technically gotten fired by the town, or downgraded to pay point zero or whatever. But we are still a team. We still have a job to do, and that job is to protect Silverlake in the event of disaster. To save lives and property from destruction. Whether or not we get a salary for it is immaterial. It's who we are; it's what we do. Paid or not, we are Silverlake Fire and Rescue. Are you with me?"

Only two of the guys, Mick and Old George, nodded reluctantly. The others looked shell-shocked at the concept of working for no salary. He couldn't totally blame them. But he forged onward.

"This community may seem a little ungrateful right now, but we can't take that to heart. We have to look at the town budget as just numbers, plain and simple. Numbers are not politics, and numbers are not weapons. Most of all, numbers are not the enemy. Neither is the town council. It's composed of people, people who are just trying to make the columns add up correctly.

"If they can't make the numbers work, then we cannot hold that against them. But *we*, as firefighters, *can* work.

"We can work in the face of the naysayers and the disrespecters and the haters. We can work as *volunteer* firefighters, because we love our town; we love this community, and we want to keep our citizens safe. So I ask you again: Are you with me?"

All of the guys nodded this time. "Yeah."

"A paycheck certainly makes things easier, but it doesn't change our core identities or values. Neither will getting other jobs during the day. We are all more than friends; we are brothers. And you guys are my heroes. I couldn't get up in the morning or go to sleep at night without knowing that I can rely on you to have my back and to save my ass—"

"Hear! Hear!" yelled Tommy.

Jake broke off; the atmosphere was thick with emotion. Of course, being guys, they had to dispel it.

"Dang," said Mick with a smirk. "This is all so touching that I'm gonna have to cry."

"Shoot, I'm gonna write a poem," Old George said in a soulful tone.

Hunter clutched his hand to his heart, a big grin on his face.

"Sing, boy, sing!" Tommy said, inciting the dog. Not-Spot thrust his snout into the air and howled.

Jake broke into laughter and flipped all of them off, including the dog, who grinned right along with the rest of them.

Grady flipped him off back. "That's better."

Mick shifted his weight and then adjusted himself. "Phew, you were in danger of getting sentimental there, dude."

"Anything but that. So anyway, guys—"

But Jake's last words were cut off by the earsplitting fire alarm, and they all sprang into action. It was what they did; it was who they were—paycheck or not.

Chapter 23

CHARLIE LEFT CITY HALL, MOVING LIKE A ROBOT, AND went straight to Lila's office. "Hi," she said, standing in the doorway. "I'm sorry to bother you at work, but . . ."

Lila looked up from her computer and homed in on Charlie's face. "What's wrong?"

"Everything." Charlie slumped into one of the chairs opposite Lila's desk and hugged her handbag to her chest.

"That's a pretty sweeping statement—"

"I mean it." And Charlie told her what had happened.

Lila stared at Charlie, aghast. "You did *what*?"

"I know . . . but Granddad was literally having a heart attack over it. He had one at the hospital when I refused. So to calm him down, I promised him that I would speak his words for him at the meeting."

"Poor Jake," Lila said.

"I didn't know how to tell Jake. I tried, at one point, but the timing didn't work. And then last night . . ."

Lila held up a hand, her face a classic portrait of disgust.

"No more information on boinking my brother. That's gross. I get it—you two have been aflame with lust for each other for years, but . . . gross. So, you told him this morning. Jeez. I think I would have snuck out without a word. You're braver than I am."

"I wanted to sneak out, trust me. He was asleep. I could have. I started to. And I almost called you for a ride."

Lila eyeballed her until she squirmed. "But?"

"I felt that I couldn't put you in that position. Jake would never speak to you again."

"Thank you. No, he probably wouldn't. I'm not sure I should let you even sit across from me, telling me all of this, Charlie. What a mess!" Lila seemed caught between sympathy and horror. "He's only just begun to forgive me for not cutting things off with you in the *past*. Now this?"

"I'm sorry." Charlie fidgeted with the straps of her bag. "I didn't know who else to talk to."

"Lucky me. It would be so much easier if you were shallow and had just used him for sex. Why can't you be shallow?"

"Huh? Uh . . ."

"But you're not. You just have to be a decent person, don't you?" Lila shook her head. "That pisses me off, because you've really gone and done it now. I hate to tell you this, but you're in love with my stinky brother."

Charlie stared at her, mute. And finally nodded. "I'm in love with your stinky brother. It sucks, but I pretty much always have been."

"And I don't see a way to happily-ever-after on this, Charlie, since you just torpedoed his job!"

"I never thought the vote would actually go against them," Charlie wailed.

"Idiot," Lila said. "As your friend, I mean that in the nicest possible way, you understand. But this is bad. I'm kicking you out of my office now, okay? I need to think."

Charlie nodded and stood up. "Okay." She had just pulled open the door to Lila's office when they both heard it: the bellowing and honking of the fire truck as it rushed by, all lights flashing, Jake at the wheel.

Something besides Charlie's life was on fire. But what?

Lila's cell phone rang. She registered surprise at the caller ID and then picked up. "Hey, Deck. What's going on?" As she listened, her face drained of all color. "Oh, dear God. Promise me you won't go anywhere near it. Promise me. Jake and the guys just passed by. I'm on my way." She grabbed her purse and sprinted around her desk toward Charlie and the door.

"What is it?" Charlie asked.

"The Old Barn is on fire! Bridezilla took lanterns out there, because we told her no candles. I'm going to kill her with my bare hands . . ."

Chapter 24

J*AKE.* T*HE* O*LD* B*ARN WAS BURNING, AND* J*AKE WAS*
heading right into it. Charlie's heart beat a staccato
rhythm, and she could take only shallow sips of breath as
she raced after Lila, who was heading to the alley behind
the office where she parked her big silver Suburban.

Scenes from the fire at her grandparents' house flashed
in and out of Charlie's mind. The nightmarish black smoke
silhouetted against the malevolent yellow flames behind the
bay window. The horrible popping and groaning, then the
obscene crash when the roof over the family room collapsed. The screams of the onlookers. Jake, crawling out
with Grandma Babe on his back.

She shook off the images. This situation had nothing to
do with the past.

Lila's white face had taken on a green tint, and tears ran
down her cheeks. She dug into her purse for her keys and
stumbled. Charlie caught her arm and steadied her. "You
all right?"

"No," Lila said baldly.

There was no debate over whether Charlie should come. They'd been friends too long for them not to face this emergency together, no matter who would get mad about alliances.

"Everything's going to be okay," Charlie told Lila, fervently hoping that this was true. "It's going to be fine."

"Yes." Lila's normally steady, competent hands shook as she hit the fob to unlock the door and then, after scrambling in, tried to get her key into the ignition.

"Let me drive," said Charlie.

Uncharacteristically, Lila nodded and moved over as Charlie rounded the rear of the truck and then climbed in. "Declan—please, God, don't let him try to go in there."

Charlie pulled the truck out and hit the road. "Deck isn't stupid, and he knows that Jake and the boys are on the way, remember? He's not going to go in."

Lila nodded. "He must be losing his mind. He worked so hard to remodel and renovate it . . . If we lose the Old Barn because of my client . . . Oh God—I can't believe this is happening. What was Felicity thinking? How did she even get inside?"

Grimly, Charlie shook her head. "Who knows?" She took a left, speeding past Piece A Cake, where Kristina's cousin was visible through the window, waiting on café customers. Amelie's shop flew by in a blur, then the insurance agency, the hardware store, and Petal Pushers.

The Suburban was a luxury vehicle compared to old rickety Progress, and it was a lot faster, too. Within moments, Charlie was gunning it down the highway, and soon they turned into the gates of the Braddock ranch and down the formal paved drive in the front. She braked hard when Grouchy appeared, agitated, and ran right in front of the Suburban.

She rolled down the window. "Hi, buddy. Hi! Go back to the house."

Grouchy wasn't having that. He ignored her, even when Lila repeated the order.

"Go play with Cat," Lila suggested.

He barked, as if to say this was no time to play.

Charlie and Lila finally gave up, and the dog followed them for a ways, eventually peeling off after he apparently felt he'd given them enough of an escort. He sniffed the air and ran back toward the house, barking.

Charlie smelled the smoke long before they saw it. She wrestled the Suburban into the left turn down the gravel road that led to the east bend of the property. She then veered to the right, down another gravel road, and the Old Barn came into view. The entire back wall was in flames, the rising smoke weirdly backlit by the afternoon sun. Big Red stood by, hoses unspooled and snaking around the building.

"Oh God," Lila moaned. "I can't look."

"Don't." Charlie drove them closer. They could hear the shouts of the men and the terrifying roar of the blaze. A massive figure in full uniform—it had to be Grady—came running toward them, shouting something.

Charlie lowered the window.

"Get back!" he yelled. "Get out of here. We got this under control."

"Everyone's okay?" Charlie's voice came out in a weird rasp.

"Everyone." He nodded, though his expression clearly conveyed his disdain for her. Charlie tried not to let it bother her, but it did.

"I'm sorry," he said, "but we can't have you here. Go back to the main house. Deck took Felicity up. They're safe."

Lila leaned over to talk to him. "Is the Old Barn—?" She seemed unable to go on.

"We've got this under control," Grady repeated. "Gotta get back to work."

Charlie nodded and put the Suburban into reverse, backed off the gravel driveway, and turned them around. Wordlessly, they drove to the main house and got out, pulling in next to Will's haphazardly parked BMW. Deck met them at the front door, looking like he'd missed a decade's worth of sleep.

"Charlie," he said frostily. "What are you—"

Lila rushed him and wrapped her arms around him. "Deck, you're okay?"

"Yeah," he said gruffly, standing stock-still, as if unused to physical contact. Finally, he slid his arm around his little sister and hugged her close, though it didn't last long. He pulled away, his hand to his face like he didn't want anybody to see more than he was willing to share.

Charlie began to have an inkling of how Jake must have felt when her family had rejected him.

She suddenly felt not only superfluous and unwelcome, but voyeuristic. She had no right to see even a hint of the vulnerability hidden by this tough, rangy rancher.

Deck shifted his weight and ran a hand over the back of his neck. "We're all fine," he said. "Well"—he jerked a thumb in the direction of the great room—"more or less."

Felicity's uncontrollable sobbing was audible from where they stood.

Deck clenched his jaw, looking back and forth between the view of the fire over Charlie's shoulder and the hall behind him leading to Felicity. Though he wasn't about to abandon the girl, everything about his body language still communicated that he wanted to run out the door and join the boys at the fire line. Lila put her hand on his arm, maybe half to comfort him, the other half to stop him from going anywhere.

Felicity unleashed another wail of distress.

Charlie hesitated. "If you'll let me inside," she said, "I can help you with that part."

Deck leveled his gaze on her, then nodded and stood aside. It wasn't a warm welcome, but what could she expect? She left Lila with him and went to deal with Bridezilla.

"Charlie!" Felicity wailed. She was the very picture of pathetic. Mascara ran down her cheeks in twin torrents, her face was swollen and blotchy, and her artful curls were limp and shapeless. "Oh, Charlie, this is all my fault. I never meant for this to happen . . ." The rest of her words were swallowed by yet another sob.

Hug her, said Charlie's better nature. *She's crying out for comfort.*

Strangle the she-beast! said Charlie's inner beeyotch. *She's the reason for this disaster.*

Charlie summoned all the empathy she could muster. "Of course you didn't mean for the barn to catch on fire." She put her hand on Felicity's shoulder and squeezed. This gesture only produced a fresh outburst of wails. "Okay, come on. Let's go into the kitchen and make a cup of tea."

Deck's kitchen was cool and soothing, with blue walls. It was full of pale oak cabinetry and old-school white appliances with rounded edges. Charlie pulled a chair out from a corner nook and nudged Bridezilla into it while she hunted for a tea bag and a kettle. She found neither, so she settled for making coffee instead.

"Felicity, how did this happen?"

As Charlie scooped a breakfast blend into the basket filter of Deck's coffee maker, the girl blubbered something unintelligible about lanterns.

Charlie shook her head. "I thought Mick went over all of that at the safety check."

"I know, but I thought everyone was being overly paranoid, and the men were so bossy about it, and that ticked me off. I figured that these candles were enclosed in glass, so they were safe, and if they were already here, Lila would let it slide. Because it was my wedding . . .”

“So you hung the lanterns yourself? Inside?”

Felicity nodded, wiping her eyes on her sleeve.

Charlie spied a box of tissues on a corner shelf and handed it to her. “Why didn’t you wait and talk to Lila?”

“She wasn’t answering her phone.”

Charlie nodded. She herself had seen Lila ignore the insistent barking from her phone. She sometimes let Felicity’s calls go to voicemail in order to retain her sanity. Maybe that had been intolerable to a neurotic bride.

“And I guess”—more shame crept into Bridezilla’s tone—“I just didn’t want to be told no. So I drove out here in Will’s car to hang them . . . and then I wanted to see what they’d look like when they were lit. So I turned off all the lights, and I was backing up to get a picture on my phone, and my elbow caught one of the lanterns and knocked it down. The glass broke, the candle ignited a roll of paper towels, and a pile of brochures . . . I tried to grab the roll of paper towels to put it out, but it unspooled to the opposite wall.

“And next thing I know, there’s fire everywhere! I didn’t know what to do. I ran outside screaming, and Declan came running, and we tried to throw water on the flames, but we couldn’t fill the bucket fast enough. So he called nine-one-one—”

“Okay, okay,” said Charlie, even though it really wasn’t. “So Jake and the rest of the firefighters evidently have things under control. Nobody got hurt, and that’s the most important thing.”

Felicity nodded, then blew her nose. She mopped at her eyes with another wad of tissues. “But the Old Barn,” she whispered. “Is it still standing?”

Charlie wasn't sure. "They seem to think they can save it. We'll know in a little while."

"I'm so, so sorry," Bridezilla sobbed. "I never thought—"

"I know."

"Will . . . my parents . . . they're going to kill me . . ."

True. But all Charlie said was, "Do you want me to call Will for you now?"

Felicity blanched. "No! No—I don't even know what to say to him. How can I even *begin* to explain this?"

Charlie sighed. "All you can do is tell the truth."

Bridezilla curled into a ball, and her wailing escalated once more. "Charlie, I can't. Everyone already thinks I'm crazy—and maybe I am. I've lost my mind over this wedding. I just wanted everything to be perfect, and now it's a nightmare . . ."

Charlie tried to think of soothing things to say. She needed to get Felicity out of here and back to the Hotel Saint-Denis, where she and her parents were staying.

So she bent and whispered into Bridezilla's ear. "The Braddocks need some time and privacy to talk, okay? And you probably don't want to be here right now anyway, do you?"

Felicity shook her head, eyes wide and full of shame.

"Right. Then we're going to skip the coffee and sneak out the back door."

Charlie led the Nuptial Nightmare outside, allowing herself one last glance toward the ghoulish orange and smoke-filled sky. Her heart pounded, thinking of Jake and his crew putting themselves in danger, and she wondered if there was a chance the fire could slip the line and eventually creep up to the main house. But in the absence of any meaningful firefighting skills to her name, Charlie knew that the best thing she could do for everyone was to get Felicity out of sight and mind.

So she took Felicity's hand and ran for Will's car.

Chapter 25

CHARLIE'S PULSE HAD JUST DROPPED BACK DOWN TO its normal rate when Bridezilla's endless emotional faucets opened back up—with a vengeance.

"I can't marry Will," she sobbed.

Charlie's brain couldn't process this statement. It may as well have been in Swahili. She kept driving. Then she swerved onto the shoulder of the highway and braked hard. "*What* did you just say?"

"I can't get married," Felicity wailed. "I just figured it out . . . All this time I've been trying to plan the most perfect wedding anyone's ever seen, and—" At this point, her words degenerated into an unfortunate stream of howling and honking.

Charlie gazed at her, stunned. She looked around the car for anything resembling a tissue and came up with a crumpled fast-food napkin from the driver's-side door pocket. Wordlessly, she handed it to Bridezilla, who snatched it gratefully and blew her swollen red nose into it.

"It's not the dress," she bleated. "It's not the flowers, or the cake or the church or the pastor. Charlie, it's the *groom*."

Even now, with the Old Barn burning thanks to Felicity's antics, with the Silverlake Fire and Rescue crew's lives at stake, it was all still about her. *Unbelievable.*

Now she was ditching Will?

And Charlie had to deal with her, cosset her while putting aside her own fear for Jake.

Felicity looked like a madwoman crossed with the most pathetic orphan child ever. Her eyes were red-ringed, like a piglet's, and smudged underneath with the last of her mascara. Her once-perfect foundation and blush had been smeared around into a greasy, liverlike yellowish paste. Her nose could have guided a sleigh, and she had gnawed off all her lipstick.

Charlie resisted the urge to open the door and push her out onto the highway. "The groom," she said carefully. "My cousin Will? What exactly is wrong with Will?" *Do you want to return* him, *have* him *hemmed, switch out* his *color scheme?*

"Nothing's wrong with Will," whimpered Bridezilla. "It's me, not him."

You got that right, sister. But Charlie didn't say it aloud.

"Will is an amazing guy," Felicity said. "He's handsome and charming and successful and p-p-perfect for me on p-p-paper."

"But?"

"He's so proper and uptight—"

"Will?" Charlie folded her arms. "Will and three other lacrosse players put paper bags over their heads and streaked across the football field during his senior year of high school. Is that too uptight for you?"

"Charlie, don't take this wrong—"

"How am I supposed to take it, Felicity?" Charlie asked,

her temper rising. She was done with soothing, done with tact, done with this crazy girl who was risking Jake's life— and the other guys' lives—for the sake of her narcissism.

"Will is my cousin," said Charlie. "I'm the one who introduced you two in college, and I've watched you manipulate him for years now. You hounded him for a ring, threw down an ultimatum, and got him to propose. You've been planning and replanning this wedding for over a year now, you've driven everyone in this town crazy, and today you set the Old Barn on fire! Now you're saying you want to switch *Will* out, like one of your dresses or a party favor? Are you kidding me?"

"You don't have to be so mean," Felicity whined. "I already feel bad enough about everything."

"No, I'm not sure you do. Will *loves* you. Do you get that? Do you understand that you don't order that from Bloomingdale's? And you don't return it on a whim."

"Please stop with the sarcasm. This isn't a whim," Felicity said miserably. "I'm sorry that I'm upsetting you, but it's really not right. I can *feel* that it's not right. And wouldn't you rather that we figure that out before the wedding than after?"

"Sure. Whatever you say." Charlie drove Bridezilla the rest of the way to the Hotel Saint-Denis in total silence and only remembered as she pulled up to the building that they were in Will's BMW. "I need to stop by the apartment and get some decent shoes before I head back to the barn," she said. "Tell Will I'll leave the car in front with the keys in the ignition."

Felicity got out and then stared at her own feet, unable to meet Charlie's gaze.

"Please don't hate me," she said.

Charlie sighed. "Look, Felicity. I'm not very happy with

you right now, but I don't hate you. I just feel really, really bad for my cousin . . . and incredibly uncomfortable that *I* know this before he does. Why don't you take a little time to think about it before you talk to him? Are you sure that this isn't just a bad case of prewedding jitters?"

Bridezilla shook her head. "I—I don't think that's what it is."

"Well, only you know what's in your heart. But if you're truly not in love with Will, then you can't marry him. It's not fair."

"That's what I'm trying to tell you. That's why I can't go through with it."

Charlie looked at the woebegone would-be bride. "Okay. Then you have a really hard conversation ahead of you. And though a part of me wants to smack you, another part of me respects you for having the guts to tell him."

Bridezilla nodded, then sniffled and cleared her throat. "Thank you for all your help . . ." She shifted her weight from one foot to the other.

Charlie waited for her to say that she was praying for the crew and the Old Barn.

But all Bridezilla said was, "I guess I probably won't see you again, at least not anytime soon."

Wow. Just . . . wow.

Charlie shrugged, then shook her head. "Probably not," she said in the kindest tone she could manage. She couldn't bring herself to hug her. "Take care of yourself, Felicity."

Once she got to the apartment, Charlie ditched Will's BMW and flew through the door, flipping off her pumps and peeling off her skirt and blouse as she ran down the hallway to Granddad's bedroom. Within moments, she was zipping up a pair of battered boyfriend jeans and pulling on a sweatshirt, jamming her feet into sneakers, and running back out the door. She threw herself into Progress and gunned the engine. The wheels squealed in protest as she backed up and rumbled out of the parking lot.

She pressed the pedal to the metal and drove the virtual antique as fast as it would go, roaring back toward the Braddock homestead, deeply afraid of what she'd find.

Was everyone okay? Jake and the guys, battling a five-alarm fire—with the added horror of it being Jake's own family's property. With the added stress that—intentionally or not—Charlie had just demolished their paychecks.

She would never forgive herself. Never. She'd allowed Granddad to manipulate her, to play her like a fiddle.

Progress's engine rumbled like fury beneath her, the seat squeaking with every bump and pothole in the road. Cold wind blew like malice through the poorly sealed windows, even though she'd kept them rolled up. And with each yard of asphalt she hurtled over, Charlie felt like a worse and worse person.

Jake would never speak to her again—and who could blame him—but she had to know that he was alive, unhurt. The thought of anything happening to him scared her spitless.

It terrified her at a primal level, in an emotional place she hadn't even known she possessed.

She might never get to spend her life with Jake, but she knew she simply couldn't go on if he didn't exist.

How did Granddad get out of bed in the morning? How had he done so, without Grandma Babe, for the past twenty-odd years? She felt a fresh wave of grief and pity for him, a bone-deep comprehension and empathy that nobody outside the family had—except maybe Jake.

What had it been like for Granddad, to lose his soul mate that awful night, not to mention his entire home? Still, he had to move past his bitterness. He was letting it destroy not only the rest of his life, but other people's lives.

Charlie stomped on the accelerator, and Progress groaned, lurched, and rattled some more. The double yellow line in the center of the road urged her on. Fence posts, mile markers, side roads, and stop signs flew by in a blur. More wind howled through the cracks. And her heart beat in her own ears like thunder. Self-hatred streaked through her like lightning.

Jake. Jake. Jake.

Please, oh please, God. Let him be okay. Let all the guys be okay.

Chapter 26

J AKE COULDN'T BEND HIS MIND AROUND THE FACT that the Old Barn was on fire, right here in front of him. It gave new meaning to the color *burnt orange* as the fire raged against a sardonic blue sky, belching ominous black plumes of smoke into the air. There they hung, torpid and malignant, refusing to disperse.

Jake and the crew had quickly determined that nobody was inside, and then he'd done an instant clinical assessment of the situation. According to his risk-benefit analysis, the collapse zone was at the east side of the building, the first part to catch fire. He prioritized an aggressive interior attack on the blaze by three crew members, as long as they stayed away from that zone.

Old George would man the exclusion zone, keeping any curious onlookers at least eighty feet away from the structure. And Jake, along with two others, would focus on an exterior attack on the roof and the east exterior wall. He shouted the orders, and they all got to work, though for Jake himself, the scene was surreal.

The Old Barn represented a century and a half of history: It was part of his childhood; the original Silverlake Ranch.

And Declan . . . aw, man . . . poor Deck. He'd devoted months of dreaming and planning, hundreds of man-hours, tens of thousands of dollars to remodel the place. He'd crawled over every inch of it himself, sanding and painting and sealing every angle.

Deck must be going insane, having to babysit Felicity.

The fact that he was doing it anyway said that he trusted Jake and the guys to save the building, and by God, they would.

Deck had saved the place from rot and ruin. He'd also saved it from reclamation by the bank—partly thanks to Everett. Jake would do his part, too.

Nobody but Old George even realized what Jake had battled after the night of the Nash fire: insomnia, recurring nightmares, and depression because he hadn't been able to get Babe Nash out in time. George had guessed, and he'd taken him under his wing. Taught him how to deal with it: by confronting fire over and over again so that it had less power to traumatize him, and learning the skills he needed to beat it. George had become a surrogate father, and was a big reason Jake hadn't left town and lost his way, like Brandon. He was *the* reason that Jake was a firefighter today.

"You got guts, kid," George had said to him that awful night, as he lay coughing on the lawn. "You done good."

Now in the face of this fire at his own family's ranch, Jake stood in full gear, squarely in the hazard zone. His eyes stung and watered behind the shield protecting his eyes, and it wasn't all because of smoke. He blinked rapidly to clear them and aimed the powerful water hose in his gloved hands at the collapse zone near the apex of the roof, just east of it. There, a portion of the roof had been eaten through, and one of the exposed rafters blazed like Satan's own Yule log.

He knew the signs of his own anxiety. As his breathing quickened and went shallow, he reminded himself that there was nobody inside the barn. Not even a dog. No Mr. Coffee, no Dave Nash in a wheelchair. No Grandma Babe . . . No stairs to slide down on his belly, with her on his back.

His ribs ached at the memory, his shoulders felt the phantom weight of her on them, and his hands shook—though he told himself it was just the tremendous vibration from the water hose. His eyes stopped stinging and burning, since, to his shame, they'd overflowed. Jake squeezed them shut, effectively wringing them out to dry.

Jake channeled cool, blessed numbness and steeled himself again for the job at hand. This was no time to lose his shit; it was unthinkable and unacceptable.

Grady signaled to him that he and Tommy were going around the back, and Jake gave them a thumbs-up to show he understood. Mick and Rafael focused on watering down the nearby vegetation. Old George cast Jake a sharp glance, waited for his thumbs-up sign, then walked around the perimeter to analyze where they needed to focus next.

They were bringing the blaze under control. It wouldn't be a total loss, at least not the exterior. The interior—it would have to be gutted. Everything in there, even if it held together and wasn't buried in soot and ash, would reek of smoke. The rugs and furniture would have to be driven straight to the town dump.

Poor Lila—she'd chosen everything with such care, working to complement the architecture and keep the country comfort, making it just the right blend of lodge and luxury, Texas hospitality with understated elegance.

Everett would have insurance investigators and adjusters out here within twenty-four hours. It was just how he rolled . . . and, as the majority owner, it would be Everett who would push whether or not to press charges for gross negligence against Felicity "Bridezilla" Barnum.

Who would then lawyer up and try to fling the blame back on the family. On Lila, perhaps, for not being out there to supervise the space . . . It didn't bear thinking of. Any of it.

And Ace? Ace used to sneak out here to the Old Barn, climb up into the hayloft and secretly draw stuff. It was one of the only things that calmed his squirrely ass. The Austin Lone Stars probably didn't offer him much of a chance to release his inner da Vinci. If Ace ever again graced his family with his pro-ballplayer presence, he'd be torn up over the loss of his clandestine art studio.

To Jake himself, the Old Barn had been the cool, cavernous space where he'd worked with Pop on restoring his beat-up but beautiful classic red 1966 Mustang. He'd loved unraveling the mystery of all the parts under the hood and how they worked together to create forward motion and velocity.

He could still smell the clean engine oil, the undercurrents of gasoline, the leather on the seats, the mustiness of the old carpet, and the rubber of the floor mats. He could hear the rough purr of the engine as Pop had started her up; he could see their old man's toothy grin emerging from his five o'clock shadow like the sun twinkling after a storm.

Hadn't those been the days?

Jake pushed away the memories and focused on saving what was left of the Old Barn, which housed so many whispers of the past.

* * *

At last, Charlie spied the familiar iron gates with the bucking bronco that heralded Silverlake Ranch. The fire had
gotten much worse. As she hurtled through them, the scents
of hell seeped through the windows, and she saw the smoke
rising like an evil spirit against the sun, spreading malevolence in its wake. Some demon had melted a celestial box
of Crayolas over everything: The clouds were backlit with
clashing colors; they bellowed silently at the normalcy of
the blue sky above, which stretched for miles, indifferent
to the scene that played out below. Tangerine warred with
burnt orange, red bled through mustard, bruised plum battered violet, and black smothered periwinkle.

Charlie had never seen anything like this dreadful rain-
bow. And under it all was a fire of epic proportions—a fire
as big as the one that had consumed the Nash mansion
twelve years ago. The sight of a fire like this was almost
more awful in the daylight, because it couldn't be written
off as a nightmare.

She didn't stop at the main house but took the dogleg toward the Old Barn. Grouchy emerged to greet her, as he did
everyone, and when she kept on rolling, drawn inexorably
toward the fire, he chased after her, panting. She stopped near
a huge live oak about a football field away from the barn,
knowing she shouldn't go any closer.

All seven of the Fire and Rescue team were now there,
as far as she could tell. There were two other Silverlake
Fire and Rescue vehicles besides the monster fire truck: one
an SUV, and the other a medical transport van. She was,
frankly, surprised that they didn't melt in the face of the
wall of flames in front of them.

The heat, even from here, was palpable and horrific. The
same heat that had taken her grandmother and her family

home. Eaten her life, her belongings, her innocence, and half her memories. Her mouth dried, her throat got lumpy and scratchy, and her palms went damp; her stomach cramped. Her pulse kicked up, and her eyes stung.

Grouchy barked outside the window, so she absently opened the door and put her hand down to greet him. He bounced and wriggled and licked her; it didn't take him long to scramble right into the truck. She didn't try to stop him. He ran back and forth, right over her lap, on the bench seat, seeming distressed at a deep level by the fire. She couldn't blame him.

Charlie put her arms around him and hauled him into her lap, where he settled briefly, his fuzzy body shaking. She buried her face in his fur, inhaling the musky, earthy doggie scent of him. Then, without warning, Grouchy sprang up and right out the door of the truck.

Horrified, she saw a cat, his gray plume of a tail *on fire*, streaking out of the Old Barn and making right for the live oak she'd parked next to.

On fire. The poor cat's tail was on fire.

Charlie scrambled out of the truck to try to catch the cat, but it neatly dodged Grouchy and leaped for the trunk of the live oak, looking for solace in its branches.

It was a cat; it didn't know this was the worst possible thing it could do.

Grouchy barked and whined, standing up on his hind legs and bracing his front paws against the massive trunk. He wasn't going to have a lot of luck climbing the tree.

Charlie ran toward it, but the cat went higher and higher, the poor thing yowling as the fire burned its tail. She could not, would not, let it burn to death. Out of the question. But the higher the cat went, the sicker she felt.

She cast a quick glance over her shoulder at the Old Barn, to see if maybe one of the guys could peel off and help. But she knew it was hopeless. They had their hands full. She was on her own.

The cat's tail ignited dry leaves and branches on its way up. The whole tree could catch fire. She was crazy to go after the animal. But how could she not?

She couldn't let it die like this. She just couldn't. It was too awful.

Charlie ran back to Progress to get Granddad's nasty old barn jacket. She grabbed a bottle of water from the floor, shoved it into a pocket of the coat, and tied the coat around her waist as she ran back to the tree. She gauged the lower branches of the oak, found a spot she could get a foothold, and started climbing.

"Here, kitty!" she called as she went. "Come here. Let me help."

Don't think about the height. Don't think about the flames. Just climb.

Climb.

She looked up toward the cat, barely registering how fast she was going. She climbed like a possessed monkey.

The cat howled.

"Oh, baby. Come here. I'm trying to help you."

She got within a yard of it. The cat tried to turn to lick its tail, but then recoiled and howled again. Charlie felt tears dripping down her face. "C'mere, baby . . ."

The animal stared at her, wild-eyed.

A branch crackled; she made the mistake of looking down. She almost vomited.

Cat. Focus.

Should she jump?

No. She was how high up? Twenty feet? Twenty-five? She'd break her neck, not to mention every other bone in her body. And she'd come to rescue the cat . . . that was the whole point of all of this. So she wasn't going down again without it.

Charlie swung her foot over the next branch up, and somehow pulled herself to within about fourteen inches of the poor creature. It flattened itself on the tree, lashing its tail and igniting yet more branches. It wasn't going to crawl into her arms. There was only one way to help it.

She untied the barn jacket from her waist and threw it over the cat. The she wriggled up one more branch and rolled the animal in the jacket to smother the flames, wincing as it howled again. She pulled the cat-jacket bundle toward her with one hand while she clung to the tree with the other.

"Poor baby," she murmured. "Come here, sweetheart."

The cat scrabbled against her, then quieted. Then it began to meow piteously.

The flames on its tail were out. Thank God.

Thank God.

"We're going straight to the vet," Charlie said. "We're going to get you help. Right away."

But when she looked down, the tree was almost entirely on fire.

Grouchy was still at the base, now barking hysterically.

And she realized that it was impossible to climb while her arms were full of traumatized kitty. *Think fast, girl. Think!*

She didn't want to think. She wanted to vomit. She felt dizzy, on the verge of passing out. But her survival instinct kicked in.

She clung to the branch with her thighs. She lowered the cat to her lap and eased the jacket from around it; she slipped her arm into first one sleeve and then the other. Then she zipped the cat inside, gathered the bottom of the coat and tucked it into her waistband. She was, for once, glad it was tight.

The barking below had stopped. She looked down through the branches again and saw that Grouchy was gone. No, there he was: running in a blue streak toward the Old Barn. Stopping there next to one of the guys, barking wildly.

Charlie did what she could to control her rising panic.

Deducing Grouchy's message, the firefighter turned his head toward her and rapidly took in the situation. Then he shouted at the others before hurtling toward her with a ladder, the dog sprinting in the lead.

Charlie wanted to climb down toward them, but she saw nothing but flames below her. They consumed almost every lower branch of the oak. She had nowhere to go but *up*.

Dear Lord.

Higher and higher. And she could barely deal with climbing a step stool. The treetop didn't bear thinking of. She already felt dizzy and sick and trapped and terrified.

Up.

Climb, Charlie. Get your ass up higher before it gets barbecued, along with the cat. Move!

She swallowed bile; her hands and knees shook. This made it even harder to trust her own judgment in selecting each next branch. Would it hold her weight? Could she cling to it with her sweaty palms, without her own fear getting the better of her?

She compartmentalized the fear: shoved it into a box and slammed the lid. She had no use for it in this situation. She had to have faith instead.

She risked looking down again, which resulted in a different f-word coming to mind as full-blown vertigo kicked in. She had the real sensation of falling, had to tell herself it was a lie. Had to cling to her branch, feel its rough bark scraping her skin, inhale its peculiar oaky, smoky essence.

You are not falling. Not!

She hung on. The fireman with the ladder had almost

reached the tree. She noticed, almost surreally, that the ladder had orange feet. And aluminum was metal . . . Wouldn't it get hot? Wouldn't it burn them both?

Stop.

Have faith.

He'll get you down from here. He's a trained professional.

The cat wriggled against her stomach and meowed again. It seemed more terrified than Charlie. "It's okay, baby," she said. "We're gonna be fine."

The cat seemed to know she was lying. It tried to burrow into her. She risked letting go of the current branch with her left hand, and stroked its head through the barn jacket. "It's okay. We'll go to the kitty doctor next. She'll make your tail feel better, okay, sweetie?"

Meow.

Two more of the firehouse guys, working in perfect co-ordination, peeled off with a hose from Big Red and aimed it squarely at the oak tree.

The guy in full gear, with the ladder, pulled off his respirator and yelled, "Hang on! Brace yourself!"

The guy was Jake.

She had perhaps two seconds to process this before the hose blasted the branches just below her with a torrent of water.

The first in a series of irrational thoughts popped into her head: *He's speaking to me.*

Only because he had to.

"Brace yourself." *Last words he'll ever say to you.*

And you're now endangering his life.

What if a branch breaks and falls on his head? What if he burns to death trying to save your sorry butt?

"Charlie. Hello? *Charlie!*" He was yelling in that deep baritone of his, the one that vibrated into her very spine.

"Climb up to that branch—the one just to the right! Do you see it? It's sturdier."

She looked up. The cat wriggled inside Granddad's barn jacket.

"Do it, Charlie. Now! We've got to get the flames out, right where you are now."

She followed instructions.

Half a second later, water blasted the spot where she'd been.

She looked down and, blessedly, saw no fire. Just hissing, smoldering, smoking oak branches.

Then the ladder slammed into place against the trunk of the tree, just below her. Jake shot up it in a yellow-uniformed blur. His rugged, handsome face suddenly appeared opposite her: his dark winged eyebrows pulled into a ferocious squiggle of anxiety, his eyes an intense indigo, his mouth a grim slash. "Charlie, *what the fu*—"

Then he took her face between his gloved hands and kissed her, hard.

She almost fell out of the tree. But his hands moved down to her shoulders, and he held her steady, pressing her back into the trunk, such as it was this high up.

And then he found his words again. They came out in a torrent, much like the water from the massive fire hose. "Are you *okay*? What *in the name of all that's holy* are you doing *up this godforsaken tree*? Why are you here? I could wring your neck with my bare hands, you crazy—"

Meow. The cat spoke for her, to her eternal gratitude.

Jake registered that Charlie's stomach was wriggling. "Are you *kidding* me?"

"Its tail was on fire," she whispered.

"You could have died up here! Do you get that? You could have been toasted like a marshmallow! Of all the stupid, idiotic—"

"On *fire*. The cat's tail," she repeated. "I couldn't—"

Jake's expression softened. He took his hands off her shoulders.

"I don't want to hear it," he said. "We're going down the ladder now."

She looked through all the branches—it had to be thirty feet to the ground. She felt the vertigo again. She tried to moisten her dry mouth so that she could swallow. Her lips were still tingling from that sudden, fierce, possessive kiss. But there was no moisture to be had, and she couldn't get past a giant lump in her throat, one that felt like maybe it could be the cat's twin.

"I can't," was all she said. Her whole body started to shake.

Meow.

"Charlie, how in blazes did you think you were going to get down with that cat? You've been afraid of heights since you were ten!"

Wordlessly, she shook her head.

In less than a second, he had her jacket unzipped.

Meow!

"Shut it," Jake said to the cat, but his voice was gentle. He swore softly when he saw its tail, pink and angry where the hair had been singed off and the flesh burned. "Charlie, we're going down in a fireman's carry. Got it? But you'll have to hold the cat. Otherwise it'll get squashed."

"I can't! No!"

"You can. You can do this. Don't overthink it."

"But—"

Jake scooped the cat out of Granddad's barn jacket by the scruff of its neck.

It howled.

"Sorry, buddy," he said to it. Then, to Charlie, "One, two, three—"

"*No!*"

And his arm encircled her like a band of steel, tossing her unceremoniously over his shoulder like a sack of grain. All of the breath she'd been using to protest whooshed out of her, and her face pressed into the filthy, smoky, wet jacket he wore. Somehow it smelled good, like warmth and safety and . . . just Jake. She hung there, petrified but weirdly reassured, unable and, frankly, unwilling to move. She was simply glad for his confidence, his competence.

How he was balancing on the ladder with no hands, she didn't know. Then she saw his booted feet, hooked around the sides. Unable to look at the ground so far below them, she shut her eyes tightly and willed her panic to recede.

"Here. Take the cat, Charlie. He needs you. And I can't get us down without at least one hand."

She opened her eyes long enough to cradle the cat, who was clearly not eager to travel this way. "Neither of us has a choice, okay, little guy?"

Her voice seemed to soothe the animal, and it stopped wriggling, just let out a long, woeful kitty moan of distress.

"Trust me, I feel the same way," she said.

Awkward step by awkward step, the three of them descended. When they got to the ground, the other two firefighters cheered. They cheered, at least, until Jake set her on her feet and they could identify that it was Charlie Nash, destroyer of their livelihoods.

Then their voices strangled in their throats. They turned and walked away, back toward the Old Barn, which was now just a mass of smoldering, hissing wood. The fire there was finally out, too. Thanks to them.

"Shoulda brought the cat down and left Charlie in the tree," she overheard one of them say as they trudged off with the hose.

Charlie hugged the cat to her, miserable. She couldn't really blame them.

"Yeah, you're not going to win any popularity contests around the guys," Jake said finally, in the awkward silence that ensued. He took off his helmet and stuffed it under his arm.

She shook her head. "Thank you," she managed.

"I can't really say that you're welcome, but I'm glad you're alive. Saving Deck's wannabe cat doesn't redeem you, so don't say another word to me. Got it?"

If there'd been any anger in his tone, it might have been bearable, because it'd mean that he still felt something for her. But there was none.

She couldn't even meet his gaze; she just bent her head and pressed her face into the cat's fur. She finally nodded.

"Get that poor animal up to Deck," he said. Then he turned on his heel and went after the other guys.

Charlie watched him go while she battled the turmoil of her emotions. She was grateful to be alive, but she wanted to weep at Jake's callous dismissal of her. She wanted to jump into his arms and kiss him—yet she also wanted to hide away from not only him and the rest of the crew, but from herself. Could she just lock herself in a closet for the next ten years, until everyone forgot who she was?

"*Meow*," said the only creature at Silverlake Ranch willing to speak to her.

"Meow," Charlie said back. She took the few wobbly steps required to Progress, opened the driver's-side door, and fell in. She closed the door, set the cat down next to her, and started the engine. Her hands were still trembling too much to drive.

But she needed to get the cat to Declan so he could get it to the vet immediately. So she put the truck in gear and rolled slowly down the gravel road, taking in the devastation of the Old Barn as she went.

It was blackened, sodden, and steaming. The east side of

the roof had collapsed, though it looked as though most of the structure was still standing. Well, not the east wall.

The furnishings were a dead loss. Lila would be devastated. Deck, too. All the work they'd put into the place . . . up in smoke.

Charlie rolled onward, speechless. She took the dogleg in reverse and drove to the back of the main house—she wasn't sure exactly why she'd gone to the back. Maybe because she'd exited from there with Bridezilla, without saying goodbye. Maybe because right now, she only felt good enough for the back door.

As she went around to the passenger side to collect the cat, she saw Mick drive Jake up in the fire department SUV. The two men got out and hurried toward the front door.

Maybe I can slip in and find Declan and slip out again without them seeing me.

Charlie carried the cat up the back steps, turned the knob, and stepped into the kitchen. She gazed again at the blue walls, willing them to soothe her, to guide her in what to say to Declan. *Jake's all right, no thanks to me. I caused him extra-crispy extra danger! Hooray . . .*

But Declan was already with his brother. She could hear Jake's voice, rumbling in his deep baritone. Peeking around the doorjamb, she saw Declan, Jake, and Lila huddling together. Charlie stayed where she was, with her sliver of a view.

"The fire's completely out," Jake said.

"Thank God," Lila said.

"Amen," Deck muttered, wiping his blackened sleeve against his equally filthy face.

Jake was still in full uniform, minus the helmet, his dark curls in wild, sweaty disarray. His back was to her, and Lila had her arms wrapped around him as if she'd never let him go.

"Easy, sis," he said. But he bent his head and pressed his forehead against Lila's. She was openly crying.

Charlie felt her own eyes well up at the sight: the Braddocks together, as a family unit. A bond she'd thought she'd broken forever had finally been repaired. A bond that she'd helped to sever.

She felt like mud on their floor. It was poetic justice, really. For how the Nashes had made Jake feel. The family circle had closed . . . and this time it was Charlie on the outside.

She, of all people, did not belong here in this circle of love. In fact, if Jake discovered she was here, the Braddock family might well be destroyed all over again. She owed it to Lila to get out of here, as quickly and silently as possible.

"Hey," said a voice.

Charlie whirled and found Mick standing behind her, a stony look on his face. The cat meowed.

"Jayzus, Charlie, haven't you got that animal to the vet yet?" he hissed. Mick snatched the cat bundle into his arms without so much as a by-your-leave, cradling the poor thing like a baby, and headed straight through the house and out the door.

It wasn't possible to feel any lower. Charlie retreated from the Braddocks and crept back into the kitchen. She opened the door again and slunk out to the truck, watching Mick's SUV speeding away in a cloud of dust.

Why didn't I just drive the cat to the vet right away? What is wrong with me? Everything was moving in slow motion.

She turned the key. The engine flipped, then nothing. She tried it again, unwilling to scream at it, because someone would come running, and the absolute last thing she was going to do was ask one of the Braddocks for a favor right now.

One more time, and there was nothing to do but pound her fists on the massive old steering wheel. "Grandma," Charlie whispered in anguish. "How is this Progress?"

She rested her head on the steering wheel and took deep breaths.

Why did families and emotions have to be so messy? So untamable? And how had she, the pleaser, somehow become a villain to so many?

Charlie got out of Progress, shut the door as quietly as she could, and started walking. It was a long walk back to Granddad's apartment. Without socks, the sneakers rubbed blisters on her heels almost immediately. With each successive step, she winced. She walked and winced, walked and winced. She passed the Lundgrens' hog farm, the mile marker for the turnout to the cemetery, the Grab n' Go Grocery, and then the Sweet Dreams Motel.

A couple of miles more, still wincing, she found herself outside the former Nash mansion yet again. She squinted at it. *I will rebuild you,* Charlie vowed. *I will make it happen.*

But for now, she kept wincing and walking.

It had been twenty-four hours of crazy highs and lows. She'd taken on and rebuked her family over their treatment of Jake. She'd consummated and then destroyed her relationship with him. She'd accidentally torpedoed the fire department just as Silverlake had its first major blaze in more than a decade and needed its help . . .

How could she ever make it up to Jake?

Then there was the wedding she and Lila and Kristina and Amelie and Maggie had worked so hard to pull off for Will and his Bridezilla. Charlie felt bad not only for Will and Aunt Sadie and Uncle Theo and Felicity's parents, but for all the guests who'd traveled and were now arriving for no reason, having paid for plane tickets and hotel rooms and rental cars.

She thought wearily of all the waste involved in the canceled wedding. The equipment that had been delivered to the Old Barn's storage outbuilding and was waiting to be set up: the chairs, the tables, the linens, the much-disputed and dreaded but necessary extra porta-potties for the grounds.

Felicity's three bridal gowns; the flowers; the cakes; the cases of champagne; the china and crystal; the perfect, elegant hors d'oeuvres being made; the entrées; the side dishes . . . all for nothing. All that energy, all those decisions, all of that money and time and aggravation.

The blister on Charlie's left heel was bleeding, and one on the toe of her right foot was causing her agony. She began to seriously consider taking off her shoes and walking barefoot along the road—pathetic or not. She had at least a mile to go.

Oh, poor me. At least I'm not fighting a fire that threatens my life, my friends' lives, and my family business.

Behind her, she heard a vehicle approaching. She almost stuck her thumb out to hitch a ride. She was exhausted and demoralized and not feeling too proud to do it.

An older-model Buick slowed down next to her, and Dottie from the Grab n' Go Grocery lowered the window, her cheerful orange eyebrows raised. "Charlie? Is that you, hon?"

Charlie produced a lopsided smile. "Hi, Dottie. How are you?"

"I'd say I'm prob'ly better than you right now, seeing as how you look like you've been wrastlin' alligators, not to mention you're limping and you've got blood trickling out the back of your shoe."

"Car trouble," was all Charlie could think of to say past the lump in her throat.

"Well, can I give you a lift, sweet girl?"

"You're an angel!" Charlie hobbled over and climbed into the car, which smelled of fake pine and baby wipes. She collapsed onto the blue velour seat. "Dottie, thank you so much—I could just kiss you."

"Don't even think about it!" Dottie looked alarmed. "My girlfriend would get upset."

Charlie blinked. "Just a figure of speech."

"Oh, okay. Just wanted to be clear. So where're you headed? To your granddad's place, I'm betting."

"Yes." She wouldn't say one word about the fire. The news would be all over town soon enough. And there was something about Dottie's carefree demeanor that was like a breath of fresh air.

Dottie hit the gas.

"So, you're getting off early today?" Charlie asked her.

"Sure am. Going to get my hair done, then get dressed and drive to the city. We're attending a fancy charity fund-raiser, Libby and I are, at a big hotel. I'm excited. You know I've never been to a ball? Sounds so glamorous." She chuckled. "Ain't it funny, how many times I've said to someone that I've *had* a ball doing something, but . . ."

A ball. Charlie felt a weird tingle of electricity go through her.

What if all the wedding preparations and food and champagne *didn't* go to waste? What if she spearheaded a different event . . . one that the entire community bought tickets to, in support of a great cause?

What if Charlie could find a way to make amends to Jake, and Bridezilla's bomb of a wedding became, say . . . Silverlake's first annual firemen's ball?

Charlie looked out the window of Dottie's car. It was far enough away from the fire to see clear blue sky.

"Dottie, would you mind just dropping me on Main Street?"

"Not at all, honey."

Charlie smiled. No such thing as a coincidence, Grandma Babe used to say.

She was making Progress after all.

Chapter 27

J AKE WAS WIPED OUT—THE BACK SIDE OF THE CRAZY
adrenaline rush he'd had while they'd fought the
blaze. His own family property had been on fire. The ranch
where he and his brothers and little sister had grown up.
The place Declan had been killing himself to keep running
for years—for all of them.

Amazing how he'd always taken that a little for granted.
Because it, and Deck himself, had always been in the background, a safety net if he'd needed one.

It struck him anew how much they all owed their eldest
brother. And how much he needed to acknowledge that.
Thank him. Tell him he loved him for it.

But Deck didn't seem to be inhabiting his own body
right now. He was staring at the smoking wreckage of the
Old Barn, his hands shoved deep into his pockets, but Jake
could swear he wasn't really seeing it. Declan's mind was
miles away, his thoughts somewhere beyond all of them,
above in the deep blue Texas sky that slowly absorbed the

hellish smoke as if it were all just ephemeral human emotion.

"Declan," Jake said gently.

No answer.

"Deck. Did you call Everett?"

"What?"

"I asked you if you've called Rhett."

Deck pulled his hands out of his pockets and laced them behind his neck, leaning into them as if they were the only thing holding him upright. "Yeah, I've called the majority owner," he said. "He's got a right to know."

Empty. His voice was as empty as his eyes. Vacant.

"Declan, it's gonna be okay." Jake took two steps, then three, toward his brother, who didn't move, didn't even seem to notice.

"Peachy," Deck said, in that same disinterested tone.

Jake blew out a breath. Stretched out a hand, let it hover like a UFO over his older brother's shoulder. "Deck . . . it could have been worse."

Deck produced a short, unamused bark of laughter.

Jake sighed. He brought his UFO hand in for a landing and squeezed Declan's shoulder.

His brother flinched, but then let Jake's hand rest there.

Both of them stood without looking at each other, both seeming surprised at the physical contact. When was the last time they'd touched each other? Years ago. After they'd all stood, side by side, as Mama and Pop's coffins were lowered into the ground?

That in itself seemed heartbreaking.

"Deck." Jake heard his own voice crack. "Look . . ."

"I'm friggin' looking."

"No—what I mean to say is . . . I'm sorry. We . . . all of us . . . me, Ace, Rhett, and Lila . . . we . . ."

And of course, that was when Deck's phone rang. He

muttered a curse, then slid it out of his back pocket. "Yeah," he said into it abruptly.

"Declan, it's Rhett. What's going on? You said there was an emergency?" The voice on the phone was loud enough to be audible to Jake, and a little distracted.

Jake stood by, frustrated but mute.

Please don't be a jerk to Declan. Not today. Not now.

Declan cleared his throat, taking his time as he either was trying to decide what to say or else trying not to sound emotional. "It's going to take a little longer to pay back the loan than I said, and I apologize for that."

Jake grimaced and kicked the ground.

"Is that right?" Everett asked, a new edge to his voice. Oblivious, as usual.

"There's been a fire on the property," Deck said. "We've got some scorched acreage, and the Old Barn . . ." The elbow holding up the cell phone drooped, and suddenly Declan looked a hundred years old, staring again at years of his work, gone.

A string of curse words was audible, and Jake's anger got the best of him. How dare Everett get pissed about his money when Deck was in this kind of pain? Jake ripped the phone out of Declan's hand; his older brother gave it up without a fight, didn't seem to care.

"I'm going to have to call you back," Everett said, his clipped voice not so disinterested anymore. Not when money was concerned.

"You absolute piece of sh—" Jake started to say.

"Hang up the damn phone and let me call you on video," Everett roared. The screen went black as the call dropped.

Declan just stared at the boys on the team doing wrap-up duty. Tommy was all business now, soaking the ground where thin streaks of smoke still bled from the earth. Grady, looking even more massive suited up in full gear, was testing the stability of some of the walls. The others were smaller figures in the background, circling the perimeter, everybody on task.

Jake found himself choked up, not just because of the Braddocks' personal loss, but because he was so damned proud of all of them. His crew.

Too bad Kingston Nash isn't here to see all this. To see the boys still pouring heart, body, and soul into this town after putting in so much already to fight this fire.

Everett's video call chimed.

Jake had a mind to ignore the request. But on the third chime, he answered it, taken aback and stunned by the visual. Rhett looked like a stranger. Like a fancy city stranger, somebody Charlie might know from her life in Dallas.

A wave of fresh sorrow ripped through Jake as the two brothers looked at each other for the first time in years.

"What the hell happened? Show me," Everett said, cutting to the chase. "Use the camera and show me."

Jake didn't say a word. He turned the phone so the camera pointed to the scorched, smoking mess before them.

There was a pause. Jake thought maybe Everett was making calculations in his head.

But then Everett's voice, not entirely hiding a well-buried Texas drawl said, "Not the barn, moron. Show me Deck. And where the hell is Lila?"

Jake hadn't talked to his brother in a long, long time, so he couldn't be sure, but Rhett sounded a little panicked. And for some reason, that made Jake smile. He pointed the camera at Declan, keeping that vigil of his with his mind a mile away. Then he muttered, "Yours truly," and body-scanned himself, rolling his eyes when he got up to his own face. "Lila's safe. She's up at the main house. She's pretty broken up about it all, though. Obviously."

"Thank God you're all safe. Now, what happened?"

"It's . . . complicated. But in a nutshell, we had a bride who just had to have her own way. She brought lanterns out here in violation of everything we told her."

"Unbelievable."

"Yeah." Jake looked back over at Declan, who had yet to emerge from what was beginning to look like either shock or despair. "Hey, listen, there's a lot of stuff to deal with here. I gotta go."

Rhett nodded and sat back, giving Jake a bigger view of the man and his office. Jake took in the starched white shirt and the cuff links, the perfect hair. His brother picked up a crystal and gold baseball-shaped paperweight and tossed it pensively in the palm of his hand. "The insurance paper-work is going to be ugly."

"Yeah, well, somebody'll take care of it," Jake said. "Somebody always does." *Declan*.

"Do you need me to come?" Rhett mumbled at the base-ball.

"Sorry, I didn't catch that," Jake said.

"Do you need me to come home?" Rhett asked, this time making eye contact with Jake.

Jake went still. "Do you *want* to come home?"

A squeaky sound came over the line, and Rhett sat up straight, his gaze moving to whoever had just walked into his office.

"You've got a meeting," Jake said. "I'll let you go."

"I'm sorry," Rhett said. "I'm . . ." He exhaled in a whoosh.

Jake just shrugged. "I'm sure Deck will be in touch when it's time to talk money."

It might have been his imagination, but Everett seemed to stiffen at that.

"Tell Declan, uh . . ." Rhett looked off camera for a

moment, like he was trying to pull himself together a little bit. "Yeah, well, we'll be in touch. Later, Jake."

"Bye."

They clicked off, and Jake stared at the dead screen. "I'll call Ace in a few. Okay, Deck?" he said. "Declan! I said I'll call Ace in a few."

"That's fine. Whatever you think, Jake," Declan said, still in that weird, disembodied tone.

Jake nodded, slapped Declan's phone into his palm, and went to join his team.

What did he think? Jake thought he might want to fall to his knees. Jake thought he might want to shake his fists at the heavens. But as he rejoined the men of Silverlake Fire and Rescue, still giving it everything they had, he knew he wasn't going to do any of those things.

He was going to work alongside them until there was nothing left he could give.

❧

Jake had just gotten cleaned up at the main house and was about to collapse in front of the fireplace, maybe with a double Scotch, when his cell phone rang.

Mercy Hospital? *Hmm.* Maybe they had a new physical therapy patient for him. Since he'd soon have no paycheck, he should collect a few more clients.

"Hello?"

"Hi, Jake. It's Mia here at Mercy."

"Mia. How are you? This is a surprise."

"Well, of course we've all heard about the fire. Are you guys okay? Is the Old Barn okay? Were you able to save—"

"Everyone's fine. As far as fires go, this one wasn't the worst. The back wall's a loss, and so is the interior, but most of the roof is salvageable."

"Oh, I'm so glad to hear that . . . And Deck? Lila?"

"Everybody's okay. They're a little shaken up, is all."

"Yeah, I'll bet." Mia was quiet for a moment. "Listen . . . there's another reason I called. I can't reach Charlie, and Kingston Nash is being discharged, as he requested, just in time for the wedding—not that anyone's sure where that's going to be now."

"Good question. I'm sure Lila's losing her mind trying to figure that out, along with the bride." Jake couldn't even say Felicity's name. He was still trying to bend his mind around her recklessness and stubbornness. How she could have dragged lanterns out there in direct disregard of his orders—

"I know you've had a big day already, but I don't suppose you'd be able to take Kingston home?"

It took Jake a moment to register her words.

Seriously? Jake almost laughed. Almost. Evidently since the fire had taken precedence, the news of the town council meeting had not yet reached the hospital's normally busy grapevine. God really did have a sense of humor.

"Because I tried King's daughter Sadie, too," Mia said, "and Dave Nash—since I know they're in town for the wedding, but everyone's phone is going straight to voicemail. They're probably all in a powwow over the wedding."

"Yeah, I'm sure they are." Jake almost told Mia to find someone else. But he was feeling just ornery enough to take this on. To make the old man look him in the eyes—and better yet, make him dependent on him—knowing that he was responsible for Jake's unemployment. Turnabout was fair play.

"I'd be thrilled to take Kingston home," Jake said calmly. "I'll be right there."

"Great! Thank you. We need the bed for another patient."

"On my way."

Jake drove to Mercy and walked inside the building with a detached amusement that he couldn't explain. He was going to repay Kingston's crotchety ill will with kindness and good cheer.

It wasn't about feeling superior to him in any way. It was about not giving in to the old man's negative energy. That's what it was: positive orneriness. Yeah, he liked that term. He was exercising PO.

Besides, it would be the last time he'd ever see the old man. There was no friggin' way he was going anywhere near any of the Nashes again—and especially not near Charlie. She could walk her own damn self down the aisle at her cousin's wedding. And the rest of them could all drive off a cliff, for all he cared. Especially the psychotic firebug of a bride.

Jake took the elevator to the second floor and walked down to room 217, his hands jammed into the pockets of his jeans. He was determined to give Kingston only a ride, and not a piece of his mind.

"Hello, old-timer," he said.

Kingston turned his head and eyed him sourly. He had the grace to flush a bit pink, but not enough to apologize for siccing his granddaughter on Jake's livelihood. "What are *you* doing here?"

Jake smiled pleasantly. "I'm here to take you home."

"The hell you are. Where's Charlie?"

"I'm not sure. Nobody seems to be able to reach her. So the nurses called me to give you a lift."

"I ain't goin' anywhere with you. Bad enough that I let you torture me after surgery."

"Aw, King—don't be like that. Besides, thanks to you, I no longer have a paying job. So I'm starting up a local taxi service." He winked.

"What?"

"You haven't heard? Charlie did a bang-up job present-ing your case, and the town council finally sided with you. Congrats."

Kingston's head retracted a little into his pillow, so that he looked like a turtle pulling toward its shell. His rheumy eyes searched Jake's face from under those bushy gray eye-brows. What was he feeling? Triumph? Guilt? Both?

What was he looking for in Jake? Resentment?

Jake refused to show him any. "C'mon. You'll be my first fare. It seems fitting. Don't deny me the pleasure."

"I ain't givin' you a plugged nickel."

"Fine. Then it's a practice run, and you're my crabby old guinea pig. How's that?" He entered the room, unfazed by the lack of a warm welcome.

"You got some nerve . . ."

"That I do. It comes in handy." Jake looked around for the old man's belongings. There didn't seem to be any.

On the opposite wall from the bed stood a tall gray cabi-net with narrow doors. Jake opened one of them.

"Hey! Get out of there," Kingston said.

Inside, there were a few personal things and items of clothing: a blue chambray shirt, some ancient frayed khaki work pants, an even more ancient brown leather belt, and a pair of beat-up brown lace-ups.

"Get out!" the old man hollered. "You trying to steal my watch?"

Jake nodded. "That's it exactly," he said. "I've always wanted a battered Timex," he added with a mischievous grin. "Plus your wallet and this flip phone. But what I covet most of all is the huge bug-eyed sunglasses that make you resemble a giant fly. That's a look that I've aspired to for a very long time."

Kingston glared at him. "Sure, get your jollies at my expense, you smug bastard."

"Aw, Kingston. Don't be like that. Think of it this way. Thanks to you, Silverlake now has an all-volunteer fire department. Well, I'm your volunteer." Jake opened the other side of the makeshift armoire and found two clear plastic bags with drawstrings hanging from a hook. He took one and began dropping Nash's things into it.

"What are you doing? Stop that!"

"King, I'm going to take you home. So that means your things, too."

"I told you, I'm not goin' anywhere with you."

"Your choice. But the hospital needs your bed, and the next patient needs a place to put his stuff. So . . ." Jake closed the doors of the cabinet and headed for the bathroom next, to pick up any toiletries the old man had in there.

He scooped up a razor, a travel-sized can of shaving cream, a travel-sized stick of Right Guard deodorant, a toothbrush, and a half-used tube of Sensodyne toothpaste, adding them all to the bag. His gaze fell next on a box of Depends. Poor Kingston. It couldn't be easy for a man so proud to rely on such a product.

"Get out of there!" King hollered. "Leave that stuff alone."

He was probably mortified that Jake had seen the disposable underwear. How could this be handled sensitively? Jake took the opaque liner from the trash can and dropped the Depends into it, concealing the packaging from the glance of a casual observer.

"Okay, you're good to go," he said, emerging from the bathroom. "Ready?" Jake stepped over to where Kingston's discharge papers lay on a counter with a speckled laminate top. He put out a hand for them.

"Don't you touch those!" the old man barked. "Those are none of your business, you hear?" Something close to hysteria had bubbled close to the surface. "They're private."

"All right," Jake said calmly, holding up a hand palm out. "I'll let you take those yourself, then." He set down the bags and pushed the wheelchair closer to Kingston's bed. "Let's get you into your chariot."

"Let's get you outta my face." Kingston's eyes blazed with hostility.

Jake met his gaze coolly, with as much compassion as he could dredge up. "You want to call a cab from Austin or San Antone? You want to roll yourself home along the highway? Okay. So be it. I'll drop off your belongings." And he turned on his heel, exiting the room with the plastic bags.

"Get back here! You . . . you . . . thief! You've been thieving taxpayers' money for twelve years now, and now you're thieving my things!"

Jake ignored him.

"Stop! Thief! Help!"

Jake, standing just outside, heard a squeak of bedsprings, a scuffle with the bedcovers, and then muttered curses. Then there came an *oof* as Kingston toppled into the wheelchair, followed by more mumbled curses.

As Jake walked toward the nurses' station, Kingston yelled "Thief!" again, and Mia emerged, looking half-worried, half-exasperated. "What's going on?"

"Just a little motivation," Jake said with a wink. "Do me a favor and make yourself disappear." He started walking.

Kingston Nash bellowed like an angry bull.

He emerged from room 217 wild-eyed and wild-whiskered, rolling himself in the chair and spitting like an angry alley cat.

"I've had it with your impudence, young Braddock. Strutting around town, playing the hero, playing everyone for a fool . . ."

Jake stopped, turned, and waited for the old man to

catch up to him. "Great," he said. "Now we can get going." He headed for the exit.

"Get back here! Give me my stuff, or I'm gonna kick your ass."

"Gotta catch me first, King." Jake picked up the pace.

Cussing, Nash rolled after him, right out the sliding doors and into the parking lot.

"Look at you go! What a trouper." Jake approached him, dropped the bags in his lap, and then grabbed the handles of the wheelchair.

"Hey! Stop that. I never agreed to go with you."

Jake ignored him and rolled him right up to the Durango.

Like a little kid, Nash stomped one of his feet on the ground, then the other.

"Hey, those hips seem to be working perfectly now."

"Don't patronize me. And I ain't gettin' into that truck. Don't even think about manhandling me, or so help me, I will—"

"What? Gum me to death?" Jake opened the passenger-side door, then rolled Kingston up close to the running board. As the old man opened his mouth to protest, Jake shocked him into silence by picking him up bodily and dropping him onto the seat. "Think you can handle strapping yourself in?"

"How dare you? This is elder abuse! This is—"

"Don't be ridiculous."

"This is kidnapping!"

"It's no such thing, and you know it. This is a friend giving you a ride home."

"I'm no friend of yours," Kingston snapped.

"Only if you want it that way," Jake said.

Because he knew that no matter how much it hurt that Kingston had taken everything away from him, the only way Jake would really lose was if he let it break him.

And Kingston would never break him.

Kingston Nash was still shouting as Jake turned into the driveway of his apartment complex.

"I've had enough of your accusations," Jake said, throwing the Durango into park and turning off the ignition. "You're writing quite the potboiler there, King. High drama. But total fiction." He got out, slammed his door, and rounded the hood to open Kingston's. "C'mon. Let's get you inside and settled."

"Get away from me."

Jake sighed but stood aside.

The old man unfastened his seat belt, twisted, clapped his blue-veined left hand on the vehicle's door, and then swung his legs out. Grabbing the seat with his right hand, he inched down out of the truck while Jake prayed silently that he'd make it safely to the ground.

Thank God.

Kingston eyed him balefully, the breeze stirring the unruly hairs of his eyebrows, tickling their severity. His chin bristles glinted against the sunset, and though the skin underneath them was loose, the determination in his jaw defied age.

All the chips on the old bugger's shoulders seemed to clack together as he and his bony old hips took a step toward his front door, and then another and another—refusing any help from Jake.

He made it. Jake's mouth twisted in unwilling admiration as Nash produced the keys from his pocket, all the while trying to maintain the illusion that he didn't need to hang on to the doorknob to stand up.

As Jake followed with his bag of things, he tried not to see as King hesitated, casting a dour, hopeless glance at what waited for him inside. A television instead of a wife. A case of Ensure instead of a home-cooked meal. A silent silver-framed facsimile of a family.

Nash walked down the narrow hallway to his bedroom, using his hands on the walls to steady himself. Charlie's suitcase stood next to the closet. Jake averted his eyes from it, put the plastic bag on the couch, and placed the Depends discreetly in the bathroom as the old man got into bed, fully dressed, without a word.

On his nightstand was a picture of a smiling Babe Nash. Jake averted his eyes from that, too.

"You want to put on some pajamas?" he asked.

"No. Why are you still here?"

"I figured I'd wait for you to break out some floral paper, spray some cologne on it, and write me a thank-you note."

"Ha. Good one." Kingston rolled over and faced the wall.

"You hungry?"

"Go away."

Jake closed his eyes. He opened them to see Babe still smiling from the photograph, and he retreated to the kitchen. In a cupboard, he found a can of something advertised as hearty beef stew. In another, he found bowls.

He nuked the stew in the microwave, made some instant coffee, and popped a vanilla pudding free of its plastic yoke. He piled everything on an old black tin tray with a faded red rooster on it and added a paper towel and a spoon. Then he walked it all into Kingston's bedroom and set it down next to him.

"You need to eat something, old-timer."

"You need to buzz off. I can't believe you're still here."

"I can't, either. But here's the thing: I really need some lessons in how to be rude."

Kingston rolled over. "Is that so? Well, watch and learn, boy." His left eye twitched. It seemed involuntary, couldn't have been a wink. His stomach growled audibly. With a sigh, he struggled to a sitting position.

The old man said nothing as Jake adjusted the pillows behind his back for him. Then he set the tray on his lap.

"Why?" Nash asked him simply. "Why are you doing this? For revenge? Because it makes you happy to see me on the verge of helplessness?"

Jake's chest tightened. He shook his head. "No."

"Because it amuses you?"

"No."

"Are you here out of guilt, Braddock?"

Jake looked him squarely in the eye. "I have nothing to feel guilty about."

Nash held his gaze for what seemed like an eternity before he dropped his own to the beef stew. "I know." His hands shook.

So he knew? That it must have been Brandon at fault? He was finally going to admit it?

"I know you don't have nothin' to feel guilty about, son."

That word again. That word with its serrated edges.

"But I surely don't know why it is that you're here."

"I'm here, you old curmudgeon—" The word came out of the farthest reaches of Jake's subconscious. It was Babe's word for Kingston, and it seemed to startle both of them. "Because I . . . *care* . . . about you, and I always have. Always will. Whether you like it or not. Whether you're a jerk about it or not. Maybe you and your family took me in out of casual pity, not thinking about it too much. But it meant the world to me—" His voice broke, and he hated himself for it.

"It meant the world to me, to have a grandfather like you. I guess you never understood that. Maybe you don't give a rat's ass. Maybe you're just focused on everything you lost that night, and that's your God-given right. You can be as sour and crotchety and ungrateful as you want. It doesn't change how I feel. And I felt the same way about Grandma Babe. Still do. Even if I didn't love you for your own sake, I'd love you for *hers*."

Kingston had hunched himself over the tray. His face was silhouetted by the lamplight. He remained utterly silent.

"I know you'll never forgive me for not saving her—" Jake broke off.

One by one, droplets were falling from the darkened, craggy landscape of Kingston's face, right into the stew. The old man was crying.

"It ain't you I have to forgive, son. It ain't you. It's me."

Jake stared at him. "What are you talking about?"

King's shoulders shook silently.

"Hey, don't do that, old-timer." Jake set his hand on Kingston's back, rubbing uncertainly.

"I knew I needed to repair that lamp cord. I *knew* it. Dang thing was frayed all to hell. But I had better things to do . . ." He pushed away the tray and sank his face into his hands. "Better. Things. To. Do."

Utterly shocked, Jake didn't know what to say.

"And now I got all the time in the world to do 'em. Until the grim reaper snatches me off this earth and drops me into hell for killing my own wife."

Jake sat down heavily on the mattress next to the old man. "Kingston. I don't know where you got that idea, but it's not true."

"It is."

"No. It's not. Look, I don't know how to tell you this . . . and it's not as if it matters, especially not after all this time. But I've seen the report. The one Old George wrote up at the time."

Nash made a hacking noise in the back of his throat. "Yeah. The one that said 'Inconclusive. Accidental.' I know he was just sparing my feelings . . ."

"Except it didn't."

"What in Sam Hill are you talkin' about?"

"King. You weren't at fault. I wasn't at fault, either. But George gave you a doctored report. Because he didn't want you to see who was. And he didn't want anyone in your family to see who it was, either."

Nash stared at him, his jaw going slack. His mouth worked, and it took him a while to get the words out. "Why not?"

"Why do you think, King?"

The old man just shook his head.

"Because he couldn't have handled knowing the truth. And neither could you."

There was a pause that stretched for an eternity.

Then Nash closed his rheumy eyes. "No . . . no . . . *no*. Not Brandon."

"It was an accident. He was smoking out back," Jake said quietly. "He tossed the butt into a pile of leaves near the kitchen door."

"No."

"He was a kid. A sixteen-year-old kid. George was worried about what it would do to Brandon, having his grandmother's death on his conscience. He was afraid it would destroy him, and his relationships with you and his parents . . . And with Charlie."

"That wasn't George's call to make!" Kingston shouted. "How could he? I'll wring his wrinkled old neck!"

"He did it because he thought it was for the best, King. Because he's got a big heart. That's the only reason."

Nash's fists twisted in the sheets. His legs twitched. Jake was afraid he'd dump the bowl of stew onto his bedcovers.

"He did it," Jake continued, "because he was your friend. And he felt terrible, too, that the Fire and Rescue crew didn't get there in time. He felt partially responsible for Babe's death."

The old man cursed a blue streak that had his beige curtains blushing before the end of it.

"Why do you think Old George has never said a word when you've gone on your rampages at the town council meetings?" Jake said. "Never defended us. Always let someone else do the talking."

"I'm-a kill 'im."

Jake nodded. "Okay. You do that. But you might want to buy him a beer first."

"Brandon. That boy . . . he's done his best to screw up his life. He knows. He didn't need anybody to tell him."

Jake sighed.

"But all this time," Kingston said, "he's let you take the blame. That I do find hard to forgive."

Jake waved a hand at him. "Oh, c'mon. He hasn't been here. How was he to know?"

Nash looked up at him from under his bushy gray eyebrows. "He knows." His mouth flattened into a thin line. "I'm sorry, son. For what we've all put you through. Real sorry."

"It's . . . it's in the past. It's done. Let's lay it to rest." Jake looked at the photo of Babe, smiling from the nightstand. "It's what she would want. You know that."

The two men locked eyes.

Nash nodded. "Sure is." Then he did something that knocked the wind out of Jake.

He reached out and put his arms around him. Patted him on the shoulder. "I've been a right 'rageous asshole to you, boy. But I want you to know . . . you *are* like a grandson to me."

Jake sat frozen, unable to breathe.

Then he hugged the bony old bugger right back, his elbow settling right into the stew.

Grandma Babe seemed to laugh from her photograph as

he pulled away to clean up the mess. And she also issued a challenge to him: *Don't ruin a bride's wedding day. No matter what she's done, that's cruel. You promised to stand up for Will as best man, and I raised all my boys to be men of their word. That includes you, Jake Braddock.*

He cursed silently as he rolled his soiled sleeve above the elbow and supervised Kingston while the old fart ate his stew. He rewarded him by bringing him a Lone Star beer to complement his vanilla pudding dessert, and repressed a smile when it brought on a burp. He turned on the TV for him, dropped a hand on Nash's shoulder before he left, and told him he'd call to check on him later.

Then Jake looked once more at Babe's photograph. She seemed to be waiting for an answer.

"Yes, ma'am," he said aloud.

He could have sworn she blew him a kiss.

Chapter 28

FIREMEN'S BALL.

If Charlie was going to pull this off, she didn't have a moment to lose.

And it was the only way she could think of to make things up to Jake.

She'd spoken with half of Bridezilla's vendors already: Kristina, Amelie, Maggie . . . they were all on board. Maggie had even lent Charlie her old Cutlass—along with a pair of socks and a handful of superhero Band-Aids—since Progress was still at the ranch.

All the Braddocks were probably still there, too. Had the family had enough bonding time?

Charlie searched for her phone so she could call Lila. She couldn't find it anywhere in her bag—it must still be in Lila's Suburban, where everything had fallen out of her purse. Charlie sighed and turned the key in Maggie's car.

As she pulled out of the parking spot in front of Petal Pushers, she witnessed Big Red drive by at a leisurely pace,

Jake behind the wheel. It was followed by the two other Silverlake Fire and Rescue vehicles.

Charlie drove back yet again to Silverlake Ranch. She squealed through the gate and down the drive, relieved to see the Suburban sitting where she'd left it.

Grouchy came galloping up, as usual, barking a welcome and wagging his tail.

She jumped out, scratched him behind the ears, and then banged on the front door.

Deck answered it, looking drained. As if he could barely muster the energy for surprise at seeing her there again. "Charlie?"

"I have an idea," she said quickly. "Is Lila still here?"

"To be honest, this isn't a great time for company—"

Ouch. "Deck, I know I'm not your favorite person right now, but this is important. By the way, Mick took your cat to the vet. I wasn't sure you'd heard, with all that's been going on. A spark lit his tail on fire, but he's being taken care of now."

"What?" For Deck, the emotional reaction was extreme. He followed that up with a more measured, "Thanks for letting me know. Don't know if you heard this one. Will's wedding just got called off. That crazy—"

"I know."

"You *know*? How? Oh," he said. "Right. You drove Felicity back to the hotel."

"Yes. So you wouldn't have to deal with her, on top of everything else. But the wedding—that's what I want to talk with you guys about."

He didn't move. "There is no wedding."

"Well, no, but all the stuff for it has been ordered, so let's turn it into something else."

"Listen, Charlie," he began in a shut-it-all-down tone.

"Lila!" she yelled past him. "Lila! I need to talk to you."

"Haven't you and your grandfather and the rest of the Nashes done enough damage?" Deck asked. He was quiet enough, but he was also gritting his teeth. "Can't you let Jake have his sister back? Don't make it worse for them."

"This is *for* Jake. This thing. This redo of the wedding. I want to turn it into a—" She tried to rush by him, but he clamped his hands on either side of the doorway.

"What the hell are you talking about?"

"Lila!" she shouted.

"What?" Her friend finally came around the corner and into the hallway. "What's going on?"

"We have a chance to do something really great here— change the wedding into a firemen's ball! To raise money for Jake and the guys. There's food, booze, flowers, linens, tables, and chairs—but we have to get the word out. We have to . . ." Charlie let her voice trail off in surrender as Lila just stared at her.

But then her friend flashed a huge smile, ducked under her brother's arm, and rushed Charlie, wrapping her in a bear hug. "Brilliant. That's just . . . brilliant!" She hugged her, and Lila and Charlie jumped up and down, like little kids.

Deck dropped his hands and took two steps backward. "Women are nuts," he said to nobody in particular. "Totally nuts."

"There's so much to do." Charlie's voice faltered.

"We'll work all night if we have to. You can stay with me and Amelie when we're done, and then we can all get ready together tomorrow," Lila said.

Charlie bit her lip, searching for ideas.

"I can talk to Mayor Fisk and get a mass e-mail out," Declan said. The girls turned and stared at him. "Maybe we can get the cheer squad to start a telephone blitz to older people," he added. Into the silence, he said with a shrug, "Jake deserves this."

Lila let out a whoosh of breath. "Thanks, Deck."

He gave her a curt nod.

"So, here's what we're going to do about the Old Barn,"
Lila said. "We'll simply set up behind it. There's a huge tent
coming tomorrow anyway. It's the perfect backdrop, because it will reinforce the need for the fire department!
But . . . what if people have plans?"

Charlie squared her shoulders. "They can cancel them.
This is too important. Stress that. We can have a hospital
and a fire department, but we have to raise the money—and
everyone has to help. It's their town, their responsibility.
And it's also a way of saying a big thank-you . . . to Old
George, Jake and Mick, and Grady, Tommy, Hunter, and
Rafael for being there all these years. And for all the extras
they do."

Deck nodded slowly, thoughtfully.

"So you'll get Mayor Fisk's office to help?" Charlie
asked Declan.

"Yeah. And I'll bet First Presbyterian's women's auxil-
iary will step up to the plate for the phone calls, since the
Fire and Rescue guys put their new roof on . . ."

"Perfect," Lila said. "Charlie, let's go down to the Old
Barn and take inventory on what got damaged, what we
have, and what's still coming. Now, how can we get an entire town to keep a secret?"

ॐ

Charlie and Lila stepped gingerly through the wreckage of the
blackened, sooty Old Barn. Horrified, Charlie stayed silent.

"Oh no. Oh no . . ." Tears sprang to Lila's eyes and ran
down her cheeks. "Poor Declan. He worked so hard on it all."

Charlie hugged her, rubbing her back. "So did you. I
know you did. On the interior."

Lila shrugged that off; she just mopped at her eyes with her sleeve.

The whole place smelled awful, of burned electrical wiring, melted plastic, exploded chemicals, and smoked cedar combined.

Most of the roof was gone. Most of the windows were intact, though a few had blown out, due to the heat and expanding gases.

They picked their way through the filthy, wet debris, without much hope of salvaging anything. The furniture was history, even though most of it was still standing. It was soaked from the fire hoses, and the burned smell would never come out of the stuffing or fabric. Same went for the rugs. The framed black-and-white photographs on the walls were trashed.

The kitchen was in decent shape, which was good news. The fire hadn't reached it. But a check of the storage closet revealed devastation: puddles of melted candles and white chocolate; broken porcelain and glass; and gelatinous red tatters on wire hangers.

"It looks like someone hung bacon in here," Lila muttered.

"What is . . . ?!" Charlie pointed and dissolved into giggles. "It's the horrible Vegas hooker bridesmaid dresses, with their matching gloves!"

Lila stared for a moment and then shrieked with laughter. "Wait, where's my phone . . . I have to get pictures of this."

"I honestly cannot think of a more fitting fate for them. Can you?"

"Nope." *Snap, snap, snap.* Lila documented the ghoulish remnants of the gowns.

"You should send the pictures to Amelie. It'll make her day."

"Already done." Lila chuckled, and then went silent again.

Nothing else was funny. The destruction was hard to take. They picked their way through the rest of the mess more soberly and then stepped out the rear door of the barn, where they made another odd discovery.

"Look: The porta-potty melted."

"That's nuts. Who knew it could?"

"It looks like something out of a Salvador Dalí painting—like those melting watches."

"It's *so* weird-looking . . ."

Lila's cell phone rang while they were examining it. "Lila Braddock," she answered with a sigh. She listened to the caller for a moment, then her eyebrows shot up. "The Barnums did *what*? Reversed the charges? You've got to be kidding me. Wait, why does this surprise me? Bridezilla had to get her freakishness from somewhere. I am so sorry."

Charlie's mouth fell open. *Who?* she mouthed.

Caterer, Lila mouthed back. To the person on the phone she said, "Wait, wait, wait. It's not a total loss. You have the fifty percent deposit, right? That cleared? Okay, good. Well, we have a plan. Let me tell you about it. I was actually just going to call you, along with a lot of other people . . . I can at least get you a tax write-off on your loss."

Lila explained the firemen's ball concept. Her phone kept ringing, and she explained it to the wine/liquor vendor, the equipment rental people, and the tent people as well.

Meanwhile, Charlie called and ordered another porta-potty. It was the least she could do.

Chapter 29

O N THE EVENING OF SILVERLAKE'S FIRST ANNUAL
firemen's ball, the sky was tinged rose as the sun set,
bathing the trees in gold and giving its blessing to the event.
White tablecloths fluttered in the breeze, and the tent was
lit with a thousand tiny white lights. Every table held a bouquet of velvety red roses and two battery-operated candles.

If the dark silhouette of the Old Barn in the background
looked a little like a haunted house, that couldn't be helped.
Charlie had vetoed Lila's idea that they put plastic jack-o'-
lanterns inside.

The band was set up under its own small awning. To
Charlie's bemusement, they struck up Springsteen's "I'm
on Fire," playing it with gusto until Lila intervened and told
them to maybe wait until after the guests had had a few
drinks.

Charlie nervously smoothed the skirt of the stunning
white cocktail dress that had been Bridezilla's first choice
of wedding gown. Amelie had laughed like a loon when she

heard the news that the wedding was off, and had volunteered to add a panel to the back of the size four frock so that size ten Charlie could wear it. No charge.

Lila looked equally stunning in the red lace number, her dark hair pulled up under the mantilla, her lipstick siren red. She walked over to Charlie, spread Bridezilla's fan open, and fluttered her eyelashes. "You look gorgeous."

"Thanks. You too." Charlie looked around and swallowed hard, pressing her fingertips together so that her hands wouldn't shake. What if Jake didn't come? What if nobody else showed up, either?

"Lila, I'm starting to freak out. What if we only raise nine dollars tonight for the cause?"

"Amelie's coming, so we already have fifty dollars," Lila said. "And so is Deck. And I'm here, and you're here. So that's two hundred." She checked her watch. "Vic the plumber is coming, because I told him you'd dance with him."

"What?"

"Get over it. He thinks you're hot. One dance."

"But—" Charlie subsided at Lila's squint.

"The whole knitting circle is coming," she continued. "Everyone off shift at Mercy is coming. Anyone remotely mobile is coming from the nursing home—the bus is bringing them. Oh, and the porta-potty guy agreed to buy a ticket and stay if *I* save *him* a dance . . . He's almost here with the replacement you ordered. Who knew that hand sanitizer was flammable? I can't believe that Jake never told me that."

Charlie plucked nervously at her skirt again. "What if Jake doesn't show?"

"He'll show. Jake may be pissed at you, pissed at the entire Nash clan, but he would never take out his anger on an innocent bride. No matter how much of a pain in the butt or a walking fire hazard she may be."

"What if he's heard that the wedding's off?"

"What if you discovered the word 'optimism' in the dictionary, huh?" Lila's cell phone chirped. "That's Kristina—she's here with the cakes even though the Barnums stiffed her, too. I need to go help her get them in."

"I can—"

"You can go to the bar and get yourself a glass of wine. Everything is in place except that damned porta-potty. You've worked harder than ten men, and now you need to relax. Look—" Lila pointed. "People are starting to pour in. We'll have a good crowd here before Jake and the boys show up."

She was right. A steady stream of cars was turning down the drive. Grouchy was having a field day, welcoming them all.

The band struck up "Peaceful Easy Feeling" by the Eagles, and Charlie headed to the bar, as ordered. She was stunned to find her cousin manning it.

"Will?" She stared at him.

He lifted an eyebrow sardonically. "Lila pressed me into service. And, hey, I'm not one to miss a party—especially one that my psycho ex's parents have already paid for part of."

Helplessly, Charlie began to laugh.

Will did, too.

"So . . . you're okay?" she asked.

"I'm better than okay. I'm weirdly relieved. I was feeling a lot of stuff, a lot of emotions, as we arrived in town, but it wasn't . . . uh . . . good stuff. My stomach was in knots. I had a headache that wouldn't go away. I couldn't do a damn thing right for Felicity, either. She was driving me crazy."

"I know the feeling," Charlie murmured. She reached across the bar and hugged him. "Still, I'm sorry. I just want you to be happy."

"Me too. And that wasn't going to end happy." A shadow crossed his face, but it was quickly gone. "By the way, I know my dad can be an ass, but did you have to toss a drink in his face?"

"Yeah, Will, I kind of did. Sorry, but he was way out of line. Nobody should question Jake's actions or motives that night. He was braver than any of us—and he still is, by the way. He will still show up this evening to help you out as a groomsman, knowing that he'll have to face the whole damn family again."

He searched her face, then finally nodded. "I know, Charlie. That's why I'm here to help out. We owe him. We owe him big. So, what can I get you?"

"A glass of chardonnay, if you don't mind."

"Coming right up." Will smoothly uncorked a chilled bottle of wine and deftly poured it for her. He'd bartended in college for extra money, and he hadn't lost the skill set. "Here you are."

"Thanks." Charlie accepted the glass and pressed it to her lips as she stepped aside for the line of people that had grown behind her, people who were equally surprised to see the onetime groom playing bartender.

The chardonnay was cool, sunny, and oaky on her tongue. She watched Will for signs that he was devastated underneath his easygoing surface, and saw none. The tightness around his mouth was no longer there. The anxiety etched around his eyes had vanished. He was no longer a deer in Felicity's headlights; he was a dear behind the scenes. He tipped back his head and laughed at something someone had said. When someone else asked where the bride was, he took it in stride. "Don't have a clue. Washing dishes to pay back her parents?"

Charlie's hands had stopped shaking when she turned around. The entire town, it seemed, was pouring down the Braddocks' gravel drive. There was Mayor Fisk; and Jean-Paul with a massive covered dish from his restaurant; and

Dottie with her partner, Libby. There were the Adlers and the Wrights and the Ramirezes and the Giardinos. The people just kept coming.

Bridezilla's massive four-tiered cake had been transformed for tonight: a sculpted red fireman's hat sat on the top instead of the prototypical bride and groom. Kristina had outdone herself, adding small marzipan dalmatians and red fire hydrants and little yellow ladders here and there. And as for the groom's cake, she must have remade it from scratch. It was shaped like a fire truck.

Kristina was a mad genius. Charlie grinned and turned to check on the caterers, but of course she didn't need to, because Lila was in charge. The caterers were calmly setting up their buffet stations. Thank God Felicity hadn't insisted on a sit-down dinner.

Feeling useless and on edge, Charlie took another sip of her wine and choked on it as she spied a familiar red Durango coming down the gravel drive. Instantly, she felt sick. She couldn't face Jake. No matter how much money they ended up raising tonight, he would still never forgive her for her stint as Granddad's proxy.

She pressed her lips together, flattening them. Granddad should be here. He, of all people, owed it to Jake to be here. She didn't care if she had to pay for his ticket herself, but she was going to go get him, drag his bony butt here by force if she had to.

A brilliant excuse for getting out of Dodge! But she couldn't get to where Progress was parked without heading straight in Jake's direction. Ugh.

Charlie homed in on the one thing that hadn't gone swimmingly: the blue plastic porta-potty being unloaded in the middle of the party. Something, Lila claimed, went wrong at every event. Oh well. Better a late porta-potty than none.

Charlie hurried over to the man sliding the awkward,

unglamorous thing off a flatbed trailer. He had a long gray ponytail that matched his baggy gray sweatshirt. "Hi," she said, producing her most professional smile. "Does anyone need to sign paperwork for this?"

"Darlin', you are a sight for sore eyes," Porta Man said with a leer as the fake diamond in his ear winked in the dying sun. He looked her up and down, then whistled. "You can sign anything you want."

"Ha," she said awkwardly.

"Preferably on my naked body." He waggled his eyebrows.

"Funny." Charlie turned to retreat but realized that Jake was only a few yards away. Oh God. Had he seen her? She spun back toward her admirer.

"You know, this is only a side business for me," he said, too casually. "My real job is day trading . . ."

"Oh, really? Great. That's great." Wait. Was she hallucinating, or had Jake been pushing Granddad, of all people, in a wheelchair?

Charlie craned her neck and peered out of the corner of her eye. Dear Lord, that *was* Granddad. But when had he been discharged from the hospital? And why would he be escorted by Jake Braddock? Willingly?

Porta Man touched his earring in what seemed to be a gesture of self-love. "And I actually own a number of properties out in—"

Jake had stopped at the cake table, looking confused. Then he saw the huge banner that stretched across the back side of the damaged Old Barn: WELCOME TO SILVERLAKE'S FIRST FIREMEN'S BALL! His mouth fell open. And his gaze homed in, unfortunately, on Charlie.

Instantly, Charlie wanted to disappear. He didn't look delighted or excited. He didn't look enchanted by her. He looked almost angry.

"Excuse me," she said to Porta Man. And she sidestepped him, closing herself neatly into the blue plastic cube he'd unloaded. With a trembling hand, she secured the door and trapped herself inside.

Oh, nice move, Charlie. You coward!

At least it was completely clean, smelling of disinfectant. And she still had her wine.

Even nicer. Drinking in a porta-potty. That is classy with a "k"!

Charlie aimed an imaginary middle finger at the mocking voice in her own head. Then she raised the glass defiantly and gulped.

What is wrong with you? Wearing another woman's reject wedding gown, hiding in a public toilet from the man you've always secretly loved . . .

"That's ridiculous," she said aloud. "I do not love him."

But she did. There was no escaping it. She loved Jake Braddock. She loved the way he always looked just a little bit rumpled. She loved the subtle threads of silver appearing here and there in his dark curls. She loved the faint shadows under his eyes. She even loved his outrage when she'd defended him to her family.

"I *can't* love him," she said to the blue plastic walls, which didn't appear particularly interested. "I don't even live here. Our history is way too complicated. And I just destroyed his job."

The blue plastic remained unmoved by her protests.

Why did I do that? Destroy his job?

Because you were spineless.

I wasn't! Granddad was having a medical episode! A heart attack!

Because he was throwing a tantrum, like a two-year-old, over getting his way.

She was making herself crazy.

Charlie nearly jumped out of Bridezilla's wedding gown as a none-too-gentle knock came on the door.

"Hey, you done in there yet? I really need to pee." Lila's voice.

"Go away!" ordered Charlie, as a text came in on her phone, which she'd jammed into the bust of her gown. Brandon: I'm not gonna make the wedding.

Surprise, surprise.

But I'll try and visit soon.

Now that *was* a surprise.

"Come out of there, Charlie the Chicken. That's a public facility, not your personal meditation chamber. And there's now officially a line. Your grandfather has to go."

Charlie leaned her forehead against the blue wall and banged it gently, once, then twice. Then she drained her wine, shoved her phone back into its hiding spot, faced the door, and unlocked it. She squared her shoulders and pushed the door open slowly, coming face-to-face with an exasperated Lila.

Jake and Granddad stood behind her. All three of them raised their eyebrows at the wineglass in her hand. Several other party guests looked on.

"Oh, shut up," she muttered, feeling a flush rising from her neck to her forehead.

"Didn't say a word," Lila said. But her tone was full of irony.

Stone-faced, Jake pushed Granddad forward.

"When did you get out of the hospital?" Charlie asked Granddad. "And since when are you two getting along?"

"Since some people don't answer their phones and have started drinking in the john," the old man jibed. "Which means other people have to come get their ailing relatives."

"Granddad, I'm sorry . . . I was busy . . ."

"What the hell happened to Will's wedding?" he barked.

Charlie sighed. "It's complicated. Ask him. He's bartending."

"Gonna greet the guest of honor properly?" Lila asked, changing the subject and inclining her head toward her brother.

Jake remained expressionless.

"Uh . . ." Charlie stepped out of the loo and edged around him, so close that she caught his scent: leather, the outdoors, freshly mown grass.

He didn't turn a hair.

Lila blundered on. "Jake, this whole event was Charlie's idea, you know . . ." Subtle as a heifer at the hairdresser's.

Shut up, Lila!

Charlie stole a sidelong glance at him, but his expression remained enigmatic. She could discern no warmth and no forgiveness in those black Braddock eyes. Well, what had she expected?

His sister kept flailing. "She's worked very hard to pull this off . . ."

"Oh, clearly," Jake said after a pause during which even Lila squirmed. "She deserves a medal of commendation."

Ouch. It was all Charlie needed to hear. She turned away, ready to flee again, just as Granddad cleared his throat.

"Young Braddock, my granddaughter's not at fault here—"

Charlie stiffened. *No.* She was done with being spineless. *It's time to own up to my part in this and take responsibility. Like it or not.* She turned back around. "Yes, actually she is."

They all stared at her.

"I *am* at fault. Granddad is about to say that he bullied me into standing up for him at the town council meeting. But the truth is that I should have told him no, especially since I didn't feel comfortable doing it.

"And, Jake, I should have given you a heads-up long before the day of the meeting, but I was afraid to mention it because . . . the timing was so awkward . . . and I didn't want to upset you. So because neither of those options was *emotionally comfortable* for me, I avoided them." She swallowed and wiped her damp palms on Bridezilla's dress.

"That's on me. And I have to face up to that. I allowed myself to be manipulated by you, Granddad, because you threw a tantrum. And by doing so, and then by sticking my head in the sand, I blindsided and essentially betrayed you, Jake—*for the second time.*" Tears welled in her eyes.

Don't you dare cry. Suck it up.

She swallowed the lump of shame blocking her throat. "I can't tell you how sorry I am."

No reaction from Jake.

"I'm sorry," she whispered again, wishing he would say something, anything. Wasn't owning up to your failings supposed to bring relief? Freedom from guilt? Praise of some kind from somewhere?

Charlie stood there, miserable. Maybe God was up there cheering, but she couldn't hear Him. That was for sure.

"So you think a *party* makes up for it?" Now the raw anger escaped him and shimmered accusingly in the air. His eyes blazed with contempt.

"No," she said, her voice low. "No, I don't. I don't think it comes anywhere close to undoing the damage. But . . . I love you, Jake. I always have. I always will. So . . . I had to start somewhere."

He just stared at her.

Say something. Say anything. Say you love me, too.

But not a word crossed his lips. His mouth tightened; he clenched and unclenched his hands.

Enter Porta Man, who spied Lila from not so afar and lumbered back over. "*Mamacita!* You are looking *muy bueno*. You promised me a dance, remember?" He gestured at the blue cube. "For delivering the Johnny-on-the-spot?"

Lila squinted balefully at him from behind her fan. "Right. Hello, handsome. Nice timing."

❧

Charlie walked away, looking forlorn and defeated. Jake was pissed at himself for being pissed, but he couldn't help it, which pissed him off even more.

"That went well," said cranky old Kingston Nash.

"Shut it, old-timer," growled Jake.

"Wish I could, but I'm too dang old to have tact or restraint. I did have a full-blown tantrum and worked myself into a heart attack. So excuse her if she freaked. Now, don't be a dumb-ass. You love her right back—it's as plain as the nose on your face. And take it from a long-married man: If you love her, then it really don't matter if you're offended or if she's wrong. It's your job to get over yourself an' make it right. You get what I'm saying?"

"No."

"Well, guess what? I don't care. Because I gotta pee. So take your mind off things and get me into that bathroom, or you're gonna have to change me like a baby."

Reluctantly, Jake laughed. "Okay," he said. But his eyes stayed on Charlie as she moved away through the crowd.

"I'll help him," said Mick from behind. "You go on."

"Aw, great. Another pervert who wants to see me with my pants down," groused Kingston.

"Yeah, that's it." Jake nodded his thanks. "Mick has been dying to get a glimpse of your dried-out old salami," he said, and then went after Charlie.

"Oh yeah," Mick said. "For years now . . ."

Charlie's head was down, her pale neck vulnerable as

she sped off, his Goodbye Girl. She was already a least a
hundred yards ahead of him, making for the bar. Damn, the
woman could walk fast when humiliated.

Her voice echoed in his head. *I had to start somewhere.*

Jake looked around at the hundreds—if not a thousand—
who'd come out to show their support for the Fire and Rescue
crew. He was honestly floored. Touched beyond belief. And
they had come out at her request. For him.

He felt awkward, weird, as if he saw them all from under
a body of water. Like a psychological school of fish, a flood
of emotions circled right under his skin, looking for a bite.

People grinned at him, high-fived him, raised their drinks
to him, and slapped him on the back. Ordinarily, he would
have loved it. But it slowed his progress toward Charlie.

He thanked them for coming out tonight, for their support. He felt his mouth moving, heard words coming out in
his voice, but they didn't seem like his own.

I love you, Jake. I always have. I always will.

When he finally bellied up to the bar, Charlie was gone.

❦

Charlie sat on a hay bale behind the Old Barn, forlorn in
Bridezilla's remade gown. It wasn't very comfortable; the
straw prickled her backside. Noises from the party reached
her: music from the band; the clinking of glasses; the chime
of cutlery against plates; the murmur of voices; and the ring
of laughter.

Her last visual had been of Lila getting Carolina
Shagged by Porta Man on the dance floor. Will had given
Charlie a second glass of wine, which she now nursed
along with her regrets. A lot of them.

A goat stared at her from a small pen nearby, occasionally asking her, "Meh?"

"Don't ask me," she said. "You're clearly smarter than I am."

"Meh," said the goat again.

"What's the meaning of life?" Charlie asked it.

She almost fell off the hay bale when it answered, in Jake Braddock's deep baritone. "The meaning of life is a girl who drives you crazy."

Jake stepped into view, and her heart did a slow roll. *Oh.*

"She wears silly boots to climb ladders," he continued. "And she falls off them. She refuses to stay in the past, where she belongs. She won't speak to me for years but stays friends with my annoying little sister. She lets herself be bullied by a foul-mouthed geezer, but she throws drinks in my defense . . . right before going on the offense. Worst of all, she says goodbye when I want to say hello."

"She sounds like a real pain in the butt," Charlie said weakly.

He nodded. "You have no idea."

"I might."

"She is the kind of person," Jake said, "who would trick a man into wearing a tuxedo to a nonexistent wedding so that he looks like a complete moron."

"Or the star of the show," she offered.

"And what a show it is." For the first time, his lips curved into a smile, and Charlie felt that the sun had come out after a long, cold winter.

"How did you pull this off?" he asked.

"Uh. I'm not sure?"

"You must have had all of twenty-four hours."

"Lila was instrumental in planning it, too. So was Declan."

"Traitors," he said softly but without any heat.

"But it takes an entire town to turn out like this, Jake." She gestured toward the party. "All of Silverlake, young and old. And they did it for you. Because they love you."

She was taken aback when tears sprang to his eyes.

"I love them, too." His voice was gruff. "But more importantly . . ."

She waited, breathless.

"Thank you, Charlie."

That wasn't exactly what she'd been hoping he'd say. Ridiculous, the disappointment. "You don't need to—"

"Yes. I do." He inhaled sharply. "I'm sorry for being harsh. I was hurt." He shifted his weight from foot to foot. "Now. What you said back there . . ."

She waited, still unable to breathe.

Nothing.

Okay. He wasn't going to say it back. Well. That was fine. That was just *fine*. She'd get over him. She'd leave tonight. Right now.

This was excruciating. Awful. The hay dug more needles of pain into her backside, the silk of Felicity's cast-off dress offering little protection.

Abruptly, Charlie got up. "I'm not sure what you're talking about. Don't worry about it."

Jake stared at her as if she'd sprouted a rhinoceros horn. "You said it in front of witnesses, you know."

"Yeah. Heh. In the heat of the moment. By the porta-potty. You know. Just flush it."

His eyebrows drew together. He stepped closer to her, and she backed up.

He came closer still. She sat down again, wobbling on the hay bale.

He leaned over and put one hand to either side of her. He smelled so wonderful and she was so very tempted to kiss him, and yet she was so humiliated that she could die. Right here, right now. Not happy. But with the memory of his face seared into her mind. At least there was that.

"Charlie?"

"Wh-what?"

"You said, 'I love you, Jake. I always have. And I always will.' Did you not say those words, in front of God and everyone?"

Slowly, she nodded.

"And did you mean them?"

Mute, she nodded again. *Oh, kill me now. Someone. Something. Anything.*

But then, miraculously, Jake's expression relaxed. And it told her everything she needed to know.

Charlie felt all the tension and misery drain out of her, making her one with the hay bale as a thousand little stalks impaled her backside. One hundred percent worth it, though.

Because then Jake cupped her face in his hands and kissed her, his mouth gentle on hers. "I love you, too, Charlie. I always have. And I always will."

"Well, why didn't you just say so?"

"Because it was more fun to watch you fall on your face in the mud? Run you down with my truck? Make you chug wine in a porta-potty?"

"You're a very sick and twisted man, Jake Braddock," she said severely.

"True. But you wouldn't have me any other way . . . and I'd walk through fire for you."

Oh, Jake . . .

He kissed her again.

Charlie kissed him right back—until the goat downright blushed, the bright silver moon pulled a cloud over its eyes, and the hay bale told them to get a room.

At last, Jake pulled away. "Since you've gone to all this trouble, don't you think we should at least attend the party for a while?"

She nodded.

"And then, Charlie . . ." Jake looked off into the distance, toward the welcoming lights of the main house. "Maybe you'd walk me home."

She smiled as tears gathered in her eyes, and she took the big, warm hand he extended to her. "Yes, Jake. I can't think of anything in this world that I'd rather do."

Acknowledgments

To Louise Fury for working a miracle. (She is a whirlwind of energy, hard work, humor, and tolerance for crazy authors.) To Kerry Donovan for making this book the best it could be; Claire Zion and Cindy Hwang for believing in the series; and the multitude of other people at Penguin Random House for creating magic behind the scenes. Thank you all.

Keep reading for a special preview of
the next book in the Silverlake Ranch series,

Home with You

Coming from Berkley in Spring 2020!

E VERETT "RHETT" BRADDOCK WAS NOT THE TYPE to hear voices in his head, especially not over the smooth, steady purr of Scarlett, his unapologetically red Porsche. Scarlett always sounded like she ran on single-malt Scotch and sex, not gasoline. But hear voices he did on the afternoon that he pulled into Silverlake, Texas. His hometown had changed.

Silverlake still retained the charm of a small Texas Hill Country town, but it had gotten spit-shined, more picturesque.

He couldn't argue with the changes from a business point of view. Clearly, the town was doing better than it had been when he'd been unceremoniously booted out of it. But it just wasn't the same.

Rhett took in all the storefronts as he cruised down Main Street. Piece A Cake. Obviously a bakery. Amelie. Looked like a fancy dress shop. Sunny's Side Up—thank God, something was the same, besides Griggs' Grocers.

The Tooth Fairies? A dentist. Schweitz's . . . he sighed with relief. Schweitz's had a new coat of paint and an awful garden gnome outside with a pint in his hand, but it was still there.

Oh, and something else was familiar: Silverlake's famous sparkling Fool Fest garlands. He couldn't help grinning. They were a bonus for April Fools', strung between lamp posts lining the main drag. *Better watch out,* Pop used to say with a grin, *Silverlake fools are fair game all month.*

Mama had been a glue-gun-carrying member of the town's holiday committee, and before everything changed, every spring the living room down at the ranch was festooned with tinsel, ribbon, fake flowers, and crepe paper jesters in a mess of harvest colors. The good folk keeping up the tradition of hanging the awful decorations used to say the neighboring towns that mocked them were just jealous.

That last year in Silverlake, Rhett had been telling his family about his rodeo dreams for the New Year. They'd been telling him something else.

As he idled in front of a florist called Petal Pushers, which hadn't existed in his time, he heard, quite clearly, Pop's voice ricochet through his brain. "Son, I ain't gonna tell you again. You get your butt back in that desk chair and fill out those applications."

So he had.

He heard Mama's voice say, "Rhett, you're special. The places you are gonna go . . ."

So he had.

Colonel Akers, his high school algebra teacher: "Sure, you stay here at Silverlake High, you'll be valedictorian by a mile. But life isn't about the easy choices, son. I can't teach you any more than I know myself. Full scholarship? Go. Go to Deerville Academy and push your own envelope. Strain that crazy-smart brain of yours."

So he had.

Declan's voice came to him, too, booming over all the others after their parents had died. Stoic, acerbic, an older brother learning how to be a father on the fly. "You'll get on that plane to Connecticut if I have to knock you out, hog-tie you and toss you in the luggage hold. The horses will always be here. That scholarship won't. Go to Deerville. Go to Harvard or Yale. Go to Wharton. And go to Wall Street."

So he had.

Except not all of the horses are still here, are they, Deck?

Not at Silverlake Ranch. When he'd found out Declan now only kept a few horses on the property, it felt like a slap in the face. That wasn't the hardest slap, though. Rhett's mouth twisted as he remembered one particular conversation. His brother had dropped it casually into a discussion about interest rates. Deck had had the unmitigated gall to give Rhett's old rodeo horse away to the Holt family—without even talking to him about it!

At least the new deal Rhett had just struck with Billy Holt would let him ride Frost whenever he wanted.

Rhett allowed himself a small smile at the thought of Declan's face when he told him what he'd gone and bought this time.

Still idling in front of the ridiculously named florist, Rhett leaned back in his seat and closed his eyes. The leather interior suddenly smelled all wrong. It was buttery and processed, a cologne and not a hide. It wasn't something he thought about in Dallas, but in Silverlake, the difference was notable.

Real leather smelled like a well-worn saddle, a bridle or a harness soaked in a horse's sweat. Real leather wasn't a pale cream color; it was dark and chocolatey and rough in places where a man's calloused hands hadn't buffed it to a working shine.

He clenched the stitched, cushioned steering wheel. German engineers didn't know what reins felt like between a rider's fingers, and probably didn't care.

Scarlett had cost upward of $300,000, and there were plenty of days Rhett thought she was worth it; he certainly enjoyed her company more than any woman he'd dated in recent memory, and she was nothing if not loyal. Still, he'd trade her in half a second just to be home before the accident, fifteen again and back on Frost, his silvery Appaloosa. He couldn't wait to see the old boy. He'd rather see him, in fact, than his brother Declan, though he was worried about him after the devastating loss of the Old Barn. What did that say about Rhett, exactly?

His mouth twisted as he glanced at the passenger seat next to him. Three Red Delicious apples knocked heads in a plastic bag. A bunch of carrots roped together stared up at him eagerly. In the footwell, six Shiner Bocks patiently waited for him to free them from their plastic yokes, condensation staining the top of his crocodile-hide briefcase, which lay outraged on the floor.

The beer was for Frost, who loved it. Pour that dark, fizzy liquid into a bowl and Frost would slurp it right down, twitching his velvety muzzle when the bubbles popped on his tongue. Then he'd show his teeth in a big horsey grin.

Damn, Rhett had missed him.

But you didn't trailer a horse and a western saddle the size of an armchair up to Deerville Academy in Connecticut. And you sure didn't talk to anyone about 4-H or rodeos—especially when they'd already started mocking the fact that he went by Rhett.

Where's Scarlett, Rhett?

I got her right here, boys. He smiled, and gave the dashboard a pat.

Of course, if he wanted to see Frost, he'd have to see Julianna Holt, too. A blessing or a curse? Rhett's smile faded at the thought of her. He'd messed that situation up but good. You didn't screw around with your best friend's little sister, and he'd gone and done just that—only weeks ago in Dallas. He'd bolted from her bed in the morning. And ever since then, he'd been trying to come up with any acceptable explanation to give Grady. Problem: There *was* no explaining to Grady, who'd kill him if he ever found out—and worse, Rhett couldn't stop thinking about Jules. He needed to erase her from his mind.

❧

"You're leaving?" Jules had mumbled, still half-asleep. She opened her hazel eyes and peered at him, the sleepiness chased away by hurt.

"Yeah," Rhett had said, trying not to look at her. He hadn't intended for anything like that to happen, but seeing Julianna Holt all grown up had done something to him that he never could have anticipated, so he went with it. And now he had to make it stop. For even though these last few hours felt about as right as anything Rhett could remember, reality had shown up with the morning sun. And reality was, Rhett had just had a one-night stand with the one person he should have never, ever touched. "You're Grady's little sister! What in the hell was I thinking?"

"Grady's little sister," Jules repeated mechanically. Her face was blank as the white sheet over her hot, curvy, delicious little body.

"You can't tell him, Jules. Promise me. You won't say a word. To anybody. If he finds out, he'll never forgive me."

She lay there, frozen under that sheet.

He almost said something then, knowing how he looked, like a careless man who broke hearts as a habit. But that's what he needed her to think.

"Right," she finally said. There was a pause. "Don't you worry 'bout a thing, Rhett." She said the words slowly, steeped in some emotion that he still couldn't read, no matter how he angled it, how many times he replayed that sentence or her expression in his head. "I won't give your dirty little secret away to anyone—not even my brother."

⁊

Rhett stared out the car window at the riot of flowers in the Petal Pushers window.

That night had been one of the best nights of his life. He should have left differently, though.

Wish I'd never done it . . .

Nah. I'd do it all over again. Twice. At least.

Stop it, Rhett!

Rhett turned off the ignition and stepped out of the car, letting the door close on its own.

He shoved his hands into his pockets, looked up and down Main Street, and then headed into the florist shop. He owed Julianna Holt one big apology, and he'd better do it before he set foot on her family property.

Inside the florist, a gal was arranging a huge bouquet of yellow roses with some fancy greenery. He couldn't help but stare at her bare arms, which sported full sleeves of tattoos: flowers of every imaginable variety. The tats were works of art, and though he wasn't usually a fan of them, they suited her. She raised her eyebrows at him, taking in his custom-tailored suit, white shirt, and gold cufflinks. "Can I help you?"

A bouquet. He'd send Jules a bouquet. The one he should have sent a lot earlier, if he'd been thinking of anyone but himself and what Grady might do to him for getting naked with his baby sister.

"Yes." He smiled his megawatt, let's-close-this-deal-already smile at her. "I think you can."

She waited.

"I need . . . I need the most beautiful, the most special arrangement you've ever done in your life."

Her eyebrows shot up to her hairline. Her eyes themselves focused on his pricey watch. "Do you, now."

"I want the best."

"Looks like you're used to it," she drawled.

He should have left the damn watch in his glove box. "What's your name?" he asked, trying to decide how best to win her over. *Charm-offensive boosters activated.*

"You don't remember me?" She said it too casually.

Oh, hell. "Uh . . ." Nobody he'd known in high school had those distinctive tattoos. "Sorry."

"Maggie," she said, her gaze shifting from his watch to Scarlett, which she could see through the storefront window. That wasn't exactly admiration in Maggie's eyes. "And you are Jake and Declan's brother, Rhett. I heard you'd become some kind of banker . . . you've been busy, huh?"

"Maggie Cooper? Of course . . . sorry. It's just that you've changed a lot."

"So have you." She looked him up and down.

Rhett Braddock, Some Kind of Banker. Managing partner of a venture capital firm, actually. I turn millionaires into billionaires—myself included. But we can go with banker. "Yeah, guess I have." *Note to self: Consider borrowing clothes from Jake.* But why should he hide his money? The money that "made" him—even though he'd made *it.*

"Well, Rhett, what kind of bouquet can I do you for?" she asked.

He stared at her blankly. "I don't have a clue."

"What kind of flowers?"

"I don't know. The best."

"Yeah. You told me." She waited.

He shrugged.

"Okay. So what exactly are you trying to say with these flowers?"

"I . . . uh . . ." Rhett stumbled over this. "That . . . hello . . . and I'm sorry?"

"Hello and I'm sorry. And it's got to be the most spectacular, beautiful arrangement I've ever made."

"Yes." It wasn't what he really wanted to say, but it was all he could give.

If Rhett could tell Maggie to write what he *really* wanted to say . . . *You have no idea how sorry I am that our one-night stand will never be more than one night.*

Because it never would.

Grady was family. Closer than his own. Grady had been there for him when Rhett's parents died, when Declan sent him away, and all those tough years back East. Grady had gotten him through the bad times, and messing around with his little sister was *not* how to repay the debt.

And so Jules? Well, Jules wasn't allowed to matter. Jules couldn't matter.

"Done," Maggie said, finishing up the order description on her pad. "Who's it for?"

"Julianna Holt, out at—"

Maggie's hand froze. She looked up from the pad, and whatever nice she had left after considering his watch and car and clothes, well, it all just drained away. "I'm familiar with the address." She dropped the order pad on the counter, and then crossed her arms over her chest. "I don't think Jules knows yet."

Rhett studied Maggie's aggressive tapping of the pen against her bicep. "Knows what?"

"That you're taking over her place."

Aw, Jeez. Small towns. No secrets . . . Rhett cleared his throat. "That's not exactly how I'd put it. Word travels fast."

"Yeah." Maggie said coldly. "So what's your budget for the flowers?"

"Whatever it takes."

She gave him a too-sweet smile. "Mmm. If it were me? It would take *a lot*."

They stared each other down for a moment before Rhett shook his head, letting loose a bark of laughter. He fished out his wallet and forked over his black Amex. "Obviously, I need it delivered today."

"Obviously. Women *love* flowers," Maggie said in saccharine tones as she processed the transaction and handed back his credit card. "I'm *sure* this will make *everything* all right."

Want to read more of Rhett's story? Get to know all of the delicious Braddock brothers and their wild child little sister? Come visit Silverlake at lizakendall.com. Kick off your shoes and stay awhile! xo Liza

Ready to find
your next great read?

Let us help.

Visit prh.com/nextread